"DON'T YOU KISS BACK, JOAN?"

SHE FELT HER FACE BURN. "Nay."

"Never?"

"Nay." She wished that did not sound so selfish. Her gaze lowered to where her hands splayed over his bronze chest. "I have never wanted to."

He lifted her chin so that she had to look at his face again. His expression took her breath away. Intense and knowing. Hard and soft and warm, just like his body. "That is not true. You want to now."

Maybe she did. Maybe that was what entranced her. She certainly did not want to run away.

Gentle pressure on her head. A strong arm guiding her. Not to his mouth. Lower, until her lips rested on his chest, above her palms.

The slight taste, the scent, made her thoughts blur. All of her senses filled with him. She did not really decide, it just happened. She kissed, and moved her lips and kissed again. A rich pleasure began beating through her like a rapid breath. She moved her hand and kissed again.

+ BY +
DESIGN

Madeline Hunter

Bantam Books
New York Toronto London
Sydney Auckland

BY DESIGN
A Bantam Book / January 2001

ISBN 0-553-58223-2

Published simultaneously in the United States and Canada

Bantam Books are published by Bantam Books, a division
of Random House, Inc. Its trademark, consisting of the
words "Bantam Books" and the portrayal of a rooster,
is Registered in U.S. Patent and Trademark Office and
in other countries. Marca Registrada. Bantam Books,
1540 Broadway, New York, New York 10036.

PRINTED IN THE UNITED STATES OF AMERICA
OPM   10 9 8 7 6 5 4 3 2 1

FOR WARREN,
WHO STILL BRINGS ME FLOWERS.

BY DESIGN

CHAPTER 1

SHE LOOKED LIKE A STATUE of calm dignity placed in a sea of vulgar chaos.

The market roared and splashed all around her motionless body. Peddlers of skins and barrels, of pigs and fish, crowded the small space that she had claimed for her wares. Her ragged gown, of a pale silver hue and displaying remnants of elegant needlework, contrasted starkly with the practical browns and flamboyant colors filling the square. Along with her blond crown and braid, the gown created a column of light tones in a very mottled world. She was all gentle fairness, except for her skin. Bronzed from the sun, it possessed a golden sheen that brightened her blue eyes.

It was the respite of pale serenity that first caught Rhys's attention as he walked through the market in front of the Cathedral. Then the unveiled hair. And the eyes. He had already slowed to see her face more clearly before he noticed her wares.

She did not hawk them. She stood silently behind the

crude, upturned wooden box that showed what she sold. Her delicate face remained impassive, as if she did not notice the bodies jostling by, sometimes pressing her—sometimes deliberately. He was not the only man to notice that this tattered dove was very pretty.

He did not recognize her. Most of the vendors were old faces, seen here regularly. She was an alien most likely, and not from the city. She had come for the day to make a few coins.

He felt a little sorry for her. Despite her rigid poise, she struck him as vulnerable, in danger of being broken. He doubted that she was doing well. The box was low, no higher than her knees, and the wares were almost invisible. He had to stroll very near in order to inspect the items set out on it.

Crockery. He had no interest in such things, but he did have an interest in her. He casually lifted the closest cup and a spark of hope lit her cool gaze.

The cup was simple but well made. Surprisingly, it was not ordinary sunbaked terra-cotta. It had been fired, and its shine indicated that it had been glazed.

"The walls are very thin. Do you have a potter's wheel?" he asked while he examined it. And her. She really was very pretty, but up close he could read fatigue in her lax expression, and discouragement in her blue eyes.

"Nay. I just used coils."

"With great care, though. The shape is very regular."

His interest attracted others, as was the way with markets. A stout woman, a wealthy merchant's wife from her dress, paused and peered down critically. Something caught her eye. Poking her chubby hand amidst the cups, she lifted a small figure.

He had been so distracted by the potter that he had not noticed the little statues. The merchant's wife held a standing Virgin, maybe a hand's span tall. It had been carefully modeled with swelling drapes, and painstakingly painted with colored glazes.

The woman examined the little figure, running her fingers along the face and back, holding it upright to judge its look. Rhys made his own inspection alongside.

"How much?" the woman asked, sharp-eyed and ready to bargain hard.

"Eight pence."

"Eight pence!"

"Five, then."

The woman groaned and sighed and dawdled and debated. Finally the five pence emerged from her purse.

The potter seemed well pleased.

Rhys dipped into the wares, moving some aside. Two other statues were there. A Saint Agnes with her lamb, and a Saint Catherine with her wheel. She might have just repeated the figure and changed the attribute, but she had not done so. Each was unique in pose, and very realistic.

"Do you seek to buy something?"

Her voice had a little edge to it. Her blue eyes regarded him skeptically.

He knew what that look revealed. He had not been the first man to loiter around, pretending to be interested in crockery.

"You craft the statues, too?"

"When I have the time, and the clay."

"They are all fired."

"I know a tiler who lets me use his kiln."

He lifted the Saint Agnes. "What are they for?"

That flustered her. "They are statues."

"Aye, but what is their purpose? The cups and bowls have a purpose. Everyone needs them. What is this saint for?"

"Devotion."

"There are churches for that, with much larger statues."

"Some people might like to have one in their homes," she said defensively.

"Have you sold many?"

She grimaced, conceding the point. "At most one a day when I come to market."

"Then you should charge more than five pence."

She rolled her eyes. "If I sell only one at five pence, I will sell none higher."

"You will sell just as many, but receive what they are worth, and they will be more valued by those who buy them. These are not practical things. Most will give you nothing, but those who will pay five pence will pay a shilling." To prove it, he fingered a shilling out of his purse and placed it on the box.

She eyed the coin hungrily, then glanced at him, suspicious again.

Her caution did not insult him. A pretty thing like her, alone in the marketplace, probably received a lot of propositions. "For the statue only. But I must warn you. I am a freemason, and I may steal the pose for a stone saint someday."

Her gaze raked him with a quick assessment. He knew what she thought. He did not look like a mason today. His dress was too fine for work. A man did not wield a chisel and hammer in a long tunic and tall boots.

Rhys drifted away, carrying Saint Agnes. He looked down at the little figure and laughed at himself. A man who could make stone statues hardly needed to purchase clay ones.

He supposed he had bought it as a form of praise, from one craftsman to another. And as a type of flattery, from a man to a woman. There had been a bit of pity to it, too. He liked the idea that he had made the day a success for her.

He laughed again. A shilling for ten minutes with a pretty woman. Still, even without the statue, he would not have felt cheated.

He ambled across the square to a busy tavern. Ducking below the low swinging sign, he entered its shadowed, cool depths.

He purchased two ales and took them to the table near the unshuttered window. It was hotter here, but he could admire the statue in the light. He placed it on the rough planks, and edged it around with nudges of his fingertips. She really was very skilled.

He looked out the window. As the crowd flowed he caught glimpses of her. That gown looked very sad. A lady's old finery, probably bought thirdhand. Maybe the bits of embroidery had not been so frayed when she got it.

A thick body slid across the window opening, blocking his view. A face peered in. A blond beard lowered in gape-mouthed surprise to find him looking straight back from a handspan away. The man glanced over his shoulder, then hustled in the door.

He came over frowning, sat on the opposite bench, and shifted it back so his head was not at the window. "What are you thinking of? The whole city can see us here."

"If they do, they see a builder and a bishop's clerk sharing a table at a crowded tavern. Drink your ale, John, and no one will think twice of our company."

John wiped his brow with his sleeve. "I had to wait for you a long time. The sun has been roasting me."

"You are fortunate that I came at all, since I know what you want and have no interest in hearing it. And I am late because I have been at Westminster, awaiting an audience with the Queen. She wants to talk about adding to one of her manor houses, and has had me cooling my heels all day. Let us be quick with this, since I must go back and wait some more."

John's face fell. "A manor house? You can not think to leave London, surely."

"I can, and I will if there is work to be had elsewhere."

"But the plans . . . your reports . . ."

"I have nothing to report, not that I agreed to provide such things. But you can tell Bishop Stratford that I have heard nothing. No gossip. No worry. Nothing. As to the plans, I doubt that there are any worth supporting. There are only frightened men talking and hoping, which is something of a relief. The last plan was poorly conceived and ill executed, and it was only by God's grace that my role in it was not discovered."

The blunt talk made John nervous. He stuck his head out the window to be sure no one lurked against the wall.

Rhys took the opportunity to look for the potter again. She appeared to have another buyer.

John leaned over the table with a serious expression. Rhys deliberately angled away so they would not look like two conspirators plotting treason. Which was what they were, for all intents and purposes.

"I will confide in you," John said. "Wake is raising an army in France. Lancaster and my bishop are sending him money. By next spring—"

"It will not happen. The barons have made peace with Queen Isabella and her lover Roger Mortimer. This will not be like three years ago, when the country rose up to welcome Isabella's invasion in order to help her depose her husband and crown her son. For one thing, the current king is not the enemy. His mother and her lover are, the same leaders whom we embraced as saviors in that great rebellion."

"They have become usurpers!"

"As some of us worried that they would. Anyone who

knows Roger Mortimer feared his ambition. The barons were supposed to control him, but they have proven weak and divided."

"Mortimer ignores the council. He even sets himself above the young King and must be brought down."

"Then it is King Edward's fight."

"He is a boy—"

"He is eighteen."

John flushed to the roots of his short, fair hair. "They have bought you. They give you the status of a master builder and let you design a few structures, and like a dog thrown some bones you forget your old loyalties."

Rhys barely suppressed the urge to reach over and grab John's fleshy neck. "I have forgotten *nothing*. I risked more than you in that rebellion, *clerk*—only to see a bad king replaced by a bad queen and her hungry lover. Only to see the unity of the barons shatter at once as they hastened to gain from the change. If you want to know who has been bought, look to the castles of the realm." He swallowed his anger and looked across the square again. "I grow weary of it, John. I am out of this, and seek only to practice my craft. If the Queen wants me to rebuild a manor house, I will do it."

John began a low-voiced cajoling. Rhys did not listen. His attention had become distracted by a commotion in the marketplace.

Two groups of youths had come down two lanes at the same time. One, made up of squires in their lords' liveries, displayed the arrogant high spirits of young men who expect the world's deference. The other, a ragtag gang of footloose boys such as plagued the city, showed the surly anger that breeds in men with nothing to do.

The crowd subtly shifted to avoid both groups, but as fate would have it they crossed each other's paths in the middle of the square. Neither gang would walk around the other.

They faced off. Sharp words were exchanged, then shouted insults. Eight rich faces sneered. Seven poor ones snarled.

Rhys ignored John's exhortations and drank his ale. The crowd spread, making room for the drama. There would be a fight, to be sure. A bit of excitement to enliven the afternoon. A spectacle to discuss for the next few days.

That was what marketplaces were for.

He mentally put his money on the city youths, even though they were outnumbered. This would be a street brawl, not a tournament in armor. Besides, it was important to show loyalty to one's own in these things.

"How much?"

Joan examined the man admiring her Saint Catherine. Skinny and pale, with a rabbity face and a richly draped hat, he looked wealthy enough to buy impractical things.

She let him look longer while she contained her excitement. To think that she might sell all three statues today!

He really did seem to like it. "A shilling."

His gaze snapped to her in surprise.

"It took a week to make, and is fired. You will find no better," she added quickly, wishing she had not been so rash. Of course that mason had just been flattering her, hoping for something more for his coin. She would lose this sale because she had almost believed what he said about the value of her wares.

"A shilling," the rabbit mused. "Your husband puts a high price on his skill."

"The skill is mine."

He instantly looked at the statue with new eyes. Critical ones. He would imagine that he saw every imperfection that he expected in work done by a woman.

That often happened. She could invent a craftsman

husband and tell the buyers lies, but her pride would not let her. The statues were *hers*. *She* had made them.

"Five pence," he offered.

It was what she had gotten for the Virgin. She should be glad for it. But this man's sudden disdain irked her.

"A shilling. It is worth much more, and I will take no less." She regretted the words as soon as they snapped off her lips. Still, a rebellious part of her felt that this man did not deserve her Saint Catherine and that she would break it to pieces before she let him have it for five pence.

To her surprise, he did not walk off. It astonished her even more when his fingers went to his purse. A shilling landed on her box as he turned away. If he had thrown down only five pence, she would have grabbed it just as quickly. In truth she could not afford the pride that still plagued her.

She tucked the money into her bodice, between her breasts. It joined the moist weight of the other coins there. Almost three shillings today. A fortune, thanks to that tall mason.

She remembered his keen-eyed gaze admiring her cup. And her. For once she hadn't minded that so much, despite his intimidating size. He hadn't leered. Those blue eyes had revealed a man's interest, but not the naked hunger that she knew too well.

And he had truly appreciated her craft. She could tell from the way he touched the wares. That had not been a lie, even if it might have been an excuse.

She had been a little rude to him. She wished that she could thank him now. He had been right about the statues. As a mason, he probably had some experience in how such things were valued. It had been generous of him to tell her.

A nice man. Handsome, too, with a firm jaw and angular face and a well-formed nose. He wore his clean dark hair bound at his nape the way laborers did, to keep it off their faces. Kind eyes. Deep blue. The skin at their sides crinkled when he smiled. Little lines had formed there, and at the edges of his mouth. Maybe he smiled a lot.

She discovered that she was smiling now, too. It actually felt strange, but a lovely lightness had entered her heart, and she couldn't stop herself.

Almost three shillings. Maybe . . . maybe . . .

Some youths entered the square off a nearby side lane, and she immediately spotted her brother Mark's blond head among them. Thank goodness for that. He had disappeared after setting down her box here at dawn, and she had worried that she would have to carry it back across the river herself.

She tried to catch his eye but he managed not to notice. He stuck with his knot of comrades, looking as though he planned to cross the square and get swallowed by the city again. His friends were trouble. They all wore the hot-eyed, tough expressions of young men looking to fight with the world.

She could not ignore the fact that Mark fit right in. Realizing that blotted the sun right out of her mood. Not only anger and hardness matched him with the others. His garments did, too. Little more than rags, his tunic and hose had already been patched and frayed when she bought them off a servant. She could afford no better. Mark had grown so much these last two years that it had been all she could do to keep him in any clothes at all.

He hated that green tunic. He resented what it meant. Every morning when he dragged it on, her heart ached for him. Day by day she watched his anger grow, and felt the storm building in his soul. When they were together, his silent thunder quaked right through the air, into her.

She watched him aim across the square, and a flutter of panic beat inside her. She was losing him. To this city's alleys, and those bad youths, and the despair wrought by poverty. At fifteen, he was no longer the boy who had trusted his big sister, and his lost faith cut like a knife. He no longer believed her reassurances that things would change for the better. Maybe he guessed that she did not believe them herself half the time.

But sometimes she still did. Like today. Her breasts cradled almost three shillings. Perhaps she could still make it right for him. Eventually.

Mark's head stopped. So did those of the other boys. The crowd began milling in abruptly different patterns. She rose on her toes to see what was happening.

Sick worry instantly twisted her stomach. Mark and his friends had confronted a group of squires. Things were fast getting ugly. The crowd oozed away from the impending brawl, forming a thick circle that quickly blocked her view.

Fear and frustration shot to her head. Hadn't she begged him to stay out of trouble? Weren't those her very last words to him this morning? Now he would get himself beaten or broken, or saints knew what!

She stomped into the crowd and pushed her way through. By the time she popped out from the front row of spectators, the fight was underway.

Clouds of dust rose around the melee of swinging fists and fumbling strangleholds. Mark was big enough to hold his own, but her quick scan saw a red bruise under his eye before a set of knuckles crashed into his jaw.

She looked desperately around the crowd. None of the men seemed inclined to stop it. In fact they were shouting encouragements and laying wagers. The two gangs had become a form of blood sport.

Something amidst the confusion caught her eye and froze her blood. One of the squires, a young man wearing Mortimer's livery, took a bad blow from Mark to his handsome face. He crumbled to the ground and grabbed his nose with a scream of pain. For an instant he lay there in astonishment. Then flaring hatred lit his eyes. As he scrambled to his feet, his hand went to his belt. Suddenly a dagger was slicing through the air.

Everyone saw that the fun had turned deadly. The crowd quieted and the youths stopped. The squire glared at his enemies and jabbed the air to move them away. The street boys edged back, but refused to run.

Mark didn't move at all. She knew why, and groaned that fate could be so cruel as to taunt him with a challenge from one of Mortimer's servants. He stood there arrogantly, daring the squire to try it.

They faced each other in the spreading silence, and it seemed as if invisible ropes wanted to pull them together. She saw—nay, she *felt*—the exact moment when her brother's death became inevitable. Fury split in her head. Fury at Mark, and at this city, and at this crowd that did not give a damn about any of these boys.

She walked right into the lines of fighters. She strode forward until she stood between Mark and the squire. Ignoring her brother's wrathful order to get out of the way, she shook her finger at the squire's bloody face.

"A fine bit of chivalry you show. You draw a weapon against those who have none? Your strength can not best him, so you reach for the easy advantage. It is clear that you will become the most cowardly of knights. Considering the colors that you wear, I am not surprised."

The squire's gaze raked her with confusion, but a sneer twisted his face when the assessment was complete. Not a lady, that look said. For all the fine talk, just an impoverished nobody.

"Get out of the way, bitch. And watch your tongue or you will hang from a gibbet at the end of these colors."

"A big threat from a mere lackey no more than six and

ten in years. Your lord will do nothing at your request. He does not even know your name yet."

"I said *move.*"

"I will not. We already know that you are a coward. Are you such a great one that you will use that dagger against a woman?"

With exasperated anger he sheathed his weapon, but only to free his hand. He reached for her and shoved.

Another hand appeared out of nowhere. It grasped one of the squire's arms, stopping him abruptly. Long fingers squeezed. The youth's whole body jerked and his grasp fell from her. They squeezed some more and a wince of pain broke the squire's sneer.

It was the mason. He stood there at complete ease, calmly crushing the squire's arm.

"She is right. You are a coward if you will lay hands on a woman," he said.

"You forget who you deal with," the squire spit, thrusting the colors of his sleeve under the mason's nose.

"I deal with a boy who does not know when he has lost a fair fight." A steely glint sparked in the mason's blue eyes. He did not look nearly as kind as he had at her box. "These hands can break stone, boy. Your arm will be an easy thing in comparison. Take your friends and be gone."

He released his hold. The squire stepped back, red-faced. "My lord will hear of this!"

"Not if you are smart. This city has laws against drawing weapons on its streets. Your lord will not take kindly to you causing trouble within these walls. Now go, or I will tell Mortimer about your behavior myself."

The squire joined his friends. Donning their arrogance, they swaggered away laughing, as if they had won the day. With their departure, the market flowed again, going about its business.

The mason turned to the motley gang of street toughs.

The command was unmistakable. They began to melt into the crowd.

Mark made to join them. The mason caught him by the scruff of the neck as he walked by. "This belongs to you?" he asked, swinging him around to face Joan.

Mark looked ready to fight again. The mason's tight mouth suggested he almost hoped it happened.

"Aye," Joan said miserably. She had never seen her brother so angry. He would never forgive her the embarrassment of her interference.

"I thought so. Same hair. Same rash bravery." He set Mark aside. "You should collect your wares and leave for today. If someone went for a constable, you do not want to be here when he comes."

"We will go at once. Thank you for your help."

Mark stood there, brooding and seething. The mason eyed him severely. "Help your sister, boy."

That did it. Mark's fist flew. The mason merely caught it in his left hand. Joan had never seen a man move so quickly.

Her brother's fury got darker. The mason just held his fist in a firm grasp, gazing back. Her embarrassment grew so intense that she wanted to disappear.

The mason's expression softened a little, as if he comprehended something of the turmoil that rumbled in her brother. "Your sister saved your life. That squire was set to gut you. Now, be a man and get her out of the city."

The worst of Mark's anger broke, as if he heard some truth in those calm words. He dropped his fist and walked over to her box.

"I am sorry for that. He is very proud, and does not like me playing the mother any more," Joan said. "Again, I thank you with all my heart."

She went to join Mark. The mason fell into step with her. "You two are alone?"

"Aye." Saints, but they were alone. She doubted that any two souls in the world were more alone than Mark and she.

Mark had set the crockery on the ground and turned up the box. A pile of rags waited, but he would not touch them. His pride drew very clear lines about these things. She did not mind. She had taught him herself where the lines should be.

She knelt and began wrapping the crockery so it would not break on the walk home. To her shock the mason dropped to one knee and began to help. There was something disconcerting about his strength next to her. The warmth of his nearness flustered her in a foolish way.

His hands lifted a cup gently and rolled it in an ancient cloth. She almost stopped him. She did not want him to see and touch those pitiful bits of dirty rag. He might recognize them for what they were, the remnants of a life that had been shredded and despoiled. Suddenly, unaccountably, she knew that she would want to die if he pitied her.

"You sold the last statue," he said while he took a bowl from her hands and carefully packed it in the box.

She nodded while she quickly wrapped the last cup. "I asked for a shilling, as you advised. You were right. He paid it."

He smiled over at her. She felt herself blushing under his subtle, meandering gaze. She grew more flustered yet. Her hands became clumsy, and the cup rolled out of its rag, down her lap, and onto the ground.

He took the rag and made quick work of the cup. Rising, he offered his hand to help her up.

She looked at that hand, and something sad swelled her

heart and burned her throat. It was just a simple gesture, but it had been years since any man had freely given her even this small courtesy.

She accepted and got up quickly. Her palm felt the dry warmth of his, and the calloused skin. He did not dress like a mason, but he owned the firm hands of one. And the broad shoulders. He was not a bulky man, but a tight strength was evident in his tall, lean lines.

Mark lifted the box and they headed across the square. Once again the mason walked beside her.

She did not want him following her. His help touched vulnerable memories that she could not afford to acknowledge. He reminded her of old times when someone always protected her, and no one expected her to be strong, and no man ever dared to leer. He weakened something in her core, and made her wobbly and nostalgic. She could not afford the luxury of his kindness any longer.

"My brother will stay with me. Again I thank you, Master . . ." She realized that she did not know his name.

"Rhys."

"I thank you, Master Rhys."

She said it with a note of farewell, but he did not leave.

"You need not walk with us. We have delayed you too much as it is."

"I will see you out of the city. Those squires may have decided to regain their pride with an easy revenge."

Her mind saw again the danger Mark had faced, and Rhys's brave help.

The memory halted abruptly at some details ignored in the fear of the moment.

"That squire acted as if he knew you," she said.

"I have seen him about Westminster."

"You live there?"

"I live in London, but my work takes me to the palace most days."

Her heart began a slow thudding of caution. "You said that you would report him to his lord. Was that an idle threat?"

"I pass Mortimer most days. If I wanted to speak with him, I expect that I could." He did not say it boastfully. She had asked a question, and he simply answered it.

"You practice your craft for him?" She heard the bitter accusation in her tone. It gave voice to the sudden heat in her head. He had helped her and she should be grateful no matter who he was and whom he served, but terrible emotions much older than this day started churning her heart.

He angled his head to see her face. A bit of that steely glint had returned to his eyes. "Aye."

"Have you worked on his castles? His fortifications? Do you repair the walls of the keeps that he destroys while he rapes the realm?"

"Rarely. Castle walls do not require tracery and statues."

"But you serve him nonetheless, as surely as his knights and his archers."

"I serve the crown."

"The crown is under his foot."

"The squire was right, woman. You speak too freely."

"It is the only benefit of poverty. Freedom to speak since my opinion is meaningless. At least I am not a lackey to a butcher, like that squire." *And you.*

He heard the last words even though she did not say them. His face hardened at the insult, but he did not respond to it.

His presence no longer felt comforting and protective. Rather the opposite. If he moved among the court he was dangerous. If he served Mortimer, even as a craftsman, his honor and character could not be trusted.

That saddened her. It had been nice to believe in him for a while. It had been beautiful to think that he was generous.

"Do you live outside the city?" he asked.

"Aye."

"In Southwark?"

"Aye." She did not hesitate with the lie. He had asked the kinds of queries she got from men who soon offered a bad bargain. He might be smoother than most, but he was no different. One could know a man by whom he served, and he served the worst. He no doubt expected her to repay him, and not with crockery. He liked her in that way. It was in the warm looks he gave her.

That worried her. She did not want the interest of a man who passed Mortimer every day. She did not want him remembering anything about her, least of all where she could be found.

At the gate she stopped and faced him.

"I thank you," she said, trying to make it friendly but dismissive.

"Are those the only words that you know? Besides sharp talk that is both dangerous and insulting?"

"What other words do you want?"

"Not the offer of your favors, as you fear. However, since I risked a fight with a dagger, learning your name would be nice."

"Forgive me. It is just . . ."

"I know how it is, pretty dove. You are wise to be careful."

"Joan. My name is Joan." There was no danger in giving it. There were thousands of Joans in London.

Mark called impatiently from the gate. Rhys backed

away and made a vague bow. "Until we meet again, Joan. And try to stay out of street brawls."

She watched with relief as he strolled back into the city. She also experienced a stab of wistful regret. There had been a few delicious minutes there when he had made her feel like the girl she had once been.

They would never meet again, if she could help it.

CHAPTER 2

RHYS FOLLOWED THE PAGE into Queen Isabella's anteroom. Three days of waiting had finally resulted in the meeting she had demanded.

She sat in a carved chair while one of her ladies dressed her brown hair. Luxury surrounded her: colored Spanish tiles and intricate rugs, Flemish tapestries and jewelled silver cups. She let him stand a long while, until the last strand of gold was woven into her coiled plaits. An inspection of her long face in a mirror, a few adjustments for perfection, and then she finally acknowledged him.

Her lidded gaze showed the confidence of a woman who had played an audacious game and won. Rhys did not dislike the Queen. But for her bad judgment in men, the forced abdication of her husband almost four years ago might have saved the realm as she had promised.

"I am told that you are the mason seeing to my window in the chapel here. I am also told that you supervised part of the new fabric at Windsor last year," she said. "I have a small manor house that I want to enlarge. Master Stephen suggested you might be right for it."

"That is generous of Master Stephen." Oddly so, since Master Stephen, the Queen's principal builder, had a grown son who would also be right for the work.

"Then let us discuss it." She turned her head. "Mortimer, would you join us?"

A movement in the chamber's darkest corner caught Rhys's attention. A man was reading parchments at a desk there. He rose now and strolled to the Queen's chair.

Rhys's jaw tightened. He did not dislike the Queen, but he hated Roger Mortimer. He hated the man's pomposity and arrogance. He hated his lax mouth and curly dark beard and puffy eyes. He despised the way the man abused whatever power he had. He resented like hell that he had helped raise him up.

Mortimer stood by Isabella's side and placed his hand on her shoulder. She slid her own up and entwined her fingers in his. The gesture symbolized the strength of her affection, which had led her to cling to the power she should have handed over to her son by now. Under this man's influence the Queen had become an extravagant, weak woman.

"This manor house is very small," Isabella explained. "I am thinking of a new hall, fit for my retinue, and new chambers, too. You will have to go there and see how things are and then consult with me. But I want it made ready so that we can stay there on our way when we visit the Welsh marches."

The Welsh marches. Mortimer's private realm. He had managed to grab the whole region, and Isabella had elevated him to Earl of March. Rhys had grown up on the Welsh borderland. The only good thing about the current situation was that it kept the man here, and away from those holdings where no one and nothing checked his ruthlessness.

"Where is this property?"

"Wessex."

"Do you know if there is a quarry on the lands, or nearby? If not, the cost will be very high."

"I can hardly be expected to know of such things as quarries. You will have to determine that. As to the cost, we will discuss that when you return."

"And if, upon my return, you decide that the cost is too great?"

Mortimer smiled with benign condescension. "You are concerned that this project will not materialize, and that you will invest your time and journey for nought. You will be very well compensated, for any work that you perform for us."

At that moment Rhys knew for sure that this audience was not really about building.

It was Mortimer who made the overture. He tapped his chin thoughtfully. "You are familiar to me. How do I know you? Ah, I remember now. Aren't you the mason who served as messenger for the Queen's cause? We were told how useful you were. How you also would pick up bits of information while you went about your craft."

"Very few bits. I am, after all, only a mason."

"A freemason?"

"Aye. I cut statues and tracery and moldings back then, and still do between building projects."

"Your guild is a powerful one. One hears rumors about it. It is said that your members know more about what occurs in the realm than our own sheriffs do."

"We travel for our craft, and we gossip like all travelers. But any pilgrim knows as much as we do. Now, as to this manor house, when do you want me to go and inspect what needs to be done?"

"Well, that depends, doesn't it?" Isabella said.

"Does it, my lady? On what?"

She sighed with exasperation. "Do not be as dense as the stone that you cut. We want to know what is being said, what rumors and stories you hear. There is treason everywhere, and we need to know of it. You are to tell us those bits of information that you pick up as you go about your craft. We want to hear word of any barons' meetings, brought to the city by masons traveling through. If you serve us well, the work on the manor house is yours, and much more."

So there it was. An outright bribe.

"Much more," Mortimer echoed. "Indeed, the Queen is considering a whole new palace there, and not just an enlargement. She wants the Church to establish a new bishopric too, and build a cathedral."

A very good bribe. A magnificent one. Every mason dreamed of becoming a master builder, and every builder dreamed of planning palaces and cathedrals. He had to give Mortimer his due. The man certainly knew how to buy someone. No wonder he had most of the barons eating out of his hand.

"I doubt that anything I hear will be news to you, or of any value."

"Let us decide that. Such things are more complex than a man like you can understand."

Despite the bribe, they were really not offering a choice. "I will do my best, of course."

They dismissed him then, and turned their attention to each other. The thick doors closed on their mumbling. He walked down to the hall, wondering how long he could put them off with little bits of nothing.

He almost did not notice her.

Lost in his thoughts, pacing the city lanes, he passed the stocks without looking up. He was vaguely aware that a crowd had gathered to watch some poor wretch being punished, but it was too common an occurrence to distract him.

He paused to purchase a new pear from a bushel on the corner. It was while he paid that he chanced to glance across the small crossroads. And then he noticed that the pale hair at the stocks was a familiar color, and that the dove grey gown of the young woman imprisoned there was covered with tattered bits of embroidery.

Her head and hands hung limply from their holes. He looked up to the sun. It had passed its peak, so she had been there for hours already. He wondered if she was even conscious.

He ambled over and pushed through the taunting crowd until he stood right below her. The stocks were set on a platform, and his head came level with her knees. He moved aside the rotting food that had been thrown at her, and lifted the objects dumped at her feet to announce the reason for her punishment.

Tiles. He examined two broken pieces and saw the problem. They had not been fired properly, and must have cracked as soon as they were laid. She had said that she used a tiler's kiln, not that she made tiles herself. He found it hard to believe that the woman who took such care with her crockery and statues could be responsible for such shoddy work as these floor pavers.

He looked up. He could see her face from here. Flushed from the strain of her position, it was set with determination. He angled to see better, and she noticed him. She shut her eyes, and moisture leaked to their edges.

He stepped to the side. From there it was obvious that she was too short for the stocks. She was stretched up on her toes, and even so she practically hung by her neck.

A man approached closely. Grinning like a rat, he circled, enjoying her vulnerability. When he got to the back he playfully yanked at her skirt. The old fabric split as if it were made of nothing but air.

The rip exposed her creamy leg from thigh to foot. Delighted by his fortune, the man grabbed at flesh. Instantly infuriated, Rhys reached, swung, and threw him into the street.

Her new humiliation enlivened the little crowd. Some youths decided she would make good sport now. Taunting and circling, they tried to grab, too. Rhys had to knock heads together to put an end to it.

He looked up into her face again. Tears streamed down her cheeks. She was broken. Well, she had lasted longer than most.

He strode back over to the pear seller. "How much? For all of them? And the bushel?"

Astonished, the woman named her price. He paid it, and carried the bushel into the crowd. After tucking a few pears in his tunic, he upended it. Fruit poured into the street.

The spectators scrambled to grab the free food. While they picked and fought, he brought the bushel to the stocks. Hopping up, he set it beside Joan. "Kneel on it. It will raise you up."

She tried, but could barely move. He lifted each leg and carefully bent it onto the bushel. Her body released a deep sigh of relief and a pitiful groan of pain.

He dipped his head low by hers and offered a pear. "Can you eat?"

She shook her head, and winced. He moved her braid aside and saw why. An ugly red welt circled her neck and jaw from where she had pressed against the stocks. If she had lost consciousness or her precarious balance, she might have strangled. This was not intended to be a death sentence, but sometimes it was.

He moved behind her and tied her skirt together. "I

will stay here, Joan. No one will touch you again. No one will hurt you. It will be over soon."

Her slender shoulders shook and he heard a muffled sob. The sound twisted something inside him. He would have liked to stay up there, blocking her from view, but that would not be permitted. Right or wrong, the sentence had been ordered and she would have to serve it. He patted her back, trying to give comfort, but that only made her cry more.

"Have heart, pretty dove. I will be right there below, where you can see me."

He hopped off the platform and took up a position in front of her. Crossing his arms, facing the street, he stood sentry lest anyone try to harm the poor woman in any way.

It was his kindness that broke her. She had fought the humiliation and pain with pride and anger, but she had no defenses against kindness. He had given her permission to be weak, and she had crumbled.

She could see his head and back all the time. He just stood there waiting, as if he had nothing better to do. On occasion he turned and looked up, checking on her with a concerned expression and a few words of reassurance.

It hurt to swallow, but at least she did not have to struggle for every breath anymore. Her body felt so stretched that she wondered if it would ever be right again.

At her feet lay the tiles that had put her here. Not her tiles. George had supervised the kiln the day they were made. He had been drunk, but not drunk enough to spend the day sleeping it off as he usually did. Every now and then he liked to play the great craftsman. Usually she found a way to keep the flawed results from being sold, but he'd sold these anyway.

He probably guessed they were bad. That was why he had insisted that she bring the next wagonload. So she would face the complaint, and not him.

A movement below snapped her alert. The mason was leaving. She couldn't blame him. It had been hours. She lifted her head a bit so she could see him walk away. It meant that she could see the little crowd too. People came and went, pausing to enjoy the spectacle. No one stayed long. It was hot in the crossroads. The hours in the sun had made her light-headed, and added the agony of thirst to the long list of tortures.

The desertion of her protector emptied her out. Her heart clutched desperately, trying to find some remnants of strength, but there was only weakness inside her now. When they took her down, what would they do with her? Leave her in a heap on this platform? Throw her in the dirt outside the gate? She couldn't walk, she was sure. She doubted that she could even crawl.

She stared at the tiles through blurring eyes and cursed George. The little spike of anger produced a tiny bit of strength. She grabbed at both with what was left of her sense. In the little whirlwind of fury that filled her head, she forgot where she was.

How dare you insult me? How dare you lay hands on me? My father will hear of this. My husband will kill you. . . .

But someone did lay hands on her. On her shoulder. Still half crazed, she turned her head to bite and fight. The black fury died in an instant, and she was back in the stocks, glaring at the mason. He stood beside her again, holding a tumbler.

He looked in her eyes with concern, and held the cup below her face. "You are getting sick from the sun. Put your lips to this and sip what you can. It is very full, and you should be able to drink some of it."

It was ale, not water. She gagged out more than she

took in, but a little made it down. The wonderful trickle of thick fluid cooled her throat.

"Close your eyes." She did so, and the rest of the ale poured over her hot head. "The fountain is too far away, so this will have to do. The sun is beginning to set, Joan. Hang on a little longer."

She wasn't sure that she wanted to hang on. It would be very pleasant not to.

But it appeared that Rhys did not plan to give her much choice. He retook his place at her feet, only this time he faced her. Speaking as if they conversed over a tavern table, he began telling her stories from old legends. While the sun moved and the ale dried on her head, his voice kept her in the world, but a very small one where only the two of them existed.

Twilight, and chilling coolness.

The crossroads were empty now. Two men mounted the steps to the platform. One worked the key on the stocks, and the heavy wooden arm swung up over her head.

She tried to remove herself. She couldn't. When she made to straighten her shoulders it seemed as though she was pushing against stone.

Firm hands grasped her waist and lifted her away. She began sagging, falling. Arms swept her up before she hit the platform.

"Why you be wanting to bother with this gutter slut, Master Rhys?" a slurred voice said. "Just set her down. One of her kin will come for her."

"No one is here. I will see to her."

"As you like it, but there's easier ways to get to heaven than helping such as her."

"Probably so."

She hurt all over. Hurt so badly that the arms under her

shoulders and knees felt like iron vises. Moving her neck the slightest bit pained her.

Stairs, and then darkness. Silence, except for his boots.

"Are you awake, Joan?"

"Aye." She could not hear whether her voice came out or not. Nor was she entirely sure that she was awake. The passing buildings seemed very dark, just a blur of shapes.

"Have you any kin besides your brother? Any friends in the city?"

She managed to shake her head.

"Then I am taking you to my home. You can rest there."

She began to drift, vaguely conscious only of Rhys's arms and his chest and his breath on her hair, and the rhythm of his stride through the city.

Lights. First one, then three, then more. The flames flared right in front of her nose. The smell of tallow began clearing her head.

The candles lit his face as he bent to ignite the last one. He appeared even more handsome than usual in their glow. Suddenly she could see a chamber. A kitchen, of good size. Very clean.

Rhys had set her down on a bench against the hearth, and had moved a table nearby. The candles burned on it. He brought over a cup and some bread. "Here is some ale. Try to drink and eat. Soak the bread if your throat hurts too much."

Her arm felt like lead, but she moved it slowly and took the cup and bread onto her lap.

He shrugged off his tunic and strode to a nearby niche. He rolled a tall hip bath out toward the hearth. She nibbled her soaked bread and watched his lean body move.

He kept encouraging her to eat while he went about his business. He built up the fire, then left through the garden door and returned with buckets of water. Back and forth he paced until the bath filled. He set the last water by the hearth to warm.

"Can you talk now? Is your throat any better?" he asked, while he fetched himself some ale.

"A little." It came out a raspy whisper. She gestured limply toward the bath. "For me?"

"Aye."

That would mean moving. "Nay."

"Aye. No one knows more about sore bodies than masons, and you will thank me on the morrow. Also, I do not want to insult you, but between the ripe fruits that hit you and the ale that I threw on your head, you smell terrible."

"You mean it is me? I thought it was you."

He laughed, and seemed pleased at her little joke. Reassured. He leaned against the hearth and looked down at her across the bath. "I did not know that you made tiles, too."

She felt some obligation to explain, but tried to keep it ambiguous. The food had restored her enough to remember that she had to be cautious with this man. "I work for a tiler. They were his, not mine."

To her dismay, it was all he needed. "Across the river? The tile yard outside Southwark? Old Nick's place? I know the wares. Builders trusted the father, but do not buy from the son."

"The wares can still be trusted, if George stays drunk and does not interfere. Some days fate is not so kind. He is impatient with the kiln, and does not fire it right."

"So George let you be punished for his bad craft. How came you to work for such a man?"

"His father was alive when I started. Nick taught me. When George inherited the yard, I stayed."

"And your statues and pots can be made there. Is the clay his? Do you use some for your own wares?"

She had thought herself too exhausted for any emotion,

but she was horrified that he had guessed this. "I manage the yard. If not for me, George Tiler would have no money to spend in the taverns and brothels that he makes his home. Aye, I salvage and use scraps. Are you going to have me branded a thief now? Compared to the stocks, that will be a quick, minor pain."

"I doubt George pays you what your skill is worth. If you have found a way to balance the scales, it is not my concern."

His bland acceptance did not reassure her. She hated that he knew this about her. She told herself that George owed her the clay, and wood for the kiln, but in her heart she knew it was a form of theft. Rhys probably thought badly of her now. Suddenly that seemed a worse punishment than the stocks. It made no sense. If he worked for Mortimer, he was certainly of dubious character himself. Still, she found that she could not face him.

She set the cup on the table. "I will go now. I am much better."

She staggered to her feet. He was beside her in an instant, gently pressing her back down. "You will stay. You will eat, then you will bathe, and then you will rest."

"Your wife will not thank you for this charity. When she learns my story she will think that you befouled her spotless home."

Rhys lifted the pails and poured their hot contents into the bath. The moist steam wafted to her, and even that vague touch of comfort soothed. Her muscles practically sighed audibly. It had been ages since she had enjoyed a *hot* bath.

"I should thank you. Again," she said. "They are not the only words that I know, but they are the ones I find myself saying a lot to you. You are a kind man."

He strolled over to a shelf and opened an old box. "Do not think me better than I am. As it happens, I do not have a wife," He returned to the tub with a chunk of soap. "There is no one here to help you with this bath but me."

Any inclination to remember him as a protector disappeared in a blink. Something in the way he stood there caused it as much as his words. Suddenly they were a man and a woman alone at night in an empty house. To her shock she realized that thinking of him that way did not disgust her as it did with other men—as it definitely should with one of Mortimer's lackeys. Rather the opposite. The flutter of caution beating in her blood possessed an appealing excitement that confused her.

"I hope you are not overly modest."

"Modest enough that I can not permit your help in this."

"I do not see any other way."

"If there is no other way, I will not bathe."

"If you do not you will be crippled for days."

"Then I will do it myself."

"Your spirits have returned, but I doubt that your strength has. You are sure that you can manage alone?"

"I can. Leave me, and I will."

He went to a chest and brought out a towel, and placing it and the soap on the bench. "I will be outside in the garden. Call me when you are finished. You may be able to bathe yourself, but you can not make the stairs on your own."

"The stairs?"

"To the chambers. To sleep. I am hardly going to carry you all the way back to the tile yard tonight, and if you try to walk you will not even make it to the street."

"I can not permit that either."

He gave her a slow smile. "I am not above seducing you, Joan. But there would be little pleasure in it when you are so hurt that you can not move."

With that, he was out the door.

This man must think that she fell off a turnip cart this morning. Everyone knew that men were capable of pleasure even if the woman was half dead. She would let the hot water restore her some, and then make her way back across the river. She certainly could not stay here all night.

She slowly eased up. Her legs rebelled with a hollow pain, but they finally held.

Her gown laced up the back. She tried to reach for the knot. Her arms, half frozen from being up in the stocks, simply would not go backward. She could barely get her hands past her hips.

It was ridiculous. Absurd. Her mind did not feel nearly as infirm as her body acted. Irked by her helplessness, she forced her arms to move.

Something pulled and twisted and shot with pain. Her vision blanked for an instant and her shoulder hit the hearth wall. Sliding down its rough surface, she sank into a huddle on the bench.

She waited for her head to clear. She debated her situation, and with a heavy sigh gave up her pride. Forcing her hoarse voice as loud as it would go, she called his name.

He came immediately, carrying two more buckets of water. He had known she would fail. He had been waiting.

He set the water near the hearth. He walked over and sat beside her. Without saying a word, he began undressing her.

CHAPTER 3

RHYS PULLED DOWN THE LACING of her gown. The crossing lines had probably once been silver ribbons, but now crude hide strips held the back together.

He tried to remain uninterested, but it proved impossible. Her condition made his arousal especially pointless, but undressing her affected him anyway.

Joan tried, too. Her expression chilled into something half stern, half sleepy, and very distant. Still, her embarrassment was palpable. And provocative.

There was something practiced to her pose. He guessed that he was not the first man to disrobe her. That did not surprise him. She looked to be in her early twenties. It would be rare for a woman to reach that age without at least one man in her past.

He decided to leave her in her shift so they could pretend some modesty. Only the grey fabric gaped to reveal that she wore nothing underneath. A creamy stripe of skin glowed from her neck to the dimpled hollow at the base of her spine.

"Hand me the towel," she said, going very rigid.

He passed it to her. Turning away, she lowered the gown from her shoulders and unfolded the linen to shield her breasts. He found himself facing an elegant back, slender and lithe, with a subtle firmness that spoke of physical labor. It tapered nicely, then began a subtle flair at her hips. The bunched gown obscured the progress of those curves.

He rose and helped her to stand. The tattered gown slid down. Its slippery descent revealed the rest. Nipped waist. Rounded hips and bottom. Shapely legs.

His mouth went dry as her beauty unveiled in the candlelight. The gaoler had been right. There were easier ways to get to heaven than this.

She turned quickly, clutching the towel to her chest. Its thin fabric molded to her curves, and the lower edge fluttered along the top of her thighs. Stark nakedness would have been less erotic.

She eyed him cautiously, alert to her vulnerability. But something else passed between them, too. It was in her eyes and her embarrassment and the vague parting of her lips. He knew women well enough to recognize the signs. Whatever else she thought or felt, she was not entirely indifferent, either.

That made it harder. He suppressed the urge to splay his hand on the curve of her waist. Instead he lifted her lovely, smooth nakedness in his arms. "You do not have to be afraid. I am not unmoved, but I am not going to try to do anything about it."

She clutched and stretched the towel to be sure it covered the essentials. "Because you would lose the grace of being a Good Samaritan?"

"Aye, and because you still smell." He carried her over to the bath. "You have to put the towel aside now. We want it dry for later."

"Don't you have another?"

"It is the only one here."

"Close your eyes then. Now, lower me in without looking."

"I do not think—"

"Put me in and then go around behind me."

"I will try, but you must sit on the bottom and it is deep. Steady now . . . you are not light, and doing this blind . . . don't . . . hell."

Once Joan touched water she tried to release herself. In the confused grappling that followed, she thrashed, he grasped, she sank, and he fell. He ended up braced above her with his hands on the bottom of the bath.

Water sloshed up to his armpits. Pretty breasts faced him a hand's span away. Soft and round and gently full. The tips were rose colored in the way of fair women. Rosy and tight. He did not bother pretending that he didn't notice.

She instantly covered herself with her arms and sank down until her breasts were submerged in the dark water. The fire showed just enough ghostly, fluid femininity to keep his blood rumbling.

"Please. Behind me."

He grabbed the soap and threw it to her. Water dripped off his sodden shirt, making pools on the floorboards. He stripped it off, fetched a dipper and a clean rag, and knelt behind that beautiful back.

"Leave now. I can do it."

He ignored her, because of course she couldn't. Using the dipper he poured water over her head. "Give me the soap."

Joan unplaited her long braid and he washed. She had a lot of hair, and it took a long time. The soap turned the water milky, finally obscuring her body. Except the top of her back. And the sinuous line of her shoulders and neck. And the bent knees popping up, catching the firelight.

She began washing. It pained her to move her arms so much, but he knew that she would not let him do it for her. Just as well. Stroking those limbs, even to clean them, would not be a good idea.

He brought over one of the buckets of hot water. Using the rag, he made a wet pad that he pressed to her neck.

She startled, and recoiled from the heat. But the shock soon turned soothing and she accepted it. He could feel her loosening beneath his hand. The protective hunch of her shoulders slowly dipped away.

"You said that you are alone, Joan. Are you widowed?"

"Not exactly. I was betrothed once. He is dead."

"You chose not to remarry?"

"I have no interest in finding a husband. Marriage can interfere with a person doing what needs to be done."

He understood what she meant. He had avoided it himself because of things that needed to be done. It was odd hearing a woman say it, though. He wondered what purpose had led her to reject a normal life.

He remade the compress and held it to her back, below her shoulder, where her position in the stocks would have caused the worst knots. A little groan of relief escaped her. It sounded for all the world like a woman being pleasured.

He pushed her wet strips of hair out of the way so he could do the other side. "How came you to London?"

She slid up so he could reach better, crossing her arms over her body lest he try to peek.

"My family died, except for Mark. We came here because I had met Nick Tiler a few years earlier where I lived. He had come to make pavers for a manor house in the region, and had let me play with the clay. I hoped that he would give me work, since he had said back then that I had a talent with it." She shrugged. "I could think of nowhere else to go."

"Where was your home?"

"The western marches."

"We have more in common than crafting statues, then, since my family hails from there as well. You crossed the breadth of England? That is a long way for a woman and a boy to travel by themselves."

"I had no idea how long when I started. It took three months and the little coin I had. But Nick accepted me, so it was not a lost journey."

All the way from the marches with a young brother in tow. He was impressed. He had made that journey himself when he had been about Mark's age, with a father to protect him and enough coin for inns. Even so, it had been hard and sometimes dangerous. He had been running from trouble and seeking a free future, and only those goals had made it worthwhile. He doubted he would have done it just to find work in a tile yard.

He placed the hot compress on the edge of her back and pressed in to her ribs below her arm. His fingertips grazed the soft swell of her breast. She stiffened in objection, but the comfort of the heat defeated her.

"When I was a young apprentice, my master's wife used to do this," he explained. "After a few years my body grew accustomed to the work. If I had really hurt myself, she also did this." He placed his fingertips below her shoulder bones and firmly circled.

She arched in shock. "That hurts!"

"It becomes a good hurt. Stay still."

She accepted it, and then welcomed it. Slowly the knots softened and she grew limp. Her head lolled on her knees.

It probably would help her legs, too. And her arms. She would never permit that, but an image of it stuck in his head. He saw her lying naked on a bed while he slowly worked his hands over her entire body.

"This is a fine house," she said, to distract them both, as if she guessed his thoughts. "Wider than most in the city."

"Too wide for one person, is what you mean. I came into some money several years ago, and put it in land as most do. I built the house with an eye to selling it."

"But you did not?"

"I will someday, I expect. But there is a well, which is convenient, and a good-size garden where I can work. I have grown accustomed to both luxuries. And it is the first city house that I planned, so I have an affection for it."

She raised her head and peered around the kitchen more alertly. "You built it yourself?"

"The stonework."

"You designed it, too? Are you a builder?"

"I assisted a master builder for a few years, and began serving as one myself around the time I bought this property."

She twisted to see him. It pained her enough that she grimaced, but that did not stop her. Nor did the fact that her crossed arms hardly covered her breasts effectively. "Is that how you serve them? Mortimer and the Queen? As a master builder?"

Her blue eyes flashed with anger. She used the accusatory tone she had adopted when he walked her to the city gate three days before.

"It is how I serve the crown."

"So you say, but it is really them."

"For now, it looks like it is."

"They spend the realm's wealth on their luxuries. Have you helped them in their extravagance?"

"There are many builders to the crown. My projects have been few, and not very extravagant at all."

"But you hope for more and better ones."

Her belligerent goading irritated him. "It is my craft and my skill and how I eat. Aye, I hope for better ones."

She was picking at something that he resented her broaching. Bad enough that he debated his choices in his heart. He did not need this woman forcing them into words.

She did not retreat. "You said that day that you do not work on their castle walls, but one day you will be asked to, won't you? Not to carve tracery, but to plan and design the keeps and the fortifications. When Mortimer steals an estate, he calls one of his builders to come and improve the defenses that failed in his assault. One day that builder will be you, won't it?"

"I doubt that. I am not one of his favorites."

"You tell yourself that, but you know the day will come. You are young for a master builder. That means that you are more skilled than most. When it comes to the walls that hold up power, skill is what matters."

"You do not know what you are talking about. Skill is rarely all that matters in this world."

She glanced with scorn over his face and body. "I think that you have already made your choice, in your heart. You will do whatever is asked if the coin is right, and say that you only further your craft. You will probably tell yourself that it doesn't matter, that it is not one man's act that makes the injustice continue."

He resented like hell that knowing glance. A little fury whirled in his head. "If I tell myself that, it will be because it is true. I am a mason, woman, not a knight or baron. Masons build structures. Others build the power and the world."

"Masons are like the men who make siege machines.

They may not lift a sword, but there can be no war, and no power, without them."

"You have an unholy anger about something far above you. Like all ignorant people, you see the world too simply, and voice stupid opinions too boldly."

"I am not so ignorant and stupid that I do not know a lackey when I see one."

Lackey. "What you see is a man fast regretting an impulsive act of charity and growing sore angry at being insulted in his own house. Do not blame me for the injustice in this realm. If you think that a mason can change any of it, you are mistaken."

"Anyone with heart and resolve can change it. Masons and farmers and even—"

"And even tilers? If you believe that, you are worse than mistaken. You are a dreamer and a fool."

She reacted as if he had slapped her. "Better a fool than a willing victim! Better dreams that give purpose, than resignation that deadens one's will!"

She looked half mad, almost desperate. He heard accusation in her cry, but also something else, as if she proclaimed this for her own sake rather than to insult him. Still the insult was there, and his anger rose in response.

Not a normal anger. It had been mixing with a spiking desire all during this argument.

He wanted to silence this bold, ungrateful woman who slung insults more scathing than she realized. Not with his hand or words, but with a kiss. He wanted to embrace her rebellious passion and transform it into a more immediate fire.

The image of a fevered taking entered his head while she glared at him. It did not help that the argument had made her indifferent to her nakedness. The clear view of her breasts and thighs only made his imagination more vivid. The hot, tumultuous fantasy defeated his control in a way the physical intimacies had not. Her challenging expression only inflamed the urges he had been battling.

He either had to reach for her and make it real, or leave.

He was angry. She didn't care.

Her head split with livid indignation. How dare he call her a fool. What did this mason know about her, and her dreams. How could he possibly understand any of it. No doubt so long as his fees were paid, there was no injustice in the world worth righting to him.

He looked at her as the silence echoed with her furious words. Looked long enough for her to realize that more than anger had set his face in its severe expression and more than fury caused those steely glints. His gaze drifted over her, and she suddenly grew alert to what he saw. She had forgotten about her nakedness in the heat of her emotions, but he had not.

He was going to reach for her. Reach in anger and desire. She could see the impulse in those blue eyes.

Good. Then she could hit him. She wanted to. She needed to beat away the doubts to which his cruel words had given voice. Doubts that lived in her own heart, but that she kept silent lest they rob her of any reason to live.

He moved. For a breathless instant she braced herself.

He did not reach. He rose to get the last bucket from the hearth. He poured its steaming contents in to renew the bath's heat. He strode from the chamber.

She collected her emotions and calmed herself, and slid down in the water. The last bucket had made the bath wonderfully hot again, and it soothed her soul as much as her body.

She could not have really gotten its benefit if he were

still nearby, even if she had not seen his danger in those last moments. Her body may have loosened under his compresses and fingers, but in her core an awareness of him twisted and knotted the whole time he knelt behind her.

He had not reached for her, but he had wanted to. Not just at the end, but from the moment he carried her into this house. Nay, from the first time he spoke to her. It was just there, thick, like the moisture rising from the bath.

Eventually . . .

The water suddenly lost its warmth. A chill shook her down to her toes.

It was time to leave this house.

Pushing herself up, she tested her legs. They no longer seemed detached from her body. Carefully, she stepped out of the tub. Bending to grab the towel almost made her fall, but she snatched it up and quickly dried herself.

She could walk now. Slowly. Stiffly. She made her way over to the bench. Grasping the bench for balance, she bent for the gown.

She held up the befouled, tattered garment. It smelled. It clumped around the knot where Rhys had tied its torn skirt. Mending would not fix that, nor would another dunking in the river ever get it clean.

She had looked like a fool in it, a poor woman displaying herself in her better's rags. But it had been all she had to wear, and now she had nothing.

She needed to purchase a new garment. It would take one of her precious shillings, and she would get little more than another rag in the bargain.

That frustrated her so much that she gritted her teeth to contain it. The shillings were not for this. She did not slave in the heat merely to feed and clothe herself. She scrimped and worked for a purpose, for a dream. Only the dream stayed forever that, out of reach, no matter how she struggled to realize it, because the need to survive kept thwarting her.

A dreamer and a fool. Rhys's words echoed in her ears, and some of the anger returned, mixing with the frustration. She blinked back tears of resentment.

It was not foolish to dream of justice. And somehow, someday, she would make the dream real, for herself and Mark. She would find the money, enough to hire a champion to fight for her. She would send a brave knight to avenge the worst of it, and maybe even to give them back the lives that had been stolen from them.

She would make it right, or she would die trying.

She threw aside the towel. Turning the gown, she lowered it to step in. The firelight flickered over a few stitches of embroidery.

She stopped and stared. The fight went out of her, and a profound sadness took its place.

The tiny stitches grew and melted as her vision blurred. She had seen that decoration perfectly worked along the shoulders in a shimmering vine of ivy. The gown had been so beautiful in its unique dove color. So marvelously impractical, as befitted a wedding gown.

Now it was filthy and ragged, like the life it symbolized. Only a stroke of perverse luck had brought it with her from the marches. She had been wearing it on the night that she had left because a man's lust and vanity had turned his humor cruel.

This gown, Joan. I want you to wear this one tonight. And you will come to my bed. You will come in this gown, and remove it while I watch, and then you will kneel naked at my feet and beg for my favor.

She heard the words again, as if they whispered in her ears. Heard them and lived them. Her breath shortened, as if a gripping fist squeezed the air from her. Tears blinded her.

Her mind grasped desperately for the life-giving dream that was all that kept her strong.

A movement broke through the sickening memory. A presence loomed beside her.

Rhys stood there, holding a long bed linen. His gaze slid down her nakedness, then up to her face. Concern entered his blue eyes, not anger or lust.

He draped the linen around her. His arms circled her shoulders until the cloth wrapped her. They rested on her a moment, like a tentative offer of comfort. Strong arms. If she sank against them she would never fall.

He stepped away and gestured to the grey rag hanging from her hand. "You can not wear that. It is no longer fit for more than wrapping your crockery."

"It will do for a day or two, until I purchase another."

"You can not sleep in it. We will see what we can do with it on the morrow."

She shook it out, and made to step in. "Nay. I will—"

"You will not. Nor will you try to walk home as you thought to try."

"My brother . . ."

He pried the garment from her hand and set it aside. "Let him worry. I wager you have done so often enough when he did not return of a night. Tomorrow he will be so relieved that you are safe that he will obey you for a few days. Do not argue with me. You can not return tonight. It is too late and you need to rest."

He did not wait for her response. He lifted her in his arms and carried her out of the kitchen.

Darkness, and stairs. She could see nothing, not even him. But she felt his arms through the drape, cradling her shoulders and knees. And she felt his chest and his breath.

He lowered her. Onto a bed. A feather bed. It had been years. . . . She sank into it. Her body groaned with pleasure. Then it froze as caution snapped her rigid.

A feather bed. Probably his bed.

She began to protest, but boots sounded on the boards. "Go to sleep, Joan."

She waited until his steps grew distant. He had gone back down the stairs. The hills of feathers supported her like clouds, tempting her sorely.

Her eyes adjusted to the dim moonlight. She could see out the window. A patch of sky showed above the pointed roof of a house across the lane. A few stars spotted the blackness. They glimmered and multiplied as she grew drowsy.

Rhys emptied the bath and brushed the wet floor. He hung out the towel and his shirt. Bending to finish the job, he plucked up the gown.

In his mind, he saw her again as she had looked when he entered with the bed linen. She stood before the fire, completely naked, her damp tresses hanging like vines over her breasts and back. She had been incredibly lovely, and utterly still. She had been staring at this gown as if it had sent her into a trance.

He would never forget the expression on her face. Burning anger. Quivering disdain. Not for the foul gown. For something else, in her head and heart.

She had appeared completely lost for a moment when she faced him. So lost that her nakedness had not mattered to him, any more than it did to her. The hard words they had exchanged suddenly meant nothing. He would have taken her in his arms to offer some comfort, if the moment had not passed.

He folded the gown and placed it on the bench. Cloth was very expensive. It might still be of some use to her.

He walked back up to the bedchamber. She should be

asleep by now. He doubted that she would stir for many hours.

She lay on her side with the linen wrapped under her arms, draping her in ghostly folds down to her ankles. Her drying hair spread all around her, a halo of gold catching the moonlight. She appeared like a sleeping angel.

He pulled off his boots and stretched out beside her, along the bed's edge. He had work to do in the morning, and could not afford the soreness of sleeping on the floor. She would wake long after him anyway, so sharing a bed would not frighten her. It was big enough for two, and she was dead to the world.

He was not, however. Nor was he dead to her. It took longer than it should for him to fall asleep. Having her beside him seemed oddly normal, considering that she was almost a stranger. Other women had lain there sometimes, women with whom he had greater familiarity. They had always been intrusions of sorts. Distractions, sometimes sought and sometimes not, from other, more important parts of his life. Joan did not disturb the bed like that. She balanced it, as though her weight had been designed to fit the void waiting there.

She turned in her sleep, and huddled against him like a hurt child seeking protection. Her knees pressed into the small of his back and her breath warmed his shoulder.

He did nothing to move her, or himself.

CHAPTER 4

THEY STAYED CLOSE BEHIND THE PRIEST. *The carnage that they passed made her want to retch. She kept squeezing Mark's hand to encourage him to be brave. Comforting him was all that kept her composure intact.*

They tried in vain to avoid the pools of blood. All around them soldiers were stripping the dead of weapons and clothing. Sickening sounds of celebration rang through the yard. So did the wails of other women and children who had entered the yard to claim their fallen menfolk.

The priest paused and cried out to God. He turned to her, his expression woeful. "Joan, do not—"

"I will see him and say a prayer over him. Stand aside."

He hesitated, and then moved to reveal the man that he had blocked from view.

Her breath caught. Mark began crying. She embraced him, but did not look away.

Her father lay there, his armor streaked with sticky reds. His helmet was gone, and a defiant expression still masked his face.

A dark canyon slashed his throat and shoulder from where the death blow had cleaved out his life.

His sword was not in his hand, but in its scabbard.

The horror of it numbed her. She had seen death before, but not like this. Her mind dazed as her spirit tried to retreat.

A voice. A call. She barely heard it while she fought to believe this was just a dream.

A touch on her shoulder. The sights and sounds in the yard assaulted her again. She snarled resentment in the direction of the man who touched her.

The priest's hold fell away, but he pointed toward the keep.

She turned. An armored knight stood in front of the door. She recognized him.

Guy Leighton. The victor. The conqueror.

It had been his voice. His call. He gestured now to the priest. And her.

The priest gently took her arm, urging her forward. "God never abandons the weak," he whispered. "His kingdom is not of this world. All that is here passes."

She glanced back at her father. The image of him lying there would never pass.

She shook off the priest's hand, and walked forward. Mark found some strength too, and pulled out of her embrace. The commotion in the yard quieted a little, and soldiers parted to form an alley through the destruction.

The victor waited. With his visor down he was all steel and blood, nothing more. He still held his unsheathed sword.

She stopped in front of him.

He gestured to a squire by his side, and the youth reached up and removed the helmet. Not just steel and blood anymore, but a man with eyes fired by hell.

The gaze of those eyes rested on Mark. Her heart started a horrible pounding. There was still death in this knight. He enjoyed the power of killing.

Mark saw it too, but did not break. He straightened, as if daring the man to do it. Perhaps like her he half wished to be spared the misery of remembering this day.

"He is just a boy," she said. It came out no more than a whisper. "You do not need to do it."

The hot gaze shifted to her.

A long gaze, with different fires slowly replacing the ones of death. Just as hellish, though. Just as dangerous. She had never been so alone, so unprotected, as she was during his meandering inspection.

He reached out and lifted her chin with the steel of his gauntlet so he could inspect her face more directly.

"Aye. Perhaps I do not need to do it."

A pain in her shoulder shocked her, and lifted her abruptly out of the depths of sleep. She lurched toward consciousness in a confused, drowsy daze. She vaguely felt the feather bed beneath her. She sensed the body beside her.

Guy Leighton.

The nightmare suddenly grew real and immediate.

A horrible desolation gripped her. A desperate sense of being trapped spread in her chest, becoming so intense that she could not breathe. The suffocation panicked her. Her whole body shook while she struggled for air.

He rose and turned. Her heart groaned in despair and shrank to something very small.

"Joan? Is something wrong? Are you ill?"

The quiet voice penetrated her desperation. The last shadow of sleep broke away. She suddenly saw more sharply, more clearly, as time and place fully asserted themselves.

Not Guy.

Relief drenched her. Wonderful, grateful relief. She

might have been dragged on shore after almost drowning, so physical was the sense of salvation.

Of course not Guy. There was no danger of that. She was free. She and Mark had escaped.

The man looked down at her. Hair framed his face and lights glittered within the dark shadows of his eyes. Not Guy. Rhys. He must have joined her after she fell asleep.

She closed her eyes and went very still, hoping he would think her asleep. She knew that was not really necessary. Rhys would not hurt her. If he had not done so yet, he would not now.

He settled beside her, and fell asleep again.

She should leave this bed, but her relief was so thorough that it left no room for fear. She found his dominating presence very reassuring.

The memory of the nightmare wanted to stay vivid and alive. It kept nipping at her mind and flashing its horror. Surely it would return if she slept.

She instinctively sought the comfort of Rhys's calm strength. She snuggled against it, as though it served as a protection against the old horror intruding. In his sleep he moved his arm until it circled her, giving shelter.

That should have frightened her, but it did not. It made her feel deliciously safe.

The feather bed felt wonderful. Clean and undesecrated. She listened to the regular breathing close to her ear, and its comforting rhythm lulled her back to sleep.

The sounds of the city woke her. They poured in the open window with the bright sunlight. A lovely cool breeze flowed over her body.

Her naked body. She glanced down at the bed linens bunched around her.

She blinked away the sleep and remembered where she was. And she remembered the half-waking nightmare. She felt again the terrible panic before she had realized that the man beside her was Rhys.

She looked around the chamber while she resisted the temptation to drift off again. For a man who owned a wide house, he lived simply. The room only held some clothing chests and a bench.

She sat up. Last night's stiffness had eased somewhat. She could move without much pain now. She tried her back and her neck to see how things were, and gazed down at her nakedness again. She had slept beside him like this.

A stack of cloth at the edge of the bed caught her eye. She reached for it. Garments. Three gowns and a shift. She shook out the top one for inspection. It was a simple green robe with no decoration, but of good quality cloth.

The noise from the lane captured her attention. So did an aching hollow in her stomach. The day was half over. She had to be on her way at once. She had already stayed too long in this house owned by one of Mortimer's servants.

She got up and put on the green gown. It had belonged to a larger woman. One shoulder threatened to slip down her arm. The short lacing at the neck did not help much no matter how tightly she pulled it. Making do as best she could, she lifted the other garments in her arms and left the chamber.

The solar also contained little furniture, just a chair and table and some benches. She peered in a chamber at the other end of it. A small workroom, it held only a table and bench. He did not appear to be a man much interested in objects. She got the sense of a solitary person, concerned with other things besides comforts and typical routines.

She went down to the lower level. No shop faced the

lane, but only a large, fresh-looking hall. It filled the space below the three chambers above.

She passed into the kitchen attached at the rear. Spotless. Unused. Chinking sounds came from the garden and she followed them.

She would thank him for his help and leave. Her legs still ached, but they would get her back to the tile yard.

Rhys straddled a bench in the shade of a hawthorn tree. Propped in front of him, on an inclining board of good length, lay a stone woman. He bent over her with hammer and chisel, carefully chipping at the folds of her drapery.

He appeared to be carving a saint. Parts were merely roughed out, but other sections had been almost finished.

It was hard work. Even with the breeze, his bronzed chest showed a sheen of sweat. He wore only hide leggings. One did not risk cloth to rough stone and sharp chisels.

He straightened and inspected while he brushed away chips. She recognized the angled head and measuring gaze. That was how she made her little statues. Thought, and then work. Decisions, and then action.

His kind eyes could grow incredibly intense at times like this, when he contemplated something. Admiring his profile, she realized that his handsome face came from good bones and would not fade with age, unlike the faces of softer men.

He bent and turned a wheel below the bench. The saint inclined higher until it was almost upright. He swung off the bench and lifted a different tool.

He noticed her and paused. His gaze was more direct, and more familiar, than one expected from a new friend. The events of last night, especially of sharing a bed, had changed things. They had created a primal intimacy that he did not appear inclined to ignore.

A memory from the night broke into her head. Of her

cuddling beside him. Of him holding her. He remembered, too. It was in his eyes and manner, as if she had granted him certain rights with that embrace.

She had been stupid. Broken and weak and careless. She must leave here. She would fetch her old gown, change into it, hand him back these garments, and go. There was danger in this friendship with a builder to the crown.

He gestured to the tree. "There is ale and cheese here. Come and eat."

She heard a bit of a command in it, as if he guessed her impulse to bolt. Maybe he saw the fear. Not just the big one that she lived with every day, but also a new, small one. This handsome man with his rock-hewn strength kept giving her sanctuary, but he also made her feel very vulnerable.

The hollow ache in her stomach made the decision for her. There would be nothing to eat at the tile yard. A little more time could not hurt. She walked around him and found a crude table tucked by the garden wall. Simple planks had been set atop stone blocks. Bread and cheese and drink waited under clean cloths.

Rhys continued with the chisel. She liked watching him work. He possessed a different strength from a fighting man, leaner and more defined. Carving stone had created flat slabs and tight ripples.

He paused for a long inspection, then set down his tools. He walked to a well near the far wall and poured water over his head and body. Dripping with little rivulets that meandered down his chest, he came back and sat next to her.

He pulled the tie from his hair and raked his dark hair back with his fingers. Sunlight dappled through the leaves, dancing over the angles of his face and making his blue eyes bright.

The latent mood of last night's events intensified. In the daylight and cool breeze, they seemed dreamy, but very present. His closeness flustered her. She almost jumped out of her skin when he reached over and casually began untangling the knots from her hair.

She poured him some ale. "Which saint will it be?"

"Ursula. It is for the parish church. I said if they bought the stone, I would work it." He smiled, and those charming crinkles formed. "The priest promised me an indulgence in payment."

"But no coin, I'll warrant."

He laughed. "Aye, from a parish church, no coin. Of course."

"I hope the indulgence is very large."

"Huge. Between the statue and my virtue last night, I should go straight to heaven."

She decided to ignore the easy reference to last night, but she knew in her heart that he was not speaking of his Good Samaritan acts.

"It is hard work. My statues are child's play in comparison."

"They are different, but no easier. I am clumsy with clay. Look." He reached to a box near the wall and lifted a small, dried clump. It was a model for his saint, but only in the roughest of ways. "I only need the large shapes as a guide. The rest is in my head. Just as well. I can not mold, nor work so small."

"And I can not imagine chipping off stone that can not be put back. What if you make a mistake?"

"Well, we masons try very hard not to do that." He pushed the board of cheese at her. "Eat." He took up the ends of her hair again, combing with his fingers. He wasn't really touching her, but it felt like he was, and she grew far too conscious of it. He acted as though what had already passed between them made this informality a minor matter.

She should leave. Now. Her soul knew it.

But the cheese tasted wonderful and rich and her stomach felt very empty. She barely resisted gorging down the whole chunk.

"Eat it all," Rhys commanded gently, as if he could tell.

"You think to fatten me up?"

"I think that you give your brother most of your portions and that eventually it will hurt your health. In a while I will go to a tavern and get some meat. I'll wager that you give your brother all of that when you get it."

"I am beginning to feel like a stray dog on whom you took pity. A bath, some food, a bit of grooming. If you give me meat, too, I will fill this gown before I leave. Where did you find it? Did you walk down the lane asking charity for me?"

"I have a friend in the ward. She owns an inn nearby and has a generous heart. I visited while you slept this morning. She was glad to share her good fortune." He looked at the gown sagging from her shoulders. "I knew they would be too big, since Moira is more . . ."

"Womanly?"

"You are womanly enough, Joan. She is just very . . . abundant." He combed his fingers a little higher. Closer.

She touched the other garments that she had placed on the table. "Abundant in her goodness, too. Is she your lover?"

That truly amused him. "If she were, she would hardly give me gowns to clothe a woman who had just slept in my bed."

She really could have done without his mentioning that. Having it hanging in the air around them was bad enough.

"Just an old friend," he continued. "Her husband is a

lord, and would gladly kill me if I even contemplated more."

Her husband is a lord. The peace left the garden at once. The cool breeze turned chilly. This was what she feared. Even in kindness, he might endanger her. "Nay. And I can not accept these garments, either. I will put on my old gown before I leave, and you will return them to her."

"I can not return them. That would insult the giver. Nor do I have any use for them myself. You might as well keep them."

"I do not want her charity. I do not want yours, either."

He smiled down at the hair in his hands, then set the tresses over her shoulder while he looked right into her eyes. "Charity implies selfless giving, Joan. Moira has such pure motives, but we both know that I do not."

His quiet frankness dismayed her more than an unexpected grope. She had lots of experience with crude or sly advances. Her anger always served her well then.

At least he had given her fair warning, but then, in all honesty, that look when she had emerged from the house had, too. She began to rise. "I must go now. The day is old and I have tarried too long."

His fingers closed on her wrist, stopping her. "You do not have to run like a rabbit from a wolf."

She nodded down at his grasp meaningfully. "Don't I?"

"I spoke of nothing we did not know already. Nor does this only come from me."

"You are certainly a boldly confident man."

"Confident enough. And not so bold, just experienced enough to know when I waste my time, and when I do not. Now sit. The day is half gone, and you are still sore. The tile yard will be there on the morrow."

He held her until she sat, then released her. She picked

at the remnants of the cheese, and decided to be as frank as he. "Are you saying that I should stay until the morrow?"

"Aye."

She nodded in resignation. "You expect repayment, then. So, Master Rhys, what price do you put on a bath and a bed and some ale and cheese?"

"I do not know. How much coin do you have?"

"None, and you know it."

He smiled thoughtfully. "Ah. Then we must find another way."

"Not the way that you want, trust me on that."

"I was teasing you, Joan. You are a very suspicious woman."

"Not too suspicious. Just not green."

"You know in your heart that I expect nothing as payment. If I did, I would have tried to claim it by now. Last night when you did not leave my bed, or this morning while you lay naked in my arms."

Speaking bluntly of that again provoked an alarming reaction in her. A little streak of physical warmth spiraled down from her heart. It felt a lot like the usual caution, but enticingly exciting.

"I was hoping that you would be good enough not to speak of that."

"That would mean pretending it had not happened. I am not so good as that."

"I did not seek your bed. Nor did I expect to share it with you."

"You knew that I was there. You woke, and saw me."

"I do not remember that. I must not have fully woken." She lied baldly, not daring to admit she had permitted such a thing.

"Fully enough, but it is of no account. We both know that I want you, but I would not take you in payment even if you offered."

She should have felt more relief, but the wanting sat between them now, like a ghost given substance by his honesty. Her heart beat rapidly in response to its presence. "What, then?"

He stroked his fingers into her hair until he held her head. He looked at her with a man's warmth. Not bold, but confident and experienced.

"I ask only for a kiss, and not in payment at all."

CHAPTER 5

"NAY?" HE ASKED SOFTLY.

She almost stopped him, because it would ruin everything. The memories of his kindness would die.

Maybe that would be for the best. It should destroy this stupid, girlish fluttering that filled her now. And it *would* be a payment of sorts. She could leave, not feeling that she owed him anything for his help.

"Aye. But only a small, short kiss."

"We will stop whenever you like."

She braced her whole being for the assault. And so the gentleness confused her even more. Just a warm touching of lips. A careful caress of his mouth on hers.

To her bewilderment, it didn't disgust her. It awoke a quivering tingling in her cheeks. He kept doing it, making that one kiss into a dozen touches and nips, and the sensation spread through her face and down her neck and began to descend further. He might have been teasing her lips with a feather.

He stopped. She glanced up at him, afraid of what she

would see in his eyes. Their expression astonished her. A
brittle desire showed, but not feral hunger. Deep warmth
softened his male interest, turning it to something that did
not insult, but flattered.

They still sat apart, their angled bodies meeting over
the space. He kissed her again.

Firmer. Harder. Not a request but a demand. The
quivering sensation lowered like an inner flush, sliding
down all of her. A flood of tingles swam inside her.
Everywhere. In her head and her legs and her breasts.
They pulsed quickly. Her utter astonishment left her
helpless.

It was not supposed to be this way.

Rhys leaned back against the wall and eased her toward
him. The pitched angle made her unsteady. Light-
headedness did, too. Her balance tottered. She fumbled to
catch herself, and her palms landed on his chest.

Delicious heat flowed into her hands. Just enough to
sooth, and make her skin sensitive to his skin and taut
muscles. He was hard and soft and warm, all at the same
time.

He kept her there, merely holding the back of her head.
Only his outstretched arm supported her leaning body as
she braced against his chest. He stopped the kiss and
looked in her eyes. His deep gaze made her tremble even
more than that kiss had.

"Don't you kiss back, Joan?"

She felt her face burn. "Nay."

"Never?"

"Nay." Her gaze lowered to where her browned hands
splayed over his bronzed chest. Bits of moving sunlight
danced over their skin. "I have never wanted to."

His fingers gently snaked through the hair of her scalp.
He lifted her chin with his other hand so that she had to
look at his face again. His expression took her breath

away. Intense and knowing. Hard and soft and warm, just like his body. "That is not true. You want to now."

Gentle pressure on her head. A strong arm guiding her. Not to his mouth. Lower, until her lips rested on his chest, above her palms.

The slight taste, the scent, made her thoughts blur. All of her senses filled with him. She did not really decide, it just happened. She kissed, and moved her lips and kissed again. A rich pleasure began beating through her like a rapid breath. She moved her hand and kissed again. His arm lowered to embrace her and his mouth pressed her hair. She sensed a tenseness rise in him, but it did not seem threatening. Her misgivings had been defeated, vanquished by the delicious physicality enlivening her body.

She impulsively kissed up the indentation in the center of his chest, to his collar, and then his neck. He held her to him, encouraging her. When she turned her face up, he was waiting.

Not gentle. She did not mind the passionate expression of his arousal. It only increased her own reactions to where they almost overwhelmed her. Something mad and yearning boiled in her. She had never been so aware of her own body, and its involuntary responses kept startling her.

Rhys moved her. It happened so neatly, so naturally, that she barely noticed until she was inclined across his lap, looking up at him, with her hips pressed against his thigh. Raising her shoulders with his arm, he kissed again. His calloused palm caressed her face, then wandered lower to her neck and arm.

Her body shrieked at his touch. Fear and visceral desire mixed together chaotically. She almost stopped him, as she should have long ago. But his mouth moved in nuzzling, biting ways on her neck and ear. A new intensity blocked everything from her mind except how good it felt.

His firm caress kept moving. Down her side, brushing

the side of her breast. Along her waist. Edging her hip and leg. The parts of her body near his hand stirred with shameless anticipation. She grasped his shoulder to steady her reeling senses. When he claimed her mouth again, she kissed back gladly, welcoming a way to release the craving that grew and grew.

He lifted her higher, until she almost sat. The kissing turned fevered and insistent—for her, too. Her own willingness, her wanting, mystified her. A physical compulsion had taken over, and it insisted on having its way. He controlled it with his arms and his kisses and the astonishing arousal of his hand.

He touched her face and thumbed her lips gently. "Open to me, Joan. If you do not, I will go mad here."

Despite the dizzy sensuality, she hesitated. But a tantalizing caress along her hip and thigh, and the luring breath exciting her cheek, sent her spinning again. Trusting it would not be too horrible, she complied.

It wasn't horrible at all. It created a deep, startling intimacy. The connection left her shaking, and emotionally exposed.

Something changed in him, too, as though he sensed her vulnerability and had been waiting for it. He pressed her closer, until her breasts crushed his chest. He encompassed her hips with his other arm. The possessive embrace contained her with a gentle domination.

He deepened the kiss, pulling her higher. His embrace turned into caresses that moved freely, now claiming instead of seeking. Down her body, then up, teasing at the anticipation and making the desire anxious. His hand brushed her breast. His palm and fingers closed on her.

Incredible pleasure. Insistent and alive. It submerged any thoughts of refusal. He touched in ways that only made her want more. And more. And more. She could barely think because of the power of that wanting. It took possession of her.

His fingers sought the gown's lacing. "I almost did not leave this morning when I woke to find you naked in my arms. I must have gazed at you an hour. I want to see you again now, awake and aware of me." The loose neckline gaped, wide enough for him to slide it down her shoulder and expose her breast. The breeze tickled, and then his rough palm made the wanting still worse.

She hung around his neck, afraid to let go. He played at the tip of her breast until a frantic madness unhinged. She gasped again and again as it only got stronger.

He stopped their constant, hungry kissing and looked at her while he made the craving intense and aching. His expression made her heart skip, and then race.

"You have never wanted this before, either, have you? You are surprised. Not by my touch, but by the pleasure."

She pressed her eyes against his shoulder to hide her embarrassment. Rhys already knew this part of her better than she did.

His head dipped. "Let us see how surprised I can make you." His tongue flicked at her breast, tantalizing her with new excitements. She closed her eyes and tried to contain the delirium.

He would not let her. He used his mouth and teeth to push her beyond all control.

It almost happened. She almost drowned in it. Her body wanted to, and the rest of her had no voice. He beckoned her toward recklessness. The strong comfort of his arms and the knowing touch of his hands promised that the rest would be as wonderful as this.

She believed it. For awhile longer she abandoned herself to it. To him.

That caress again. Firm and possessive. Along her body, her stomach, her thighs. Reaching low and warming up her bare leg. Higher, creating pulsing trembles that made her ache. Higher. Warm and confident and knowing. Higher, until her whole body rocked with yearning.

A touch. A gentle, masterful touch.

One heavenly moment of incredible pleasure absorbed her, and then the ecstasy crumbled. Her body and soul recoiled from the sensation in horror. The pleasure turned dangerous. Instantly, with devastating clarity, she knew that she had gone too far. He had lured her in deeper than her past would let her go.

She grasped his wrist and moved his hand away.

He froze, still holding her to him.

He touched her chin and made her look at him. "Why?"

"You said that we would stop whenever I wanted to."

"I would have sworn that you did not want to."

"You know a woman's mind so well?" She disentangled herself and scooted away. She felt ridiculous. She hastened to relace her gown. "I offered one kiss only."

His gaze pierced her. "You offered more than that, pretty dove."

"Not what you sought."

He smiled and raised his hands in surrender. "I apologize for misunderstanding. The fault was mine."

She looked away and sighed. "Nay. It was mine."

The passion's memory still drenched them both, making things tremendously uncomfortable. She couldn't face him.

One kiss. It was supposed to sever the connections born of last night's bath and bed. Instead it had intensified them, and woven new, stronger ones. She had traveled farther with Rhys in less than one day than she had thought herself capable of going with anyone, ever. That bewildered her.

"I must go now."

He rose. "Nay. You offered me a kiss and I offered you a good meal. I will be back with it soon. It is the least I can do after you have been so generous."

She suspected that he mocked her. She couldn't really blame him. They were neither of them children, even if she had acted like a frightened one.

"Are you saying that you still want me to stay for dinner?"

He gave her a thoughtful look, as if he debated his response. "I find that I want you to stay as long as you choose to, Joan."

He walked to the house, leaving her alone. She was grateful he had left.

She fought to shake off the confusion their lovemaking had evoked. She should leave before he returned. This house and garden were seductive. So, it turned out, was he. She hadn't expected that.

She thought about what waited for her across the river. There wasn't really any choice but to go back today. He might tempt her from the poverty and worry, but never from the purpose and goal. It was why she lived now. Hot baths and feather beds would never assuage the spiritual needs. Even kisses of surprising pleasure could not do that. They might help her to forget for a while, but until she got justice she would know no peace.

She had liked forgetting. She had not thought it possible. He had created a fantasy of pleasure that had obscured everything else. For a time. Up to a point.

Boot steps paced from the house. She looked up, dismayed that Rhys had returned so quickly. Only it wasn't Rhys. A red-haired youth walked over to her.

"Is your master here?"

He thought her a servant. "Nay. He works today." It

seemed a sensible lie. She did not want the youth waiting here.

He looked her up and down. "A dedicated man if he leaves such as you to wield his hammer."

Not just a servant, but a leman. Well, that was common enough, too. "He will not eat if he does not work."

A wolfish grin broke over his face. "Who needs bread if there are other delicacies."

"Leave this property now, you rude boy. If you have business with him, come back later."

He resented her tone. Rich or poor, high or low, they always did, as if they expected her to be flattered.

He pulled a parchment out of his sleeve and tossed it on the table. "See that your master gets this, woman."

He strolled back to the house.

She picked up the parchment. Its folded ends were sealed. She recognized the device impressed in the wax. She had seen it before, on the banners unfurled by Guy's army.

The seal belonged to Mortimer himself. And it appeared that Rhys knew him well enough to receive private messages.

An unholy fury reddened her mind. That device had always heralded disaster for her. The power behind it had ripped her life from her grasp.

Hot resolve instantly stiffened her. She would get it back, all that she could, for Mark if not herself. She would avenge the crimes, at least. She could not touch Mortimer, but she could demand justice about the bastard pig Guy Leighton who served him.

Nothing else mattered, suddenly. Not the kindness nor the care. Not the sweet pleasure under the tree. The last day might never have happened. Rhys was what she had accused him of being, a lackey to an evil man who hired butchers to do his bidding. It had been a mistake to forget that.

She carried the parchment into the kitchen and set it on the table with a cup holding one corner. Her old grey gown lay folded on the bench by the hearth, and she picked it up. She glanced down at the green robe she wore. It had come not from him, but from that lady friend. She would keep it, but not the others.

She looked around the kitchen, and fought off the memories of last night. His hands undressing her and his arms lifting her to the bath. His concern when he found her naked by the fire. The sense of protection last night, and the flutters of excitement when he looked at her.

In her desperation she had clung to the help, forgetting the cost and danger. Nor had his generosity been pure. He had just been biding his time. The giving had not been selfless. He admitted that himself, and had proven it just now.

He wanted her to stay. She knew why. She was not reduced to that yet, though. And if she ever bartered that way, she would expect more than simple comforts in return. She would demand much more than this mason even knew how to pay.

She hurried through the hall. She stepped out on the street, and ran down the lane.

CHAPTER 6

A MASON WHO WANTED TO LIVE did not refuse
Roger Mortimer's call. Still, Rhys waited a day before re-
sponding to the summons. He decided that would be long
enough to remind Mortimer that he dealt with a free citi-
zen of London, but not so long as to anger the most powerful lord in the realm.

He found Mortimer on a bench in his private garden at
Westminster, alone with a young woman. The lady appeared distraught, as if she feared that she was being
forced to play a game which she could only lose.

Rhys knew that look. Its familiarity evoked painful images from his youth.

Relief veiled her eyes when his arrival interrupted
them. Mortimer dismissed her, and she darted to the garden portal.

Rhys experienced an intense, visceral reaction to the
little scene. The way that Mortimer used women disgusted him. He brought all his power to bear on the weak
in order to get what he wanted.

He was not alone in it. Many lords thought it their due to have whatever women caught their eyes. But Rhys had first seen it happen to a woman desired by Roger Mortimer. He had been only fourteen at the time, and the injustice had branded his young heart. He had watched that woman's anguish as Mortimer trapped her into submission. He had heard her screams while she birthed the dead bastard of the man whom she loathed.

Details surged, specifically and clearly, out of the place in his memories where they had retreated long ago.

A beautiful woman, dark haired and fair skinned, slowly descending a staircase . . . His uncle sitting by the fire, refusing to watch . . . A silence so deep that one could hear the starving stomachs growl.

No one went to support her in the short walk to the waiting knight outside. Everyone's life depended on her accepting the shame, but the women did not want to be touched by it. The men did not want it to appear that they agreeably handed her over.

This final injustice infuriated him. If his father and uncle would not fight, they could at least give her comfort. And so he had gone to her, so she would not be totally alone.

Before they reached the knight, she had spoken. "Tell my husband that I will remain untouched in the ways that matter."

He had admired her strength, but the cost of that resolve had been high. When Mortimer finally tired of her, she returned with a soul so numb that nothing could ever touch it again.

He stood in the grass twenty paces from the bench. The vivid images had dazed him, and had darkened his mind the way they still could when they unexpectedly emerged.

Mortimer gestured him forward. "You take your time, mason. I sent a summons for you two days ago."

"I was not there, and had other matters to attend as well. Please do not send messengers to the city again. I am at Westminster often enough for you to find me here."

Mortimer's mouth pursed in annoyance. "You are overbold for a craftsman."

"A timid man is of no use to you."

Mortimer did not invite him to sit on the bench, but Rhys did anyway, to show just how overbold he could be. He resented this summons. Like that woman, he sensed that he was being drawn into a game that he could not win.

"I have nothing to tell you. It has only been several days," he said.

Mortimer considered that. "It is too quiet." He squinted thoughtfully. "Do you know Addis de Valence?"

"I have met the Lord of Barrowburgh a few times." He had more than met him. Addis was married to Moira, the woman who had given him the garments for Joan.

"I am told that he is in the city. In the heat of the summer. No lords use their London houses now."

"Sir Addis is no enemy to you. He fought bravely for the Queen's cause. He held London for her. He took no part in Lancaster's uprising against you two years ago."

"But he has not come to court. He has not presented himself to the Queen."

"He is a rough man, not given to little courtesies. He has a new son. Perhaps that distracts him."

"You know much of this man whom you have met only a few times."

"His house is in my ward. And I know his wife fairly well, from before their marriage."

Mortimer grinned lewdly. "Do you now? A lush woman, nay? Serf-born, it is said. Such women are the best, the most passionate. She caught my eye, I will admit. If you know the wife, you can visit there. I am most curious about Addis. He keeps his own counsel too well. One never knows where he stands."

"I doubt that he will confide in me. We are not friendly."

"You served together in the Queen's cause. That makes a bond. Use it, and your friendship with the wife. See what you can learn. Something is brewing. I can smell it." Mortimer appeared truly concerned. "Find out what it is, and you will have more than you ever dreamed. Whatever you want."

There was nothing more to discuss, so Rhys gladly left. The meeting had unsettled him. Even without the Queen's favor, Mortimer was lord to a quarter of the realm. He was not a man to cross. He was also the kind of patron every builder needed if he sought to make his mark.

More than you ever dreamed. Whatever you want. He dreamed of palaces and cathedrals and town halls. He dreamed of carving statues the way he imagined them and not the way the priests demanded. He dreamed of leaving a legacy in stone that would stand through time, so that ages hence people would see it and wonder whose mind and art had brought it into being.

Whatever you want. The words repeated in his head, over and over. He would not be the first man to align himself with power for his own purposes. Nor the first to put aside principles to achieve his goals.

Fortunately, he would not be tempted to. Nothing was brewing, and if anything ever did, Addis de Valence would not be in the middle of it.

He collected his horse and headed home. He took a long route, meandering from market to market, more aware than he wanted to admit that he was hoping to see a blond woman selling crockery.

She had been filling his head for two days. He kept seeing her face and body. Images of her breathless surprise always provoked an immediate arousal. The parted red lips and the glistening eyes and startled gasps could immerse him in a sea of desire.

I have never wanted to. Maybe not before, but she had wanted to with him. It had been very natural to have her in his arms under the tree. She fit in them as surely as her body had molded against his in her sleep.

He could not remember ever being so interested in a woman. Not just in bedding her, although that impulse also was stronger than normal. He wondered about her. She had been seasoned by loss and life, and experience had produced a rich complexity that intrigued him. He worried, too. Twice now she had needed help. If it happened again she had no one but a young brother to look after her.

Certainly that tiler she worked for would not aid her. He might even send her into the city again with more flawed goods, and her punishment the second time would be worse than the first. Someone should explain to George Tiler that letting a woman answer for his bad craft was cowardly, and that abandoning her to be thrown in the gutter after a day in the stocks was despicable.

Aye, someone should definitely have a few words with the man about that.

It was all that he needed. Just an excuse, like his consideration this morning that he needed new cups, and that fired, thin-walled ones would be nice.

He abruptly turned his horse and retraced his path. He aimed for London Bridge, and the town of Southwark.

The tile yard stood on a finger of land that jutted into the Thames about a mile upriver from Southwark. As Rhys neared, he could see workers carrying trays of tiles out of a long thatched building, and others waist deep in a huge vat, stomping to separate clay from soil. The workers were women, all of them wearing nothing but sleeveless shifts and kerchiefs.

A small cottage backed up on the road, and tiny shacks flanked the water's edge around the works itself. Rhys tied his horse to a dead tree behind the house and walked around it to its door.

A sandy-haired man rested in the shadow of its eaves, slouched on a bench beside a bladder hanging from a peg near the door. His red-stained beard and liquid eyes declared him drunk already, and it was barely past midday. He watched the women while he sipped from a chipped crockery cup.

He did not notice his visitor until Rhys stood beside him. For a moment he appeared uncertain whether to welcome or resent the interruption of whatever he contemplated about the women. Rhys had no trouble imagining what it was, and that sent his temper churning.

"Who are you?"

"My name is Rhys. I am a mason and builder."

George brightened. "Then you come looking for tiles. Welcome, welcome." He gestured to the bench for Rhys to sit, then held up his cup with a questioning expression.

Rhys looked down on the dirty, wine-stained drunk. He remembered Joan suffering from thirst in the stocks, and deadly anger leaked into his head. "I find wine too drying in the summer. In fact, I find it over-warm out here. Can we speak in your cottage?"

"There's a fine river breeze here, and the view is very pleasant." George smirked lewdly toward the half-naked women.

"I would prefer the cottage."

George shrugged and led the way into his home. Rhys followed, and closed the door behind him.

"Now, how many tiles you be needing, Master Rhys?"

"I did not come to buy tiles."

"Not tiles, eh? Odd you should want to come in here, then, if what you want to bargain for is out there. Or maybe you already know which one you favor?"

So George did a little whoremongering on the side. Rhys resisted the urge to end the conversation at once by breaking the man in two.

"I did not come to buy a woman, but to speak about one. Four days ago one of them spent the day in London's stocks with your tiles at her feet."

"She fired them wrong, and tried to hide the results in among good ones. I assure you that my goods can be trusted. It was a rare occurrence that will not happen again. When she returned, I chastised her soundly."

Rhys's temper snapped. He reached for the neck of the tunic in front of him. With a sweeping swing, he crashed the stunned tiler up against the door. Holding George by his neck, he forced his face into the planks.

"If you beat her—"

"Nay! Not beat . . . I did not . . ." George's squashed face twisted with fear. "I spoke with her is all."

"Even that took gall. You sent her in to take your punishment, you bastard. You did not even come for her when it was over."

"I didn't know! She didn't come back, and I figured she'd run off, to escape her debt to me. Had my wagon, didn't she, and all those tiles. I thought she'd stolen it all, not ended up in the stocks."

"If you thought that you would have looked for her." Rhys pulled George away from the door and held him up by his tunic's collar. "What debt? You spoke of her debt to you."

"I have her mark. She signed an indenture. Five years."

He threw George aside. "Find it. I want to see this mark."

George nodded nervously and poked and dug in a trunk. Finally a stained folded parchment emerged. He offered it with a shaking hand.

Rhys held the document to the window's light. It looked legal. The little fool had indeed put her name to it. It bound her to the tiler for five years in return for ten shillings and the use of a cottage.

He hated indentures, and the way they took advantage of the desperate. A person should not have to choose between freedom and survival. It was not an apprenticeship that Joan had acquired with her mark, as was the decent use of such things. She had signed herself into slavery for little more than shelter.

Fury sliced through his head. He truly wanted to punch George's face in. The tiler cringed, as though he could see it was coming.

"A handsome bargain for you, George. She is more skilled than most master tilers, certainly more skilled than you."

George looked insulted despite his cowering pose. "She is skilled, but hardly like me. She is useful to the works, but not so much more than the others."

"I think that she runs the works, while you sit and get drunk and leer at her. And let other pigs leer, too."

"I run the works. It is my craft, like my father's. She is useful, but not necessary."

"Than you will not mind losing her." It was out before he even knew he was thinking it.

George frowned with confusion. Rhys put an iron grip on his shoulder and waved the indenture in front of his face. "You gave her ten shillings and a hut. I say that is worth no more than one pound altogether. Don't you agree?"

George appeared ready to agree to anything if it kept him alive. Rhys hadn't decided that part yet.

"I will send you that much. A man will come with the money tomorrow, and you will sign this over to me. Do you accept?"

"I accept."

"One more thing."

"Whatever you want. Just don't—"

"Did you ever force her, or sell her to some man? While she lived on this property and slaved for you, did you hurt her?" He pictured that as he asked, saw her fear and helplessness, and almost moved his grip to George's neck.

"Never! I swear to God and all the saints that I never once ever—"

"You told me that you sell these women."

"She wouldn't have it, for coin or not. She hates men, she does. Why, once I just suggested, friendly like, that we might share some ale, and that night I woke up to find her in here with a knife at my throat telling me to get no ideas. She can be ill-tempered and ornery that way. Hell of a thing, if you think about it. It's my property, isn't it? Who's she to—"

"If I find out that you did, if you ever insulted her or let others do so, I am going to come back."

"If she says that happened, she is lying. I never—"

"Stay here. Do not come out until we are gone."

George sank into a resentful sulk. "Aye, but for a man who claimed he didn't want to buy a woman, you've done so a bit too thoroughly to my sense of trade," he muttered.

Rhys stepped out of the cottage, into the sun. There, with George out of sight, the fury began to thin, making some room in his mind for other things.

Like the stark realization of what he had just done.

He looked toward the tile works. Joan noticed him. She strode toward George's shack, but stopped halfway down the path. She stood there, regarding him curiously, with her hands on her hips, looking as ill-tempered as George had warned she could be.

He stared down at the dirty parchment in his hand. He could not believe he had just bought this. It had been a mindless impulse born of anger. In one moment he had been condemning such things, and in the next . . .

The rash act stunned him. Not just because he did not believe in freedom being bought and sold, but because of the responsibility and ties it entailed for him. He had avoided such chains. They interfered with a man living as he chose and doing what he must.

He should turn around and undo this. Now. At once.

Joan crossed her arms over her chest. She appeared very curious now, and a little suspicious.

He pictured her in the market and the stocks. He imagined her fending off George and his drunken friends. He saw images of her brave and broken.

He tasted her lips again, and the softness of her breast, and felt her body snuggled against him in the bed and pressed to his chest in an artless embrace.

He walked down the finger of land toward her, knowing he made the choice for many reasons, and that only half of them were rational and honorable. Nor did all of them have to do with protecting her.

Then again, the urge to protect was often coupled with the desire to possess.

She watched him come. She managed to be very lovely even when garbed in a clay-encrusted shift and a dirty kerchief. The peevish expression on her face did not strike him as especially becoming, however. He suspected it would not get friendlier very soon.

"What are you doing here?" she demanded when he drew near her.

"I came to purchase some of your crockery."

Her expression softened. "You did?"

"Aye."

"What did you want with George, then? I think that you also came to browbeat him about me, about what happened." She did not sound as if she welcomed the interference.

"That is true. I also came for that. But things got a little tangled there."

"How so?"

"I truly came to purchase some crockery." He held up the parchment. "But as it happened, I bought you instead."

CHAPTER 7

"YOU BOUGHT ME?"

"Not you, in truth. Only your indenture."

"You can not do that."

"I can, and I have."

"Then go back there and undo it."

"Nay. The bargain is struck."

She thought that her head would split. She pushed past him, hotly eyeing George's cottage. "When I am finished with that lazyboned, besotted weakling, there will be no bargain."

He caught her arm and set her back a few paces.

She shook his grasp off and faced him. He returned a hard gaze that said she would not pass.

"Surely you did this as a jest."

"Nay."

"Then why?"

"I did not like the idea of you indebted to such a man in any way, let alone with your freedom."

"A chivalrous impulse. How generous. Since you interfered to protect my freedom, give me my mark. When it is mine, I will make George pay me the wages he should."

"I am not leaving you here. George sells these woman as whores. Eventually he would sell you that way, too."

"He would not dare—"

"He has no scruples."

"And your scruples are very confused, if you buy me to prevent my being bought by another."

A vague acknowledgment of that passed in his eyes, but his firm expression did not soften. "Let us get your property. You are coming with me. My horse is behind the cottage."

Vision half blurred with anger, she looked from him to the cottage. A terrible thought entered her fevered mind.

He had come here intending to take her away. It had been his real purpose. The indenture had only made it easier, and prevented her from having a choice. He had brought a horse to make the trip back to the city with her more convenient.

Why? He had recently been summoned by Mortimer. What if, in talking as men do, Rhys had mentioned the tiler named Joan. . . .

She forced down the fear that rose in a nauseous wave. What if he had? There were many Joans, and a poor one had no consequence. There was no reason for Mortimer to suspect that Joan the tiler was the same Joan who could bear witness to his worst crimes, and give substance to the rumors about them. Maybe he assumed that other Joan was dead anyway, and had forgotten about her.

She hoped that was so, but she could not count on it.

"Is your brother here?" Rhys asked.

Her heart skipped a beat. Many Joans, but fewer who had a brother named Mark. Fewer still who had walked here from the Welsh marches three years ago.

"Why did you come today? Who sent you?"

"I am beginning to think that the devil sent me. We will get your things now. If your brother is not here, we will leave word for him to follow when he returns."

"I will not go with you."

"Would you rather slave and whore for George?"

"If a woman whores, it does not matter who the man is. Do not expect my gratitude that it will be you instead."

"I do not intend that."

"Then perhaps you expect some other benefit from this? To gain favor with someone?"

"I expect nothing but trouble from this. I will gain favor with no one, and only get lectures from the wardens of my guild and the priest of my parish. Now, let us be gone from this place. The sun and your hot mood are burning away what little good humor I have left."

He strode forward, pulling her along. She shook off his grasp again and marched alongside, barely containing her worry. Even if this had happened as he said, she and Mark would be much more vulnerable living inside London's walls.

And she would be gone from the tile yard. She would not miss the work, but she would sorely feel the loss of the kiln. How could she earn coin if she could not make her wares?

The other workers watched as she and Rhys headed to her hut.

"Only women labor here?" he asked.

"We are cheaper. He pays almost nothing. The women who come here have no other choice, except the brothels."

"Except that this serves as a brothel at night."

"They tell themselves it is different. They all think that they will leave someday."

"Like you thought it, no doubt. But you are still here, aren't you? Does he pay you? Even with the indenture? Even though you refuse to work at night?"

"Just enough for food. The indenture is of no value if I starve to death."

He muttered a curse. "Why did you sign such a thing?"

"To survive." She pulled open the flimsy door of the shack. "When Nick died, I was desperate. Nick had let us live here for free, but George would not. We needed a roof over our heads, and some coin. It had been my hope to buy the parchment back in a year, but . . ."

But. Just like *maybe*, it had thwarted her again and again. Her life had been a series of both words for three years.

She pulled on the green gown. It did not take her long to pack her property in one homespun sack. A few shifts, dull and brown from the washed-out clay. The tattered rag of grey fabric. Two crockery cups and bowls. The crude tools she had made to work details into her statues.

She reached under her pallet for her hidden coins, and for her eating knife. She carefully lifted a wooden board from under the only bench. It held her new statues. She carried over the box that contained what was left of her wrapped crockery, and contemplated the little saints.

"Roll them in the grey gown and shifts," Rhys said.

"There is no point. I will have no way to fire them."

"There are other kilns. Use all your garments if you need to. We will leave word for your brother to carry the box when he comes."

She halfheartedly tried to protect them, knowing it was useless. He crouched and helped, rewrapping the one she had begun.

"You should not have done this," she muttered. "I have always dealt with George. He needs me here. The works will fail without me."

"The day will come when he needs coin more than you. Then you would have found a strange man entering this shack, and no recourse but submission or a beating." He rose and held out his hand. "Come. You are done with this place."

She peered around the shadowed, crude shack that had been her home. Despite their poverty, they had been safe here.

She had to know what she faced. "Did you truly come today to purchase crockery? And just to reproach George?"

He stood beside her. His tall strength dominated the tiny space, and her. "Aye. But I also came to see you, to be sure that you were well."

"Do you swear that was all? That you did not come here planning to take me away?"

He did not answer at once. She waited, the caution that she knew too well pounding its low beat in her blood.

"I do not think that I planned to take you away. But I can not swear it."

His hand appeared again. She wished that she could trust him. She rose on her own. "If you are an honest man, I fear that you will regret this. If you are not, I certainly will."

"It appears that we will both be taking a chance."

"It appears that you give me no choice but to do so."

He lifted her sack and opened the door. "That is true, Joan. I give you no choice. You will come with me now."

Her brother followed a few hours later. Rhys heard him call into the house from the street, seeking Joan.

He left the small workroom and went down the stairs to the door. Smells of soup and bread filled the hall. Like the kitchen clutter Joan had already caused, such ordinary things were interesting novelties here.

Mark stood in the street, holding the wooden box. He was big for his age. Already his shoulders had broadened, giving his youthful frame a loose, wiry appearance. His blond hair hung straight to his shoulders, and his eyes, surprisingly dark in one so fair, gave Rhys a very unfriendly inspection.

"So it is you," he said.

"Aye, it is me."

Rhys brought him to the kitchen. Joan stirred some soup at the hearth. He walked out to the garden, leaving Mark with her so that they could speak privately.

He went over to the bench where the statue lay propped. He had begun working the face yesterday. He always did that near the end. His saints were famed for their humanity, because he did not rely on the traditional formulas for their poses and characters. He waited for the faces to emerge in his mind. When they came to him, they were composites of many that he had seen in the city, of eyes and mouths and expressions branded on his memory.

This Ursula would be dignified and soulful, showing both the confidence of her high birth and the acceptance of her suffering. Not above it all, like too many carved martyrs.

Mark came out of the house, carrying the box. He put it on the table under the tree and faced Rhys. A little cocky. A little defensive. The man of the family was ready to discuss terms.

"She says that I can stay here, too."

"I will hardly leave you in the alley."

Mark considered that, then speared him with a knowing gaze. "You have no wife."

"It appears not."

"She will not whore for you." He looked away. "I will not, either."

"I am looking for no whore, least of all you."

"No matter what you call it, she won't do it. As long as you accept that." He pulled two folded sacks from the top of the box. "I brought our beds. Good thing that I did, eh? Even a mason would not have three. They need straw, though."

Rhys gestured to the far portal, and led Mark to the stable.

The youth's eyes widened in delight when they entered. "Do you own a horse?"

"That one there."

He entered the stall, and began checking teeth and legs as though he knew what he was doing. "He looks to be a good animal. What, about six years?"

"How came you to learn about horses?"

"My father had one. We were not always so poor."

Not poor at all, if the father owned a horse. "You can take over caring for him, since you know what you are about."

"If you don't use him every day, I will exercise him, too."

Rhys imagined the young man happily galloping through the city lanes, wreaking havoc. "Let me think about that. Now, the clean straw is over there."

"I will tell Joan where it is."

"Nay, you will do it yourself."

Mark looked shocked. "I do not stuff pallets."

"You do if you want to eat."

"You do not understand. She will not permit it."

"*You* do not understand. It is not her say now, but mine. If you live here, you will work. There will be chores every day. You will care for the horse and tend the garden. The stable roof needs rethatching, too. You will not live off your sister's labor anymore."

Mark resentfully grabbed an armful of straw and sulked all the way back to the house.

They found the meal ready. Two bowls waited on the kitchen table. Rhys wandered into the hall. There, alone on the long table, stood the last bowl and cup.

He went back to the kitchen. "Move your crockery in there with me."

"Servants do not eat at the master's table," Joan said primly.

"This master does not choose to eat alone. It is why I always went to taverns. Move them."

It was a silent meal. Joan kept her eyes on her food, as if she did not want to see her surroundings. Or him. Even when he complimented her cooking, she did not respond.

Mark did not notice the awkwardness. He wolfed everything in sight, and would have taken the last of the bread if Joan had not smacked his hand. Remembering the relentless hunger of that age, Rhys broke off a small piece and pushed the rest to him.

Joan grabbed the bread from her brother, and slammed it back down in front of Rhys. "It is yours, not his. Stop mixing things up. Stop acting like this is other than it is."

He pushed the bread back to the boy. "Take that, and go stuff the pallets."

Mark darted glances to them both. Suddenly alert to the tension, he left quickly.

Rhys rose, and looked down on Joan's bowed crown. "I must go meet some men, Joan. When I return you will explain to me what you think this is, since you seem to know better than I do."

He did not come back quickly. Joan spent the whole time in a turmoil, waiting for the sounds of his return. She worried that he would not come back alone, but with guards who would take away her brother, and probably her, too.

Several times, while she washed the cups and cleaned the kitchen, she nearly succumbed to an onslaught of panic. She almost called for Mark to tell him they must run. Rhys had gone to Westminster, to report that he had them. The meal had just been a gesture to lull them into complacency. To fatten them up for the kill.

Run to where, though? That consideration always intruded, and forced more rational thoughts. She had no real evidence that he knew who she was or the crimes she could prove. None at all. She was letting her imagination unhinge her judgment. If Mortimer suspected, he need not have sent Rhys to the tile yard. His guard could have found her there as easily as here.

She debated it back and forth, over and over, trying to decide what to do. The sun set on her agitation, taking the choice out of her hands. Mark laid their pallets near the kitchen hearth, and soon fell asleep on his.

She paced the hall, sick to her stomach, listening through the silence for the sounds of horses and boots.

Finally she grew exhausted from the fear. She went out through the garden to the well, to wash off the clay and the soils of cooking.

The city had gone to bed. It was very quiet now, very peaceful. That calmed her. Hidden by the night and the wall, she slipped her arms up through the gown's broad neckline, and let the bodice and shift fall around her hips so she could wash more thoroughly.

The cold water felt good. It enlivened her skin. The night air dried her with a subtle chill, making her very alert.

Suddenly she sensed him. He was here, in the garden. Sitting at the table, under the tree. She did not turn and look, she just recognized his presence.

He had been there all along. He had returned through the garden portal much earlier. The whole time that she washed herself, he had been silently watching in the moonlight.

She quickly pulled her shift up to cover her breasts. She heard him move, and rise, and walk toward her.

"You should have said something, and made your presence known," she said accusingly.

"I couldn't. My heart was in my throat."

She fumbled to find the shift's armholes. He came up behind her and reached around, doing it for her. His arms encircled and enclosed even as they aided. Heart pounding, she shoved her arms through.

Rhys's fingertips brushed her shoulder, making her tremble.

She stepped aside, so he would not seem so close. "Did you go to Westminster?"

"I went to the Guildhall. Why did you think I had gone to the palace? No one works there this late."

"I thought perhaps you went to answer that summons."

"I did, but not tonight."

She still fumbled clumsily with the gown. He watched. She got the sense that he could see more of her than she of him. His attention left her so exposed that she might have been standing naked beside him.

"If you know about that summons, you were still here when the messenger came. I have wondered about that. Did he offend you? Is that why you left?"

She finally got the gown up. She set it on her shoulders with relief, but still felt naked. "He was offensive enough, but that is not why I left."

"Then why?"

"Because I did not want to stay. I did not want it to continue. But it appears that you did not understand that. Your vanity has put too much weight on a few kisses. I meant nothing by them."

"I have kissed often enough to know what they meant. Have you?"

"Often enough, as you say. To my mind."

He reached out and brushed his fingers on her mouth. "Except that you never kissed back before, because you did not want to."

She turned her face, but his hand did not fall away. His fingertips lingered on her skin.

Best to have it out now.

"You want me to sleep with you, don't you? You lied at the tile yard. You said that you did not intend that."

"I will never force you, pretty dove. But I will not pretend that what passes between us is not there."

She forced herself to angle away from his touch, and break the contact. "Nothing passes between us. I do not like men in that way."

"You like this man in that way."

Hands reaching for her. Gently closing on her shoulders. Turning her, so that her hips now rested against the well.

He caressed her arms down to her hands, and pinned them wide apart on the ledge, leaving her spread and vulnerable, and standing so close that his chest brushed her breasts. "Something most definitely passes between us, Joan. At the very least, a very promising pleasure does."

He kissed her neck, then her ear, then her mouth.

More than promising. Astounding. It flowed and tingled and sunk low quickly, as if she had been waiting for it. She realized that she had. Anticipation had been a part of her worry and her fear, and even her anger, complicating all of her emotions.

Craving impulses awoke, and grew and grew. He gently bit her lower lip, demanding more.

It frightened her. A chilling sadness intruded on the pleasure, as though invisible hands pulled her out of it. She could never permit what he wanted. Neither the past nor the future would let her.

He stopped, as if he sensed her retreat. His hands caressed her arms up to her shoulders. "You are a confounding woman."

"Perhaps I am just a virtuous woman. There are a few left in the world."

"I do not think of these things in such commonplace ways, Joan. I don't believe that you do, either. But if I am wrong, and I offend your virtue, say so. Look me in the eyes and say that you think this is sin, and I will never touch you again."

She could not. He would hear the lack of conviction and know that she lied. Her ideas about right and wrong, about virtue, had long ago been abandoned. This was not wrong in that way. If anything it was too right.

Rhys took her face in both his hands.

"You think that you know what *this is*, Joan. I am more curious about what this might be."

His rough, gentle hands reminded her of the care in the market and at the stocks and in the bath. His words lured her with memories of the bond forged that night and then explored the next day under the tree. The yearning spread intensely. Her heart ached from it so badly that she wanted to weep.

She removed his hands. "I cannot let this be anything more than it is. I will not be staying in London much longer. There are things that I must do soon."

"What things?"

"Things close to my heart that I do not speak of. I have nothing to give you but the service that you have bought. There is nothing I can take from you except a few nights of shelter."

"There is friendship and pleasure, in the very least."

"If I ever lie with a man, it will not be for that."

"What then? You said you did not want marriage."

"Nay, definitely not marriage. That bondage is even

more permanent than the indenture. If I wanted that, I could have had it by now, and spared myself three years in the tile yard."

"Then for what do you save yourself, if not affection or security?"

I want a man killed.

She almost said it. She came so close that she knew he was weakening her, and luring her to confidences that would jeopardize everything.

"I save myself for myself, and for duties and plans much older than your knowledge of me. I will not let you interfere with them."

She slipped from between him and the well and began walking back to the house. He fell into step with her.

"We have not settled what services you expect," she reminded him, seeking refuge in practical things so as to hide her unsteady emotions.

"They will settle themselves. Only I do not think of you as a servant, so do not insist that I treat you as one."

"Then I am your guest?"

"Since you will not be my lover, I suppose that you are."

"You offer an odd hospitality. Normal guests can leave."

"I will not hold you against your will. You can leave when you know where you will be going, and that you will be cared for, and it is not back to the tile yard."

"Those are a lot of conditions."

"They are the ones that I set. Buying that indenture gave me obligations as well as rights. I am responsible for you now." A new firmness entered his tone.

"I do not accept either the obligations or the rights. I will leave when I choose, without any explanations to you." They entered the kitchen. "However, I do not expect to do so tonight, so you need not keep watch."

With his departure, she sank down on the bench against

the hearth. She felt as though she had been holding her breath for hours.

She should wake Mark and go. She would be free of Rhys, and the confusion he kept evoking in her.

But how would they live once her coins were gone? She had only two things to sell to ensure their survival. Her craft and herself. She knew not where to find work in the former, and she could not stomach the notion of resorting to the latter.

He knew that. He knew that necessity would keep her here more surely than any indenture. Aye, he was a man, and in this no better or kinder than most.

But they were safe here for a while. She was certain now that Rhys did not know yet. But someday he might. Then what? Keeping silent might cost him dearly, while exposing them would ensure a powerful man's favor. She would not count on any man risking himself for her, even a man who wondered *what this might be*.

She looked over at Mark. His stomach was truly full for the first time in years. He had not gone looking for trouble in the city tonight. This place would be good for him.

They would stay while she planned what to do next. She would start learning about other tile yards and kilns. Free of George, she could earn coin for her skill now. Maybe in a few weeks . . . maybe . . .

CHAPTER 8

JOAN SLOPPED SOME WATER onto the plank floor-
ing and stretched to scrub a corner of the solar floor. She did
this every day, even though it hardly needed it. Only Rhys
used these upper chambers, and he spent little time in the
house. Still, she did it along with other extra chores. She did
not want anything unbalanced in this arrangement.

This effort would be especially noticeable today. It had
rained, and only now was the afternoon sun emerging.
The light breeze blowing in the window carried the mix-
ture of freshness and fetid damp that only a summer storm
could cause. The floor would not completely dry before
Rhys returned this evening.

A burst of laughter and a scuffling of footsteps rose
above the city sounds. A raucous noise of youthful horse-
play tumbled into the house from the street and began
rolling up the stairs to her. Mark stumbled into the solar,
still nudging and jostling another boy by his side.

"This is my sister, Joan," he said, playfully aiming another elbow. "This is David."

David looked to be a bit younger than Mark. He was shorter and slighter, and had not yet begun that quick, manly growth that had occurred with Mark in the last year. A beautiful boy, though, with golden brown hair and deep blue eyes.

"He's a mercer's apprentice, and lives a few lanes over," Mark explained while he and David paced around the chamber, curiously examining its contents.

"Shouldn't you be at your trade, then?" she asked the boy, rising from her knees to greet him.

"My master went to Westminster today, to show some silks to a lady. The older boys went with him, and he closed the shop." He peered into the bedchamber. "Not much here for a house so big, is there? Always seemed odd, just one man in such a place. It is not so grand as my master's house, but it is overlarge for one person."

"Well, there's three here now, isn't there. For a while," Mark said in a superior tone. He had obviously decided that age and strength dictated the pecking order in this new friendship.

David looked out the window. Something caught his attention and a peculiar, almost hard expression veiled his face. For a moment he reminded Joan of the street toughs that Mark had known. It would be just like Mark to find a new friend who had a taste for trouble.

He kept watching—long enough that she got curious. She threw down her rag and went over to him and looked, too. When it was clear that she saw nothing of special interest, he pointed.

"Over there, in the shadow of that narrow alley. There is a man there. I saw him when we came in, and he hasn't moved. You should tell Master Rhys that there may be a thief who is interested in this house."

She squinted. Slowly a darker form took shape in the dark shadow.

"He may have learned that it is empty most days," David said. "He may be waiting for it to be empty again."

A little spike of fear stabbed her stomach. Aye, it might be a thief, or just someone loitering around. Or it might be a man sent to learn about the woman who lived here now.

She knew that made no sense, but she could not control the fear with rational arguments. It had always possessed a life of its own. Worry began tightening inside her against her will.

"See what I found," Mark announced.

She pivoted to see him standing beside an open chest, beaming with delight. He held a longbow and a quiver of arrows.

"I'd seen the butt in the stable, but thought it belonged to a neighbor. There is a fine dagger in here, too."

"Are you tired of eating? Do you yearn to sleep in a field? You know that you should not go into his chests. I do not want us thrown out before I have found another place where I can work."

Mark smirked while he admired the bow. "He is not going to throw you out, and he knows that you will not stay if I can not."

If his friend heard the insinuation, he did not show it. He joined Mark at the chest, and lifted the dagger. "All citizens own some weapons, to defend the city. These are very fine ones, though."

Mark headed to the stairs. "I'm going to get the butt. It has been so long, I wonder if I have any eye left. Should be easier to use than the last time. I've grown a lot since then."

"Nay, you are going to put them back where you found them," she scolded.

"They will be back before nightfall. If he finds out, just blame me." With that he disappeared down the stairs, with David and the dagger following.

She knew when she had lost an argument with him. He was showing off for his new friend, and he would never back down now.

She went to the window overlooking the garden. The butt emerged through the portal. Mark set the straw-filled disk atop a bench against the far wall. Pacing down the length of the garden, he took his position, sighted an arrow, and let it fly. A whistle speared the evening's peace.

A pang in her heart matched the thud of the arrow hitting the butt. She knew the sound of longbows too well. It had been years since her ears had rung with their sickening song, however. Hearing it again reminded her that this was not child's play, for all of the boys' laughing and joking.

Both worry and pride filled her heart. Mark had a good eye. Most boys could not handle a longbow until they were fourteen or so, but he had been big for his age, and strong, and their father had put one in his hands the year before they left.

She returned to her scrubbing. Periodically, she rose and peered down at the shadow across the street. The man in the alley did not move.

His relentless presence preyed on her mind.

By the time the floor gleamed dark and wet from end to end, she had worked herself into a state of agitation.

She hated this worry. Hated what it did to her. Well, she had no intention of spending the rest of the day being owned by it. If the danger was real, she would find out.

She carried the bucket down to the garden and poured the water into the garden. "Put the weapons back in the chest now," she ordered the boys. "Then come back here. I have something for you to do."

Maybe it was her tone that got their obedience, or perhaps they had tired of their game. A tempest of youthful exuberance swirled into the house and up the stairs, then back down to her.

"The man in the alley across the street will be leaving soon. I want you to follow him and see where he goes."

David aimed at once for the garden portal. "We'll wait a few houses down and take his trail there. Come on, Mark, I'll show you. We won't lose him. These lanes and alleys are my kingdom."

She strode through the house and out the front door. She marched across the lane, right into the shadow and right up to the man.

"They hang thieves in London," she said, branding her memory with his portly body and blond beard and round face. His garments were simple but well made. He was a successful thief, if he was one at all.

Her abrupt confrontation unsettled him. "Who are you, woman, to dare to accuse me of such a thing? I am no thief."

"Then why do you lurk here? Hiding like this?"

"I neither lurk nor hide. I needed to piss. There are men who do that openly in the lane's gutter, but I am not one of them."

"If you piss, the good Lord gave you a bladder as big as a lake, seeing how long I have watched you here."

The man puffed up with indignation. "Hell of a thing, when a servant goes threatening a peaceable man. And a woman servant at that. Watch how you speak to your betters, or I will have you punished."

"By whom? This woman answers to no man. Be off with you, or I will fetch my carving knife and take some of the hot air out of you."

"Hell of a thing," he muttered. But he angled out of the alley, and headed down the lane.

She waited in the kitchen for Mark to return, the simmering worry making her anxious. Acting boldly did not mean that she truly felt very brave.

The boys were a long time coming. Finally they strolled

into the garden, well pleased with their adventure. She met them beside the shrouded saint.

"He went to a tavern and drank some ale by himself," Mark reported, sinking down on the workbench. "Then he walked west, and headed toward Newgate."

"Did he leave the city?"

"Nay, he went to another tavern. Only this time he sat with a man. We waited for him to leave for a long time, but finally gave up since dusk is falling."

"Did the other man wear any livery?"

Mark turned serious. He suddenly understood why she had sent them trailing the man. "Nay, he wore no livery."

It wasn't much information, but at least their quarry had not gone to Westminster, or met with someone in Mortimer's household.

David had been eyeing the column of canvas propped on the workbench. He lifted its edge and peered at the statue underneath. "The man he met wore no livery," he echoed, ducking his head for a better view. "But from the cut of his garments and the fashion of his hair, I think that he was French."

"You cannot know that for certain," Mark said, a little peeved that his friend had gleaned more than him.

David smiled and shrugged and continued examining the saint. Something in that smile told Joan that he did know that for certain. A mercer's apprentice would have an eye for such things.

"Well, if the other one was French, that is odd," Mark muttered.

Joan agreed. It was very odd.

Rhys packed his tools and prepared to head home.

To Joan.

He ruefully acknowledged that he thought of it that

way. Carving tracery required great skill but little thought, and so half of his mind could dwell on her while he worked. It was not something that he entirely welcomed.

She was quickly filling his world. The house and the garden. His chambers. She impressed her presence, like so many feminine footprints in wet clay. He returned to his home at sunset every day, amazed anew at how she now marked its spaces.

Having her in the house was a form of torture. An entrancing little dance of silent desire waited for him every evening. Mutual desire, that she refused to acknowledge. He watched her place her feet very carefully, so that she did not sway too near him no matter how he moved.

He waited for the misstep that would send her into his arms.

He slung his sack of tools over his shoulder and followed the other masons out of the abbey work yard. As he neared the portal he saw the red-haired youth, whom Mortimer had been sending too often with impatient summones. The page did not wear livery.

The boy did not even have to speak anymore. Rhys merely fell into step beside him and accepted the escort to the little private garden where Mortimer liked to hold his meetings.

At least no fearful woman sat beside him this time.

"No word, mason?" Mortimer asked peevishly.

"Please remember that I must still earn my bread. I have work that occupies me. And of course I can report no word if no words are being spoken."

"They are being spoken. What have you learned about Sir Addis?"

"I told you that his wife is lying in from the birth of her child. It is too soon to visit her without raising suspicion. In a few days, perhaps."

Mortimer bit into a pear. He sucked at the juice noisily

while he contemplated the craftsman standing before him. "In a few days, then. As to you earning your bread, I have had a thought about that. A new project. Edward's little queen is dissatisfied with their chambers. She wants a new wall put in, and some other changes. His mother is inclined to permit it, to keep the girl happy."

Rhys felt as though a rope had just been slipped around his neck, and that Mortimer had begun to haul him toward a chasm.

"Wouldn't the King prefer to choose the builder on his own? That is customary."

"He is too young to know of such things. One builder is the same to him. It will take some time, I think, to build that wall. A good long time, when you will be in the chambers often, doing your craft."

Aye, often. Frequently enough to become invisible. Seeing who came and went, and hearing the odd word or two that might reveal much more than intended.

And Mortimer would be waiting for all of it. It would become very hard to put him off with little bits of nothing.

He faced another dance now. He might enjoy the one of desire that filled his nights, but he would hate the one of survival that would mark his days.

The burden of that turned his mood surly as he rode back to the house. He wanted no part of this. He had pulled away from politics and intrigues after the rebellion, but like a fool he had let John and others lure him back to help with the ill-fated revolt against Mortimer two years ago. That disaster had thoroughly resolved his disillusionment. The failure of the barons to support Lancaster and Stratford had proven without a doubt that he could not change much in the world, since the most powerful men shifted their loyalties as it suited their gain.

He did not want to be listening for Stratford, and he sure as hell did not want to do it for Mortimer. He desired only to be left in peace to practice his craft. He wanted to walk the city lanes without looking over his shoulder, and when he reached his home every night he wanted to make love to a pretty tiler with sun-bronzed skin and silken hair and an indomitable spirit.

A spirit that he felt even as he put the horse in the stable and crossed the garden. A spirit that, in his dark mood, struck him as a distracting challenge as he crossed the threshold into the kitchen.

Joan noticed him at once. She was bent over a pot in the hearth and could not see him, but with his footfall she shifted ever so slightly, as if to make room for his presence.

A subtle retreat. The announcement of a boundary. The first step in the dance.

Usually he found her art at the game intriguing.

Tonight it raised the devil in him.

She always knew when he had returned to the house. Even when he came in the front way and she did not hear him, she felt his arrival. This house might be too wide for one person, but as far as she was concerned he filled it very completely.

And so she knew he was at the stable before she heard the sounds there. Sensed him walk toward her through the garden even though she did not turn to look. Felt him at the threshold as surely as if he had touched her shoulder.

It was always thus, and it badly unsettled her, but this evening that presence seemed stronger and less benign than usual.

"Where is Mark?" he asked. "He did not come to care for the horse."

"I'm sorry, I had forgotten that you took the horse. He met a new friend today. A mercer's apprentice. He is eating supper there."

He walked across the kitchen toward the hall. She kept her nose to her stirring and instinctively eased to one side to give him more room to pass.

His steps paused. "Stop doing that. You insult me with it, as if you think if I get within ten paces of you I will pin you against the wall and ravish you."

"I do not—"

"The hell you don't." He strode out. She listened to him go up to the solar.

Goodness, but his mood was stormy. She wished she had not relented to Mark's request to eat with his friend.

Rhys came back down, and Joan quickly spooned out the soup and carried the bowls into the hall. He stood there drinking the ale that she set had out to wait for him. He had removed his hide tunic and thrown on a sleeveless cloth one instead.

He watched her every move as she set down the soup and walked back to the kitchen for the bread and cheese.

Aye, she should have never let Mark eat elsewhere. This big house suddenly struck her as far too small. Forcing down a peculiar wariness, she carried in the food and took her place.

He sat at the end of the table as always. She tried to edge away a bit without being obvious. It didn't help much. It was just the two of them, knees almost touching, close together. Much closer it seemed than when Mark joined them.

She kept her eyes on her soup and tried to ignore the sense that she sat beside a rumbling storm cloud.

"I have grown fond of your brother, but I am glad that he eats elsewhere tonight," he finally said. "You tote him around with you in the evening hours and make sure he is always by your side. It is pleasant to take a meal with you like this, without your human shield between us."

She had not thought her use of Mark had been as obvious as that.

"The floor upstairs is wet," he said. "It often is in places, but not like today."

"It was damp today because of the rain, so it did not dry very fast."

"You do not have to scrub all of the floors every day. It is excessive."

"I don't mind the labor."

"I do. And it will damage the planks over time."

"I won't be here long enough to damage any planks."

"I know why you do it. All of that scrubbing. To prove that you earn your keep, so—"

"Since the scrubbing is to your benefit, and the keep is your cost, I cannot see why you should mind."

Except for the glint that entered his eyes, she might have thought he had not heard her interruption. "To prove that you earn your keep, so I will not expect other payment," he finished.

At least her sore knees had not been acquired in vain. Only she had not expected to speak of it.

"I told you that it would not be like that, Joan. Have I done anything to frighten you, or to make you think that I lied when I said that? Have I treated you with anything except respect?"

"Nay. But . . ." She caught herself.

Rhys gazed right into her eyes. "But it is always there. That is what you were going to say, isn't it?"

"Aye, always there. Whenever you return and even when you are gone. Like a mist so thick one can catch it in one's hand. You spoke too boldly at the well that first night, and look what it has done. I am not afraid of you, but you make me wary."

He reached out. Half mesmerized, half shocked, she watched that hand come. A touch. The gentlest caress on her cheek. "This does not just come from me, pretty dove. It never has. Nor from my honesty at the well. You are as wary of yourself as of me. You know that it would be good between us."

For a moment she could not move. The warmth of his rough palm seemed to hold her in place, and flush into her skin and blood. A luring, enlivening warmth.

She pulled back and rose and walked to the end of the table so it formed a barrier between them.

"Here you are, the first night my brother is not present, being overbold again. If I keep a human shield nearby, it seems that I do with good sense. You insist that you have shown me no disrespect, and then proceed to indeed show it to me."

"There is no disrespect in a touch of affection."

"It is not just affection. You said that first day that you are not above seducing me, and I think that is what you think to try tonight."

"There is no disrespect in wanting a woman, either."

"There is if she is not interested, if she does not want it."

He gazed down the length of the table at her. She found his expression unfathomable.

"You keep saying that you are not interested. You are very sure? Because I just saw something in your eyes and felt a tremble beneath my hand that said otherwise."

"I am very sure." Except that she wasn't. Something inside her had lurched hungrily at the promise offered in that touch. A false promise, she knew. Hopeless. But her womanhood had responded anyway.

And Rhys knew it.

"Then come sit and finish your meal. If you truly are not interested, you are safe with me."

He was teasing her. Challenging her. If she retook her place he would touch her again, maybe only once, to test her lack of interest.

The mood between them tightened terribly, enticingly, with his invisible pull and her feeble push. He did it deliberately, like a declaration of power. Only the table's barrier kept her from sliding across the tiles to him.

"So," he finally said. "At least we do not have to pretend anymore. But if this is so strong that it is always there, in the air that we breathe, I am wondering why you deny it."

"I explained that. I will not be here long."

"Aye. You have somewhere to go and something important to do. Another thing that we have in common. Unlike most men, I understand that, since I have known it myself. But it looks like you will not be going soon. Since I do not seek to bind you or stop you, what is it that you fear will happen in my arms in the meantime?"

"Disappointment."

A very direct look. A slow, sensual smile. A dangerous light in those blue eyes.

"Well, Joan, I promise to do my best."

She had impulsively spoken a confession, but he had heard a challenge. Just as well. It would humiliate her to explain.

"If I ever want to find out how good your best is, I will let you know." It took all of her trembling poise to say it.

The light of challenge flickered again in his eyes. He regarded her too warmly, that storminess surging. She half expected him to get up and walk to her and put her rejection to the test.

He didn't. He relaxed back into his chair, and she sensed that the worst had passed.

She began collecting the bowls and tray.

She moved quickly, dreading the arm that might reach out for her.

Dreading it, and waiting for it. Waiting too hopefully, she ruefully admitted. He knew that, too. She could feel that he did.

She turned toward the kitchen with her burden.

"Running away?"

"Aye."

"I wonder what you would do if I did not let you."

The notion appealed to half of her, but the other half instantly bared its claws. "I would hate you."

"That is what I usually decide. When I don't, it is the dead of night and I am dreaming."

"You imagine me compliant, then?"

The smallest crinkles formed, but the smile was hard and the gaze very direct. "Compliant? That sounds tamed and defeated. Nay, Joan, I imagine you as I have known you. Moaning with pleasure and only wanting more."

She closed her eyes and shook off the spell he had cast. She turned away from him and strode to the kitchen, trying to appear dignified despite her wobbly legs.

No steps followed. Relief pounded through her, but something else, a thwarted yearning that she could not deny, beat beneath it.

It seemed that avoiding one kind of disappointment meant swallowing a different, more confusing kind.

CHAPTER 9

VENDORS JAMMED the market. Not just food sellers, as was normal for this section of the Cheap. The season for market days and festivals had arrived, and merchants and craftsmen from all over the region would stop in London as they traveled from one fair to the next.

Joan pushed through the crowd, carrying her basket. This was not the market closest to Rhys's house. She had decided to obey his order and not scrub the floors daily anymore. Instead she used the time to venture about the city when she bought provisions. It gave her a chance to visit the shops that sold crockery and tiles, and ask about the craftsmen who provided them.

She slowed as she passed a potter's cart, and gave his wares a sharp examination. Kiln fired. She had noticed several others with such cups and bowls in the markets these last few days.

"These are very fine," she said, lifting a bowl. Not just kiln fired. He had used a wheel. "You are not from London. Is your home nearby?"

"Kent."

Kent. Not far away at all. "I see some tiles in your cart. Do you make those, too?"

"They are my brother's. We share a kiln."

"Will you be here all week?"

The potter shook his head. "There's a fair day down toward Canterbury next week. I'm heading there in two days, to get a good spot. If it's tiles you want, come there. My brother will be with me."

She studied the potter's greying hair and soft face. He seemed friendly enough. And safe enough. She broached the subject she had already raised with several other craftsmen today. "Do you make all the pots yourself?"

"I've two apprentices, and some workers to prepare the clay, but most of these here are mine."

"I make pots too. Not on a wheel, but many cannot tell, they are so fine. I am looking for a place to ply my craft. I have worked in a tile yard, too. Perhaps you or your brother need another worker."

He looked her over curiously. "You expect coin, or just shelter and board?"

"Coin. My craft is very good."

"Everyone's craft is good, to hear them tell it."

"I can show you. I have some cups that I made. I will be meeting another master tomorrow at the Cathedral to show him my skill. I can meet you, too, if you want. You will find none better than I. It will be a bargain for you, since I work as well and hard as any man, but cost much less."

"I'll not be standing in a Cathedral bidding over a woman. I take ale at that tavern over there at dawn. Bring these cups of yours before I leave the city, and we'll see what's what."

She promised to meet him, and picked her way through the crowd. A heady excitement enlivened her step. What luck that she had chanced upon two potters looking for workers today. In a fortnight she would be gone from this city. Considering what had happened at that supper with Rhys, that wouldn't be soon enough, but it would have to do.

She aimed out of the market, making plans. She would leave before Rhys woke, and bring only the best of her cups. If she baked tomorrow's bread tonight, there would be food for him in the morning, and by the time he could question her about her absence, everything would have been settled.

Boots fell into step beside her. A familiar presence warmed her side. Startled, she looked over to find Rhys smiling down at her.

"You are far from home, Joan."

"The fowl in the neighborhood market were skinny. I decided to visit this one. And I may be far from home, but you are farther from Westminster."

He relieved her of the basket's burden. "I often come back to the city after dinner. The other masons use the time to sleep, but I do not need it. I am going to a scribe's shop to buy some parchment. Why not come with me? It is an interesting place."

Since he would carry the basket, she went along. A scribe's shop would be a nice diversion.

It was several lanes off the market street, tucked among other shops that looked very fine. She peered in their windows as she passed. A goldsmith's and a furrier's. Rich fabrics could be seen beyond a mercer's shutters, and she recognized a golden brown head among them. David, Mark's new friend, saw her and hailed a greeting.

"My master lived in this area, so most of these craftsmen are old friends. This scribe passes on some of his parchment. It saves me the trouble of finding it elsewhere, since I do not need much," Rhys explained as he led the way in.

His friend looked to be a very successful scribe. Most worked at tables in the Cathedral, not in a shop. This one even had an apprentice.

She peered at the scrolls and sheets and the book that the apprentice illuminated with colored inks. Rhys purchased two sheets of creamy parchment. She watched a lot of coin change hands.

Outside the shop he set down the basket and carefully folded the sheets.

"It is very expensive," she said.

"Aye. My one indulgence. Other men buy jewelled knives or rich furnishings. I buy the stuff of dreams."

"That is when you aren't wasting your silver on unwilling women."

He smiled. "I told you, Joan. You are the stuff of dreams, too." He tucked one of the sheets into the basket. "That one is for you. I will give you a quill and some ink. I expect that you miss your craft."

"It will be a sinful waste. Quills and ink and drawings are not the stuff of my craft." *Or my dreams*.

"It is all design. It is all a manifestation of the same craft. If you make mistakes, you can scrape them off. I will show you how."

He strolled back down the lane, and paused at the goldsmith's shop. "Now that I think about it, what we really want is in here."

"Gold? Oh, aye, that is truly the stuff of dreams."

He crooked his finger and beckoned her to follow him inside.

The only gold visible was a miniature saint being worked by the master at the back of the shop. A small vise held it while he filed along its delicate lines. He welcomed them and continued his labor, but he kept glancing up at her and breaking into boyish smiles at her attention.

"It is hollow," Rhys said. "It has no back and will be attached to something—a reliquary, I would guess."

The goldsmith nodded. "Aye, a reliquary for the Blackfriars."

"To make it hollow, and less wasteful of the gold, he makes a core of clay. Then the saint is molded in wax, then covered with plaster," Rhys explained. "He heats it all, the wax melts, and the molten gold is poured into the cavity. When it cools and hardens, he breaks away the plaster, lifts it off the clay, and he has his little saint. All precious metals are done that way. It is how church bells are cast."

"Then I must finish it, which is what I am doing now," the goldsmith said. "Perhaps someday you will make a bronze statue, Rhys. The Queen is rich enough for it."

"Even she is not that extravagant. And I do not mold, I carve." He gestured to Joan. "But my friend here works clay. Perhaps you have some extra that you will sell us."

She looked at him in surprise, and then at the goldsmith with unabashed hope.

The goldsmith set down his file and debated it. "I don't have much, and there's other figures to do." He glanced at her and broke into one of his smiles. She smiled back and he flushed. "Oh, aye, I guess I could sell a bit."

She watched in wonder as some more coins appeared. Rhys took the small clump and dropped it in the basket. It wasn't much, but it would make a statue.

Or two cups. Newly worked undried cups that she could bring to the potters tomorrow, to prove that the skill was truly her own.

"I had better carry this back to the house for you," Rhys said. "The clay makes it very heavy."

That was very kind of him. He often was kind. Except when he was buying her indenture. Or threatening to seduce her. Maybe he was being especially nice today to make amends for the other night.

He brought the basket into the kitchen, then left through the hall. She grabbed the clay and carried it out to the table beneath the tree. She sat and peered at the lump, poking it with her fingers. It would be nice to make a statue. She had imagined several the last few weeks that wanted to be formed. Since she could not fire the clay, she could make one, then reuse the clay and make another, over and over.

Nay, it would be best to form the cups. Not so much fun, but more useful at the moment.

Her contemplations utterly absorbed her, and so the nearby steps startled her.

Rhys had not left after all. He set a quill and ink pot on the table.

She looked at them, and at the clay. She thought about the parchment still tucked in the basket. It had been very pleasant today, visiting the shops and walking and chatting.

She pressed the pliable mass and her fingers sank in. It felt so good. "Thank you for this. For helping me find it. I will pay you what it cost."

"It is a gift. I could not bear being cut off from my craft. I am sure it is the same with you."

Her heart warmed at his thoughtfulness, but she did not want him giving her gifts. She would find some way to repay him, even if he never knew.

Maybe she would begin a statue at least, and then later in the day reform it into cups.

"Joan, Master James and Master Neil will not be waiting to meet with you. Both men have decided that they do not need a pretty worker after all."

His quiet words penetrated her euphoria. She stared up in shock. "You saw? You followed me? You spoke with them after—"

He suddenly looked less kindly. "It is well that I did. Not every man who works clay is as pliable as George. If they agreed to meet with you to discuss such a thing, it was not your skill at your craft that they sought to buy."

"It would be once they saw my craft."

"Your skill is high, but theirs is higher."

"Exactly. I could have learned from either of them. I might have had the chance to master the wheel, or to learn to use slips. You had no right to interfere!"

The glint flashed in his eyes. His face turned stony and severe.

All at once she understood. Anger shot through her. "You did not do this to protect me. You did this because you have decided that you will not let me leave." She lifted the clay, and threw it back down. "You sought to appease me with this."

He did not respond, but his hard expression answered plainly enough.

"What did you say to them? With what words did you undo what I had carefully begun?"

"I said that you belong to me." It came out simply and firmly.

Fury pounded in her head. She felt her jaw clench. "Nay, mason. I belong to *me*, and never forget it."

His eyes burned. He lifted her off the bench. His expression made her heart jump. "Aye, you belong to yourself only, Joan, and I never forget it." He pulled her into his arms. "I never forget anything. I never forget this. Nor do you." His mouth claimed hers in a forceful, demanding kiss.

It was her breathless confusion that permitted the deep kiss, not her free will. He had caught her unaware, that was all. She frantically told herself that as he plunged her into a chaotic whirl. The strained attraction yanked her in, rendering her helpless.

Biting kisses. Their anger made it heated and contentious, a fevered series of challenges and triumphs and defeats, with the latter entirely hers.

When his mastery was complete, when he had proven to her the power of the desire, he took her face in his hand and looked in her eyes. "Aye, we neither of us forget. I can be in my chamber, and you in the kitchen, and it is there." His expression was far too knowing. Still severe, still angry. "So tell me, Joan, about how you belong to you alone, and how I have no rights or claims. But first tell me why this frightens you so much that you would risk your safety to escape it."

Anger flooded her again. Anger at herself, for ever permitting that first kiss under this tree. Resentment of the weakness that had led her to seek sanctuary in a man, any man, let alone one who wanted her in this way. A man about whom she could trust only one thing for certain. That he desired her.

The anger was mostly with herself, but there was some for him, too. For the way he kept cornering her, and asking her to face something that she did not want to look at.

Something dreadful and numbing and hidden. Something shriveled and invisible, but not dead.

She grabbed the anger and threw it at him with reasons she could speak of. "You act like you protected me with this interference, but it is not that, mason, anymore than it was when you took me from the tile yard. Since you have failed, since I will not be your leman, just let me leave."

"You want to make this base, but you know it is not. If I sought a bedmate I could have taken the coin I gave George and bought whores for years."

"Then buy them." She pushed away, hard. He let her loose. Good that he did, for she was ready to pummel him if he held tight. "Buy them, Rhys, because this will never be."

"It already is. And we both know it."

"Nay, it is not. Nor will it ever be. Never. Nor will I be in your home much longer. I want to earn coin with my craft, not just mold for my amusement. I will find a place where I can. When I do, I will be gone, and all the pleasure in the world will not stop me." She strode toward the kitchen, desperate to end this.

"I think that you fear that it *will* stop you."

"Stand aside and see if it does." She snapped the challenge over her shoulder. "You know *nothing* about me. Who I am and what I fear have nothing to do with you."

She went to the tavern and the Cathedral the next day, but neither of her potters was waiting for her. Whatever words Rhys had used, they had been effective. Probably his size and strength had spoken eloquently enough.

She tried to ignore the clay he had given her, but it beckoned like a siren. By marketing time she had destroyed the cups made in a rebellious fury the day before, and begun one of the saints that she had already molded in her mind's eye.

Mark accompanied her to the market, none too pleased to do so. Rhys was clever, she had to give him that. He had given Mark an additional chore. He had commanded her brother to carry her market basket so she would be free of the burden. Of course Mark refused to wander the whole city doing such woman's work, visiting shops and visiting craftsmen. By saddling her with her brother, Rhys chained her to the neighborhood market.

They returned with provisions earlier than normal. They entered through the garden portal and brought the food to the kitchen. Mark headed to the hall.

He was going up for the bow. He used it every day while Rhys was gone, and she had ceased arguing about it. He was restless despite his work in the stable and garden. Aiming at the butt for an hour usually pulled him out of his surliness.

She did not hear him on the stairs, however. Instead he returned to the kitchen.

"No fun today," he muttered. "He came back early. He is up above. I heard him walking about. Best plan on more than bread and cheese for dinner."

Actually, she had planned on little else. Now she would have to go marketing again. She strode into the hall, intending to say a few pointed words about giving her some warning if he expected to take his midday meal at the house.

She heard the footsteps at once. She froze, and listened intently to their weight. Her nape prickled.

Not Rhys. She knew his steps very well. Too well. When he was here the pulse of her blood matched their rhythm, and when he was absent they echoed in the emptiness.

She slipped back to the kitchen. "It is someone else, I am sure," she whispered.

Mark's eyes lit with excitement. "I will go see. No point in having us about if he gets robbed while we sit in the garden."

"You are not going up there unarmed."

"I've my two arms and fists."

"I am coming with you."

He began to object, but she let him know with her eyes not to bother. Gesturing her to stay behind him, he eased through the hall.

The steps above paced to the far end, where the little workroom was.

She tiptoed up the stairs behind Mark.

The intruder must have been occupied in the workroom, because no one was waiting to jump them in the solar. Mark slid over to the chest that held the weapons. He lifted its lid and pulled out the bow and an arrow. While he fitted the shaft to the string, she grabbed the dagger.

Muffled sounds, like a rat rustling through debris, came from the workroom. Mark quietly walked to the threshold of the little room, raised his weapon, and barged in.

"So it is you," she heard him say.

"Jesus," a startled voice cried.

"Joan, go raise the cry and get a constable. We've a thief here. No doubt he has already filled his tunic."

"A thief! I'm no thief. Strip me if you want, I've taken nothing."

"They can strip you when they hang you."

"Hang me!"

"Out. And don't try to run. This shaft will find you if my sister's dagger does not."

Steps moved. "Jesus," the thief muttered. "Hell."

A man came into the view. Portly and well dressed with blond hair and beard. The man from the alley.

Mark followed him out, the head of the tense arrow a hand's span from his back.

"Careful with that, boy. Ease it up a bit, will you? One slip and—"

"And you are dead. Don't forget it."

Joan greeted him with the point of the dagger. "Mark will keep that trained on you while I go and get the constable. If you steal from this house, you have stolen from others."

"I swear that I am no thief." The man sank onto a stool, looking panicked. He nervously patted his tunic. "See? Nothing."

"Then why are you here? What is your interest in this house?"

He looked at her cautiously and a little pleadingly. He nodded toward Mark. "Tell your brother to take his sight off of me, will you?"

She guessed that he wanted more than that. There had been an offer to explain in his eyes. "Mark, take the bow downstairs in case he tries to run. I will hear what this man has to say before we go for help."

Mark didn't like it, but the idea of thwarting a dramatic escape must have held some appeal. He relaxed the bow and carried it down the steps.

Joan let the intruder see her dagger plainly. "If there is a reason I should not go for the constable, you'd best explain."

"It is not the constable whom I'd like to avoid. It is your master. I would prefer if he did not know I had been in here."

"I am sure of that."

"Nay, it is not what you think. Not theft. My name is John. I am a clerk to Bishop Stratford."

That stunned her. Stratford was a powerful bishop, equal to any lord. "What interest could a bishop have in Rhys? Is this intrusion Stratford's bidding?"

"Nay. He does not know . . . I had hoped to find out for certain, before I went to him. . . . Hell, this is a tangle, and I fear that I will get strangled by the knot."

"Better to be strangled by a tangle's knot than a thief's noose."

"Oh, aye, better that." The reminder helped him decide. "Look you here, woman. What do you think of that man who struts around the royal palaces, and leads the King's mother by the nose? What is your opinion of the Earl of March?"

"Mortimer? I hate him."

He blinked at the flat, firm way that it came out. His

expression lightened. "Well, my bishop hates him, too, as do I. There are some who intend to bring that man down, you see."

"I am glad to hear it. What does that have to do with this house?"

"I have some concern that your master might interfere with our plans. I was seeking to learn if I am right."

"A mason cannot interfere with a bishop's plans. I think that you are lying."

"That is where the tangle comes in. See, I know Rhys. Thinking him sympathetic, I told him things that I should not, over some ale as is the habit with friends. Now I worry that he may have betrayed that confidence. I have reason to think that he has met with Mortimer."

"He is a builder for the crown. Mortimer would have projects. If they met, it was probably just for that." She let her tone mock him, but a tiny shiver of worry skimmed through her. Rhys had gotten a summons that day. He most definitely had met with Mortimer at least once.

"Aye, it could just be that. But I would like to know, wouldn't I? Because if it was something else, if my misspeaking had been repeated, I'll need to tell the bishop and others, which will sore displease them. On the other hand, if it is just a project of some kind, I need not raise the whole story, need I?"

He smiled at her hopefully. "So, you can see why I would rather no one know I was here, can't you? If I have to start explaining, it will just make the tangle worse."

"Did you find anything here? Any indication that your confidence was broken?"

"Your brother interrupted me. Maybe I can just . . ." He turned expectantly toward the workroom door.

"Nay."

She should hand this man over to the city. She should tell Rhys that John had been here, and what John thought.

But older loyalties and fears surged, smothering any new ones that she might have to the mason who fed her.

Fed her while he bided his time, and tried to lure her into more than she would ever give him. And found ways to keep her from leaving.

Her hesitation gave John new confidence. "I can see how you might find it wrong to let me poke about. But maybe, if you favor the bishop's cause, if you see or hear something, or happen to find something while you do your cleaning and such, just by accident, you might let me know."

He wanted more than accidents. His eyes said so, despite his words.

"I only ask because so much is at stake. We only want that man brought low, and his crimes undone."

Aye, crimes. Terrible crimes. She knew how terrible.

"There would be gratitude. Such help would not go unnoticed, or unrewarded," he ventured. "A few shillings, at least. It would be a shame to have important plans undone merely because I did not know if I could trust an old friend. It would be good to know what Rhys is, and where he stands. You see that, don't you?"

Aye, it would be good to know what he was for sure. Which Rhys was the real one? The good, kind one offering protection, or the lackey who used blue eyes and physical comforts to seduce a woman?

John eased up from the stool. "Best if I leave now. You will call down to your brother, won't you? Tell him to let me pass?"

She did not stop his path to the stairs. And so she made a decision of sorts, or part of one.

"Do not come back here," she said.

"I will not. But if you should want to speak with me, I can often be found at the first tavern on the Cheap just past the cathedral."

She doubted that she would ever want to speak with him. He was wrong. Rhys might serve Mortimer as a builder, but not as an informer. Nor did she think it likely that she would even look for what John sought, let alone find it.

She was almost sure of all of those things. Almost.

CHAPTER 10

THE MAN LOITERING inside the chapel yard when Rhys returned to work after dinner in the abbey wore no livery, but he looked familiar. Rhys had seen him around Westminster.

The red-haired page must be ill. "Are you waiting for me?" Rhys asked when the man caught his eye.

"Aye. You are wanted."

He was not brought to the garden this time. Instead, his escort took him into the palace through a back entry and up a narrow set of stairs. After snaking through several chambers, he found himself between two guards outside the royal apartments. The door opened, and suddenly Rhys was looking right into the face of the King of England.

"Here is the mason," his escort said.

"You would be Rhys," Edward said, gesturing him inside. "I have heard of your skill." He swept an arm around his chamber. "My wife and I desire some changes made, and my mother tells me that you are the best."

The chamber served as an anteroom to the royal apartments. It had been furnished richly enough, but not as opulently as that of the King's mother. Isabella and Mortimer kept the King's household short of funds.

Edward sat in a cushioned, carved chair that barely fit his unusually tall frame, and gestured for Rhys to sit in another nearby.

Edward looked him over. Rhys did a bit of looking, too. The youth who had been crowned three years ago had grown into a tall and strong eighteen-year-old. Tawny hair hung to his shoulders, and a short pointed beard made him look a few years older. It was said that he had more in common with his grandfather than his father, but the way he accepted the way his mother and her lover usurped his power did not speak well of his character.

"Most of the changes are in the other chambers, not this one. My wife wants our son kept near her, and desires a small part of her bedchamber partitioned for that. The floors as you can see are only plank, and she finds that too poor. She had tiles in her home in Hainault. She would like similar ones here."

He rose and led Rhys into the royal bedchamber. "There is one other small change I would like." He pointed to a wall. "I want a door there."

That wall stood at a right angle to the one which held the main entry in the anteroom. The entry through which he had just come, and outside of which stood guards—guards loyal to the Queen.

Mortimer had said nothing about a new door. Rhys gazed at that wall and knew for certain that he did not want this project.

"You do not need a freemason to do the partition or door. A rough mason is better skilled at such things."

"I have been assured that you are discreet. I would prefer that the work be done quietly."

He played dumb, hopefully. "One can not cut away stone blocks quietly."

"There will be the tile work making noise too, and the new partition, and my mother will assume it is that. She has given her approval for those changes, in the hopes of appeasing my wife. Who is to say what makes which sound?"

Hell. "I am honored that you have seen fit to seek my craft, but perhaps another . . ."

"I have been told that you are the best that I can find for my purposes. My mother trusts you because you aided her cause, but I know what she does not—that you also aided the men who later tried to curb her power. Aye, Master Rhys, you are the mason for this project."

Short of saying that he had been recruited against his will to spy for Mortimer, there was no way out of this.

"I will of course do the work. I can begin at once. As to the tiles, does your Queen have a preference for the colors, and do you want me to get them from Spain?"

"She knows exactly what she wants. If you must wait to get them from Spain, then do so, but I prefer to patronize English craftsmen if we can."

Edward led the way into the adjoining apartment. The brown-haired Philippa sat in her own chamber. Not a great beauty, it was true, but she possessed a sweet expression, especially now as she held their son.

She described the tiles she had known in her father's home. Rhys asked for some parchment and a quill and quickly drew one. They made arrangements for his access to the chambers, and then Rhys took his leave.

He did not return to the abbey yard. He headed home, so there would be no chance of being called by Mortimer this day. He had a good excuse, since a last-minute change in the design for the window's glass required some recalculations regarding the fitting of the stonework.

But he aimed for his workroom for another reason. He also wanted to trace on parchment his accumulated knowledge of the organization of the palace chambers. If memory served him correctly, the wall waiting for a new door separated Edward's chambers from those of the Keeper of the Privy Seal.

He wondered who and what would pass through the new door once it was cut.

Joan made sure that the soup was simmering, and took the evening's bread out of the oven. She left a few pence and a pitcher on the table to remind Mark to go buy the ale when he returned. He was never home during these evening hours. That was when his new friends, the apprentices like David, were finally free and he always went in search of them.

Arming herself with a broom and a rag, she headed upstairs. She aimed for the little workroom.

In her two weeks here, she had not cleaned in there. Although Rhys had not forbidden it, she sensed that her intrusion would not be welcomed. But she had decided to intrude today, and not just to sweep.

The chamber was quite small. The long table cramping it sat below a window that overlooked the street, and the sounds of the city flowed in.

It was full of parchments. A shelf held rolls of them, along with her little Saint Agnes. More covered the table. They appeared just strewn about, but something in the way they lay suggested that she would disrupt things if she got tidy.

She had no intention of disturbing them—at least, not too much.

It would be good to know what he is. Aye, it would be. She did not like living here not knowing, and John's suspicions had been unsettling her.

One top sheet showed a small church, a stone doorway, some window tracery, and a town gate. The images angled this way and that, as though some idea had come to him and he had simply grabbed the closest parchment and jotted it down. It also showed ciphers and symbols.

Relief bubbled in her. Just drawings for his projects. Not what John suspected, whatever that was.

Still . . .

She gingerly lifted the corner of one and peeked below. Then another. A pang of guilt stabbed her. Rhys may have interfered with her life and plans, he might speak of protection when he really meant lust, but he had done nothing to hurt her. John was probably just a suspicious fool. She should not let his accusations affect her.

John's words echoed in her head. For a just cause. To bring an evil man down.

Maybe just a few more, near the top, just to be sure . . .

Steps sounded on the stairs. She knew who it was. Felt it. She looked to the window in panic. There was at least an hour of light left. He should not be back this soon.

She grabbed her broom and began sweeping.

He entered the chamber, darkly handsome in his sleeveless work tunic and leather leggings.

"You are back early today." She reached the broom into a corner to catch a cobweb. Her heart pounded from the close call.

And from his presence. She always felt a bit on her guard, a tad too aware, when he was in the house. His behavior the other evening at their meal had only made it worse. No matter what they spoke of, another silent dialogue continued between them without stop. An intimate one.

"The fool who is in charge of the glass changed his design, so I must change the placement of the tracery."

He kicked a bench over to the table and sat. He rummaged through the parchments until he found a fairly empty sheet. Opening a box, he pulled out a wooden instrument shaped like a V.

She swept closer to get a better look at it. "What is that?"

"One draws circles with it. Look." He set one arm of the implement straight upright, and then moved the other around. A grey line appeared in a perfect circle. He moved the arms closer. "See, bigger or smaller. Try it."

She set the broom aside, and took the tool and made a circle herself.

"A little image of infinity," he said. "No beginning or end, and perfect in form, all points equally distant from the center."

"That is a very poetic way to think of a circle."

"If you work with geometry for long, it does seem like a type of poetry. My master used to say that God was in numbers. Sit here and I will show you something almost magical."

She slid onto the bench and he handed her a measuring straightedge. "First you will make a perfect square." Following his instructions she drew one with a burnt stick that he retrieved from the box.

"Now take the tool's point and place it right in the middle of the bottom line. Open it until the drawing stick is on one of the upper corners. Now draw the arch of a circle down outside the square, but stop when you get to the same spot as the bottom line should go. Continue the bottom line of the square out to that point, then finish out the rectangle."

She had a bit of trouble making the point stay put while she turned the other arm. He covered her hand with his and reached around to guide her curve.

His touch and closeness made her heart rise. He flustered her enough that it took a while to get the drawing right. "It seems like a lot of trouble just to draw a rectangle."

"It is a special one. It is called a golden rectangle. The addition on the side of the square is another rectangle of the same proportions as the big one. And that can be again broken into a square and yet another golden rectangle. And so on."

She sensed a depth that caused a little chill, as if her mind had brushed against something profound. "It just keeps going, you mean? Another image of infinity. One cannot help but be awed by it."

Rhys seemed pleased that she saw that. "Builders use the golden rectangle all the time. It gives pleasing proportions that the eye finds harmonious. It is often the basic measurement used to start cathedrals."

"It is like magic. Perhaps your master was right, and God is in numbers."

"Many apprentices hate learning the geometry it takes to be a mason, but I always thought it allowed me to see a small bit of how the Creator's mind worked."

Most people turned to prayer to learn that, not numbers. He did not speak of learning God's will, though. He meant comprehending the mystery.

She had never before known someone who contemplated such things.

She sensed that this was not something that he explained with frequency. He was letting her see a small bit of how *his* mind worked.

"I sometimes think that I experience a bit of His mind when I work the clay," she said, hoping it would not sound too earthbound in comparison. "When it is going very well, and my hands can not err, and the figure takes form just as my mind sees it. At such moments it is like a trance, more spiritual than being in church. Wordless and pure, but not nearly so solid and absolute as these numbers."

"Aye, but is very similar. Only it is not the Mind that we know when our craft moves us in that way. It is the Soul."

He understood exactly. That astounded her. She had not realized that it was the same for everyone who made forms with their hands. Rhys had also known that special ecstasy.

Acknowledging that they shared this most private of experiences touched her more surely than any hand could. He might have invisibly caressed her soul.

The mood warmed her, and stirred a wistful yearning. They had much in common. They were both far from the place of their families, and they had tasted the power of creation. From the looks of this house, with its scant furnishings and lack of wife and children, he lived as though he also was on his way to somewhere else, to do something that needed to be done. She almost asked him if he had decided where and what it would be.

He gazed at her with intimate comprehension. This moment of special empathy did not need words. It wove a spell between them that she found impossible to deny or break.

Expectation pulled, trying to draw them together. It tightened with a palpable force the longer they looked. She thought that she would fall into him as surely as she had that day under the tree.

"Are you waiting for me to kiss you, Joan?"

She averted her gaze, embarrassed that she had let him think so.

His hand cupped her chin and turned her face back to him. His thumb gently stroked her lips, making a tiny tremor beat in them. He gently pressed that little pulse, letting her know he understood what it meant. "I think that you are."

She pulled back and rose, sad that she had to deny the sweet closeness they had just shared. She turned and walked toward the door. It seemed very far away.

A movement behind her. An arm stretched, blocking her way. A hand, strong and bronzed and masculine, pressed to the wall, making the barrier complete.

"I cannot let you run this time, Joan. I am not so good as that."

He warmed her side. Not touching, but she felt him anyway, and her heart started pounding. She kept her eyes on that hand and arm.

"Look at me, Joan."

She dared not. She should duck beneath that arm and truly run. He did not really restrain her here. But her legs had no strength for it. Neither did her will.

Warmth on her hair, her temple. Not a kiss, just his breath. Still not touching, but closer somehow. All of her alert to him. Expectant. Twisting tightly.

His quiet voice, so close it could have been soundless and she would have heard. "Turn to me, pretty dove. I am not above seducing you, but it should not be like that."

She turned her head to that voice. To explain that it should not be any way at all. That was why she did it.

His kiss silenced whatever words she might have spoken.

A wonderful kiss. Warm and promising. An invitation to explore the connections born in this chamber.

Her womanhood fluttered to life at once. It slipped out of the chains forged by the past and took to flight. Wings beat in her heart, her body, her blood. Its hopefulness made her want to weep.

Maybe . . . maybe . . .

He knew. He turned her to him, and his arm slid behind her in embrace. His hold supported her like a rock and bent her into him.

Palm against her cheek, he enlivened her face and neck with his mouth and breath and teeth. He began to control the wind beneath those fluttering wings.

Tempting. Luring. The mood of what they had shared here still surrounded them both. He offered more than mere pleasure with his touch. He always had.

But it was the pleasure that mesmerized her. It just built and built, filling her with a compelling anticipation. It cloaked thought and fear in the most wonderful way. It drenched her in glowing light and spring breezes.

He looked down at her. No triumph flickered in those kind, eyes. Confidence, aye, and strength, but none of the demeaning lights of a conqueror eyeing the vanquished.

"Don't you kiss back, Joan?"

The question from the garden. Memories flashed through her whole body. The glory of that journey. The devastation waiting at the end.

But Rhys had already lured her onto the path again, and the freedom felt so good, so right. Released from their bonds, the wings would not be still. They beat more frantically as he gazed into her eyes, and the disappointment seemed a small, impossible thing.

Maybe . . . maybe . . .

She embraced him, and kissed back.

He drew her closer, and his kisses became more fevered. He sought a spot below her ear and played at it until her senses began splitting. He kissed her again and this time entered her, obliterating what little hold she had on who she should be.

With permission granted, he did not ask for it again. A caress, firm and possessive, smoothed down her side, as claiming and intimate as if she were naked. The sensation took her breath away. She arched as that warm path pressed along her waist and hip and thigh.

Kisses on her neck. And lower. Careful, deliberate, hot

kisses. The solid strength of his arm arched her higher as he trailed those kisses down to her breasts. He tantalized her, moving his mouth around their swells.

Her mind blanked and she grew frantic. Nothing but an anxious need existed in her. A delicious need that was one with the pleasure.

It grew so intense that she begged. With her embrace and an offering thrust of her breasts and a guiding pressure on his head, she mindlessly asked for more. Almost with her voice, too, but the audible sighs that filtered into her dulled senses were eloquent enough.

He made her wait a little longer, making it worse. When his kiss returned to her mouth, she almost cried in protest. But his hand replaced his mouth on her breast, teasing her with gentle caresses.

The screaming need pushed her into shamelessness. She kissed back insistently, madly.

A touch. A subtle brushing against her nipples, first one, then the other. Two instants of exquisite relief, no more. Just enough to send her reeling into abandon. Just enough to remind her of the pleasure he would give her soon.

Not soon enough. He pressed her against the wall. It took forever for him to unlace the gown. An eternity passed while he slid its wool and her shift off her shoulders. The cloth sagged down to her hips.

He looked down at her nakedness and then in her eyes, while his hand smoothed over her bare breasts. Knowing warmth gazed at her. And maybe, this time, a few lights of triumph in response to her gasps.

"I told you, Joan. What is between us does not just come from me."

His head lowered. His fingers flicked at one tip, and his tongue at the other. Pleasure streamed sharply and deeply into her stomach and loins. He sent her to an astonishing place. A different world, one of bliss.

For a while. But the pleasure quickly ached with need again, and with an impatient urge for something else. A different part of her began that begging demand. Despite her besotted state, she knew that he was indeed seducing her. He was using the pleasure to lure her step by step, until she would be hungry not for a touch but for all of him.

She didn't care. It should worry her, but there was no room for that. She had lost this game with that first kiss and that first "maybe." The word seemed to echo all through her while those wings soared higher on their passion. The glory of their flight was all that she knew.

Nay, not all. Something else intruded. A distant sound, vague but familiar. A commotion of voices and steps. It rumbled lowly on the edges of their private world, then got louder. She tried to ignore it, but it shook the peace and entered the house.

It was halfway up the stairs before she clearly grasped its source. Mark and David. Coming up for the weapons, assuming that Rhys was not yet home.

Reality flashed starkly. She pushed, putting space between their bodies, and stared down. At her nakedness, and the strong hand holding her breast. At the intimacy she had sworn to avoid, and the evidence of her foolish weakness.

At the terrible mistake of a woman seduced by hope, grabbing at what she could not have.

Rhys released her. Without a word he strode into the solar. She heard him pace to the stairs. She heard the whirlwind halt in mid-bluster as the boys saw him. She heard the silent denial of entry to the upper chambers, and the feet retreating through the hall and out into the garden.

But she heard more than that as she frantically redressed herself. She also heard the past in her brother's voice, and the truth in his steps.

She relaced her gown. She glanced up to see Rhys leaning against the doorway's jamb, watching her. She could not look at him, and kept her attention on the knot that she tied.

She felt her face burning. She did not know what to say, only that she could not speak the words that he wanted to hear.

She looked down at the table, and the golden rectangle they had made. Her heart twisted. "I wonder about this magic that you showed me," she said, tapping the parchment. "The rectangle keeps getting smaller and smaller, until it disappears. It stops then, doesn't it?"

"Nay, it continues invisibly."

That seemed impossible to fathom.

"It works the other way, too. It can get bigger and bigger until it covers all of creation."

That was even harder to imagine.

She went to the door, hoping he would let her walk away from what had just happened.

It was not to be. He pulled her into his arms. Not a restraining embrace, but a firm one. He kissed her, and a melancholy echo of what they had just shared whispered through her.

"I should not let you go," he said.

Mark's voice, teasing his friend about some girl, rang from the garden through the solar's windows.

"I should not let you go. I should kiss you deeply and hold you to me and carry you to my bed. I should undress your lovely body until you are naked, as you were that first night, and as you have been in my dreams. I should lay you down and make love to you, because I think it is very clear to both of us what this might be." He kissed her again. "Come to me tonight."

A vise of yearning squeezed her heart. It felt so good to be in his arms. So good to pretend for a while.

She touched his face. Something in her grieved, threatening her composure.

"Ah, Rhys, it would not be as you think. It would only bring us both unhappiness."

She forced herself to step back, and away, and through the threshold. She grabbed onto the clarity of her brother's voice as it wafted on the evening breeze. She let it pull her through the solar.

She paused on the stairs, breathing deeply to swallow the tight knot inside her throat. Then she continued, lest Rhys hear her hesitation and guess her confusion. She trod down, heavyhearted, as soulfully disappointed as she had known she would be.

Not just in him, and what she might learn that he was.

He spoke of what this might be as if glory awaited them, but she knew differently. If this continued, she could not look in his eyes and only see warmth. Eventually she would face the full reflection of herself too, and there were crippled places in her heart that she dared not scrutinize.

He might give her pleasure, but eventually it would shatter, no matter what kind of man he was. He dreamed of them together, but she never did. And if it ever happened, if she imagined in her sleep that Rhys or any man was taking her, she did not doubt that the sensation of being trapped and drowned would wake her immediately.

CHAPTER 11

RHYS BEGAN WORK ON the new wall in the royal chambers. His presence created an intrusion for the first few hours of the first day, no more. Many servants came and went. He simply became the one who stayed.

Invisible. Insignificant. An obstacle to walk around, much like a chair or bench.

He let the work absorb him. He decided to face the new stone exactly like the old, so the new wall would appear part of the original fabric.

It almost distracted him from thoughts of Joan. Fevered thoughts, full of the sounds of her pleasure and the taste of her skin. Curious ones, too, that wondered about the way she denied something so right. He contemplated the barriers that she kept shoring up between them. Barriers not just to passion, but to a luring peace and unity that he sensed possible with her, waiting just out of reach.

He avoided beginning the new door. No one had suggested he be hasty with it. He wanted to believe it led only to an empty chamber that Edward planned to use as a wardrobe, and began convincing himself of that.

He heard nothing for days. No tidbits worth offering anyone. He began to feel a little smug. Mortimer's eternal worrying might have merely brought Rhys Mason into the King's favor, with no cost or danger. Well, let the Earl of March worry. Maybe it would be bad for his health.

And then, a word. Just one. Muttered by a young knight entering the Queen's bedchamber with the King. Part of a conversation mostly over when the young man came to take his leave of Philippa. A single clear word amidst a flow of almost silent ones.

Addis.

It was not a word he wanted to hear. Especially since no barons had passed those royal guards to enter these chambers, but only knights new to their spurs. Friends, with whom a young king would drink and whore. Not the kind of men who could lead conspiracies.

Nor the kind of men one would expect to find in the circle of Addis de Valence, the Lord of Barrowburgh, and casually speaking his name.

His hammer fell a little harder after he heard that name. He tried to pound its sound out of his head, and convince himself he had heard wrong.

He tried to tell himself that he could ignore it. But Mortimer also had spoken that name, and had voiced suspicions.

He broke off his work a little early and rode back into the city. Mortimer was expecting him to visit the home of Addis de Valence. It shouldn't be put off any longer.

Rhys stuck his head through the doorway to the inn's hall. A woman sat near the far window with a babe at her breast.

"Are you alone, Moira?"

"Addis is in the solar, if that is what you mean."

"Aye, that is what I mean." He strolled over and peered down at the tiny infant. "He looks to be a healthy boy. Two sons in three years. Your husband must be pleased."

"Pleased enough that he plays with one while I feed the other. Let me call for him, so that he can greet you."

"Nay, leave him to his son. It is you that I come to see, and he knows it." He pulled a bench against the wall and sat where he could watch her in the twilight leaking in the window.

Abundant chestnut hair tumbled around her body. The babe suckled with sleepy contentment, as though he knew his mother's goodness. Moira had a heart that would nurture the world if permitted. If he ever carved an image of Charity, he would use the memory of her as she sat thus, giving succor.

He had almost loved her once. Not the way he did now, as an old friend. She had been the only woman before Joan about whom he had wondered what might be. She had been Addis's serf then, and her lord desired her. Rhys thought it was the same story he had witnessed as a boy, and probably wooed her more quickly because of that. What he had not known was that Addis owned her heart more securely than her freedom. She had loved the son of Barrowburgh most of her life.

Her lord loved her, too. He ultimately married her despite her low birth, and let his sons have her blood. Rhys did not like Addis much, and the tension over Moira still hung between them. His respect for the man increased tenfold, however, when that marriage had occurred.

"It has been over two weeks since you came last, Rhys. You were very busy?"

"Aye. A window at the abbey. The donation came from the Queen, and the abbot wanted it done fast, lest the funds get diverted to some extravagance. There were ten of us there."

"Then you were not in the city at all these days."

"I only returned at night."

The fading light caught an impish glint in her clear blue eyes. "To be with your tiler?"

Hell. "Moira . . ."

"Nay, nay. You do not need to explain to me. I can not help but be curious, though. You have had women before, but this is the first time that you have taken one into your home." The baby had fallen asleep. She shifted him, and covered herself. "It is said that she is your housekeeper now."

"How do you hear such things? You are still lying in. You have not even been to the church yet."

"I have servants. I have visitors. They are sworn to bring me any gossip worth hearing. Imagine my surprise to learn that the best tidbits were about you." She lifted the infant to her shoulder and patted. "Some say that you bought her, but I have let it be known that you are the last man to do that."

She smiled expectantly, waiting for his gratitude. He stared blandly through the window. Out of the corner of his eye, he saw her face fall.

"Rhys, you *didn't*."

"It is not—"

"You? The man who stood up to Addis about his claims on me? The man who has taken no apprentices because he does not believe in bonds lasting even ten years?"

"I have taken none because the responsibility for them restricts my movements, not because—"

"The man who helped depose a king, because he said the abuse of power had infringed the people's rights? *You* have bought a woman's freedom and made her your leman?"

"It is true that I bought her indenture, but I do not hold her to it. And she is not my leman."

She frowned at him skeptically. "Truly? She does not share your bed?"

"Truly." And then, because it was Moira, he smiled. "Not that I haven't offered."

She gave him a very motherly look. Sympathetic, but far too knowing. "It sounds like you are tempting the devil."

"Aye, I am certainly doing that." And he was. The devil inside him. The voice that, late at night, calculated the odds of success if he pursued Joan more aggressively, and that weighed the strength of passion against that of her resolve. And of her fears. Only his suspicions about the latter checked him now, not his much-vaunted principles.

"Perhaps you should send her away," Moira said. "I will give her work here, and take the brother, too."

"Nay."

He said it sharply enough that she frowned with disapproval. "So you do not hold her with the indenture, but with her need for food and shelter."

I am inclined to keep her with me any way I can. So there it was, admitted bluntly. He had never thought to see the day when he understood why Addis had forced Moira to remain his bondwoman, but he did now.

"Do you care for this Joan? It is not just temporary lust, I hope."

He laughed. "There is plenty of lust, Moira. Enough that I am not sure what I think about the rest."

"You must bring her to the baptismal feast next week. I must meet her and look her over."

"Look who over?" a voice asked from the shadows.

Rhys twisted to see Addis de Valence walking toward them. He had known Addis would come. He had been waiting for him.

"So it is you, mason. One of the women said that a man had snuck in the gate. Sly and silent, she described him."

"Greetings, Addis. I came to admire your new son."

"And my wife, I'll wager."

"A fool's bet for me, and easy winnings for you." They treated it like a little joke, but a low note in Addis's voice said that he still had suspicions about Rhys's interest in Moira. Which was why he had come down from the solar.

"Look who over?" he repeated.

"A woman," Moira said.

"Your woman? The pretty one you have taken into your home?"

The Lord of Barrowburgh normally did not partake of town gossip. Moira must have told him.

Moira rose with the baby cradled against her bosom. "I must put this little one to bed. Do not leave, Rhys. I have a rose gown and veil to send back to Joan." She carried the infant away, leaving him alone with her husband.

"Your woman sounds proud," Addis said, sitting in the chair Moira had used. The last of the light hit the left side of his face, revealing a deep, long scar slicing from his dark hairline to his jaw. "That is good. Some men prefer timid women, but I have always thought that was because such men are too weak to handle anything else."

"She is proud enough." *And she is not my woman.* He would not get into that with Addis, however. Unfortunately, Moira would probably tell him all about it.

"How do you fare, Rhys? Has your work been taking you to the palace of late?" Addis asked casually, like an old friend catching up. Except that they were not old friends.

"Aye. I just finished a window. One of the Queen's donations. Now I am honored to do some work in the King's chambers. Did you recommend me to Edward, Addis? He said that men he trusts spoke for me."

"I may have done so."

"Did he mention that his mother had first put my name forward?"

"He may have done so."

"I do not think that I should thank you for this. You have put me into an impossible situation, and one that I did not seek on my own at all. I am treading on the edge of a precipice as it is. This only makes my path narrower."

"You speak as though you do not know where to put your feet, or your loyalties."

"When I risk my life on my loyalties, I like it to be my own choice, and for a worthwhile reason."

"You speak as though someone expects something of you. That would be Mortimer, I guess. What does he want?"

Addis spoke as if he assumed the expectation had not yet been met. And so Rhys answered more honestly than he might have. "Information. He smells something, so he says."

"Indeed? To where has he turned his nose?"

"Well, Addis, at the moment, in the direction of you."

A silence pulsed while he absorbed that. "He was specific about this?"

"Most specific."

"He must be too idle these days if he sniffs in my direction. I am the least of his concerns."

"You are not in his pocket. He will be suspicious of any baron who is not."

It had grown dark, but Addis looked as if he could see Rhys very well. Gold lights flickered in his dark eyes. "Did you come here today to learn if his suspicions are correct?"

"I came to visit Moira, and to greet your new son."

"But if your visit were known, Mortimer would assume that you had at least tried."

"Aye, he would assume that."

"I think that you are practiced enough in walking that precipice. You will not fall. Visit as often as you need to keep Mortimer satisfied."

It was the offer of a comrade, if not a friend. It was not the rebellion that had forged this bond of trust between them. It was Moira. "You should probably visit the Queen."

"Then he would suspect that you had warned me, and start sniffing at you. I am safe from the man in ways a mason can never be. I have no business with the Queen, and will not inconvenience myself to feed her vanity."

A woman entered with two candles to give them some light. Addis waited for her to go before speaking again. "You have no loyalty to me, but you would never allow Moira or her children to be hurt. I think that you came this evening not just to visit my wife, but to alert me to Mortimer's interest in me."

"I might have mentioned it before I left."

"I am grateful for that. I am glad that you waited until Moira was not present, though. I would not have her worry about something that has no significance."

He lounged comfortably in the chair. The scar gave him a face half handsome and young, and half old and menacing. His last words rang with a peculiar note. And a request.

There it was, the word or tone or sigh that spoke more than intended. It was what Rhys had been waiting for, and the real reason he had come. He now knew for certain that Mortimer sniffed for a reason, and in the right direction.

The Lord of Barrowburgh had brought his family to London during this hot summer because something kept him from waiting for cooler winds.

Rhys slept fitfully, and eventually not at all. The meeting with Addis had forced him to see the truth. Something was indeed brewing. Now that he admitted it, he remembered other words and pauses and shielded glances—things he had deliberately ignored, but could no longer.

John had spoken of an army being raised in France. It had sounded preposterous, since Queen Isabella was French, and would surely learn of such a thing. But there were regions where her influence did not extend, places like Brittany or Bordeaux, or other areas John might have called France but which were not loyal to the French royal family.

He considered his situation, and annoyance made him restless. Should some action occur, Mortimer would never believe he had not known beforehand. And if it failed, John would undoubtedly tell Stratford and Lancaster that a certain mason could have helped and did not. He might claim more than that, come to think of it. He might assume that the mason had betrayed them. Addis might assume it, too.

Which that mason could do, with a word or pause or glance of his own, intended or not. Nothing explicit, but enough for a shrewd man like Mortimer to surmise the truth. It might even be for the best, if it ended this foolishness before lives were committed.

Damn. He had known this kind of danger before, but then he had accepted it of his own will.

He swung his legs and sat on the edge of the bed. It was nights like this when he regretted not having married. It would be nice to hold a friend now. A little feminine softness might distract him.

The chamber felt confining, as though its walls cornered him as surely as the situation that he contemplated. He pulled on some clothes and headed down to the garden, seeking the limitless sky.

As he passed through the kitchen, Joan stirred on her pallet. He paused and looked down on her, and his spirit was soothed immediately. The concerns of this night became something to worry about another day.

He enjoyed watching her sleep, even though he could not see much in the darkness. He relished it all the more because she would be gone soon. He did not doubt that now. Her denial of what had passed between them in the workroom had proven it. It would not be anything that he did that would send her away. It would be something in herself that had nothing to do with him at all. She had made that very plain.

He wondered what it was. He almost envied her this goal that consumed her. He remembered her that first night in this kitchen, crying out a rebel's yell for justice and ignoring the realities he threw back at her. It had been hot, youthful belief clashing with weary, old experience. She had reminded him of himself ten years ago. He had probably been harsher with her because of that.

Whatever it was, it would take her away. Pleasure and affection would not hold her. Nor would the comfort of this house. She resisted the hold of both, just as she did not mingle with the neighbors or find a more private place to nest at night. She wanted no ties to bind her. He understood that. He had lived it. It was easier to be brave if you had nothing to lose.

She spoke of needing coin. He should just give it to her. It was what any friend would do.

He should, but he would not. The affection he had for her was not just that of a friend. She was right; the help and kindness were not selfless on his part. He had never pretended otherwise. He had been honest about that, with her and himself.

She looked so lovely sleeping there. This house was a friendlier place for her presence. She might refuse the closeness he sought, she might deny what this might be, but he still liked having her here. And walking that precipice every day would be easier if the path led to her every night.

She needed coin. She would leave in order to find a way to get it—unless she could find it here. Well, he could help with that. Not selflessly, not immediately, but help all the same.

Her own sleep had grown restless, as if he intruded on her dreams. She turned on her side and huddled, as though a nightmare had claimed her.

He reached down and touched her shoulder. Her body stiffened. He shook gently. She flipped onto her back and shrugged him off.

He could tell when she woke. He sensed her gazing up at him.

"Come with me, Joan."

"Nay."

She had misunderstood. "Not to my bed. Out to the garden. I want to speak with you."

He left, not knowing if she would follow. Since that day in his workroom, she had worked hard to reestablish distance.

He waited among the flowers at the far wall, where no tree or house obscured the sky.

She came. The moonlight glowed gently off her hair as she walked toward him. "What do you want?"

"I have a proposition to make. You said that you sought out those potters in the market so that you can earn coin. I know a way for you to do so."

She turned on her heel to retrace her steps. "When I told you to go buy whores, I did not mean that I would be one for you."

"I would never debase our friendship by offering money for that. It is a different proposition that I have."

That stopped her. "Go on."

"It is my new project. It requires tiles, but I am no tiler.

I can judge the quality once they are made, but not the works that will make them. I will need to commission these, and must be sure that the yard can do the work well if I strike the bargain. If you visit those yards with me, you will know if the craft will be as it should be once those tiles are made."

She idly swept her hands through some tall growth while she thought about it. The gesture made her appear childish. "You would pay me to do this?"

"Aye."

"How much?"

"Whatever you say it is worth."

"I would visit the yards with you, and judge the kiln and the skill of the workers, that is all?"

That wouldn't take long at all. "I would want you to visit again a few times once the commission is given, to see that it is being executed properly. And the chambers have plank floors, so you should probably see if they need any work before the tiles are laid."

"Where are these chambers?"

"At Westminster."

Her sweeping arms stopped. "Mortimer's chambers?"

"Nay. The King's chambers."

"Your new project is for the King? Truly for the crown then."

"You could say that." You could, and it would be partly right. At least half right, and maybe more if he could pretend ignorance where he was not.

She strolled through the flowers, thinking. "I will visit the yards. I want ten pence for each one that I judge. If I am still here when the tiles are made, I want ten shillings to supervise the quality. But I will not go to the chambers with you. Find a man who lays pavers to judge the floor."

"It would be easier if you did it."

"I do not want to go to Westminster. I would feel foolish there, among such grand people."

"You would be with me, and I am hardly grand. No one notices such as us."

"Nay."

"As you like it. In a few days then, we will begin visiting yards."

"One of the potters in the market, the one from Kent, has a brother who makes tiles. His wares looked good."

"Then we will start with him. There is one other thing. In two days Moira's new son will be baptized. She has asked that you come to the feast."

"You said that her husband is a lord. Will there be knights and such there?"

"There are few in the city. It will mostly be people from the ward. She has shown you kindness. You must come and thank her. You know that you must."

She didn't like it. He could feel her agitation over the idea. Maybe she worried that attending with him would only convince the neighbors of what they already suspected, that she served him with more than food and scrubbing.

"Aye, if it will mostly be people from the ward, I will go and thank her. I would not want to be thought ungrateful," she said, turning back to the house.

She said it with resignation. And a note of worry.

CHAPTER 12

MOIRA NOTICED THEM immediately when they entered the big hall. She hurried over, her clear blue eyes taking Joan in, then glancing at him in approval.

"I scolded Rhys for not introducing us sooner," she said, taking Joan's hands in her own. "Come and meet my husband and son, and the child whose birth we celebrate today."

Addis stood by the cradle that held the infant. His little son Patrick hovered protectively, beaming with delight at all of the adult attention falling on him and his tiny brother. The Lord of Barrowburgh examined Joan with blunt curiosity, and she paled a little under the strong man's inspection.

Moira lifted the drowsy baby from his nest. To Rhys's surprise, she did not place him in Joan's arms as one would expect, but in his own.

It moved him more than he expected. He gazed down at the fresh innocent face, and awe swept him. He knew that Moira had put the child in his arms to make an argument for lifelong bonds and love. It touched him that she worried for his happiness.

The child made what could be a smile, and he smiled back. He looked up to find Joan watching. Her face remained calmly pleasant, but a sheen of moisture filmed her eyes. He sensed a ripple of unhappiness shiver out of her.

Moira must have sensed it too. She took the child from him, but did not offer the bundle to Joan. Instead, she put the baby back in its cradle, and then eased Joan away toward a huddle of talking women.

Which left him alone with Addis.

"Your son grows already, Addis. How did you christen him?"

"Did she not tell you? She asked that I name him Rhys."

He strolled away as he said it. Considering the startling news, Rhys had no choice but to follow.

"I am honored."

"She said that your friendship has been selfless, and that you once pointed her to the path that led to her happiness."

He remembered that day. It had not truly been selfless. A smart man did not marry a woman whose heart was owned by another. If he had accepted what Moira offered, the Lord of Barrowburgh's ghost would have shared their bed every night of their lives.

"She wanted you as godfather, too, but I could not permit that."

"That goes without saying."

"Does it? If you think it is because of your birth, you do not know me well."

Their casual walk brought them to the end of the hall, near the kitchen. Addis opened the door and led the way through. With more determined steps he aimed for the garden, towing Rhys along.

He finally stopped in a sunlit patch of high grass and wildflowers behind a big tree. "I let Moira think that I found you unsuitable to stand up for the child, but it was not that," Addis said once he had secured their privacy. "I do not want it thought that you are bound to Barrowburgh in that way. The babe's name is a smaller matter, but an official affinity would not be convenient right now, for either of us."

"You do not have to explain. The name is honor enough, and more than I deserve."

Addis nipped a tall yellow flower off its stalk. He had positioned them both so no one could see from the house. "Edward wants to know if you are loyal to him."

"Of course. He is my king."

"It is not a common loyalty that he speaks of."

Addis had been full of surprises today, but this one startled Rhys the most. "Are you saying that he is joining with Lancaster? That the army being bought in France will fly his banner?"

"He will not tie his fate to either Lancaster or that dream of an army. He gathers men to his side whom he personally trusts, and will act in his own name and in his own time."

"Has he gathered many?" He knew the answer. He would have known if half the realm supported the young king.

"A handful so far, no more."

"He needs barons and knights, not masons."

"He needs the mason who cuts that door to be sworn to him. Surely you know that. He needs the mason who feeds Mortimer information to offer the right food at the right time."

"I think that you lure me into danger, Addis. And the cause sounds hopeless."

"There is not so much danger. It is not treason to serve an anointed king."

"I will be sure to explain that to the executioner."

Addis laughed. "As will I. Are you with him?"

The request made the passion for justice that had once burned hotly in his blood flicker alive. He tasted the excitement of affecting his world, not just acceding to it.

But that old passion met competition from the numbing disillusionment that he had worn for two years. And from the compelling desire to discover what might be with Joan. The quelling effect of that latter emotion proved surprisingly strong. For the first time, he had something to lose.

"I will not betray what you have told me, and I will keep the door a secret. Beyond that, I cannot commit to this."

Voices disturbed the garden's quiet and drew their attention. Moira and Joan had come out from the house, and together they admired the flowers while they chatted.

"How can you risk her and the boys' future?" Rhys asked.

"She does not know, but if she did she would have it no other way."

He meant that it was the price of wedding the son of Barrowburgh. But she did know, and Addis knew that she did, but they pretended otherwise. She had made it easy for Addis to get Rhys alone because she wanted men she could trust beside her husband.

Joan bent to smell a late rose. Moira said something that made them both laugh.

"How can you take the chance of losing it all?"

Addis glanced over in a way that suggested too much had been revealed by the question. "I do not intend to lose anything. But if I do, I can work the fields with my own hands and be a happy man if my wife and sons are beside me."

"And if you lose your life? What then?"

Moira noticed them, and called that the feast would soon be served. They began walking toward her.

"That is an eternal danger for a knight. I will confess that I have always slept better knowing that should the worst happen, there is a mason who I know will never refuse my family sanctuary."

Something more than a normal friendship existed between Moira and Rhys. Joan could sense it in the warmth they showed each other and in the freedom with which they spoke. She wondered if Rhys had once loved this serf-born woman.

Maybe he still did. She couldn't blame him. Moira was lovely. Comforting and giving and full of heart. She would have been good for Rhys. He would have been happy with her.

That was what her mind said, but her heart was not so kind. It resented the ease they showed with each other. It twisted when they kissed on greeting, and kept twinging all through the feast.

She really didn't care, of course. It was none of her concern if he pined like a fool over a lord's wife. But when she found herself sitting with Moira as the feast wound down, curiosity got the better of her.

"You seem to have known Rhys a long time."

"Not so long, but he is one of my dearest friends."

"You met him while you lived in London?"

"Soon after I first came here. I served Addis then. I was his bondwoman." She did not pretend that it was something to be forgotten.

"So you were neighbors in the ward then? You met Rhys in the marketplace?" Joan hoped that she would not learn that it had been similar to her own first encounter with him. Not that it really mattered or would have any significance.

"Not in the market, and not as neighbors. He came to the house one night. He brought some men. It was right before the rebellion, and they had come to ask Addis to join with them."

Joan just stared at the clear blue eyes of the woman who cradled an infant in her arms. Surely she had heard wrong.

"These men came to ask Addis to join against the King? To foreswear his oath of fealty?"

"Addis foreswore nothing. His home had been taken while he was on crusade. He had made no oath to the last king."

It was not the information about Addis that mattered. "But Rhys brought them, you said. He was with them."

"Of course he was with them. All of London was with them. The whole realm was with them."

Not the whole realm. Not her father. "If Rhys brought men to Addis, he must have been closely involved."

"He was one of a handful of London citizens who helped more, and risked more, than most."

"How much?" It came out too sharply.

Moira eyed her curiously. "Perhaps you should ask him to tell you about it."

"It is not secret, is it? How much was he involved? How much did he risk?"

"He risked everything, as Addis did, and all who stood tall to stop what was happening. If they had failed, it would have been treason and they all would have died."

Success or not, it still had been treason. A treason that had put Roger Mortimer in power, and sent Guy Leighton to the Welsh marches.

Resentments and anger instantly deluged her. For a moment she could not even see.

"I fear that I have distressed you," Moira said gently. "I thought that you knew. Everyone in London does. Rhys was very valuable to the cause, and when the Queen landed he rode to meet her, as bravely as any knight. He was one of those present when the King abdicated in favor of his son, along with Addis and myself and members of every degree, from bishops to serfs."

Joan almost could not absorb it. She had been so stupid. So blind. No wonder he worked at the palace, and had been elevated to master builder at such a young age. No wonder Mortimer sent a summons for him, and met with him. It had not been skill with stone that had brought him into that circle.

He had helped depose a king, and had been gifted with status and prestige for his role. He had raised Mortimer up, and had been rewarded for his help.

He had chosen the winning side, and had benefited.

And men who had chosen the side of honor had been destroyed.

Bits and pieces of horrible memories flashed through her head. Arrows of pain stabbed her heart with each one.

She had known from the start, but had ignored the signs and her instincts to be wary. John's suspicions were right. Rhys had served Isabella and Mortimer once, and would again. He would not want his patrons to fall, and would warn them if he heard of plans to bring them down.

She lifted her dazed gaze from the ground. Moira was watching with concern. And too much interest.

She forced composure on herself and made her expression go bland. Addis de Valence had also supported the rebellion, and Roger Mortimer. She suddenly felt very vulnerable in this house.

"It was bigger than one man, Joan." Moira said it as though many moments had not passed. "As to what happened after the abdication, these things take their course and can not always be directed. Least of all by a mason."

That did not soothe her. She experienced fear and agitation such as she had not in many months. The old vulnerability and caution possessed her, and Moira's words did not assuage them at all. No words could.

Rhys walked by, talking to a merchant. She could not believe that she had been so stupid, and been so easily blinded by a handsome face. He was worse than she had thought. No mere lackey, he. While her life was being torn to shreds, his hands had been among those grasping the edges of the fabric.

It overwhelmed her. It filled her head until she felt half crazed.

She could not sit here any longer. She could not chat about neighbors and children and pretend that nothing had changed.

She rose. "I must take my leave now. Please tell Rhys that I feel unwell, and have returned to the house."

"Let me send for him, so that he can take you back."

"Nay, do not." It came out harshly, like a command. She took a deep breath to calm herself. "Please do not. I would rather be alone, so I can rest."

Moira let her go. Rhys did not see her departure, and did not follow.

CHAPTER 13

"I HAVE DECIDED to judge the chamber floors after all. I will come and look at them for you."

Joan said it while Rhys broke his fast two mornings after the feast. It was the first conversation that she had initiated in all that time. They were not the words he had been waiting to hear.

Accusations. Insults. That was what had silently screamed off her during her silence. He knew why. Moira had told him that Joan had learned about his role in the rebellion.

He knew how she felt about Mortimer, and the power that the rebellion had handed him. She had made her opinions about that very plain that first day in the bath.

Still, her reaction had been extreme. He had spent the last two days thinking about that, putting together bits and pieces. A word, a look, a sigh.

A hatred, a quest, a denial.

It would not be the way that you think.

"I could come today," she said as she fussed around the

kitchen, finding chores to do so she could avoid seeing him.

The quick offer surprised him. Her retreat these last days had been complete. It wounded him more than he liked to admit. He did not like the notion of living with her like this, as two strangers. He did not want only the service he had bought, even if that was all she had ever claimed to offer.

And so, although he had sworn to himself ten times over that he would not invite her anger and accusations, he did so anyway.

"Moira told me that she told you how she and I met."

A sharp look, one that could slice steel. "Aye, she told me. How you aided that butcher. Do you still?"

He told himself that he read too much into her piercing gaze. Still, she waited as if she wanted to know.

He looked right back, and hoped she believed him since it seemed to matter. "Nay, I do not."

Something passed in her eyes. A slight softening. A moment of wavering. Then blankness.

A word. A look. A pause.

A quest and a dream.

"Why do you have this hatred of Mortimer, Joan?"

"I do not approve of what he is doing. I am not alone."

"Your emotions far exceed the usual discontent. Moira said that you grew very distressed at the feast, and you have treated me like an enemy since."

She instantly looked very wary.

"How did your family die? You never said."

He should probably leave her to her memories, but having begun to wonder, he now discovered that he needed to know. "Do you blame him for it? After the rebellion he knew no restraint on the marches. Did his army attack your town?"

"Aye," she said bitterly. "I blame him for it."

And you. It was there in her tone and the glare she shot him.

"Your brother knows horses, and says that your father owned one. You lost more than your family, didn't you?"

"Aye, more than my family."

"What happened?"

"I do not speak of it."

"Nay, you do not, but I ask you to now."

Her eyes glinted fiercely. Her mouth hardened, as though she clenched her teeth. "His army came, to take by force the estate of a lord who had stayed loyal to the last king. My father joined the fight. He died when the castle fell. So did every man who defended the keep. The new lord was a vile man, one of Mortimer's favorites. He took everything belonging to anyone who stood against him, all in the name of the crown. So Mark and I left that place and came here."

She got through it only by speaking quickly. Glinting anger flashed behind her blinking lids.

"Your fall was farther than I guessed. I assumed you were a townswoman, a craftsman's daughter. But your father was landed. He was not a poor freeholder either, was he? A yeoman farmer, from your tale. No wonder your brother knows horses, and thought it below him to stuff pallets."

"Do not pity us. I can not bear that from anyone, least of all a man who was in part responsible, but pretends he was not. A man who hides what he really is."

So there it was.

"I did not lie to you."

"You did. You let me think that your craft alone had brought you your position, but it was something else."

"In part it was something else. I like to think that my skill with stone helped."

"You deceived me."

"Nay. The mere mention of Mortimer distressed you enough to avoid talk of it, and what had happened years ago had no meaning between us."

"How could you support such as him? How could you put that man in a position to do what he has done?"

"It was not about him. We supported the Queen and her son, and we fought to rid the realm of a king who was the pawn of men without honor or scruples. Perhaps in your father's home you did not see how it was back then."

"Are you saying that I was blinded by comfort?"

"I am saying that you were young, and protected, and isolated from the injustice."

"That certainly changed, didn't it?"

"Joan, what happened to you and your family pains me. But there was no way to know that would happen and the last king had to fall. I will not apologize for helping to bring down a monarch who was not fit for the throne."

"How comfortable you must be in your lofty principles. How reassuring to know that you did the right thing as you saw it. How easy to play the dangerous game when you made sure that you had nothing to lose except your life."

"That is hardly a small thing."

"I have learned that sacrificing one's self is much simpler than sacrificing those you love. You formed no family and put down no roots, so that you never had to face that dreadful choice. You could ignore the innocents who might be trampled, because none of those innocents belonged to you. Well, I do not remember those times as noble men doing great deeds in the name of high ideals. I see only a castle yard filled with blood, and brave men butchered as they stood in surrender, and a conqueror with eyes like those of a devil who has escaped hell."

She turned abruptly and paced back to the hearth. He

watched that back, stern with repudiation, and knew that all the talk in the world would not absolve him.

He retreated into practicalities—for now. "If you are willing to check the floors, come to Westminster today at tierce. I will meet you at the gate and take you to the chambers. Afterward we will go out to Kent, and see about that tile yard. I have learned that it is not far from the city."

He expected her to object. A woman who had decided to despise a man would not want to spend that many hours with him.

She considered it, and nodded. Slinging a cauldron's handle over her arm, she left to go to the well.

He had a good look at her face as she passed. Determination set her expression, and fires lit her eyes.

A word. A look. A sigh.

She set out well before tierce. She left the house not long after Rhys. She made her way to the Cheap and walked down its length.

John was not in the tavern near the cathedral. She sat on a bench at a table in a dark corner and bided her time. If he did not come this morning, she would return another time.

The woman who laid down ale gave her a quizzical glance and she shook her head in response. She had no coin for ale, and would not for a long while. But she would soon have coin for other, more important things.

John entered the dark chamber. He looked around. Joan had the sense he did not search for anyone in particular, just a familiar face. Whatever he did for Bishop Stratford, he used this tavern as his private study.

He saw her, and ambled over. He slid onto the bench across from her. "Been some time. Didn't think you'd help."

"You did not tell me that Rhys had aided the rebellion. I might have come quicker if you had."

"Didn't expect it to matter. That was different. Lots helped. I did. But some of us seek to undo our mistake, and others only seek to benefit from it."

"And you fear he is one of the latter."

"I wonder, is all. He was with us, but is no longer. Loyalties change." He paused and stroked his beard. "Do you know if his have?"

"I looked in the house, among his things, yesterday. I looked at all of the parchments in that workroom. I found nothing." It had been harder than she expected. Guilt and fear of discovery had quickened her blood the whole time. That she examined parchments that revealed his inner eye, his imagination, had intensified the unexpected sense of betrayal. Even as her act repudiated their connections, what she saw tightened them.

Some of the designs had been predictable and finished, but others, sometimes no more than meandering lines, had displayed fanciful moments. Whimsical and free. Impractical or impossible. Statues that moved the way stone never could. Doorways in shapes that would never be built.

She banished those images from her mind, and closed her heart to the man who had made them. "You said there would be coin."

"But you found nothing."

"I finished what you began. You now know what you went to that house to learn. You seek evidence one way or the other, and I have brought it."

He frowned, but conceded the point. He fished in his purse, and a shilling landed on the table.

"Nay, I want three. I risked much doing this. If he discovers it, I am in the street."

"Such as you will never be in the street. There are other men who need . . . housekeepers."

His little leer got her back up. "Four shillings, now."

He began filling with indignation, ready to bluster. "I say it is worth only one."

"Then you are a cheat, and I will help you no further. Go tell your bishop of your stupid mistake in talking too freely. Face his wrath at having his plans undone, and possibly for nought."

That took the air out of him. "You think that you can help further? It has become vital to know what he is. He works in the King's own chambers now. If he is in Mortimer's pocket, the King must be warned."

Aye, important to know what he is, and not just for the King's sake. "I live in his house. I will be helping him in his craft, even at the palace. If he is aiding Mortimer, I think that I will know soon." She tapped the table. "But if I do this, if I learn that he is, I want five pounds, not a few shillings."

He chewed on his lip and mulled it over. "Aye, five pounds, woman. But do not think to feed me air."

"I would not fabricate a story. If I were such a person, I would have brought you scraps today that I had written myself."

She rose, feeling soiled by his presence and by the grime in this tavern. It was still too early to meet Rhys, but she wanted to be away from this man. "If I learn anything, I will leave word here for where to meet me. The whole city probably knows that you sit here every day, and I do not want to be seen with you."

His face hardened at her tone. "'Tis for God's justice that we do this. For a good cause."

She grabbed the coins, turned on her heel, and left. Aye, for God's justice. And her own.

Entering the town of Westminster took all her bravery.

She had never come here, not even to sell her wares. As she approached the palace, her blood began the horrible pulsing born of the old fear.

She held onto her resolve, and found a portal where servants came and went. If she discovered what John wanted, she would have the coin that she needed at once. If she did not, her work for Rhys would at least bring her some, and her visits to tile yards would provide the means to arrange to earn more.

She would ignore the way all of this made her heart heavy. She would remember that he had helped reduce her to such scheming, and that such a man should not be given trust, let alone loyalty.

She approached a stout woman carrying a pail and asked where she might find the King's chambers.

The woman raised her eyebrows. "None goes there unless they are called. If you've a petition, wait for the days when it's done, or see his people."

"I do not come to petition, or to see the King. I'm to meet a mason who is working on the fabric."

"Ah, that be Rhys. We all know him. Face and body like that, the women notice. Odd that he should tell you to come to the chambers, though. Not done, and he isn't there now anyway. I just saw him elsewheres."

"He did not tell me to come to the chambers, but to meet him at the gate. But I am early, so I thought—"

"Come with me. I'll show you where he is, but you are to wait and not go in."

Pail swaying, she led the way up some stairs and through some passageways, then pointed out a window. Down below, in a small garden, two men sat on benches against the wall. One was Rhys.

"Who is the other man?" She suspected the answer even as she asked it.

"You are an ignorant one, aren't you? That is Roger

Mortimer, none other. Now, I'll show you where to wait below, so your master passes when he leaves there."

She barely heard the woman. She kept looking at the two men. They appeared very casual with each other—not the way an earl spoke with a mason, and gave commands about some project. More like friends. Or confidants.

Anger tightened through her. So did sorrow. The sadness proved more powerful. It strangled her heart and filled her throat and brimmed up to her eyes.

The woman gestured, and led her back down below. She did not stay where she was told Rhys would pass, however. As soon as the servant left, she hurried through the palace, asking for directions back to the portal through which she had entered.

She plunged out into the open air, and sank against the wall. The sadness wanted to overwhelm her. Containing it was harder than controlling the fury she had known when Moira told her about Rhys and the rebellion. That anger had been sharp and hot, a fire burning in her head. This felt like a flood of melancholy that threatened to drown her.

Somehow, she battled to the surface. As always these last three years, she clutched onto that which gave her a purpose.

She pushed away from the wall, and sought different directions. Not to a place inside the palace.

She would have coin soon. A lot of coin. Five pounds.

Joan was not at the gate at tierce. Rhys waited a long while at a spot where she could not miss him, eyeing the veils and faces of the women who passed.

She had not wanted to come. Most likely she had changed her mind again.

He did not know what made him turn and look to the

far yard, and the spot where the curving outer wall disappeared behind the buildings. He just did, as if an invisible voice had reached his ears on the breeze.

He knew it was Joan despite the distance. He recognized the brown gown that still hung too loosely, even though she had gained some weight in his house. He saw the elegance of her stroll, and the familiar tilt of her head. He saw it all, as if she stood right in front of him.

A man walked beside her. A knight, wearing armor. He must have come from the practice yard.

Rhys did not go to her, but stayed by the portal, watching. Joan walked a few paces aside, angling her head this way and that, examining the strong man none too subtly. The knight stepped closer, and made to touch her face. She turned slightly, but did not run away. A discouragement, but not a complete repudiation.

His chest tightened. The grip of jealousy surprised him. His thoughts heated, and burned open new paths.

Maybe he had misunderstood. Perhaps her mood the last two days had nothing to do with him and what she had learned at the feast. That resolve in her face and eyes might indicate something else. He could have been seeing the decision of a woman to achieve her goal any way possible. To barter with other than money if necessary.

Perhaps it would not be the way he thought because he could not repay her with what she really wanted.

She backed away from the knight, taking her leave, waving him away. He imagined her words. *Come no further. A man waits for me, and he will be displeased to see me with you. He likes to think there is something between us, and that he has claims on me, although I have told him often that it isn't so.*

She strolled toward him with a perky step. Joan the tiler was well pleased with her visit to Westminster.

He did not mention what he had just seen. He brought her to the King's chambers and she paced over the planks,

noting those that needed work. It did not take long, since
the Queen was ill and they could not enter her rooms. And
so they were on the road out of the city, into the Kent
countryside, before midday.

Every moment she was with him, a stew of emotions
simmered in him. Jealousy and anger and curiosity and
concern. The words and looks and pauses flashed in his
memory again and again, lining up this way and that,
forming links to various conclusions. Some were infuriat-
ing, some worrying, and some tinged with resentment. But
all of them were tragic.

He suspected that he now knew where she was going,
and what she had to do. He also thought he had guessed
one of the reasons that drove her, and why she assumed
that it could never be the way he thought.

He hoped to God that he was wrong about the last part,
but he did not think that he was.

Rhys did not hover nearby at the tile yard. He let her ex-
amine the kiln and wares and speak with the workers on
her own. He was taking ale with the tiler when she finished, so she ambled over to the property where the
brother who was a potter plied his craft.

She dawdled there, watching the wheel and asking
questions about some special light grey clay that he had. It
came from soil near Dover, he explained, and made finer
cups than ordinary stuff. It seemed to her that it would
make nice statues.

She asked about work, but halfheartedly. That would
not be necessary now. She would have her coin, and very
soon. And five pounds would be enough. That knight had
been happy to talk with a woman who smiled at him, even
if she was lowborn. He had assured her that if the cause
was just, a champion could be had for five pounds. His

manner had implied that if the woman was fair and willing, one could be had for no coin at all. But she had always known that.

Rhys was waiting by the wagon when she emerged from the potter's shed.

"The work is good, but the yard is small," she explained as she climbed to her seat. "I do not think they can make as many as you need while the weather holds."

"We will check some others before deciding, then."

That would mean more such journeys, some farther from London than this yard in the city's environs. That would mean spending more long hours beside Rhys.

He had been thoughtful and quiet all day. She had probably spoken too rashly in the morning, when he asked her about her home. She had just blurted it out, giving voice to the horrible memories and images that had plagued her since Moira's revelation.

He had said that he no longer aided Mortimer. For a moment he had convinced her.

Her mind had rejected that at once, but deep inside her, something had wanted desperately to believe he had spoken honestly.

She glanced at his profile, so handsome in its clear planes. His blue eyes were full of the shadows of thought, and maybe also those of anger and displeasure. He brooded over something. Perhaps his meeting with Mortimer had not gone as planned.

Nay, it was not that. She just knew it. Looking at him, sitting with him, being near him for the first time in two days, unsettled her. His closeness undermined her resolve and cracked her certainty. She thought about the two men in the garden. What had she really seen? No so much. Nothing damning. Her feelings of betrayal after hearing Moira's words had made her assume more than she should.

She saw his eyes again in the morning when he said he did not aid Mortimer. Saw their intensity, and heard the firm statement. He had spoken the words as clearly as one does a vow or oath.

Her fear and anger repudiated that, but her heart said that he had not lied. Right now, sitting beside him, sensing the man more than knowing him, her heart's voice spoke the loudest.

She would not discover what John sought. She would never see those five pounds.

Accepting that surprised her. There was no disappointment. Instead, a gentle lightness entered her mood. After two days of tight rancor, this new certainty soothed her spirit at once.

Which only made his brooding seem darker.

He noticed her watching him. It pulled him out of his reverie. The way his mouth hardened made her wish it had not.

"What did you want with that knight, Joan?"

He had seen. His deep mood had to do with her. He was jealous. "I arrived early, and went to watch the swordplay in the practice yard. I only complimented him on his skill."

"A long compliment."

"I asked him some questions, too. It was not what you think."

"What do I think, Joan? That you looked like some loose woman fawning over a handsome young man?"

The insinuation made her burn with embarrassment, and with indignation. "So you want me loose only for you? You should have made that clear."

The glint turned steely. "Aye, only for me. It has been clear enough, even if we never speak of it."

She decided that not speaking at all might be a good idea.

Except he would not permit that. "What questions did you ask him?"

"About his horse. His life. Such things as that."

"I would not be evasive, Joan. I have learned to tell when you lie."

"If I lie, it is because you are too curious."

"You asked about his life and his horse. Did you ask about his purse?"

"Why would I do that?"

"Because you examined the man as if you sought to buy him."

His insight stunned her. How much did he suspect?

"Except it could not be that, could it?" he continued. "Even if you harbored some childish plan to avenge your family, you could not afford such as he."

Childish! "Of course not. See how silly you are being."

"Of course, you might think to pay with other than coin, but you did not have to wait three years for that. Unless you have suddenly grown impatient."

"We spoke the usual pleasantries, that is all. What I said to Sir Gerard is not of your concern. It had nothing to do with you."

It was the wrong thing to say. Lightning flashed in those blue eyes.

He angled the wagon off the road, beside a copse of trees. He jumped down and came over and lifted her out. She hurled objections at him, but he ignored her. Face set like stone, eyes sparking, he dragged her in among the trees. "Aye, it has nothing to do with me. You tell me that often. Where you are going and when you will leave and what you will do and what is in your heart has nothing to do with me." He pulled her against an oak, into his arms. "But it has everything to do with me, because this does."

He kissed her. Hard. Furiously. A kiss of demand and

claim. An assertion of the ability to possess her passion if he chose.

It frightened her. Not the heat, nor the iron hold of his embrace. Her reaction frightened her. For all of her outrage and shock, that kiss defeated her at once. Even as she struggled, her body grew pliant. The inner voice of denial faded, drowned out by an onslaught of visceral affirmation. Those wings of her womanhood took to flight and soared, soared, glorying at the dizzying height made possible by the winds of his storm.

Nothing mattered. Not her misgivings or her plans or her decisions. That world ceased to exist when he kissed her. It always had. She had no resistance against the beauty of that. Her heart longed to have the hard things obscured.

He ended the kiss, but did not release her. He rested against the oak, and pulled her closer. He eased his knee between her legs until she straddled it, her toes barely skimming the ground. His eyes glinted as he saw her reaction to the firm pressure.

"This part of your life definitely has to do with me, Joan. To my mind that means the rest of it does too."

"You have the poorest part, Rhys. The weakest way to make a claim."

His knee kept pressing her, keeping her arousal alive, reminding her of where this might have gone. Should have gone. "It is the oldest way between men and women, pretty dove. The first way. And if you did not join me in this pleasure, I might not think to claim more of your body or your heart or your mind."

He spoke of so much. Of what this might be. Her heart twisted. It could never happen, not with her. The first way, the oldest way, the way essential to the sharing he meant, was blocked to her.

She had to make him understand how hopeless this was. How painful. "It is only pleasurable up to a point for me, and then that dies. I have told you from the first that I can not give you what you want, that I do not like men in that way."

She expected more surprise. Instead he only wrapped her tighter with his arms, and looked down at her. A long, thoughtful gaze. Too long, too thoughtful.

"Did you give yourself to your betrothed, Joan?"

The question shocked her.

"Did you?"

"Nay."

"So you were a maid when he died?"

He prodded at something bruised and sore. She recoiled from the intrusion.

"I do not think that you are a virgin now, though. Am I wrong about that?"

She gritted her teeth. "Nay. Now are you contented? Will you leave this alone?"

"I want to know why you are afraid of this. Why does the pleasure die?"

She fought to control the dreadful emotions that his questions tapped, but they started oozing into her heart.

"Did something happen when that army came? After your men were killed and you were unprotected? Is that why you want to earn coin and meet a champion? Do you dream of avenging the loss of more than your family and home?"

She could not answer. She could not face him. She wanted him to stop asking about this. Wanted it so dreadfully that she desperately raised her face to kiss him. To distract him.

He accepted the offering, but did not kiss back. He broke it gently, as though he knew what she was about.

"Joan, were you raped?"

Mortification poured through her. Utterly engulfed her. Her throat and eyes burned as she struggled to suppress the onslaught of disgrace. Fear and disgust and deadening sadness blew through her.

And anger, too. At Rhys. He could not leave it alone. He had to dig and dig until he undermined her feeble defenses. He had to throw her back into it, just to satisfy his vanity that her denial was not a repudiation of him.

Barely controlling the pointless tears that she had sworn never to shed again, she roughly pushed out of his arms. She faced him, more furious than she had ever been in her life.

He wanted to know? He needed to know? Then let him know, damn it.

"It was not rape. I was not forced." She started striding back to the wagon. "I went willingly. I sold myself."

CHAPTER 14

THE DEVIL IN HIM had taken over, and now he sorely regretted it.

Joan rode the rest of the way in utter silence. Unmoving. A figure carved in stone, with all of her humanity drawn in beneath a hard surface.

He turned and glimpsed her eyes. Shadowed with pain, they peered inward and noticed neither his concern nor her surroundings. He knew that look. He had seen it before, on a dark-haired woman carrying a dead bastard in her womb.

They got back to the city an hour before sunset. Joan hopped out of the cart when he stopped by the stable, and scurried into the house. He unhitched the wagon as Mark arrived to take care of the horse.

"What is this?" Mark asked, lifting a large twine sack. "It is awful heavy."

Rhys had forgotten it was there. "It is clay."

"Clay? For Joan? Let me go tell her. She looks unhappy. This will brighten her up."

"Nay, hand it to me. Let her be alone now. Take care of the horse, and then go visit your friend David."

Rhys carried the bag into the garden and put it on the table. Since the sunlight was still strong, and since Joan needed her privacy, he uncovered the statue. Angling it low, he straddled the bench by the face and took up his fine rippler to finish the mouth.

Ursula, the virgin martyr. She had died rather than lie with the pagan leader of the Huns. Eleven thousand young women had perished with her, in the name of Christian purity. He decided that he did not like Ursula and the other virgin saints much, even if he loved this statue. What message did her story give to the Joans of the world who had to bargain with the devil in order to survive?

He lost himself in the work as he had hoped he would. And so he did not notice her in the garden until she set the cup of ale on the table.

Despite her unhappiness, she had gone to the tavern. The fresh ale had become a little ritual, and every evening it waited for him in the hall when he returned. If the night had grown cool she usually built up the fire in the hearth there, too, and placed the master's chair nearby. He rarely used that, though. He normally carried the ale back into the kitchen, and spent the time before supper with her and Mark.

He glanced at her face, and her sadness tore at his heart. He had guessed her story, but he had never suspected how raw her soul still was.

Too raw. She had accepted the things she could change, and had ignored the ones she could not, but that did not weaken the worst sorrows. A grief that was not embraced would have its day eventually. It slowly ate its way out of its hiding place, destroying whatever lay in its path.

She began to return to the house, but noticed the sack.

He watched while she considered it, and poked its side curiously. She peeked inside. He returned to his rippler.

Nothing. No sound at all. Finally he looked over.

She still peered into the sack, but her expression had lost its deadness.

"You bought this for me?"

"The potter from Kent had extra. He was willing to give me some."

"It is very fine clay. And it is a lot."

"You can put some in water to save, nay?"

She pulled the sack down and stared at the lump, as though she did not remember what to do.

He got up and found a wide board. He set it across the other end of the bench. "You can work it here."

"I have no kiln."

"For a price, George will let you use his. And even if you can not fire them, it is the craft that gives satisfaction as much as the product. At least it is for me."

"Aye, for me, too."

He returned to his place. She contemplated the clay. Clawing away a big chunk, she carried it to the board. "It is too stiff. It requires kneading."

Ignoring his presence, she unlaced her gown and slipped it off. Bare-armed and bare-legged, wearing only her shift, she straddled the bench and sank her hands into the grayish mass.

She did not lose herself in it, though. He might be gone, but her own thoughts were not. They silently quaked through the air. He felt her sadness as surely as the tool in his hand.

The clay proved very stiff. Almost unyielding.

"It needs a little water, nay?" he asked.

"Probably," she said dully.

He rose and got some from the well, brought it back, and straddled the other side of the board. He dripped some on, and then lent his own hands and strength to the chore.

They kneaded together in silence. Her movements were rote and not very effective. Her bare knees peeked out from the hitched up shift, but she neither noticed nor cared.

"You knew," she muttered.

"I guessed. I was not sure."

"How?"

"Things that you had said. Bits here and there. I am somewhat practiced at hearing the thoughts behind a word or two."

"So you had to ask, because you hoped it was not true."

"That it is true matters not to me, Joan. Not in the way that you think."

She glanced up with complete disbelief, then slammed her fist into the clay. "Well, it matters to *me*."

He debated his course, and hoped that he chose the right one. "When I was a boy, just younger than Mark, a woman I knew caught the eye of a powerful man. He was the son of the local lord's overlord, and accustomed to having what he wanted. She refused him, but he did not relent. She was freeborn, of a craftsman's family, but it did not matter."

She did not look at him, but her fingers stretched tensely through the clay.

"He might have just caught her alone and forced her, but that was not his way. Instead he made her suffer. Not just herself, but her family. He saw that no one sold them food or gave them work. He threatened everyone who might help, but he never directly hurt her. All of her kin went hungry, even the children."

Her hands stopped. She stared at the clay. "What did she do?"

"What could she do? She went to him. Willingly, as his

vanity wanted. But there was no will in it at all. If he had held a knife to her throat, it would have been more her choice than it was. Nor did he welcome her as a lover. He made her bargain for her family, so she would know his power. It was the first of many degradations."

She closed her eyes. A tremor shook her body.

He slid his hand over hers. "For what were you forced to bargain, Joan?"

She barely moved, but the hand under his clawed into the clay. "For Mark," she whispered. "For my brother's life. He would have killed him, and no one else could stop it."

Jesus. He grasped her hand tightly, as much to contain his own emotion as to soothe hers. She did not have to say who "he" was. It had not been some knight drunk on victory, but the man who flew Mortimer's banner. "You had no choice, darling. See that, and know the truth of it, and never say that you sold yourself again."

Her shoulders bowed lower. The memories began defeating her.

He reached for her. "Joan . . ."

She threw up a hand to ward him off. "Nay. Please do not. Leave now. Please, leave me alone."

He rose, reluctant to abandon her like this. She appeared terribly limp, and tragically, pitifully alone. He thought that his heart would break for her.

He caressed her head with his fingertips as he passed, lightly enough that she would not feel. But he did. "I am sorry, Joan. I should have seen it sooner. I fear that whenever I touched you, it only made you remember."

She kneaded with all her strength, praying the clay would absorb the horror as smoothly as it did her hands. It didn't happen this time. The despair just grew and grew, filling her until it choked her chest and throat in its demand to come out. She used all of her strength to keep it contained, but its devastating power surged relentlessly until her hands and the clay blurred from the tears streaming into her eyes.

It was time, whether she wanted it or not. For over three years she had never really faced the despair, but she had no choice now. His questions had opened the frail scabs, and it just started flowing, like blood from a putre-fied wound. She could not stop it this time. None of the old sanctuaries served her well enough. Not the anger or the hatred or even the clay.

She had often sought escape in her craft, but now she found release. She pounded and jabbed viciously as the emotions racked her. Gasping sobs groaned out of her so forcefully that they pained and bent her whole body. Tears fell like a waterfall onto the mass that she pummeled. The memories forced themselves into her mind so vividly that three years might have never passed.

Images of Guy, of his demands and touch, were the least of it. The real hell had not been at night, except when she woke and experienced the suffocating sense of entrapment. She had faced what occurred with her body long ago. Reliving the rest of it devastated her, though. The numb-ing of her soul. The lonely helplessness. The self-hatred and disgust. The sense of being so unclean that no bath could purify her.

She fought acknowledging all that, fought so hard that her body ached. It filled her anyway. It poured out of the places she had hidden it, swamping her until she groaned in surrender.

Sobbing uncontrollably, drowning in bleakness, she continued blindly attacking the clay. Her mind kept run-ning away, trying to find shelter, but there was nowhere to hide.

Her head hurt. She thought that her chest would burst.

The sobs choked her so badly that she couldn't breathe. She folded her arms over her body in a frantic attempt to hold herself together.

It felt like grief, the worst grief she had ever known. Giving it a name made it a little better, but also more intense. Facing the loss broke her heart. It sharpened the pain with a biting nostalgia.

She careened, pressing her folded arms into her bent body so hard that she hurt herself. She finally mourned for the life torn from her. Not the comforts, but the happiness and the innocence. The trust and faith. She mourned for her childhood, and the girl she had once been.

It blew through her like a deadly storm. She lost her mind for a while and only scathing pain existed. Pain that threatened to tear her to shreds.

Slowly, like all tempests, it eased a little. She tried to regain some control. Swallowing the anguish shot cramps through her body. Forcing back the tears seared her eyes and thickened her throat.

Calm came slowly. It brought a new knowing and a new acceptance and the vaguest relief.

She grew aware of herself, and the bench and the clay. Twilight had fallen on the garden. She unfolded her arms and slid her hands onto the mass on the board between her knees. Her violence had created lumps and pits and jagged valleys.

She squeezed and smoothed until she had a round, flat form. A compulsion to work it slid through her. Like the line of the sun spreading over a field after a storm, the hope of solace peeked through her misery and beckoned her.

She had found comfort in her craft before. Perhaps she could now. It was the one good thing to rise out the destruction. She would make something beautiful, an image from the old days, and give form to what was left of the part of her that had once known goodness.

Sniffing back the threatening sorrow, she let her hands move. She would not make a statue this time, but a plaque in relief. She scooped and modeled, making the forms rise and swell.

It absorbed her completely. Peace came, melancholy but secure. The light grew so dim that she could not see what she made. It just emerged, flowing directly from her soul to her fingers, skipping her mind. It felt so right, though. It would be perfect. Beautiful and perfect and good. A little monument to who she had once been and to what she had once known.

"What do you have there?"

It was Mark, coming toward her from the garden portal. She straightened and realized that dark had fallen. "I don't know for sure. A face, I think. Father's, I think."

He went very still. She instantly regretted saying that. She did not want to draw him into her unhappiness.

"Bring me a candle, would you?"

He went into the kitchen and came back with a small taper. She took it from him. "Go and get some sleep now."

He gladly obeyed. He would not want to see their father's face. He carried his own wounds, and licked them his own way. She lowered the little flame. Its flickering light sent the smallest glow over the clay. Her blindness had produced something fairly crude, but the visage was distinct.

Not her father's face. It was not an image from her girlhood, but a man from her present.

It was Rhys.

CHAPTER 15

HE WENT TO THE SOLAR window again and again. The sound of her grieving drew him there.

Night fell, and still she sat, straddling the bench. Not the soulful careening of before, though. She worked the clay now.

That was a hopeful sign. Her hands would express what her soul needed to know. Creating something from base materials was a spiritual act as well as a physical skill. There could be healing in it. He had realized that as a boy, and it was a big reason why he would never put aside the chisel, no matter how many buildings he planned.

A tiny light appeared. He watched it flicker while she sat motionlessly, holding it in her hand. She appeared calmer.

He turned away, leaving her to her privacy again. He sat in the chair where he had held his vigil while he listened to her sobs rise from the garden.

She would not like to know that he had heard. He would have preferred not to, because her sadness wrenched his heart. It was empathy that had kept him here as much as affection. It was also guilt. Not just for bringing her to this state, but also for not preventing the events that had shredded her life.

His mind saw himself as a youth, resolved to make his own justice for a destroyed soul. He had not thought of it as the right thing to do; it had simply seemed the *only* thing to do. The marcher lords held more power than barons did elsewhere in the realm. The son of the man who was the law would never answer to the law himself. And this crime had been shrewd. If a woman went willingly, how could she claim to have been forced?

There had been weeks of planning and practice with the bow. Days of silent watching. When the opportunity came, however, he had experienced an instant of cowardice. That hesitation had led to failure, and then to the run across England to escape the search for the hidden assassin who had dared try such a thing.

If he had been braver and faster, Mortimer would have died that day. The realm would have been spared his ambitions. No army would have gone to Joan's home three years ago.

No henchman would have degraded her.

He had come to this city sworn to fight when necessary, and to never hesitate again. Not just for that woman, and not just against Mortimer. That commitment had governed his life and his choices as surely as the urge to build had.

But fate could be capricious. In the fight for justice, he had helped hand more power to the man whose ruthlessness he had wanted to avenge as a youth. He had made a ruler of the rapist he had once tried to kill.

All his risks, all his ideals, were thrown in his face. Worse, he had actually been an agent in the corruption of his own beliefs.

He lifted a rolled parchment from the floor by his boot. He had grabbed some of his fantasies to bring in here to distract himself from the misery in the garden. That had been hopeless. He might peer at the drawings, but he had not really seen any of then. The part of him that mattered had been down there with her, feeling her pain, praying that those tears would purge the worst of the hidden misery from her heart.

He unrolled the plan. It was an old one, done during the rebellion. With war threatening, he had turned his imagination to castles. It showed a keep and walls, with all its parts articulated. It was very detailed, in ways few of his designs ever were.

He calls one of his builders to repair the walls. Someday that builder will be you.

She had seen to the heart of it at once. Seen more than he wanted to admit to himself. Her own sense of justice, still hot and pure, had recognized loss of faith when faced with it.

Slow footsteps sounded on the stairs. That would be Mark, bringing up water for the night.

A blond crown and lit taper emerged from the stairwell. Then a delicate face and very blue eyes. It was not Mark. Joan had decided to take this chore tonight.

She watched the bucket to make sure none of the water slopped out. She stepped into the solar and began to head to the bedchamber before she noticed him sitting near the cold hearth.

She stopped, the heavy bucket straining her stiff arm. The little flame that she held cast shadows over her shift and arms and legs. She had not remembered to put her gown back on.

He peered at her face, hoping for a sign that she had conquered the memories, and not the other way around.

Her poise had returned. That was a good sign. She held

herself proudly, but he saw the fragility of that pose. He sensed that, given half a reason, she would break again.

He wanted to go to her, but she might not want that.

"Who was she? The woman you told me about. How did you know her?"

Her voice sounded distant. She continued the conversation from the garden, as if two hours of hell had not intervened.

"My aunt. The wife of my father's brother."

She paused, as if it took time for his response to penetrate and be considered. "So you were one of the family that suffered."

"Aye."

Another pause. "Did you love her?"

"She was a young bride, not much older than I. I loved her as an aunt, but maybe in other ways, too."

"You all wanted her to go to him, didn't you? So that you would not starve. Did you all despise her even as she saved you?"

He knew where this was going, and cursed the world for its simplistic ideas of virtue and the burdens they put on women. "I can not speak for the others, but I did not despise her. I honored her."

Her body tensed. The bucket wobbled. Water lapped over its edge. "Do you despise me? Do you see a woman defiled when you look at me now?" It came out firmly, like a challenge. She gazed at him, waiting to see if he lied.

He stretched out his hand. "Please come here to me, Joan."

She hesitated, then put down the bucket and walked over. He blew out her taper and set it aside, then took her hand and lifted it to his lips. "When I look at you I see a brave maid who saved her brother's life."

"Not a maid."

"Aye, a maid. Untouched in the ways that matter."

Her glance contained some gratitude, and a bit of reassurance.

She stayed there, as if she did not know how to leave. He held her hand and waited for her to decide why she had come.

"Please do not tell Mark. He does not know. I brought the water because he was asking me questions. He wanted to know why I was out in the garden, and what had happened to make me sad. I am hoping he will be asleep when I go back down."

That was not why she had come. She looked very lovely standing before him in the candlelight. A little mysterious and very alone. Somewhat childlike in her distraction. She belonged to herself, but even the strong needed support sometimes.

"Can I stay here until he sleeps?"

"You can stay as long as you want. You can stay all night. You are always welcome."

She understood the offer. She contemplated it, shyly fingering her shift. "The last time your bed was chaste."

Maybe her choice truly came from her desire to protect her brother from learning the truth. Perhaps she merely sought shelter from the loneliness of her grief. His heart did not care why she accepted. He was just grateful that she would let him comfort her a little. He was relieved that she would not be alone with her thoughts tonight.

"It will be again. As chaste as you want, Joan. For as long as you want."

Her mouth quivered into a little smile. She appeared awkward and embarrassed, but also warm and beautiful. She looked down at the crusty splotches on her arms and knees. "I am covered with clay. I will get the linens dirty."

He rose, and handed her into the chair. "Sit here and we will wash it off."

He brought over the bucket and knelt before her. He took a rag and began wiping off the drying clay.

She permitted it. Like a soldier exhausted by battle, she sat limply, her lovely legs dangling from the chair, while he took care of her. The mood of that first night, when she bathed in his kitchen and then slept beside him, emerged again in the silence.

The bed might be chaste, but it would be intimate. In her need she seemed to accept that.

He rose and held out his hand. She scooted off the chair and took it.

He began to snuff the candles.

"Can we bring one? The last time, when I woke, for a moment I thought . . ."

He lifted the longest one. "It should burn most of the night. I want you to know that it is I who am beside you."

He led her into the bedchamber and set the candle on a chest. It gave a faint light, but enough.

She stood thoughtfully, as though she could not decide how to do this. With a little shrug, she lifted the sheet and climbed onto the bed and huddled on the far side.

He smiled at her embarrassment, and undressed. He slid under the linen beside her curving back.

She had not asked to stay so she could be alone. He touched her shoulder. "Come here."

She turned into his arm as if she had been waiting for the request. She fit against him perfectly, warm and feminine, with her head on his shoulder and her breath on his chest.

Her braid hung along her arm. He lifted it with the hand holding her close and used the other to release the tie. Unplaiting her hair occupied him for some time, while he enjoyed having her there.

She relaxed. Her body grew pliant, molding neatly. She nestled closer, and rested her hand on his chest. His body stirred in a quietly pleasant way. He had promised that this bed would remain chaste as long as she wanted, and it would. But not forever. She had taken the first step to freedom, and he would guide her the rest of the way.

He spread her unbound hair over her arm and the sheet. The low light made it a glittering sea of gold.

"What happened to her?"

He did not think that this part of the story would comfort her much. "He tired of her, and she came back."

"Did she come back whole?"

She understood what had happened far too well, but then it was her story, too. "Nay."

"Where is she now? With your uncle still?"

"She died about a year after."

"Did she kill herself?"

The frank way she posed the question chilled him. "Nay." And she hadn't. But she had embraced death. She had not fought it.

"I thought of doing so. Once, on the way here, we stopped by a lake. It looked so peaceful. Soothing and placid and clean. It just entered my head to walk in and not come out."

His heart swelled. He stroked her arm with his fingertips and hid his reaction.

"But I needed to take care of Mark. He was only twelve then. That stopped me. And anger did too. Fury that we had been made victims. Instead I swore on my father's memory to undo all that I could, for Mark at least. To get our home back, and to know some justice about that man. I will, too. You were right today. I was asking Sir Gerard about champions. I save the coin from my statues to hire one. Someday I will send a knight to make that man pay for all that he did to us. I will issue a challenge to that devil, and he is so vain that he will accept it."

It was an admission born of the intimacy of the bed,

and the rawness of her sorrow. She shared her heart's thoughts, but she also gave him fair warning. She might have faced it all today, but she had not changed her mind. *I will not be staying, and now you know why.*

He would not argue with her about it now. Some other time he would point out the futility of her dream, and the necessity of putting the whole of that time aside.

They lay quietly in the poignant mood of her revelation. He kissed her head, just once, to let her know that he did not judge her badly for that moment of weakness by the lake. She had chosen to fight the deadliness and not surrender either her life or her soul to it. He admired her strength, no matter where she had found it.

"You were wrong about what you said in the garden," she whispered. "When you left. I do not want you to think that. Your touch did not make me remember."

"I am glad to know that. It pained me to think I had hurt you."

"You did not. In truth, it made me forget for a long time, up to a point. I did not think that possible. But that was frightening, too, because I can not let myself forget, can I? I can not make it right if I do not remember."

She spoke as if she was working something out in her mind—something having to do with her and him and their embrace.

He considered his response carefully, trying not to make one out of self-interest. "You must live this as your heart tells you, Joan. But if I were you, I would forget when I can, and remember when I must."

She fell silent for a long time. She barely moved at all, but he could tell that she did not sleep. The expectation of unspoken words beat in the quiet. He could not say them. It had to be her.

Just when he accepted that she would not, she surprised him.

"Do you want to kiss me?"

"You know that I do."

She thought about that. "Even though it can not be . . . even though . . ."

"Even though."

"It is not because you feel sorry for me, is it? I could not bear that."

He slipped out of their embrace and turned to look down at her face. "Do not think me better than I am. My interest in you had never been selfless, and it is not now. I think that the day will come when the pleasure does not die for you. I am vain enough to think that I can make that day come soon."

A small, crooked smile played on her lips. "I will feel very foolish, knowing that it will not be what you want."

"Whatever it is will be enough. I will make sure that you do not feel foolish."

Emotions flickered in her eyes. Doubt. Caution. Desire. She had raised the possibility, and he could not leave the decision entirely with her now. His body would not let him. If it was not time, if it was not good, they would both know it at once.

He lightly touched the mouth that had so recently gaped with grieving sobs. "I will not ask for anything more than you can give. Do you trust that?"

She nodded. He could only imagine the leap of faith that took. She had to know how vulnerable she would be.

"Then let us go slowly, so that nothing frightens you." He kissed her soft lips, testing. After a moment she kissed back. Her arms rose to accept him. Her trust flattered and pleased him, and checked the ferocious response that threatened to roar through him.

He kissed her patiently until he felt her arousal building. He resisted caressing her until her caution and embarrassment disappeared and her arms clung more tightly, and then he just gently stroked her arm, waiting until she was ready for more.

He indulged himself, tasting the delicate skin of her throat and tonguing the sensitive edge of her ear. Feeling the tiny tremors in her cheeks with his fingertips. Sensing the heat rise until she stretched and flexed and turned her face so his mouth could reach the most sensitive spots on her neck. Since he had put aside his own satisfaction, he could enjoy the languid path of this lovemaking.

He lured her lips open. Warmth and softness and intimacy absorbed him. With sensations blurring his mind, he never lost touch with her reactions. Even as he entered again and again, and forced control over his mounting desire, he remained alert to the unspoken language of her arms and body and quiet gasps. With a strict resolve he clung to his promise that nothing was going to frighten her.

A new tension entered her embrace. Her body arched in an invitation. He nuzzled her ear. "Do you want me to caress you?"

"Aye," she breathed.

He palmed down her side, along waist, hip, and thigh. She moved into it with an elegant stretch. A lovely muffled gasp breathed into him. Her passion rose quickly then. Trusting and willing, she let him bring her with him.

She was so lovely in it. He stopped kissing so that he could watch the way she molded into the long, slow paths of his hand. She turned slightly, beckoning him to her breast.

Not yet. He intended to go very slowly. He had a goal beyond this night. He would show her just what this might be, so that she would return again and again, until the day came when she gave herself to him. He would fill her with new memories, so that the old ones would no longer find room to live.

He turned her onto her stomach. She faced him, wide-eyed. He kissed her cheek in reassurance, and then pushed her hair aside so that he could look at her. The shift draped softly down her back and bottom to the middle of her thighs. Beautiful legs stretched out below.

He bent and kissed along her spine through the fabric, down to the little hollow at the small of her back. Her body flexed and her breath shortened in reaction. He enjoyed her whispers of pleasurable shock as much as the feel of her warmth on his lips.

Desire conquered her surprise. Her body moved in ways that she did not control. He moved the shift up so he could taste her skin, and bent low to kiss her thighs. She parted them slightly, volunteering a new vulnerability. He smelled her arousal, and a musky moisture touched his lips.

He had to forcibly pull himself away from what she unknowingly offered. A pounding heat entered his head and blood, and the decision to take this farther than he had planned simply happened, the natural conclusion of her ready responses.

He moved the shift higher, unveiling her. Her back dipped and her bottom rose at the exposure. He pushed it to her shoulders, and then slid it off until she was naked in the candle glow, as he had seen her that first morning and imagined her so often since.

He caressed her round, taut bottom. It tensed firmer and higher. He explored lower. Her thighs parted more. Short, anxious cries sang out on each of her breaths, muffled by the pillow.

He gently kneaded the back of her thighs, his fingers brushing closely to the source of the wetness slicking her skin. A melody of anxious pleasure poured out of her.

A touch on her shoulder was all it took for her to turn, clawing him to her in a tight embrace. She joined the kisses fiercely, opening to the hungry joining that did nothing to relieve the pounding in his head that her innocent eroticism stimulated.

Her kisses turned frenzied. Her cries rang with frustration. She pulled him closer and kept turning into his caress. She tottered on the brink of the abandon that had surprised her under the tree in the garden.

He could take her there, he could give her fulfillment, but he wanted to know she had chosen it. He caressed her inner thigh in offering, and pressed his lips to her temple to soothe her. "What do you want, love? Tell me."

No response at first. Then a whisper, no more than the spirit of a voice. "Everything. Let us try. I want everything with you."

He had not expected that. An inner voice warned that tonight was too soon, but need and triumph roared louder. "You are sure?"

"Aye. Please."

He touched her intimately, testing. In the garden, her pleasure had died with that, and he waited to see if it would again.

A flexing, defensive and cautious, tensed through her.

Then it slipped away, and she spread her legs.

No thought, then. No debate. Hunger sent a blaze through his head. He moved on top of her.

Another flexing. Somehow he forced himself to stop, waiting.

Again she conquered it. She pulled him closer, and kissed him.

He started, reining in his body's impulse to quickly grab the gift.

A tension. A chill. With his first touch it shivered all through her.

He stopped again, barely breathing from the effort it took. A primitive yell in his head urged him to ignore it.

She did not push him away. She did not resist, but he knew what had happened. She would not stop him, but they had gone farther than the memories would permit.

He hovered there, pressed at her heat, battling the desire that insisted he finish it. The urge almost overwhelmed him. Gritting his teeth, cursing himself, he pulled away and pushed her legs together.

They closed on him. That was all it took. He accepted the release, and the relief.

He opened his eyes after the instant of pleasure. Her hand covered her eyes.

"I am sorry," she muttered.

"It was too soon, that is all. I should have known that."

"I thought that I could."

"I do not want your bravery, Joan. I do not want you to force yourself. When it is time, you will know."

"At least I did not leave you . . . at least you are not . . . that would have been . . . I would have felt even more foolish then."

He kissed her until her embarrassment fell away, then pulled her to nestle in his embrace for the night.

"The next time we will not rush things, and I will see to your contentment, too."

"I am content enough. I do not think I could know more."

She could, and she would. But that would wait for another night.

He wrapped her in his arms, so that she would not feel foolish, or anything except protected. She fit against him very neatly, as if she had been molded to match him.

CHAPTER 16

SHE APPROACHED *the lord's chair in the hall. The wrong man sat in it, a man too young and too complex. He appraised her with the kind of interest that the last lord had never shown.*

Grief had killed her fear of him. The last days' horrors had turned her numb. She knew what he wanted, but she had already decided that she would kill herself first.

He looked her over possessively. It had been thus since he first saw her. She had assumed that first day that he would violate her, but he had not.

"You will sit here and eat, Joan. I will not have you pine."

She took the place beside him. His solicitous tone made her bitterness spill out. Its heat felt like boiling water thrown on the ice of her heart. "You did not have to kill Piers."

"He challenged me. It was ungrateful of him. I spared him when the keep fell, because we had once fought for the same lord. He repaid me by threatening my person."

"You forced him to the challenge. You have been too familiar with me. He is . . . he was my betrothed, my husband in God's eyes. His honor and mine left him no choice but to challenge you, despite his wounds, and you knew it."

He smiled mildly. A charming smile, but deadly in its brittle line. "Aye, your husband. Now he no longer stands between us, as fate would have it."

She understood suddenly. She saw the horrible truth. Piers had been lured into that challenge. It had all been deliberate, decided once Guy learned what Piers was to her. It had been a game to this knight, with her both the bait and the prize.

"You are a madman if you think his death makes me more willing. I only hate you the more."

He sipped his wine too calmly. His eyes glinted with triumph. "You will be mine, and you will be willing. You may bring me only your hatred at first, but that will change. Your safety depends on my favor."

"Do you think that I care about my safety? I hope that someday you know defeat, and learn how death can be a gift when all you love has been destroyed."

He looked her over again. The lust glowing in his eyes made her stomach turn.

He turned his head, and stared at something in the hall. "Not all that you love has been destroyed. I have been generous."

Her gaze followed his. She saw what absorbed his attention. Her brother Mark sat with the servants. A chill prickled her neck and shivered down her back.

His hand covered hers. "It is not mere lust, Joan. I can satisfy that without cost, and we both know it. But your beauty and manner entrance me, and I am besotted enough to want you to accept me of your own choice."

Rebellion surged for an instant, but she forced it into submission. She gave up all hope at that moment, and tasted the bitter bile of surrender.

✦ ✦ ✦

The nightmare faded away, and she knew it had been a dream even as she lived its last moments.

She drifted out of sleep peacefully. No drowning panic. No desperate entrapment. The silver light of dawn barely gave form to the man whose arm and hand rested possessively across her hips, but she did not need to see him to know who it was. Care and kindness could be felt in the weight of his touch.

She should wake him. He would be late to the palace. But the sweet protection of his embrace made the reemergence of the world gradual and manageable. The light of reality intruded into the chamber slowly, illuminating the scene of last night's intimacy.

The dreamy memories of their lovemaking summoned a flush of embarrassment and confusion.

If she had known how far it would go, she might not have let it start. She had never guessed that pleasure could consume one's whole being. She had not suspected that the right man's caress could soothe both physical and spiritual needs.

For a while. Up to a point. The memory of her failure embarrassed her anew.

She had probably made a mistake last night. In her need for his warmth and strength she had started something that she could not complete, but did not know how to stop.

His hand pressed her nakedness more firmly, and eased her nearer. She turned her head and his perceptive eyes looked back. Not sleeping. He had stayed to wait for her to wake. He had known that the new day would bring misgivings.

He kissed her breast, only in affection, but it aroused her anyway. He had discovered a part of her that would never be able to hide from him again, and he knew it.

"You will be very late," she said.

"I answer to no one there." He stretched and swung up.

He went to the door and opened it, and came back with a bucket of water. "Do you want me to speak with your brother, or will you?"

She stared at the bucket. Of course Mark would be awake by now. When he had brought the water up, the empty solar had confirmed where she had spent the night.

"I will," she said, not looking forward to that at all.

While Rhys washed and dressed, she found her shift and pulled it on. His reference to Mark spoke of his assumptions about how things had changed between them, and his expectations for the future.

She had not considered that. She had not weighed anything last night. It had just happened, and her raw emotions had not wanted to contemplate the consequences.

Her happiness took on a flavor of nostalgia. She could not stay in this house, yet deny what had occurred. Nor could she pretend that there would be more. That would be heartless and insulting.

She began to get up. "I will get some food ready."

He came over and stood by the bed's edge so she could not leave. "I will find something."

"I should . . . we should . . ." His gaze did not let her finish. He knew what she was thinking: *We should find a way to put this spilt wine back in its barrel.*

"You do not run away anymore, Joan. I will not let you. I warned you that I am not selfless in this." He bent and kissed her. "Nor will you leave anytime soon. What you have to do can wait a while."

At least he spoke as if he understood this could not continue very long. Her tangled emotions found vague relief in that.

"When you talk to Mark, tell him that there is no need for two pallets in the kitchen anymore. You will sleep here with me."

He left, and she got up and straightened the bed. She

washed slowly, wanting to delay facing her brother. She did not even have clothes here. She would have to go down as she had come up, dressed only in her shift.

She heard no shouting. Mark had not confronted Rhys. When she descended the stairs and entered the kitchen, she knew why.

Mark sat by the window, staring out to the garden. At her sound he turned to her. Her heart thudded at the sight of him. It was not a boy who pierced her with fiery eyes. A young man, face chiseled by anger, raked her with his gaze.

Nay, he had not said a word to Rhys. He had saved it all for her.

He reached for the rose gown piled on the bench beside him and threw it at her. "Get dressed."

She put it on, feeling childish and flustered under his watch. Their ages might have been reversed this morning, with him seven years older than she instead of the other way around.

"So he expects you to whore for him now?"

She could not explain what had happened last night, but it had not been that, and not only because it had been incomplete.

"He has wanted you from the start, but I thought that he would leave the decision to you."

"The choice was mine."

"Oh, aye, but a devil's choice. He gave us a decent home and decent food, and waited until we grew accustomed to it before making his bed part of the bargain. That is what happened yesterday, isn't it? The last move in his game. He said that you had to go to him or leave, didn't he? That is why you were so distraught when you returned." His jaw clenched and he glanced away. "I will not let you sell yourself to feed me. I will see us both dead first."

"It was not like that. He is not like that."

"He is a man, sister, and in this we are all the same."

"He is not."

He suddenly comprehended. His eyes burned hotter. "You have affection for this mason?"

His incredulous tone rankled her. "Aye," she said sharply.

The storm that had been building in him for three years broke. The last few weeks had seen that tempest calm, but now it swirled out of him. "Eager for it or not, you were not born to be a leman to a craftsman."

"I was not born to work clay, either. Or live in a shack. Or wear rags."

"Do you see this as an improvement? Have you found contentment suddenly in this man's house? Have you found happiness in his bed? Will you forget everything because he shows you a little pleasure and feeds you meat?"

"I did not say that."

"A good thing that you did not, because our fates are tied together. I will never forget what that fate should be, even if you can be wooed into accepting what has happened by a few cast-off gowns and a dry feather bed. I am your blood, your male kin, and I remind you that you can give yourself to no man without my say."

Black resentment filled her mind. Not just his tone raised her temper, but also the way he spoke of Rhys. "How dare you tell me of your rights over my person. How dare you accuse me of being bought. I have been humbled as much as you. If I choose to forget it briefly while I know some kindness and affection, you will not stop me or interfere."

"It is not the brief forgetting that I worry about, sister. It is the lure to forget forever. The poverty of the tile yard could not break you, but the peace and ease of this life might." He rose. "I have left it all to you too long. I am thinking that it is time that I lead this battle, rather than let myself depend on a woman's inconstant will."

"Inconstant! I have never wavered. For three years I have slaved to make it right, and to preserve your pride."

"It is not my pride that concerns me, but yours. He is making you lose sight of who you are, and where you belong. You were brought so low that this looks like salvation."

"That is not true!"

"It is written all over you." He stomped into the hall, and his footsteps sounded on the stairs. Moments later he returned, the longbow and quiver in his hands.

He went to the stable for the butt. For the next two hours, while she mixed and kneaded bread and began the evening soup, he let arrow after arrow fly. The whistles formed a sickly melody that sang of his anger.

She paused and watched him through the open door. He looked so tall now, and broad in ways she had not much noticed before. He stood like a man, and not an awkward youth. The repeated pull of the string did not tire him.

How long had it been happening? Some time, she guessed, only he had not confided to her the decisions he debated in his heart, and the memories that tormented his soul. He had run away from them, much as she had, but last night, for some reason, he had no longer been able to do so. He had turned away from his childhood and embraced his manhood in those dark hours, and she had not been there to console him.

Finally, the deadly whistles stopped. He put the butt away, and carried the longbow into the kitchen. He stood behind her while she stirred.

"How much coin do you have?" he asked.

"Not enough."

"How much?" A demand this time.

"A little over two pounds."

"Give me one of them."

She turned, hands on hips. "Nay. I earned it, and I will keep it, and I will deal with this as I have always planned to."

"Not soon enough."

She could not argue with that. The years had proven him right. "What do you want with the coin?"

"I am going to buy a sword. I should be able to get an old one for that."

"You do not know—"

"I know the basics, and can practice them, at least. I can build my strength, and look to learn more. Give me the money, Joan. It is time. In fact, it is past time."

She wanted to argue with him, but she could see too plainly that her advice had become meaningless. A boy might obey his sister, but a man does not.

She felt behind the stack of fuel for the small purse that she had hidden there. She thumbed out the precious coins. She tried to keep her heart-gripping worry out of her voice. "Promise me that you will not do anything rash. Promise me that you will give yourself the time to learn—"

"Does Rhys know about us?" He took the coins and tucked them away.

"Nay."

"I did not think so. His attention flattered you, and you knew his interest would cool if he knew."

"That is not why."

"Then why? Do you not trust him? Did you spend the night in the bed of a man whom you doubt?"

Did she? She looked to her heart and knew that she did not doubt Rhys anymore. He would not betray or hurt her for his own gain or safety.

But that only meant that now she endangered him, instead of the other way around.

"Do not tell him," Mark said. "If he does not know, he will let us stay a while longer. That will give me the time to learn."

"It will take years for you to gain the skill to meet Guy."

"Whatever time I have will have to be enough."

The worry became a heavy fist pounding inside her chest. He would get himself killed. She could not bear losing him, too.

"You must swear to me that you will make no move until you have told me," she said. "Prepare as you must, but do not let your temper lead you to recklessness. I will not tell Rhys, and we will stay, and you can practice. Will you swear this to me?"

He hesitated, then shrugged. "Aye, I will speak with you before I go to meet him."

Maybe his hot determination would dim. Maybe it would be years before he felt himself ready, and she would have the time to earn the coin to have a trained knight, a champion, do it instead.

CHAPTER 17

THE HORSE KEPT giving her trouble. Even with Saint George standing beside it rather than riding astride, the weight of the animal's bulk proved too heavy for the clay legs.

She muttered her frustration. Rhys looked around the upright Saint Ursula.

"Stone is even heavier. Have him lean against his animal and form them as one, as masons do. Then he helps bear the weight."

She studied the figures. It might work.

Rhys returned to his rippler, his face obscured again by the bulk of the saint. "And round his rump more. You are not accustomed to molding animals, and they can not be hidden with drapery. Go to the stable and see how a horse is formed. It will make yours better."

He was right. While the horse appeared fine at first glance, the parts did not really seem natural with close examination.

Now that she thought about it, Saint George had

awkward legs. Since he wore armor, she could not hide those with drapery, either. She smiled to herself. She would have to make a closer study of Rhys's legs when they were naked.

She worked on some details that would not need such lessons. The light was fading, but she wanted the afternoon to go on forever. It had been so peaceful this Sunday, working together in the garden. Mark had gone to the river with some friends, and she and Rhys had spent the day thus, with him carving at one end of the bench, and her molding at the other. Working her craft beside someone who understood it, sharing advice and occasional conversation, added a deep richness to the act of creation.

It is not the mind that we know, it is the soul. Aye, that was what kept building between them. Even in bed. The physical pleasure kept surprising her, but it was afterward, when he held her, that she felt the closest. Their bodies might never join, but they had begun molding together at a deeper level. Today, sharing this, forming realities out of base matter, they had known the soul together. A part of her spirit had adhered to him in these last days and hours, and would never be separate again.

The breeze carried a coolness that warned of summer's waning. The patch of flowers near the wall had grown to a riot of color in a last effort to make seed. Already the days shortened. There would not be many afternoons like this left.

She set the statue aside, and bent to lift more clay out of her pail. She plopped it on the board and began kneading.

Rhys set down his tools. He came over and straddled the bench behind her. With a reach that embraced her, he lent his strength to the task. His fingers squeezed through the oozing mass along with hers, sliding and gliding in wonderful, sensual touches. The strong bronze arms and hands mesmerized her. His warmth behind her sent exquisite chills down her body.

"I have been thinking about using George's yard for the tiles," he said while he bent to press a little kiss on her neck.

She twisted in surprise to look at him. "Do not be ridiculous. You know how bad those will be."

"I think they will be good enough."

"George is a besotted fool. He will pass off inferior goods if he can. One bad firing and the results will be snuck into every wagonload."

"George is a fool, but you are not. I was thinking that perhaps you should manage the yard while these tiles are made."

The happy contentment disappeared, like the illusion of a dream lost on waking. Her stomach hollowed out.

She returned her attention to the clay. "Have you returned my indenture to George so that I can make these tiles?"

"That is a stupid thing to ask."

"Not so stupid, if you expect me to manage the yard."

"I do not expect it, I only ask it. I bought the yard yesterday. It had failed with you gone, and George was glad to be free of it."

"You bought the tile yard? You own it now?" She swung her leg over the bench and stood so she could look at him.

"Aye. The only problem is, I have neither the time nor the skill to make it pay. But you do."

Her heartbeat quickened. If Rhys owned the yard, he owned the kiln.

Rhys concentrated on the clay, as if he did not realize that he had just offered her the answer to all her dreams and plans.

"Will you do it?"

"Of course I will do it. Can I fire my statues there, too?"

"You can fire them, and glaze them, and use what clay you need."

She could barely contain her joy. "I will see that you bring the King tiles equal to any from Spain. I will paint the glaze on each one myself if I have to. I will wait until they are all finished before taking my own wares to market."

"I think that you can steal a few days before that."

She threw her arms around him. "I can not believe that you did this. A kiln! I can mold statues all winter, and fire them, and sell them. And I will make certain that the yard pays. The wares will be so fine that you can ask a high price, and you will see a good profit, I promise."

He surrounded her with his arms. Pulling her into his lap, he moved her legs so that they embraced his hips and she faced him. "As will you. This is a partnership. The yard might be mine, but the skill will be yours. You will share whatever income it brings."

She searched his face in astonishment. Did he understand what he was doing? She knew the income that the tile yard saw in good years, and half of that would be almost all she needed. Next summer her goal would be within reach.

And she would be leaving him.

An eddy of sadness rippled through her joy. She nestled closer, not wanting to think about that. She held him tightly and told herself that she should be grateful if he did not understand that he had just taken the first step toward their parting.

His lips pressed her hair. She tilted her head and looked in his eyes and saw that he did understand. He just did not believe that when the time came, she would really leave.

And in that instant she knew that she would not want to. It would mean abandoning the best friend she had ever had, and walking away from the closest bond she had ever experienced. A part of her would be torn away. Even as she rewove the shredded fabric of her life, there would be new holes that could never be filled.

She tasted the anguish she would know that day. The claims of the past, of her family and her brother, would make leaving inevitable. She had sworn oaths to her father's memory that she could never forget. There was more at stake than her contentment, and the happiness that she had found in this garden and with this man.

His embrace tightened and he lifted her to a kiss. Not gentle, the way he usually started. Not careful, but fevered and deep. Passion blew through her, blending with the sadness until a heart-searing poignancy filled her. He kissed her as if he had seen the future in her eyes, and sought to argue his cause. Much of her, too much, wanted him to win the debate.

He stood, not moving her position, and carried her to the hawthorn tree and sat on the bench with her limbs still wrapped around him.

He pulled her shift off her shoulders and pushed it up her hips until it bunched thickly around her waist, covering almost nothing. His kisses stopped, but the fever did not cool. He eased her back until her shoulders rested on the table's edge and her naked body angled away from his, much like one of his statues on the inclining board.

His hands moved over her body. He might have been the molder and she the clay. He stroked and smoothed and circled, watching his hands with deep concentration. Her own hands could only reach his forearms, and she clung desperately while the sensations aroused by his determined caresses riveted her awareness.

"You always start out holding me as if you do not know if you want this, Joan, even though you do." He palmed her nipples until she arched with craving. "You cling as if you fear it even as you desire it."

The urging pleasure left her too shaky to respond.

"The abandon still frightens you. What are you afraid that you will lose when you embrace it? A past world that does not await your return?"

He slid his hands down her arms and released her hold. He placed her palms on the table until her arms spread their length from her propped shoulders. "I do not want any restraint on your passion today, not even that of an embrace."

His hot eyes examined the path of his hands down to her hips and thighs. He eased her up so he could mold her bottom in his palms. He frankly observed the rhythm of her body, as if he could see the hidden, itchy pulse causing it.

He looked to her eyes, and she knew what he was going to do. And so it did not shock her too much when he rose, and slid her back on the table until she lay there naked in the breeze, like a rustic, erotic feast. He stood over her, and his rough hands worked their wonderful magic, forming her passion into a mad delirium.

He raised her legs and bent her knees and set her feet on his shoulders. Cradling her bottom in his palms, he lifted her hips high like a sacred cup, and bent to her.

For one moment she feared the pleasure would die, but it did not. Trust helped her take a new step and accept a special freedom. The triumph produced an astonishing euphoria. Most of her senses left her. Nothing existed but the torment of pleasure and the blurred pattern of leaves and sky and sunlight above her head.

She climbed with frightening intensity until nothing mattered but her need. Her body begged and then, in the distance, her voice did, too. He lowered her hips and put his hand to her, stroking where his kisses had created a throbbing sensitivity. She looked down her sprawled, open body to see him watching her face while he brought her to a violent, long release.

It left her drifting in a foggy madness of saturated senses. He brought her back on the bench again, straddling him as she had before. His masculine scent and the hardness of his arms and chest encompassed her as she sagged into his embrace.

His quiet voice flowed into her ear. "The next time it happens like that I want to be inside you."

"Perhaps I can soon. I want to."

He kissed her temple. "Perhaps it is not the past that interferes so much now, but the future. I want you to think about that. Maybe, in living for what you must do in the future to avenge what happened in the past, you are not allowing yourself any life in the present."

She would think about it. She would. But not now. She did not want that confusion yet. She just needed to hold him in this serenity that he had given her.

So peaceful. If she stayed here forever, she might be happy. The day might come when she never thought about what had been lost, because she reveled in that which had been gained.

Perhaps she should repudiate the duty. She could accept what had happened. She could be the new Joan in a new life and a new world. The notion appealed to her more than she expected.

A slight sound broke her sated happiness. She turned her head and looked down the garden. Mark had entered through the portal, and now bent and slid something behind the high flowers along the wall.

The sword. Mark had not gone to the river at all. She had found another shilling missing, and guessed that he had taken it to pay someone to teach him. That was how he had spent the Lord's day. Wielding a sword, and preparing himself for vengeance.

He passed them on his way to the house, but he did not notice them entwined in the shade of the tree.

She tried to immerse herself again in the contentment she had just known. She fought to reclaim the innocence of it, but she could not.

She turned her head to where she could see the bench, with its big stone statue near the center and its little clay one at the other end. Despite their different sizes, they balanced each other on that long plank, and created a pleasant harmony. A perfect design.

She branded her memory with their forms, and Rhys's feel, and the sound of his heartbeat. She wanted to remember the unity of this day forever.

CHAPTER 18

JOAN'S STATUES STOOD in a dignified procession on the tall table Rhys had made for her. Everyone in the market who walked by noticed them.

A lady who had purchased the Saint George brought a friend back to consider the Saint Sebastian. That one had attracted a lot of attention. Clad only in a loincloth and tied to a tree stump, he looked up to heaven, waiting for the martyr's palm. The arrows piercing his body had not diminished his strength.

The woman eyed the naked chest far too appreciatively. Joan really did not want to sell it, and named a price of two shillings in the hope of discouraging a purchase. It did not work. There was no bargaining, and the coins instantly appeared.

Joan was sorry to see the statue go. She had followed Rhys's lessons about studying real forms when crafting their replicas. Saint Stephen's torso, face, and legs, as a result, were very familiar ones to her.

She watched Saint Sebastian being carried away, and

her heart glowed for the man who had been its model. If Rhys had never given her anything but this improvement to her craft, she would have been grateful forever.

But he had done so much more.

She spent most days managing the tile yard now. It hummed with activity the way it had during Nicholas's life. The King's pavers kept many workers busy, especially her. Still, every day she arranged to steal an hour or so to make her saints. The work was hard and tiring, but she had never known such contentment. And waiting at the house were the little pleasures of sharing bread and stories with Rhys, and eventually the perfect bliss of sleeping in his arms.

Her happy contemplations distracted her. She gazed blindly at her row of saints and thought about that feather bed, and what occurred there, and the way that she never remembered the bad experiences anymore.

She calmly made a decision. She was ready to make it complete. She would make this union all that it might be. She would forget while she could, and later, much later, she would remember when she must.

She did not see the new patron approach. She did not notice him at all until he stood by her table. Even then she did not look up and greet him, but let herself enjoy the warmth of her decision, and the way it stirred her blood. She regretted that Rhys was not at the house. If he were, she would pack up these statues and run back at once. She might even give them all away if it would hasten her return to him.

Rhys would be joining her soon. He was coming to fetch her, so they could visit the King's chambers again and remeasure the floors. She suddenly could not wait to see him.

The man did not move on. His presence intruded more and more. Still only half conscious of him, still absorbed with her joyful resolve, her lowered gaze saw him only in bits and pieces.

Fine boots. A rich, green, knee-length cotte. The stark line of a good sword.

A vague, spicy scent.

Caution roared through her, stunning her into alertness. Her instincts remembered that exotic, dangerous smell. It made the skin on her neck and scalp prickle.

She froze and refused to look higher. Fear and horror shrieked, obliterating her contentment. She just kept staring at her saints, praying that she was wrong.

A hand reached out. One finger wore a ring that she had seen before.

Her heart dropped and broke, and she knew for certain that her happiness had just been destroyed.

She recoiled from the touch on her chin, but that did not stop him. He forced her head up, until she looked into a face that she loathed.

"Why do you act as though a ghost has appeared?" he said. "After all, you are the one who is supposed to be dead."

For one despairing moment she wished that she were. For an instant she regretted not walking into that lake three years ago.

He tilted his head and studied her face, much as her patrons did her statues. "Still lovely. And much more clever than I ever suspected."

She did not move. She had never let him see her fear, and she would not now. But utter terror filled her like an unending, shrill whistle.

Guy Leighton was the devil incarnate, wearing the face of an angel. Beautiful. Almost ethereal. His golden hair and violet eyes and perfect, fine-boned face still appeared boyish when he was calm. But she had seen the fires of hell in those eyes, and the sickening pleasure he took in meting pain and death. Considering his ugly soul, his physical beauty struck her as a type of sin, a corruption of nature itself.

She had seen at once how crippled his heart was. He had sensed that she could tell. It had fascinated him, and fed both his vanity and his cruelty.

Another man ambled over to inspect her wares. Guy gave him a deadly smile. The man hustled away.

He still held her chin. He did not release it. He merely walked around her table and drew her toward the Cathedral wall, leading her like an animal.

He forced her into the shadow, against the stone, and blocked her body with his. Arm braced above her head, he scrutinized her face.

"I have been looking for you, Joan. All week I have been visiting markets in search of the pretty blond potter."

"How did you know to look?"

"A man came to me. He had been in this city while on pilgrimage, and saw you at a market. Since he had heard of your demise, he could not believe it was really you, but I did. I knew at once that you had deceived me, and not truly died while crossing that river." He lightly stroked her cheek. Her stomach turned violently. "It wounds me that you ran away after all that we had shared, and the risks that I took for you. You are an ungrateful bitch, Joan."

The last part came out in a brittle tone. He sounded like a lover who had been betrayed. He acted as though she had abandoned something beautiful. Maybe he thought that she had. The world existed for him only as he saw it.

"Too ungrateful to deserve your attentions. Everyone thinks me dead, and as you can see, I might as well be. Leave me to my humble life and let everyone assume my bones lie in that river."

He found her desperate argument amusing. "It is not so simple as that."

Nay, it was not. He had not come here just looking for her at all.

"Your brother survived, too, I assume."

He made the query very blandly, but she saw the sharp interest in his eyes. And something else. Something she had never seen before. Fear.

"He did not. I almost didn't, either. The river swept him away. I caught a tree branch, but he—"

"Neither of you crossed the river where we found the clothing washed up. It was a ruse, and your breathing body proves it."

"Nay, he died. I swear it to you."

"The man said that he saw a blond youth of Mark's age with you later. And a tall dark haired man."

A new fear spiked, this time for Rhys.

"The man was a stranger. The youth was his kin, and not my brother. I do not know either of them, and was just chatting as one does in markets."

He took her face in his hand and held it to a deep examination. His grasp squeezed her cheeks just enough to hurt.

"You are lying. You were never good at it, and three years have not taught you much there. He lives, as you do. That is most awkward, Joan. I told my lord that you had both died. It will be very inconvenient to explain the mistake."

"Then do not explain it."

He leaned against the wall so that his body lined against hers. His hold released her cheeks and slid lower, caressing her neck and shoulders. She suffered it to buy some time for Mark and herself and Rhys, but her essence cringed with revulsion.

"I have missed you. I think that I even mourned a little when word came that you had perished."

"I doubt that you have missed me at all. I am sure that your bed is never cold."

"It is not the same. You were a compelling challenge. Having you gave me wonderful pleasure. I do not think that taking a keep surpasses it."

"Nonsense. When you take a keep, you can put men to the sword."

"And when I took you I could make you feel things against your will. Surely you have not forgotten that part."

She suppressed the urge to vomit, and closed her eyes to him. She stopped breathing so she would not inhale that spicy scent. She wanted him to be gone, and for this day to begin anew. She prayed that when she opened her eyes she would be in Rhys's feather bed and discover this had been a nightmare.

Guy's fingers drifted over her face, outlining her nose and chin and jaw. "Perhaps I need not explain to my lord. Maybe we can continue the bargain from before. No one has ever understood me as you did. I have felt your absence."

She looked at him in shock, and saw that it was partly true. Not because of physical things. He could get that from other women.

His perverted vanity had always enjoyed her hatred too much. It drew him the way affection did normal people. Everything was upside down with him. Deformed. Her hatred had engrossed him the way love did other men.

He was right. She understood him very well. Even better than he guessed. He might offer the bargain again, but he would no more honor it now than he had the first time. She had never truly kept her brother safe. She had merely delayed his death back then. The accidents that had almost claimed Mark's life had forced her to see the truth. That had been the final degradation, realizing that she had sold herself for nought.

She remembered the exact moment when she had finally admitted that to herself. Pressed against the

Cathedral wall, she experienced the hopeless bleakness again. But that dark moment had given birth to anger and strength, too, and now their fires rekindled in her blood as well.

She had beaten this man once. Outsmarted him. She could do so again. She would not let fear defeat her. She would not be his victim.

He had journeyed across England because of her and Mark. He stood alone now, and had searched the markets with no retinue. He had been ordered to make sure that Mark died like her father and all the other men and squires who had defended that keep, and he had come looking for her on his own because he feared Mortimer's learning that he had failed to extinguish every witness to that massacre.

Which meant that only he knew that she and her brother were still alive.

She had to delay him. She needed time to find Mark and get out of London.

"You offer the same terms? My brother will be safe?" Her whole body rebelled against the words. She almost choked on them.

"I will shield him as I always did. It is only a small deception of my lord, and you are well worth it."

Guy Leighton spoke with sincerity. Lied with impunity. He believed the words as he said them, but would easily abandon the promises when they proved inconvenient. That had always been the most frightening thing about him. He possessed no conscience at all. No normal sense of wrong.

He took her arm. "Come with me now. I am staying at the palace, but no one there will know you. You can show me how grateful you are before we get your brother."

A spitting denial almost screamed out of her. She fought to keep the disgust out of her voice, and the resurrected memories out of her mind. "You can not think to stay at Westminster, with Mark and me in your chamber. There is no way we can be safe there."

"It is only for a short while. I leave two days hence."

"Then I will come to you two days hence. I am not yours until my brother is safe away from here, and until I see that you are committed to your side of our agreement."

"You will come now, and tell me where to find Mark."

"Nay. It will be as I say, or I will die before you ever learn where to find him." *I will die before I let you know about that house.*

"Three years have made you too sharp-tongued. This humble life has turned you shrewish. I much preferred you as you were, girlish and biddable."

"I am no longer a girl. If that is what you want, go find another."

Guy examined her as he would a docile horse that had unexpectedly shown some spirit. "Nay, I think that I will enjoy you this way. It will be exciting to have your hatred out in the open. We will meet at the Temple the day next at tierce, and leave at once from there."

"You must come alone, ready to ride."

"I did not journey here alone, and my men must return with me, but you have nothing to fear from them. Your brother and you will be under my protection as before."

He finally eased away. She swallowed a deep sigh of relief when he ceased touching her.

His gaze locked with hers, and too much passed in those violet eyes. The sick bond of the past, and what awaited in the future. Something else flickered in them, too. Tiny lights of anger and suspicion and jealousy. She knew what would happen if those little flames found fuel.

"The dark-haired man seen with you at the fair. What was his name?"

Her heart pounded horribly. She flattened her palms on

the cool stone at her back to steady herself. "I do not know. He was a stranger to me."

"I hope that you speak the truth. I trust he has not been stealing what is mine."

"Nay. You ruined me for other men."

His vanity liked hearing that. She doubted that he understood how she meant it, and just how thoroughly she had been ruined.

Guy stepped closer again, and took her face in his hands. "Do not think of thwarting me, Joan. The last betrayal was one too many, and I will not be so generous the next time. Be sure you are at the Temple as agreed, or I will hunt your brother down and kill him like a dog. Wherever you go, I will find you, and I will punish whoever helps you."

She knew that. Only it would happen no matter what she did. If she brought Mark to the Temple, he would die, and then, after a brief hell in Guy's bed, she would too, for she knew too much. If he learned about Rhys . . . Jesus, if he learned about Rhys . . .

Aye, she understood him very well. She had nothing to lose in defying him.

He pressed a kiss on her. She barely managed not to gag. He dipped in a courtly bow of farewell.

"Two days hence, sweet Joan. Do not fail to be at the Temple."

Joan sank against the wall, and desolation engulfed her. She closed her burning eyes and gripped the cool stone along her back. Some mason had hewn those blocks, and set them squarely, and they would stand through time unless another mason pulled them down.

She wished that life could be so solid and secure. Her own always seemed to be built of straw. Ugly tempests kept roaring through, blowing away the tiny structures of her happiness before she ever had a chance to make them her home.

She did not fight the discouragement. She did not try to hold in the tears that trickled down her cheeks. Mourning what had just been lost would not weaken her because, even as the emotions gripped her, she felt others waiting for their turn. Anger and resolve and fierce determination hovered on the edges of her sadness. She allowed herself to wallow for a few moments in misery, before she gathered those harsh weapons and marched forward to protect the men she loved.

The poignant heartache drowned her like a dark, endless sea. Despite the pain, she found it soothing compared to what she knew would come next. She must have leaned against the cathedral for an hour, so timeless was her immersion. Finally she forced herself to the surface, and the sunlight, and the reality that waited.

She opened her eyes. A man's intense, questioning gaze looked right back. Her heart leapt to her throat. Rhys stood at her table, holding the reins of his horse, blocking the market with the wagon.

Seeing his suspicious expression, she knew that no hour had passed, but only a few moments. He had been there while Guy spoke to her. He had seen it all. He had watched the touches and kiss, and now he was deciding what to make of it.

Rhys chose to believe an explanation that favored her. A glint of hard fury sparked as he turned to watch the receding form of a golden-haired knight dressed in green. Never taking his eyes off Guy's back, he bent and tied the reins to the table. He began striding after the man he assumed had offended her.

She ran, knowing that she flew toward heartbreak. She had hoped to find a lie that would not hurt him, but that would not be possible now. She could not let him confront Guy, no matter what the cost to her pride. She could not let Guy guess who the dark-haired man at the market had been.

She grabbed his arm, forcing him to stop. "Do not. He is a knight, and he wears his sword."

Rhys tried to shake her off. "Let him draw his damn sword, for all I care."

She clung desperately. "Do not get yourself killed because of a fool's courage."

"You are so sure I can not best him? I know what I am about. I do not let any man insult you like that, and he will know it soon."

"Are you so certain that you saw insult?"

"His hands were all over you."

"Did you hear me cry out? Was I fighting him?"

Rhys turned to stone. He looked down at her, and something new burned in his expression. "What are you saying?"

"I am saying that I will not let you fight him just because you chanced upon something I did not expect you to see."

She would have gladly died ten deaths to avoid seeing the disbelief that broke in him. She watched him try to convince himself she had not meant what he had heard. A breathless yearning saturated her heart, and she silently begged him to see her lie even though he would not be safe unless he believed her.

They stood there while the market milled around them, two unmoving forms, speaking only with their eyes. He waited for her to give the sign that he had misunderstood. She forced a display of indifference, though she wanted to throw her arms around him and explain the horrible, precarious truth.

She suffered it, for his sake and Mark's. She kept the

anguish deep inside her and watched disillusionment slowly slice his trust into shreds.

A passing man jostled them both. Rhys stepped back and glanced around. "We are becoming a spectacle. Let us pack up your wares and go to the palace."

"I do not want to go to the palace." Guy might be there, so she could not risk going, especially with Rhys. Nor was there any point in measuring floors anymore, even if Rhys did not know that yet.

"It must be done soon."

"Aye, but not today. I want to return to the house. If you have business elsewhere, I will walk."

"Nay, we will go back together, and you can explain yourself there," he said tightly, taking her arm and pushing her toward the wagon and table.

He helped her wrap the statues and dismantle the table. His wonderful, gifted hands worked quickly, and his handsome, kind face remained impassive. Except his eyes. It was all in them for her to see, disheartening her so much that she wondered if she could go through with it.

The silent wagon ride lasted long enough for his disappointment to turn to anger. She felt his mood transform beside her. She could almost hear his mind conclude that she had been playing him for a fool. She sensed his soul taking distinct, determined steps away from hers.

It broke her heart. She wanted so badly to pour out the truth and spare them both the ugliness that was coming. Instead she would have to layer lie upon lie until she constructed a wall of deception that might protect him from her danger.

Only her fear for him kept her resolve intact, and her misery hidden. Better to have him bitter than dead. If she told him the truth, if she admitted who Guy really was, he would not do the sensible thing and help her to flee. He would go meet that devil, and his goodness would be no match for evil.

She left him in the alley to care for the horse and went to wait in the kitchen. Sitting by the window, she tried to plan how she would get Mark away, but her mind would not cooperate. Her head ached from her efforts to hold in her sorrow. It wanted to break out of her, and she longed to vent the pain.

Rhys came to her slowly, walking through the garden as though he did not welcome this any more than she did. He passed the bench with its shrouded saint, and paused to glance under the hawthorn tree. That almost undid her. Her eyes filmed as innocent memories wrenched her heart.

Forget when you can and remember when you must. She steeled herself and held in the grief. It was time to remember.

He came in and looked at her, and she knew at once that he still waited to hear that he had misunderstood. Despite his anger and her bluntness, he still believed in her.

He was going to force her to say things that would make him despise her.

"Who was he?"

"A knight named Sir Guy. A famous champion. He has come to meet me in the market several times now. He claims to have fallen in love."

"He appeared little more than a youth. No more than two and twenty."

"Prowess with weapons is often greatest then."

"Did something happen to make you think that you needed his friendship? Did something frighten you, and you did not count on my protection being enough?"

"Nay, he is famous for his skill at arms. I have told you that I am looking for such a man."

"You told me that you planned to pay with coin, not by permitting what I saw."

"That could take years, and Sir Guy does not want coin from me, anyway."

"Nay, he does not, pretty dove. That was clear." He crossed his arms over his chest, as though seeking to contain the anger that had begun flaring in his gaze. "I do not believe that you can do that. I do not think you can bring yourself to it."

"I thought not either, but I find that his attentions do not affect me badly at all. It appears that things are different now."

It sickened her to say it. It infuriated him to hear it. His eyes blazed and she knew that he wanted to hit her. He would not, though. She knew that, too.

"I am glad that I could be of service, Joan. It is good that you found me so useful as you rediscovered your womanhood. I am relieved to have helped you prepare yourself for your great goal."

Even in her desperation, she could not let him reduce it to that. "I did not sleep with you for that reason."

"And I did not touch you so that when you were whole you could give yourself to another man. I see now why you would not risk that with me. If it went badly, you might not be able to do it later with another. That would set back your plans a long while, wouldn't it?"

His scathing tone cut through her. She had to avert her eyes to hold onto her composure. Her heart pounded painfully from the effort, and from blocking the fleeting memory of those sunny moments before Guy had appeared when she had decided that she *would* risk it with Rhys. Today, as soon as they returned to this house, she had looked forward to giving herself to him.

Only now here they were, speaking for the last time, and all she could offer him was insult and hurt.

BY DESIGN ✦ 227

"You speak of truly selling yourself this time. You know that, don't you?"

"Aye."

He looked away in dismay. And disgust. "Perhaps if I had offered to kill for you we would have both found more contentment."

"I never wanted that from you."

"Nay. You need a professional killer, don't you? One so jaded that he will barter death for pleasure. This will not happen the way you plan. An honorable knight will not accept such a bargain. The ones who will can not be trusted to do the deed."

"This one can be, I think."

"It will never happen. No man will stand against someone in league with Mortimer."

"Some men have. This one will."

"If he does, if he wins, what do you gain? Revenge? Nothing more, that is certain. Not your father's property, and not your old life back. Another will replace him, and nothing will change. He is but the agent. Mortimer is the power. Your quest is a childish dream. The girl who ran from the horrors of war may not have understood just how impractical a dream it was, but you are a woman now."

His ruthless logic tore at the foundations of something older than her trust in him. He attacked more than her honesty with his words, and threw more than her betrayal in her face.

"Childish dream it may be, but it has sustained me. It is all that I had to keep me alive for three years. Maybe I will only know revenge, but that will be something, at least."

The anger left him suddenly. He gave her a long, penetrating gaze. He must have found what he searched for, because resignation slid over him.

He headed to the garden door. "The past enslaves you even more than I had guessed. Go and find your champion. I can see that I have finished my purpose in your life. Offer yourself to him. If it will free you of this, I almost pray that he accepts the bargain. I had hoped you would give this up, but I can see that you never will."

He was leaving. Walking away, out of her life. She rose, and almost ran to grab him. She wanted to cry that he was wrong, that her heart had not been enchained by the past.

Except that it had been.

She needed to explain before they parted forever. She wanted him to understand. "For three years, the goal of some justice was all that I had. If I had given it up, I would have relinquished all that I ever was. What would I have held on to then?"

He barely glanced at her. But in the brief meeting of their gazes, she saw a disappointment so deep that it stunned her.

"Me. You could have held on to me."

He strode to the garden portal, never looking back. He did not pause to glance at the hawthorn tree this time.

CHAPTER 19

RHYS BLINDLY STRODE through the city, stoking his fury with visions of the knight touching and kissing Joan. Her bland admission that she intended to trade her favors for a champion's services kept shouting in his head, drowning out the sounds of his rational sense.

He knew that he was reacting like some untried boy, and that only made it worse. He resented like hell that he had let her get close enough to affect him like this. Blood dangerously rumbling and curses silently chanting, he stalked the streets and lanes, bumping into people and hoping some man would bump back so he could start the fight itching to burst out of him.

Joan had seen him for the fool he was. She had played to his sympathies and given as little as necessary to get as much as she could in return. She had held him off with one hand while she beckoned knights with the other, and planned to trade like a merchant that which she claimed unable to offer him. She had probably even lied about what had happened to her. She was nothing but a scheming, ruthless, heartless whore.

The rabid insult caught him up short. His obscuring anger broke a little, just enough for him to see the image of Joan that his hurt pride was carving. It stood in his mind in wanton glory, a combination of temptress and tease. It bore little resemblance to the woman whom he knew.

He remembered her anguish in the garden, and her shyness in his bed. Nay, she had not lied about that part.

The grudging admission offered no relief. It only complicated something that he wanted to keep simple. He wanted—needed—to think the worst. But more memories intruded, sweet and poignant ones that interfered with his efforts to let his affection turn to hate.

Still seething, still resentful, he walked on with new purpose. He made his way to the Cathedral, and to the spot where he had stood when he saw Joan in the shadow of its wall. Reliving the betrayal would surely defeat his weakness for her.

He let the memory emerge, but it came slowly, devoid of the shock he had felt, and clearer now than the reality had been.

He realized what he had actually observed there. Joan in her brown gown, pressed against the wall, her face blocked by the shoulders of a man. Her acceptance of caresses and a kiss. But no obvious welcome of those attentions. No returning embrace. She stood rigidly with pride—or maybe fear.

His mind's eye saw her beside him in the wagon and then at the house. Withdrawn, contained, stony with dignity and devoid of regret. Calm. Too calm, considering what she admitted. Face impassive and eyes so opaque that he could not read her thoughts.

He had seen her indifference as a greater repudiation

than her pursuit of a knight, but maybe it had really been a defense.

Had she truly accepted that man's touch? Or had she lied, to keep a mason from fighting with a sword-wielding knight?

He did not want to believe the former possibility, but he did not find the latter any more comforting. He did not welcome the idea that she had destroyed what existed between them because she did not believe that he could protect himself. Or her.

He might swallow the insult if it meant that she cared for him. Maybe she did, but not enough. Not everything that she said in their argument had been uttered with indifference. When she had spoken of her goal sustaining her, and of trusting her hold on nothing else, familiar flames of resolve had lit her eyes.

It was not the beginning of the argument that had sliced the deepest, but the end.

He continued his walk with calmer thoughts. He wondered about that golden-haired knight. Perhaps he really was a great champion. Maybe he had even fallen in love with Joan, and would see it through for her. Then again, he might be a boastful coward who lured women with his beauty and his promises.

Hoping it was the latter, so that he would have an excuse to beat the man bloody, he aimed his steps in the direction of someone who might know about young Sir Guy.

A servant brought Rhys to the garden where Moira sat in the grass, weaving a basket. It had been her craft when she was poor, and she still practiced it for her pleasure.

She looked up and greeted him with a serene smile that

fell a little when he drew closer. The anger still rumbled in him, and he guessed that she could see his mood.

Moira gestured for him to sit beside her on the ground, as he had often done years ago, when he came to this house wooing the good-hearted basket maker. He rarely looked back to those days, or wondered what might have been with her, but he came close to doing so now. Moira was fresh and honest, and as open a person as he had ever known. He found that very appealing at the moment.

"I am glad that you are here," she said. "I was going to send a servant to you soon. We are leaving the city this afternoon, and I wanted to see you before we left."

"Are you and the babe able to travel?"

"It has been almost a month. I am not some delicate court lady, and the babe is content to sleep no matter where he is. Addis has decided it is a good time, before the fall rains come."

She took a reed from a bucket of water and began weaving it along the top of the basket, finishing its edge. "I will give this to you to bring to Joan. I like her, but she is a complex person. I think that she and I could become good friends, but that I will never really believe that I know her."

His quick reaction was annoyance at this criticism. He reminded himself that this was Moira, who did not idly pick at other women for fun.

She turned her clear blue eyes on him. A little frown puckered her brow. "Do *you* know her?"

A day ago he would have sworn that he did, but now he wondered. "Well enough."

She smiled. "Well enough is sufficient."

They talked of simple things, of her children and his craft. Sitting with her in the grass soothed him. He had sought her out as a courtesy, but now he took his time. If she was leaving the city they might not speak again for a long while.

She guessed that he had not come just to see her. "Addis is in the solar," she said when the basket was finished. She handed it to him. "Tell Joan it must dry a few days. And you must try to visit us at Barrowburgh. Bring Joan if you can. I will enjoy her company." She fixed him with an open, sincere gaze. "You know, I trust, that our home is always open to you and yours."

He saw more meaning in her eyes than she would ever put into words. The instincts of nature beat in her serf-born blood. She could smell the danger on the breeze, and knew the risks that her husband would be taking soon. She assumed that the man facing her would share those risks.

Maybe he would. He suddenly had nothing to lose again.

He lifted her hand and kissed it. "And my home is always open to you and yours, Moira."

He found Addis in the solar, packing rolled parchments into a wooden box.

"This departure from London is sudden, Addis. I trust that you are not fleeing for your life."

"It is time to go, that is all."

"The King's plans have been set aside for a time?"

"Mortimer is watching very closely. We will disperse, to make the watching harder. But if you speak with him, tell him that you think that his suspicions are correct. Let him know that Edward grows restless."

"That will only force his hand."

"His hand was forced the day Edward came of age. Let him know that time is running out. Let us see just how bold a usurper he is."

"Are you ready for that?"

Addis did not respond. He would not explain more to a man who had not sworn to the cause. He set the box on the floor, and poured some wine into two goblets. "Sit and drink with me, mason. Speak to me of simple, uncomplicated things."

Rhys noted the shadows in Addis's eyes. Nay, they were not ready, and this knight knew it. Something was pushing things forward too quickly, either Mortimer's suspicions or the King's impatience. Addis did not exactly flee London for his life, but he took his family away to protect them.

They sat in two chairs near the hearth in the large chamber that held the lord's curtained bed.

"I saw a knight in the city today, Addis. A face I did not know."

"You know all the faces?"

"Most of them. He was young, and wearing no lord's livery from what I could tell. Wealthy, though. Too well dressed for a young man without a patron. I heard him called Sir Guy."

The name pulled Addis out of his thoughts. "Describe him."

"Golden-haired. Middle-sized. Very handsome, almost like a woman. A sword with a yellow stone in its hilt."

"You describe Guy Leighton. He is Mortimer's man, livery or not. If he has been called to Westminster, it is not good news."

"How so?"

"He is the kind of man who would kill a King and enjoy doing it."

That was indeed not good news, and not for the reasons Addis worried. Not only did it speak against Guy's character, but it suggested that Joan might get entangled in something very dangerous.

"How do you know him?"

"My first wife's brother tangled with him years ago, when he was no more than a boy. He was ruthless then, and the years have made it worse. He came to Mortimer's attention during the rebellion. Mortimer gave Guy an army, and sent him out to secure the northern Welsh marches, to take the lands that had belonged to Despenser and Arundal. He did it in the name of the crown, but really in the interests of the House of Mortimer. You have heard of the bloodbath; I do not need to remind you of it. But Leighton may be guilty of more than the usual acts of war. It is said that he even disposed of women and children if they proved inconvenient."

Rhys went very still. The words penetrated one by one, but halfway through he knew what was coming.

No great champion had pressed Joan against the Cathedral wall, but the man who had misused her.

He realized that he had been expecting this. He had come to Addis to hear it put into words. His pride had blinded him to the truth, but his soul had understood.

"There was an inquiry in one case," Addis continued. "Nothing could be proven, but a girl and her brother drowned in a river, and Guy's hand is seen in it."

The chamber felt very warm suddenly, and Rhys's body very cool. "An inquiry? That is unusual. In war, people die all the time."

"Not the children of a baron. Not the son and daughter of a marcher lord."

His blood began pulsing slowly. "Tell me about it."

"It happened three years ago. Even if the stories are true, he will not pay until he faces eternal damnation."

"Tell me anyway. Who was this baron?"

"Marcus de Brecon. His lands lay south of the Despensers'. Much smaller holdings than those, but he was a tenant-in-chief, sworn directly to the last king."

Rhys knew of Marcus de Brecon. The names of all the marcher lords were familiar to those who had lived in the region.

"De Brecon was an honorable man, and would not

betray that oath of fealty during the rebellion. And so, after the abdication, he was vulnerable. Mortimer claimed he had been in league with the Despensers, and sent Guy Leighton to disseise him. There are those on the council who insist it was an independent move, but the documents bore the King's seal—and while everyone suspects that Mortimer uses the seal with impunity, no one can prove it."

Rhys listened, but another voice silently joined the tale. Joan's voice, speaking in the kitchen, *His army came, to take by force the estate of a lord who had stayed loyal to the last king. My father owned property in the region, and joined the fight.*

"You really mean that no one will risk Mortimer's displeasure by trying to prove it. Marcus died in the battle?"

"He resisted. Leighton offered no terms, he never does."

He died when the castle fell. So did my betrothed, and almost every man who defended the keep.

"It is said that he was cut down after he had finally surrendered, that all inside the keep were massacred, but again, there is no proof. With the son and daughter dead, there was no one to petition the King or parliament for justice, and no witnesses left whom the courts would find reliable. As I said, there was an inquiry into all of it, including the disappearance of the heir and his sister. Lancaster tried to stir the barons' discontent with the story, but it went nowhere. But many think those drownings too convenient. It removed witnesses, and the boy's challenge to Mortimer's hold on the land."

The new lord was a vile man, one of Mortimer's favorites. He knew no law but his own will. He took everything belonging to anyone who stood against him, all in the name of the crown. So Mark and I left that place and came here.

Jesus.

A rush of agitation flooded him. He could not sit still,

but rose and paced while his mind accommodated this astonishing discovery.

"Their names. The son and daughter. What were they called?"

"I was not at the council when this was discussed. If their names were ever given to me, I do not remember them."

Mark and Joan. Their names were Mark and Joan.

He turned his back on Addis, and pretended to admire a tapestry on the wall so the Lord of Barrowburgh would not see what this had done to him.

Conflicting emotions poured through him. Waves of amazement followed waves of anger. She had deceived him, not by lies but through omissions. She had not trusted him enough to confide it all. She had not thought herself safe with him. At the beginning he could understand that, but later . . .

She was not the daughter of a mere yeoman or gentry knight. She was Joan of Brecon, born of the noblest blood.

I save myself for myself, and for duties and plans much older than your knowledge of me. I will not let you interfere with them.

His mind replaced the tapestry's woven images with others. Joan, watching her honorable father cut down. Joan, facing Sir Guy alone in the hell her world had become, realizing that only she stood between her brother and his extinction. Joan, eyes flaring with anger and resolve, clinging to the dream of justice so that her soul would not die.

She had been right. She could not ignore the past. She was not a nameless nobody who could forget forever. She and her brother had run for their lives, but there had always been the danger that the past would follow.

And it had. It had caught up with her today in the marketplace.

"They are vulnerable," he heard his voice say, while his mind saw Sir Guy hovering over Joan at the Cathedral. Smug and familiar. Predatory, like a hawk that had caught a helpless dove in its talons.

He shook off the image, and turned. Addis watched him curiously.

"They are vulnerable. Mortimer and the Queen. He is careless in his own palace. He watches and sniffs, but he waits for the sight and smell of an army. I walk through Westminster freely, and have been totally alone with him several times. It would be an easy thing for me to—"

"Nay." It came as an uncompromising command. "When you are taken you will be executed, and Edward will not be able to stop it, no matter how it solves things. Nor should this be the work of an assassin. It must be the King's move, and legitimate, and it must also deal with the Queen, not just her lover."

"Then let Edward move. Not on a battlefield, but in his own home. You say that he has a handful whom he can trust. Let them go with him to the Queen and Mortimer, and arrest them."

"Mortimer may be vulnerable to a craftsman, but not to the king he holds down. He is surrounded by guards when he sees Edward."

"If it is not expected, it can be done. Even at Westminster, but surely at another holding, where the guard will be thinner. How strong is Mortimer's sway over his followers? He buys them with power, and they will desert him when that is gone. The realm grows weary of his excesses, and I can not be the only one who is disgusted that I helped bring this about. A small band, Addis. A quick move. It will be over before he can marshal his support, and even his household guard will hesitate to cut down an anointed king."

Addis rose and paced. His large body circled the chamber several times while the golden lights in his dark eyes burned deeply.

Rhys watched the inner debate. He hoped that he had swayed Addis. Joan could not afford to wait for the King to gather an army.

"It might work," Addis said. "Not at Westminster, but at another castle. A small band, as you say. If they can gain access to the Queen's chambers, it can be done." He folded his arms over his chest. "Aye, it might work. It may have to. If Mortimer has called Guy Leighton to him, it could be that he is considering a quiet move of his own. Such men do not have the scruples about assassination that I do."

Guy had not come for that. He was not called. He came on his own, to find the son and daughter of Marcus de Brecon. He came to kill the boy he had already promised was dead. And the sister.

"Is the door in the King's anteroom completed?"

"Aye, it has been cut."

"Good. I think that before I take my family out of London today, I will have some business with the Keeper of the Privy Seal. But if I am going to do it, I must attend to it now." He grasped Rhys's arm in friendship. "I asked you to speak of uncomplicated things, and you have done so. We barons assume it takes an army to battle for a cause, but your simple plan appeals to me. If you can, speak with Mortimer again. Tell him there is unrest in the city, so he thinks himself unsafe at Westminster. Let him know the King has expressed impatience."

"Is there anything else you want me to do?"

Addis cocked an eyebrow. "You are with us, then?"

Aye, he was. Not for the realm, and not for high principles. Not for anything lofty or complicated. He was with them because of Joan. If Mortimer fell, then Guy

Leighton fell, and she would have her justice. She would be safe. More than that, she might have her life back.

"I am with you, but I pray it will not be like the last time. I do not want to see another bloodbath."

"Edward has known nothing but strife in his young life. He seeks to heal the realm. There will be no campaign of revenge. Except against Mortimer, of course. The King is very bitter there, and he will treat the usurper as he should."

"Then I will speak with Mortimer tomorrow, and warn him as you request. And if there is need of me, send word."

They went down to the courtyard together. Moira stood at the threshold to the hall, and waved her farewell.

Addis smiled ruefully. "She will be relieved that you are committed. She does not trust the fleeting loyalties of highborn people. She says they are like straw, quickly scattered when the wind shifts."

"You have told her?"

"She already knew. She misses little, watching from the shadows as she does."

Aye, she missed little. She had seen Joan more clearly in one afternoon than he had after several months.

Do you know her?

"She worries," Addis said. "For her sake I would like to finish this quickly."

"Let us truly finish it this time, Addis. Let us complete what we began, and finally be done with it."

CHAPTER 20

Tᴏ HOUSE WAS DARK and silent when Rhys entered the garden. No glow came through the kitchen window to penetrate the gathering twilight.

Joan was gone. He knew that she would be. She could not stay any longer. Not just because of their argument, and the words with which he had parted. She needed to run away again, to hide from the devil.

He stopped between the hawthorn tree and the workbench. He did not want to go inside. She might be gone, but her presence would not be. The ghosts of her scent and laugh waited for him. The garden was not devoid of her either, but it would be worse in the kitchen and the hall. It would be unbearably intense in his chamber and his bed.

Feeling as hollow as the quaking silence that surrounded him, he sat on the workbench. Something fell off the plank with his movement, and he groped on the ground for it. His fingers closed on one of Joan's little tools, a tiny piece of iron that she used to line patterns on her clay. A few other metal pieces still lay where she had left them, here at the spot where she straddled the bench to form her statues. Rhys pictured her, her expression intent and her hands moving, the afternoon sun revealing the shape of her body beneath the thin shift.

She must have left very quickly if she forgot to take the tools. Of course she had. She needed to get away fast if she was going to protect her brother. And maybe she thought that she protected someone else, too. Maybe she wanted to sever her connection with this house immediately in order to shield the man who owned it.

That notion left a bitter taste in his mouth. It was one thing to accept that she did not think that he could protect her. It was much worse to admit that she felt obliged to protect *him*.

She was probably very frightened. It hurt his heart to think of how she had forced herself to hide that from him. The whole time that they rode back to this house, all during their dreadful confrontation, she had been holding terror inside her. Worse than that, she had been living anew the old memories of her bargain. He did not doubt that Sir Guy had reopened the healing wounds, and probably intended to inflict new ones.

She should have told him. She should have let him help her. Did she doubt that he would? Did she think that he would run from the danger and leave her on her own? Did she worry that if he knew who she was, and what followed her, he would abandon her to save his own skin?

She should have told him, damn it. If not weeks ago, then today.

The upright plank of the workbench shielded him from the sight of the house. Early this morning he had come out and finished the saint. She waited rigidly now, in all her calm dignity, for him to cart her to the church where she would watch generations pass through its portal.

As so often in his life, he soothed his inner turmoil by turning to his craft. He rose and pulled the canvas off the stone. She loomed there, almost life-size, a black column in a darkening world. He ran his fingertips over the eyes that he had smoothed today, checking the surface to be sure it needed no more work.

His hand paused. In his blindness he felt more than he had ever seen. He slid his fingers lower, over nose and cheeks, to lips and jaw. The strokes summoned wrenching memories of touching this face before, many times, in passion and affection. Not hard stone then, but velvet flesh and pulsing life.

Saint Ursula, a virgin martyr. The daughter of a king, and of noble birth. He had carved her in rich, embellished robes as befitted her station, and he had given her the dignity and face of a highborn woman whom he knew intimately.

He left his fingertips on her lips, and they almost seemed real beneath his touch. *Do you know her?* His heart had known. His soul and his essence had seen all of it. The truth of her birth, and what she had lost, and what she fought to regain. It had guided his chisel without his realizing it. His craft had expressed what his mind did not want to acknowledge. He had not wanted to admit how hopeless his love would be.

She should have told him. Except that she had. She had never really hidden her nobility from him. The first time that he saw her in the marketplace, it had garbed her more surely than her tattered grey gown.

A vague sound penetrated his absorption. He glanced over his shoulder, then turned. Another dark column stood in the thickening shadows near the house. Another draped female form, unmoving and rigid, faced him. Not made of stone, though. Fear and worry and relief did not pour out of stone.

Joan was not gone. She had not left yet.

He did not know what to say to her. She did not trust him, and he could not help her unless she did. Even then, his interference might cause more trouble than aid. She might indeed be safer if she and Mark just disappeared again.

He realized that he did not have to say anything, because it would not matter. She had already chosen her course. She ran from the past toward her future, and neither included him.

She had not left yet. But she would be gone forever very soon.

He knew.

It was in his stance and his silence and in the way he looked at her. Joan could not see his face in the darkness, but she did not doubt that those intense blue eyes glinted with his new knowledge of how she had deceived him.

She would have given anything for Rhys to have never known. Already it changed things. He faced her differently. Not with sudden deference or restraint. Nay, Rhys did not think of nobles as his betters. It was not shock or dismay that stretched from him to her across the garden yard. She felt something much sadder coming to her. Something poignant. Acceptance and regret. Resignation, and maybe some anger.

He stood there like a man who calmly realized that he had been wasting his time.

"You are not gone."

She grimaced. He had delayed all day in returning so that he would not find her here. "I thought to be, but I could not find Mark. He should return soon, and we will leave at once—"

"I am glad that you are not gone."

He meant it. Her heart stretched. She was glad that she was not gone yet, too, even though it would be much harder now. Terribly hard.

"Come and sit with me while we wait for your brother, Joan."

She walked over and they settled on the bench side by side. She basked in the final security of feeling his warmth and strength. She was glad that their last few moments would be here in the garden, on this bench, at the spot where they had shared their deepest moments and known the soul together.

"How long do you have before he starts looking again?"

Aye, he knew. He had guessed it all. "One day. We can be out of the city by then, and well on our way."

"Where will you go?"

"North."

"Let me take you to Edward. Instead of running again, go to the King and get the justice that you want."

"I can not risk that. If I enter Westminster, I will never see the King. Nor can he do much for me. He is only a pawn. Another holds the power."

"It will not always be so, I promise you."

"Perhaps not, but it is so now. If Edward ever claims his place, I will be the first in line to petition him."

"I think that he will very soon."

"Not soon enough."

He sighed deeply. Sadly. Her own heart responded in kind. The whole garden seemed drenched in melancholy, as though the plants and trees awaited the death of something beautiful.

"I will go with you. I will take you and your brother out of the city, and bring you to Sir Addis. He knows of your story, and he will give you sanctuary."

"We can not even prove who we are. The world thinks

us dead. We will bring Sir Addis and Moira nothing but trouble, and the enmity of the Queen and Mortimer."

"Then we will flee north as you planned."

"I do not want you coming with us, Rhys. Today Guy saw me as a long-lost love, but very soon he will see me only as the woman who betrayed him. In either view, he will retaliate against you if he learns of the time I spent here."

Rhys took her hand, and stretched his fingers between hers in a firm grasp. "I do not care about that. He frightens you, but he does not frighten me. We will go together."

"Nay." She squeezed his hand to emphasize her resolve. "*Nay.*"

Silence surrounded them, but unspoken words filled it. Accusations of deception, but also promises. She wished that the latter ones could be said. Her throat tightened and her heart burned from the effort to keep strong.

She longed to embrace him and say that one day she would be safe and she would return, and they would start over, and finally discover just what this might be. Only it would not happen that way, and Rhys knew it. She wished that it could, though. She wished that she owed nothing to the past and future. She ached with the imminent loss of what they had shared. She prayed that he understood how happy Joan the tiler had been with Rhys Mason.

He pulled her into his arms. His strong embrace defeated her. She sank against him and inhaled all that he was, and tears brimmed in her eyes.

"You might have told me," he said. "You might have trusted me."

"I could not, at first. And then . . . I knew that I would only have you for a short time, Rhys. If you knew who I was . . ."

"If I knew who you were, I would also have known that

we would have each other only for a short time. You had always warned about that, but I had hoped for more."

"And I let you, and lied to myself that maybe it could be more, too. A year at least. Maybe I wanted us to believe it while we could, so this day would not shadow our time together. It was selfish and heartless of me."

"Nay, not selfish. Maybe I am glad that you did not tell me." He caressed her face, and turned it up to him. "And I am glad that you were not gone tonight, so that we can part with a kiss, and not the harsh words we spoke this morning."

The touch of his lips seared her whole being with warmth. He tasted of goodness and fairness and all that she had lost years ago. He kissed her beautifully, for the last time, lingering in a way that stirred her soul and her womanhood.

A noise penetrated their sad bliss. Footsteps padded through the garden. She clung desperately, blocking out the intrusion, not wanting to hear the sounds that signaled the end.

He broke the kiss, but held her tightly. A figure walked past them, and stopped near the statue.

Joan reluctantly turned her head. Mark gazed not at their embrace, but at the propped stone saint. He stood like a soldier, legs parted and braced, back and shoulders squared, his hands clasped behind him.

"I looked at it this morning," he said, nodding to the statue. "You completed the face."

"Aye."

"She is very beautiful, and you handled her with great skill and affection. But it is over and done now, isn't it. It is time for her to leave this garden. You are finished with her."

Rhys brushed Joan's hair with his lips, and loosened his

embrace. "Take the horse," he whispered. "Take whatever you need."

Her heart screamed a protest as he rose, separating from her.

He walked away, heading to the house, taking parts of her with him, making tears that would never heal.

Aye, it was over and done now. He was finished with her.

She tried to calm her emotions, and see past the pain. Mark waited, giving her a little time.

She had to collect herself. She had to explain to her brother just how over and done it was. They needed to be off, and find some way to get through the city gate tonight.

He shifted slightly. His right hand emerged from behind his back. A long, dark line appeared by his side.

He held his sword.

Her heart stopped, then began again with a rapid, desperate rhythm.

"He is here. In the city," he said, flatly.

No wonder he had spoken with such finality to Rhys. "I know. How did you find out?"

"The man whom I pay to train me is the father of one of Mortimer's household guards. He gossips when he is in his cups. I make sure that happens often."

"What else did he tell you?"

"That Guy's arrival was unexpected. He was not called. I think that he came looking for us."

"Perhaps not, but we can not risk it. I also learned he was here. I have been waiting for you, so that we can leave tonight."

"Nay." The word came out too calmly.

She realized what he was thinking. What he planned to

do. She shot to her feet. "You can not. It will be just what he wants."

"We do not run like criminals anymore. I do not."

"You are a boy."

"Man enough to know I have only one choice in this."

She grabbed his arm. "He knows we are here. He saw me. Do you understand how dangerous this is? He will be looking, and waiting. You will not be able to take him by surprise."

"I never intended to. I am not some coward who cuts a man down from behind."

Saints. "It will be like Piers. Do you forget so easily? Is your pride making you blind? You are no match for him. He will kill you."

"Then I will die with honor, where the whole world sees, and before I do I will let everyone know what he is, and what he did. And you will survive and tell the rest." He reached out and smoothed his hand over her hair. "All of the rest. What happened to Father and the others might be excused by war, but not what happened to you."

Dear God, he knew. He had always known. And now he would go to his death rather than live with it unavenged.

"Do not do this for me. I am alive, at least, and so are you. I do not want your rash bravery on my behalf."

"Women never do. That is why men do not ask their permission, and I do not ask yours now. I only tell you because I promised to."

"You will die. Are you still so callow a youth that you do not comprehend that? And public challenge or not, it will change nothing. *Nothing.*"

"It will change everything. Despite my youth, he will not be able to resist meeting me, and all who see him do so will know him for the murderer he is."

"At best you will wound his honor. Do you think a man like that cares about such things?"

"What matters is that *I* care about such things."

He was not listening. His pride had made him deaf. She gripped his arm tighter, until her fingers clawed. "I beg you, brother, do not do this. Do not leave me alone."

"You will not be alone. When it has all come out, the King's council will see to your safety. They will find you a strong husband, who will protect you and our lands until you have a son."

Mark did not understand. Full of youth's rash heroism, he did not realize it would not be that way at all. He had been only a boy when it happened, and he had not perceived how every move Guy had made had been directed by another man. A man who would gladly bury her brother and her and blithely ignore the questions Mark's bold act raised.

It was her fault. She had kept his pride alive, breathing on its embers whenever poverty threatened to extinguish it. She had fed his anger with tales of Guy's atrocities. She had never led him beyond that, to take into account the distant hand that had guided the whole thing.

And now it was too late. He had worked himself up all day, and made his hard decision. The path of valor shone in front of him, and he would not listen to words that insisted it would all be futile.

She could understand that. For three years she had not seen it, either. In her hatred for Guy, she had ignored the totality of it. She had dreamt of destroying the smaller evil, when a bigger one was the source of its power.

"Wait one day. Give me one day, I beg you. I will make this right."

"You can not accomplish in one day what three years could not make happen."

"I can. I know how."

"If you think to buy a champion, put the idea out of your head. You do not have the coin, and I will not permit the alternative."

"Rhys has the coin."

"He does not. He used it to purchase the tile yard. So his pretty leman could practice her craft, and be bound to him in a partnership. Twenty pounds it cost him, I heard. I doubt your mason had much more than that hidden under the floorboards."

The news stunned her. She had not thought about the cost of the yard, and the potential loss of the investment when she left. It became one more misery to add to her distress.

"I still ask for one day. I know another way to settle this. If I am wrong, if I fail, one day can not matter. In fact, it will make it easier. You will not have to go searching for Guy, because he will be waiting for you. Tomorrow next, at the Temple. He thinks that we will come at tierce."

Mark's head snapped around in shock. "You spoke with him?"

"Aye."

"You promised this to him?"

"To buy some time, so we could leave."

"What other promises did you make?" He sounded furious.

"What he wanted to hear. What he needed to believe, so he would not look for you at once."

He calmed a little, and considered the options. "The Temple at tierce. It is busy there at that time. If we meet thus, many will see it." His boyish pride liked that, as if it would make a difference.

"If I fail and you meet him, I will make sure that the whole city of London sees it."

He wavered. "It would be better than going to him at the palace, I suppose."

"Much better."

He toed at the tip of his sword. It was a childish gesture, revealing the boy who still lived inside the man. Joan wanted to gather that child in her arms, and scold him and protect him and forbid this dangerous game.

"One day only?"

"One day. I will know by tomorrow evening if I have been successful."

He shrugged. "I suppose that after three years, it can wait one day."

Relief oozed through her. Relief and numbing dread. She had made a promise, and now could avert his death only by finding a solution very quickly.

There was only one that would work.

No champion. No coin. No time. That left only her, on her own. In coming to look for them, Guy had forced her hand in ways she had never anticipated.

No more running. No more dreaming. The past pressed along her back, and her brother's sword blocked the future. In the next day it would all be over. Truly finished and done with.

She released her hold on Mark's arm, and smoothed her palm up to his shoulder. "I want you to go to David's house tonight. I want you to wait there until I come and get you tomorrow."

"Why? Does Guy know where you live? Do you worry that he will come to this house? If so, I will not leave you to face him alone."

"He does not know. But I will sleep better if you are safe and hidden, just in case. It is foolish of me, but we women are like that."

"Oh, aye, if you are going to worry all night, I will go."

"You should probably leave the sword here."

"I suppose that I should." He paced down the garden. He slipped the weapon behind the plants along the wall, then aimed for the portal.

She ran and stopped him. She gazed at him in the darkness, and wished that she could see his face clearly. She ran a caress over his strong shoulders and down his arms, and her memory felt the frame of a boy and a youth even though her hands traveled along the body of a man.

A surge of nostalgia washed her, and a new expectation of loss pierced her heart. She took his hands in hers, and lifted them to her face. He shifted, uncomfortable with the intimacy in the way of boys his age.

She stretched toward him, and kissed his cheek. "You have been my world, Mark, and my life, for three years. One day more, and I will finally make it right. You will have it all back."

He stilled suddenly. "As will you. We will reclaim our home as we left it, hand in hand."

She was grateful that he could not see her face, and the tears brimming in her eyes. "Aye, hand in hand. Go to David now."

He hesitated, as if he sensed her hidden sorrow. As if he knew. He reached for her impulsively, and clutched her in an awkward embrace against his chest.

He released her, and stepped to the portal. "I will wait for you. Only until vespers, though. I will return here then if you have not come or sent me word."

He meant that he would return for the sword. His heart suspected that he would not find her here if he had to wait that long.

She stepped into the alley, and watched as he was swallowed by the night. She waited long after he had turned off the path, imagining that she could still see him. Then she closed the portal, and went to sit among the flowers and face the only choice left.

We will reclaim our home as we left it, hand in hand.

That was how it was supposed to be. That was the dream, and the plan.

But it would not happen that way now. If she did what she had to do, she would not live to see that day.

CHAPTER 21

JOAN SAT AMIDST the flowers, unnaturally alert to
their scents. She drifted her hands through them, reveling
in the textures of their fibrous stalks and soft petals. The
white ones shone like tiny ghosts in the night, reflecting
the vague light cast by the moon.

Her senses absorbed it all, moment by moment. Reality
existed in a new way. Sharper. Immediate. It was as if God
had slowed time for her tonight, and heightened her
awareness, so that she might live as thoroughly as possible.

Strength battled with fear in her heart, but it was the
fear that fed the strength. Fear for Mark, and for Rhys. If
her brother did what he planned, someone from the ward
would recognize the bold youth, and go to Guy or
Mortimer later to tell of the house where the son of
Marcus de Brecon had been living.

She had no choice, and that was a good thing. Given
one, she would have run and run. She would have spent
her life running, and never lived in the present again.

Right now, in this garden, the present existed as it never

had before. Was it always like that at the end? Did a body's senses only completely come alive right before they perished? She plunged her hands through the flowers to the soil, and relished the sensation of cool darkness around her fingers.

There was no choice, but she did not welcome what she faced. She was not that strong. Swells of panic rose again and again, and only the fear for Mark and Rhys kept them from overwhelming her. She prayed that fear would not desert her tomorrow, or be drowned by the soul-chilling dread for herself that lapped at her resolve.

She was glad that she had not seen the solution earlier. Her childish ideas had bought her three years. Even their poverty seemed beautiful now, because it had led her to this house, and the man who owned it. The foolish dream had kept her alive long enough to know him.

Her spirit cringed from thoughts of tomorrow. She did not doubt that she would succeed. She would make sure that she did. But she did not lie to herself. There would be no escape after she stilled the hand that had moved the pieces on the board of her life.

The earth and breeze and sky knew that. They bound her to them in this precise present. They let her see and feel them as she never had before. The acute awareness of her senses and soul both soothed her and pained her.

The house loomed darkly at the other end of the garden. A man slept inside. She pictured Rhys in that feather bed, and her heart lurched with yearning for the sheltering comfort of his secure embrace.

She should stay out here in the garden and sleep in the flowers. They had said their farewells, and he thought her gone. She had already let duty tear them apart. The courageous course, the right one, would be to allow him to begin forgetting her.

Her heart would not let her. She ached for the bond she

had known with him. In this sharply real present that saturated her, she needed to cling to him, and know him and touch him as thoroughly as her fingers experienced the flowers and soil. Physically and spiritually, and totally.

Her mind argued with her heart. It warned that he would guess what she planned, and try to stop her. It said that if she did this, it would be the greatest deception, and unforgivable.

Nay, no deception. This was now, and the rest was tomorrow. Only the current world existed this night. Not the old one with its memories, and not the next with its duty.

She rose, and walked toward the house. There really wasn't any choice. Not about tomorrow, and not about tonight.

Rhys was not sleeping. As soon as Joan entered the kitchen, she saw him standing by the hearth, arms crossed over his chest. He stared at the embers like a man in a trance, and did not react to her footstep.

She saw him more completely and precisely than she ever had. A strong, handsome man, contained and complete in himself. A good man, who had been too generous with her, and who would receive only pain for his kindness.

But that would be later, and this was now. Very now. The last now that she would have. She prayed that he would understand. She hoped that sharing what might be for one more night would help him to forgive her.

A premonition of the morning's pain slid through her. A hollow nostalgia filled her. With fierce determination she forced it out of her. She reclaimed the present, and the sheer joy of seeing him again took its place.

Most of its place. The waiting sorrow could not be

completely banished. It would remain, coloring their bond. It was the sorrow that made the present so real.

Rhys's head moved slightly, and his shoulders tensed. He had finally realized she was there.

"I thought you had left. I saw you walk out the portal." He did not look at her, and spoke into the hearth.

"I came back. I sent Mark to a friend's house for the night."

"Why?"

"I doubt we would have gotten out a city gate this late."

"Then you intend to leave tomorrow instead?"

"Aye. At dawn."

"Alone?"

"Alone."

She could barely see his profile, but it was enough. The line of his mouth hardened, and his expression darkened.

He was angry. She could not blame him. Her refusal of his help had insulted him. Her deceptions only made it worse. She guessed what conclusions he had drawn while he stared into that low-burning fire.

"It is not because of who we are, Rhys."

"It is all about who we are, darling."

"It is not. I do not doubt your bravery, or your worth as a protector. But I have lost too much in this, and I will not lose more if I can prevent it."

He did not respond to that. He kept his stance turned from her, and his gaze on the glowing fuel.

"If you do not want me to stay here tonight, I will leave. I have some coin for an inn."

"Do not add to the insult. I am not so cowardly that I would throw a lady out on the street."

His sharp tone cut her. She desperately needed to bridge the distance between them. "It is not a lady who will stay, but Joan Tiler."

"There never was a Joan Tiler, just a mason too

besotted to accept that. Just a man too willing to embrace self-deceit, and never ask the real name of the woman who had not been born to the craft that she practiced."

"That is not true. When you met me, and until today, I was as you knew me."

"Nay, Joan. The ghost of the lady was ever in you, determined to be reborn, desperate for it. You never forgot. Even in my arms that past owned you." He finally turned, blue eyes sparkling with deep lights that revealed just how far his contemplations had gone. "I wonder if it was that, as much as the memories of Leighton, that kept you from giving yourself to me."

"I beg you to believe me when I say it was not."

"I think that you do not know your own mind very well. If I had been a different man, a man equal to the ones whom you lost, a knight of standing, it would have been different. You would have trusted me to right the wrong done to you. You would have seen a future with me that went beyond these few weeks."

"I can not say what my mind would have thought. I only know that it would not have made a difference to my body, or my heart. I never deceived you, Rhys."

His expression softened a little. "Except that it is all part of the same thing. All facets of the jewel of your past, and your vow to wear it again as you were born to. If I had admitted the truth to myself, I would have understood better, that is all. I would have known from the start that you could not put it aside, any of it, including the memories that killed the pleasure. If you lost hold on one part, you feared losing it all. You warned me as much that first night in my bed."

"And you told me to forget while I could, and to remember when I must. You showed me how to forget, and I did, but I will never forget what we shared."

Rhys smiled vaguely. Sadly. "I fear that neither will I, pretty dove. That is the problem that I deal with now."

He walked over and sat on the bench below the window. He gazed out, as if he could see something besides blackness. "If you must leave at dawn, you should sleep. Use the chamber and bed. I will come up and wake you at first light."

It was a gentle repudiation, but an unmistakable one. He had been glad to see her in the garden, but he was not pleased to have her here now. Her presence interfered with his building a wall in which he would contain whatever emotions he felt.

She should walk away and leave him to it. She should not ask for more than he wanted to give. But she could not sleep in that bed alone. She would lie awake all night, awaiting the dawn, dreading the ordeal to follow, and feeling the mood and presence of the man holding vigil down below.

As she felt them now. They filled the kitchen, thickening the air, surrounding her like a misty cloud. The old bonds, the physical attraction and emotional connections, still stretched between them, pulling as tautly as they ever had. Like everything else tonight, she experienced them acutely, and her heart and body stirred.

Rhys had decided it was over, but it was not. Not yet. Tomorrow would be soon enough.

"If you do not want to come upstairs with me, I will stay here with you."

"You speak of an overlong farewell, darling."

"I do not want to speak farewells at all. That is for tomorrow."

He shifted, and faced her. "Then what? My humor is not good, and I am in no mood to talk about what has happened, and will happen, until daybreak. It will only lead to arguments, and keep me from finding some peace."

"A peace that will come only if I am not with you?"

"Aye, Joan. I may never forget you, but that does not mean that I will not try."

It pierced her heart to hear him put that into words. Only her desperate need of comfort kept her brave. "That can wait for tomorrow, too, can it not? It is not speaking that I want from you, Rhys. I am not in the mood for a lot of talk, either."

He just looked at her. His casual pose on the bench did not change, but a new power entered the air. It came from him and forced her alertness higher yet, in a physically exciting way.

"Then what is it you want from me, Joan?"

"I want tonight. I want to sleep by your side one more time. I want your embrace and your kiss and your touch. I want to forget for a few more hours."

"I do not think that I can do that."

"Have you closed your heart to me already? Begun to forget so quickly?"

"Nay, and that is why I can not do it. I can not trust myself with you tonight. I have wanted you for too long, from the first moment I saw you. When I thought there was a future, my hunger could bide its time. I could afford to wait. But there is no more future and no more time, and I am not a saint. I know what is in my head and my blood now, and it would be unwise for us to do this. I do not think that I would stop, and if I ended this by hurting you, that would be a bitter memory for us both."

"Then do not stop. I do not want you to."

There, she had said it. She could not turn back now. Nor would she want to.

He did not move or make a sound. He just looked at her, but she felt his reaction. She sensed the effect of her words on him, and they way they prodded the hunger he spoke of.

Prickles of anticipation danced through her. She waited for him to rise and come to her. Surely he could not resist the way that the old pull tightened. Tensely. Fiercely.

"I told you the first day that I would not take you in payment even if you offered, my lady."

"I owe you much, but I do not offer anything in payment of that debt. I do this for myself, so that when I leave tomorrow I will know that what we had was whole. And it is not a lady who wants you. It is only Joan Tiler."

Still he did not come to her. She wished that there were some way to convince him that it would not be like the first time, that the pleasure would not die. There was no danger of his hurting her, because the only memories that lived for her tonight were those of him.

There were no words that could explain that. There were fewer yet that could convey how thoroughly the present existed for her right now.

It did not matter. This was not a time for words.

She strolled over to the hearth, and carefully placed some fuel on the embers. She poked until it caught, and the warm tongues gave off their dancing, golden light.

She plucked open the neck lacing on her brown gown. She turned to see his intense gaze. The new light sculpted his face beautifully, and the blues of his eyes appeared almost black in their depths.

The gown slid off her shoulders and slithered down. His quiet watching did astonishing things to her.

"You do not have to do this."

"Aye, I do. For myself. So the remembering is only good, and there are no regrets."

She pushed her shift straps down her arms. She lowered the fabric, exposing her breasts. Her skin had grown so alive that the cloth's brushing descent aroused her like a caress.

The shift dropped. She faced him across the room, naked but for the firelight. The slow way that he looked at her, all of her, made her suddenly shy. She brought her braid forward and unplaited it in order to hide how unsettled he made her.

He watched her hair loosen. She shook out the strands until they streamed around her.

Still he did not come to her. His gaze rose up her length until he looked her in the eyes. His expectation of what she offered could be seen in the tight planes of his expression, and the intensity of his attention.

Still he did not move, but the waiting was not unpleasant. Desire pulsed in the passing moments, exciting her as much as a touch. Despite their distance, they seemed as connected as when in an embrace.

It affected her physically. Her breasts hardened and their tips grew tight. A delicious tension filled her belly. Her throat went dry.

He could tell, but he did nothing to breech the space. A spark of challenge glittered in his eyes.

"You are going to make me come to you, aren't you?" she said, suddenly understanding.

"Aye."

"So that it is clear that it was my choice, and my decision."

"Aye."

"That is not very generous of you."

"What I want tonight has nothing to do with generosity. I want to take you, and possess you, and bury myself in you. Come here to me if you are so sure that you want me the way I want you. Show me that you really need this to be whole between us before you leave. Otherwise pick up that gown and run up to the chamber, and we will part at dawn as we did in the garden."

His voice carried enough of an edge to make her pause. He was not angry, and not really dangerous, but he warned her about what he expected. Even more than his words, his tone let her know just where his mind and his blood were tonight.

It sent a shiver through her. Not one of fear. Deep excitement quivered, humming into her limbs. It shook her so thoroughly that she wondered if she could walk.

She could. She stepped toward him. His gaze towed her closer, drawing her forward as if he pulled in an invisible rope.

Finally she stood in front of him, so close that she felt his warmth along her bare skin. She also felt the tension of anticipation in him, and the force of contained power. Her own arousal spiked in recognition, releasing hungry yearnings. They had not even touched, and she already responded to the pleasures that awaited. They filled her imagination and tantalized her body.

He straightened, and splayed his strong, wonderful hands on her hips. The warmth and roughness of his skin was like a touch of ecstasy. He pulled her between his legs and smoothed his face against her breasts.

She stroked her fingers in his hair and held him to the beat of her heart. "You did not believe that I could do it."

"Nay, not today of all days. Not after seeing him again."

"This is not about today, or him. I had decided before he found me. I was waiting for you to come, so I could tell you."

He looked up in surprise. He rose, and wrapped his arms around her nakedness. "Then this is just about us. Finally, only us."

"Aye, only us." Finally. Very finally. But the contentment of his embrace, of feeling his body pressed along hers, easily submerged the swell of regret that rose with that word.

Holding him was heavenly, but she needed more. Wanted more. They both did. It tremored in the pressure of their grasping holds, and it flowed along the paths of his long caresses. Something powerful waited. A wonderfully turbulent force built silently but palpably, straining against the containment of this restrained prelude.

He kissed her and the force broke loose with a fevered gust. Her need met his in a passion made desperate by the impending loss of each other. The hunger in her soul matched that of her body, and both were eager for all that this could be.

His hot, biting kisses promised that they would finally have that. They warned that there could be no holding back. Her fears and his decency had respected barriers for too long, but it would not be like that tonight. Finally.

Her senses filled with him. Her skin felt the textures of his skin and hair and clothes in a cascade of alert, novel sensations. His breath warmed her neck, and the touch of his tongue shot pleasure into her blood. Her arms embraced the need rising savagely in his frame, and her own desire reveled in it, soaring triumphantly, urging more and more.

It turned mad and impatient and wild. He kissed and held and touched with controlling mastery, as if he wanted to absorb her. Consume her. Her heart begged him to take all of her. Her soul longed to be joined with him.

She needed more closeness, more connection. She clawed at his clothing, anxious to strip away the interfering barriers. Somehow they got the tunic and shirt off. She pressed her palms and her lips to his bare chest and lost herself in the taste of his skin and the beat of his heart.

He lifted her into it. Held her to it. Kisses pressed to her hair and hands caressing lower on her bottom, he encouraged her wandering, circling tongue. She loved what it did to him, how his body tensed and his breath shortened. She itched for his stroking fingers to find their goal. She smoothed her palms lower to urge him on, and the muscles of his torso tightened beneath her hands.

He took his time, tantalizing her need, making her wait. Her body pulsed with craving. The need unhinged her. She looked up to find him watching her rocking body with dark satisfaction.

"Please. Touch me there. I will die if you do not."

His hand moved. Eyes alight with a new kind of passion, he watched her reaction. She let him see it. Let him hear it. Limp in the support of his embrace, she submitted to the torturous pleasure. Welcomed it.

He lifted her, and settled back on the bench below the window. "Here. Now. It can not wait for the bed upstairs."

He pulled her onto his lap, with her knees straddling his hips as they had under the hawthorn tree that Sunday. He eased her up so his mouth could reach her breast. Arms braced on the sill behind him, breeze titillating her hot skin, she hovered there while his tongue flicked and licked and his hands loosened the rest of his clothing.

Her breasts had never been so sensitive. The luscious torment left her shivering. She reached down and stroked him while he kicked off his garments.

He let her for a while. In a sweet unity of sensation they explored the pleasure. Tongue and fingers circling and smoothing at her nipples, he played with her madness until cries sighed out with each of her gasping breaths.

He removed her hand and placed it back on the sill. "No more. It is not your hand that I want surrounding me."

The position left her poised over him, vulnerable and passive, hungry and waiting.

His mouth and hand aroused her more specifically. The need centered low, where he had caressed before. She imagined that touch again, and more, and needful pleas breathed out of her. Begging words and declarations of desire poured out with abandon.

His other hand caressed her inner thighs with commanding firmness. Anticipation consumed her mind and she cried with impatience. His caress lined higher in response, and stroked deeply. Relief groaned through her. Out of her.

It was only a brief respite. His slow, knowing touches made her body come alive. The focus of her pleasure pulsed with astonishing sensitivity. It quickly turned frantic. The hunger possessed her until her legs wobbled and she cried from the intensity. All of her, her body and soul and heart and mind, all of the alertness and awareness and experience of the present, joined in a totally consuming, desperately insistent craving.

"Now," she begged. "Now, like this, do not wait. I want you now. Now."

"Aye, Joan. Now." His low voice sounded as tight as hers, and his breath as ragged and short. He took her hips firmly in his hands and lowered her.

There was the briefest hesitation just as he entered her, as if he checked her body's reaction. The pleasure did not die. She knew it would not, but tenderness poured through her at the sign that, for all his warnings, he still worried for her. She did not doubt that he would have stopped if he had sensed the old fear.

She nestled lower, absorbing the wonderful fullness, floating in the sudden calm in their passion. It still cried for fulfillment but they both waited, motionless, entwined in the closest embrace, savoring what this finally was.

Finally. Aye, that colored it. Deepened it. Her heart absorbed the mutual sorrow that made this night more important than it should be. She sensed his determination to know it all with her, since there would be no other chance.

He kissed deeply. He lifted her gently, and showed her how to move. "Now come to me, love. Let me feel you lose yourself in it. I want to be buried in your body like this when your passion sets you free."

It began slowly, a luscious savoring of their unity, a joining of more than their bodies, and saturated with connections so profound that her heart almost burst. Love and joy and sorrow and regret poured through her. Out of her. Into her. Their hearts journeyed together, and the fullness and friction and building need only brought them closer.

The pleasure grew anxious and demanding. Her senses soared and flew away until only one remained. All of her consciousness centered on him and an aching, searching reach for completion. She lost control of her body, but he did not. He held her hips, stopping her abandoned rocking, forcing her still just when she thought she could not take the torment of need any longer. And then his passion demanded more from her. The power of his desire sent her higher, pitching toward the freedom he spoke of. The pleasure tightened painfully, deliciously, and his thrusts pushed her the rest of the way. Screaming and begging, she clawed onto the reality of him as the ecstasy broke through her.

He joined her there, in the ultimate freedom. Together they knew all that this might be.

Finally.

He held her to him, in a floating, blissful world of contentment. His sated breath poured in her ear and his firm embrace bound their bodies in the glory. She experienced him very specifically, very alertly. Peace drenched her heart as she gave thanks for the gift of knowing him.

She nestled against him in the feather bed where he had eventually carried her. They had made love in the garden, under the hawthorn tree, and again on the workbench. He had led her to the places that mattered, to complete what had started at each of them, to finally know fulfillment of what had been shared.

She did not sleep, and neither did he. They did not speak, though. Their embrace held back the waiting world. She was more grateful for that than he could guess.

He turned silently, and pushed off the bedclothes that warmed them in the cool night. He moved on top of her and bent her legs and entered her again.

Weight braced on his arms, shoulders and chest hovering above her, he looked down in the flickering light of the gutting candle. She saw his expression, and knew that his mind had not been restful this last hour.

He spoke while he slowly stroked into her. "You will not leave at dawn. You will not run away. You will stay with me for whatever time we have left. I will deal with this man now, and the rest will be resolved soon."

He was not making a request. She was grateful that she did not have to respond. She did not want to speak of the dawn, and of parting, and of how thoroughly she would leave him. She did not want to think about just how little time they had left.

She encouraged his passion so that he would not guess what her silence really meant. She urged him with her touch and words to let the pleasure obscure the truth a little longer. She lost herself in the pure freedom, and lured him to do the same.

Rhys slept after that. She lay turned into him, her face

pressed to his, swallowing his breaths. She filled the last hour with the beauty of this night, and drew strength from her love. It filled her heart, swelling it with joy and sorrow and gratitude and poignant regret. She lived as completely as she ever had. A whole lifetime passed in that feather bed.

She sensed when dawn drew near. She eased from beneath Rhys's arm, and savored a long look at his face. Anguish washed through her, but the fear revived to give her courage.

She dressed silently in her simplest garments. She pinned a wimple and veil around her head in the hopes the obscuring fabric would help, even though it would not. She turned one last time to the bed, and brushed the gentlest kiss on his cheek.

Walking away proved much harder than she had ever imagined. She had to tear herself from the bed, and a part of her refused to go. It ripped from her soul and stayed there, to remain forever in that sweet unity.

The pain vanquished her composure, but not her strength. Blinking back the sorrow, embracing the empowering fear, she turned away.

She left him, finally, to go and do what she had to do.

CHAPTER 22

JOAN MIGHT HAVE BEEN invisible, so easily did she move through Westminster. Her visits to the palace with Rhys had made her a familiar enough figure that she raised no notice.

She pretended to head to the King's chambers, but darted in a different direction when the way was clear. Holding her basket close to her body, keeping her head lowered, she made her way to the little garden.

Mortimer's garden. His private retreat where he plotted his ambitions, and met with spies and messengers. And masons, sometimes.

She peered through the portal. A silk canopy stood in the center, to protect the great man from today's hot sun. Colorful flowers spread out in spokes, and all paths led to the cushioned chair on which he would sit.

He was not there yet. But he would come. The day was fair, and he would seek out this place.

The lush beauty disturbed her. Evil should recoil from the bountiful goodness found in nature. Its private places should be dark and gloomy. This garden suggested that Mortimer's soul was not all bad.

For a moment her resolve wavered. She reminded herself of the stakes. Her brother's life and future, and maybe those of Rhys, too. The barons of the realm might be too weak to stand against this man, but she dare not be.

She spied a tall hedge where she could hide and wait. She eased the portal open wider.

For Mark, and for Rhys. For her father and Piers. For all of the lives trampled and crushed these last few years. For herself.

A hand slid up her back, shocking her. Fingers closed on her shoulder, stopping her. She froze, staring at the flowers.

She scrambled to find an excuse for why she tried to enter this garden. She clutched the basket harder, praying this guard would not look inside.

"Are you lost, sweet lady?"

The voice turned her blood to ice. Not just because it belonged to Guy Leighton, but because of its dangerous resonance.

She would have preferred being caught by Mortimer himself.

She pulled her composure together. She dare not let him see her terror.

She slowly turned. Guy appraised her suspiciously.

"Aye," she said, feigning relief.

"I have been following you, Joan, while you skulked about. Whom do you seek?" His lids lowered over ominous fires. "The King?"

Saints, he suspected that she had come to demand justice. He thought that she sought out Edward, to pour out her story and beg his intercession.

"What would I want with the King? He would just think me a servant, trying to claim the place of a dead woman." She forced a sweet smile. "In truth, I was looking for you. A page directed me to your chamber, but I lost my way. I thought this garden might offer a short path to the part of the palace beyond it."

The danger dimmed a little. Just enough to give her hope. "Why did you seek me?"

"I thought about our conversation in the market, and was sorry for how we parted. The shock of seeing you unsettled me, and I was not myself. I came to thank you for forgiving my rashness, and for offering to continue to protect my brother. You risk much in doing so, and I wanted you to know my gratitude."

Her faced warmed while she said the words. She prayed that Guy assumed it was feminine delicacy that caused her to blush, and not the inner disgust that she battled.

His vanity responded as she hoped it would. Different fires ignited in his eyes. Bile rose to her throat as his lust began burning.

He had a hungry look, like that of an animal spying prey. So different from what she had recently known. So ugly compared with the beauty of last night.

She would not think about that now. She could not afford to. But the comparison caused a touch of pity to poke into her terror. Guy, for all of his power and beauty and wealth, would never know what might be.

The alertness to the present had not left her, and now she looked into those eyes and saw more deeply than she had in the past. Amidst the lust, she perceived another tiny hunger. A sad one. She suddenly knew him even better than she had before. Better than she wanted to.

Guy Leighton suspected what his dead soul denied him. He recognized the void. Her comprehension of him was perhaps the closest he had ever come to a true human connection. That was why he relished her hatred, and goaded it. That was why he wanted her, and had kept her alive, and had bothered to try to make Mark's death look like an accident.

Her new insight did not soften her heart. Pity mixed with the hatred and fear, but did not assuage them. He was lost, and she could not save him, even if what was left of his humanity wondered if she could.

His arm slipped around her, and he guided her away from the portal. "You should not be seen here. It is Mortimer's place. Come with me."

She held down the shiver of dread so he would not feel it rack her frame. She forced her feet to move. She let him lead her through the palace.

For Mark and Rhys and herself, she went with him.

She could not do it. As soon as they entered Guy's chamber, she realized it. Not for anything, not even to survive to finish this day's work.

It was a well-appointed chamber. Mortimer valued the man he had put in it.

She could not look at him. Memories invaded her head, but not of him. A different face and a different touch and a peace soaked with caring filled her thoughts and heart.

Guy had once taken from her all that was good. He had destroyed everything that made her who she was. She could not let him do it again. She would not give up what she had claimed for herself last night. She would not let the freedom be shackled again by that numbing shame, not even as a ploy to achieve the great goal.

He took her hand and drew her toward the richly draped bed. She dug in her heels.

"Nay. I did not come here for that. Not yet. I only

wanted to speak with you, and let you know how glad I am that we will be together again."

Her words rang through the silence. She heard the panic in them. She cursed herself for revealing that.

Guy liked her resistance. He always had. The contest had begun. His delight in the inevitable victory, assured by his command over life and death, made him smile.

His fingers tightened, like a reminder of how easily he could crush all she held dear. "Of course it is why you came. Our bargain was never sealed with words."

She yanked her hand free and backed up, holding the basket to her stomach like a shield. "Take the words this time, and wait one day more."

She had dared to refuse him only once, long ago, and had paid dearly for the insult. He advanced on her with an expression that said that she would do so now again.

She moved away but he kept coming. Slowly, horribly. She glanced frantically around the chamber, searching for a way to get free, looking for the dodge that would thwart him.

There was none. She was trapped. Cornered. She had avoided his cruelty in the past with submission, but she could not do that today. The womanhood reborn in Rhys's arms would not accept a new death so easily.

Finally there was nowhere else to move. Her back hit the wall and he stood an arm's span away.

"I warn you, do not touch me. It will not be as you think. Not now. Not yet."

"Of course it will, if I command it. I am glad that you have tried to toy with me, sweet Joan. I considered hiding my anger at the insult of your betrayal, but I will not have to now. It will give me great pleasure to break your pride again, as I did when we first met."

He reached for her. She shrank against the wall and plunged her hand into her basket.

His grip closed on her neck.
Hers closed on the handle of a kitchen knife.

Rhys awoke abruptly and knew immediately that something was wrong. He lay motionlessly with his eyes still closed, hoping his other senses would reassure him.

His skin detected the void by his side, and his heart took on a slow, heavy rhythm. The scent of their lovemaking surrounded him, but no others intruded. No bread baking down below. No leeks frying for soup or pottage. The house was soundless, too. Empty. The melody of her breathing was long gone from this bed.

He forced himself to look, and to move. He got up and pulled on some clothes. While he did so, he noticed how vacant the chamber suddenly seemed. Not just because she was not in it. All of her belongings, every item, had been removed.

He went down to the kitchen, his boots making very loud steps in the silence. No signs of the usual morning ritual waited for him there. No ale or domestic mess. No water warming. No Joan peering in the oven. Nothing.

The garments that she had slipped off last night had disappeared. He pictured them in their heap at her feet, like the froth of the sea giving birth to a goddess. He saw her again, both bold and shy, deciding for them both how it would be.

Other images invaded his head. Wonderful ones, of her free passion and breathless abandon. He felt her body again, heard her words of love tumble into him between her begging cries.

Joan's absence pressed on him as tangibly as her presence ever had. He held down the outrage trying to take control of him. He paced out to the garden, to be sure. He searched the workbench, and the ground around it, for the tools he had found last night.

They were gone, like everything else. Staring at that bench, he finally accepted the truth of it.

He experienced a few breaths of utter, unnatural calm. And then his head split with livid resentment.

She had actually done it. She had made it whole, given all of herself and taken all of him, and then walked away. She had let him know paradise, and then had thrust them both back into purgatory. Only it would be worse now, since he knew for sure what he had lost.

He remembered their last lovemaking. He had interpreted her embrace as acceptance. He had told her that she had to stay, and he had thought that she agreed. Every kiss, every touch that they had shared had seemed to speak a promise of tomorrow. Not forever, but some time at least. More than one night, damn it.

He paced furiously, incapable of keeping his body at rest. He wanted to hit something. He would gladly tear the tree up by its roots if it would ease the heat in his head.

She was out there, God knew where, running and afraid. She had put her terror aside for a few hours, she had tasted freedom, but now the past enchained her again. Hadn't she understood him last night when he had said that he would deal with the man?

He strode back into the kitchen, immersed in chaotic, conflicting emotions. Anger at her and worry for her. Heart-ripping love and mind-scathing bitterness. Stark resignation and hot determination. They all crashed together and mixed and merged, leading him to one crystallized decision.

Joan would not accept his help, but this was bigger than she was. She might not let him protect her, but he was not powerless to do so anyway. He did not need her permission to finish this.

She ran from Guy Leighton, but that man stood on another's shoulders, and it was time for that support to fall. Rhys had sworn to it, and only protecting Joan would have diverted him from the cause. Since she had refused him that honor—*that right, damn it*—he would set in motion the plan that Addis and Edward would complete.

He washed and shaved and prepared himself to attend on the great man. He rehearsed the words with which he would convince Mortimer to leave Westminster. He would make the usurper fear for his safety, and thus make him more vulnerable.

The whole time that he forced his thoughts to the matter, images of Joan, of last night, of what he had briefly held and just as quickly lost, hovered in the back of his mind.

He headed outside again, to get the horse saddled. At the threshold he paused, and looked back to the kitchen. He had expected her laughter and scent to haunt the house after she left, but nothing of her remained. Nothing at all.

She had taken everything with her. Every item, and even her ghost. There was no evidence remaining to prove that she had shared his life these weeks.

In her fear, the severing had been complete. And brave. And ruthless.

Rhys found Mortimer in his garden, eating fruit beneath the canopy.

He accepted the berries offered him, and drank some wine. He made Mortimer ask what he had learned, and then let him suspect that he held something back. In response to pointed questions, the information emerged bit by bit, almost apologetically. He made light of it, and spoke of vague rumors and overheard bits and pieces. He offered his own opinion that it was all much ado about nothing.

By the time Rhys took his leave, Roger Mortimer, the Earl of March, the Queen's lover and the most powerful man in the realm, was very worried. His stupid spy had just confirmed his own suspicions. The dense mason simply did not comprehend the significance of what had just been related.

Rhys aimed for the nearest palace door. Once in the building, he considered his next move.

His part in this was done. The rest would be work for the King and his knights. He did not even have to report on this meeting. When Mortimer left Westminster, Addis would know what to do.

They did not need him anymore. No one did.

Which left him free to follow his blood. And right now his blood wanted to punish a man who had almost destroyed a helpless woman.

Not Mortimer. Addis was right, and an assassin's hand should not resolve that. But somewhere in this palace another man waited, anticipating the sick pleasure that came from forcing the weak into degradation.

Joan had run away, but flight would not ensure her safety this time.

Rhys began searching for a handsome, predatory face. The fires of justice burned in him as they had not done in years. It might be the last act of his life, but he would make sure that Guy Leighton could not hunt down the children of Marcus de Brecon.

He asked a passing servant where to find Guy Leighton. The woman directed him to the chamber given over to Mortimer's guest.

There was no guarantee that the man would be there, but he went anyway. It did not matter where he found him. The privacy of a chamber would be useful, but if he had to confront him in the middle of the palace practice yard, he would do it.

A scratch on the door brought no response. He was about to look elsewhere when the vaguest sound came from within, barely penetrating the thick wood below his fingers.

He gently pushed the door ajar. Heavy breathing, marked by tiny desperate sounds, leaked out to him.

He pushed harder. The door swung wide to reveal a scene of horror.

Blood, red and fresh. A growing pool of it, spreading from Guy's body, edging toward Moira's basket.

A woman, looking down with blank, wide eyes.

He stepped in and closed the door quickly. Joan did not respond to the sound. She just kept staring at Guy's motionless body and closed eyes. Her face had gone so white that it looked more dead than her enemy's. Her arms hung rigidly, angled away from her body as though she balanced precariously. Breaths pumped out of her, carrying those tiny, gasping cries.

Blood stained her hand, and her brown gown.

She had decided to become her own champion.

She noticed that she was not alone, and turned astonished eyes to him.

And then he saw how her wimple sagged low on her neck, revealing red marks on her skin where someone had gripped her. He would have killed the man then, if Joan had not already seen to it.

"He is dead," she whispered.

"Aye, it appears that he is. Let the devil have him." To hell with Guy Leighton. Nothing mattered but saving her from discovery, and there wasn't much time. He strode to a clothing chest and yanked it open and threw items out until he found a cloak. "You have to get away from here. Did anyone see you come?"

She did not answer. She just stared.

Questions would have to wait for later. He threw the cloak around her to hide the bloodstained gown, and slid the basket on her arm. "Come with me now."

She tore her gaze away. She let him lead her to the door.

Clutching her in a close embrace, he walked her through the chambers and passageways. He chose a longer route than necessary to avoid the busy parts of the palace. He made for a stairway and a portal close to the stables.

A group of household guards approached them, heading toward the royal apartments. Rhys pulled Joan into a corner, and shielded her with his body while he pressed a kiss on her cold lips. The guards sauntered by, and shouted lewd encouragement to the lovers.

He felt the life come back to her with his kiss. Her body pulsed beneath his. Warmth replaced chill, and her pale face flushed. She grew alert to what he was doing, and pulled herself out of her shock.

He gently caressed her neck. "He hurt you."

"I would not let him . . . Not again. Not now. Not after . . ." She blinked hard. "I had a knife. It is beneath him. I cut his arm, but it did not stop him. Then it went into his side, but I do not remember how."

He pulled out of the corner and sped her forward on their escape. A fear bigger than he had ever known gripped him. Not for himself, but for her—for what would happen if he did not get her away before some squire or servant entered that chamber, and raised the cry.

"Is that why you came here? Why you left?"

"I came here to kill Mortimer, not him."

Jesus. He almost thanked God that Guy had found her, and forced her hand in a private chamber. If she had attacked Mortimer, she would be dead already.

"I should finish that now, and be done with all of it," Joan whispered vaguely.

"The hell you will. Keep walking, woman, or I will carry you."

Her lips thinned. A spark of rebellion tried to catch fire, but it died, and only sad discouragement looked up at him. "I can not, anyway. I don't have a weapon anymore, and now you have been seen with me. I do not think I am brave enough in any case. It is much harder than I thought."

His heart went out to her. Guy certainly deserved killing, and she had only defended herself. But, aye, it was much harder than she had thought.

At the stables he called for his horse. He mounted and lifted her up behind him. He barely resisted the urge to bolt across the yard and through the gate. He kept the animal to a walk only by repeating to himself that they must draw no attention.

"Were you veiled all morning? While you were with him?" he asked, weighing her danger.

"Aye."

That relieved him somewhat. Her face was not well known in the palace. Anyone who had seen her with Guy might just remember a lowborn woman being flattered by a knight.

It was possible that the servant with whom he had spoken would remember his query, however. He counted on that being unlikely. Servants rarely offered information in such situations, lest the eyes of suspicion turn to them.

He could not be sure that she would be safe, though. Someone who had seen her with Guy might speak of it. There would definitely be a search. He could not risk even the small chance that she might be accused.

They finally got out the gate. Once in the town's lanes, he moved his mount to a trot. He headed toward London, but not to stay. They would collect her brother, and then leave for good.

Her embracing arms tightened snugly. Her head lulled against his back. The aftermath of her ordeal was defeating her.

"I am so glad that you guessed," she said. "I am so glad that you followed me."

He pressed her overlapping hands against his stomach. He did not tell her that he had not followed at all, that he had assumed that she was long gone from the city. Nor did he say that he had not trailed her to Guy's chambers, but had gone there on his own, for his own reasons.

He would never need to explain that. Once the shock passed, she would figure that part out for herself.

Newgate beckoned ahead. He normally saw it as a portal to freedom, and the entry to a sanctuary. But now London's walls could prove dangerous and confining.

It was time to find safety somewhere else.

CHAPTER 23

SHE LET HIM take care of her. She seemed to accept that they were in this together now.

He left her to pack the wagon while he went to get Mark. He found him loitering around the shop where David served as an apprentice. The master was nowhere in sight, and Rhys was just as glad for that.

Mark reacted with suspicion. "She said that she would come."

"She sent me instead."

"I think that I should wait for her."

"You will come now. If it means tying you up and dragging you, I will do it."

"How do I know that you can be trusted, and that you came at her bidding and not someone else's?"

"You know. More to the point, *I* know. All of it." He turned to David. "If anyone should ask, he was not here. You have not seen him in two days. Tell your master and the others that I said for all of you to claim this."

Mark followed Rhys out of the shop. "You say that you know all of it. What does that mean?"

"I know who you are. I know that Guy Leighton let Mortimer think the heir to Brecon had perished in a river. I know that Guy learned you are alive, and came looking for you. Your sister did not tell me this, but I know it anyway."

"She truly sent you? It is over? She found a way to finish it?"

"She certainly did that."

"She went to the King?"

"Nay, she went to Guy."

Mark spit a curse. "Then she finished nothing. I should have guessed what she intended to do. I told her I would not stand for it, that I would see us both dead before she agreed to that again." He paced on furiously. "If she thinks this will stop me, she is wrong."

Rhys grabbed Mark and pushed him up against a building. "Stop you from what?"

"From being a man. From acting like the son of my father instead of some cowardly, gutter-born bastard."

"Did you tell her that you planned to challenge Guy Leighton? Is that why you and she did not leave last night?"

"I said that I would die with honor, not like some hare run to ground. I told her that we are not going to hide anymore."

"Well, you are going to hide now, boy. You are going to do whatever is necessary to save your sister. She did not go to Guy to bargain. She killed the man, and I'll be damned if I will let your callow conceit interfere with getting her away from here."

"She *killed* him?"

"It was to defend herself, but it is done just the same."

"I told her that I would deal with him!"

"As did I, but she did the dealing on her own. If I can put aside my pride, you can, too. Now, move, and if you say one word to upbraid her, if I see any criticism in your eyes, I will treat you like the man you claim to be and make you wish that you had never been born."

Rhys grabbed Mark by the scruff of the neck and pushed him forward down the lane.

Joan had finished packing the wagon when they got back. She emerged from the kitchen just as they entered the garden. She had changed her gown.

She faced her brother cautiously, waiting for his anger. Rhys saw very different emotions haunt the youth's dark eyes. Relief that she was alive and whole. Worry that she might be hunted now because his own arrogance had forced her hand. Something else shadowed his expression too. Guilt. A terrible guilt that had festered for three years.

Rhys placed a hand on Mark's shoulder. "Do not blame yourself for anything that has happened, or that you were too young to protect her. Do not feel ashamed about the sacrifices she has made to keep you alive."

Mark's eyes filmed. Rhys squeezed his shoulder. "Go to her. I will make sure that all is ready."

Mark went to his sister and embraced her. Rhys returned to the alley and waited. He could not see them through the portal, but his gaze fell upon the carved saint beneath its canvas.

Eventually someone from the ward would come, curious about his absence, and it would be found. It would be taken to the church, and set up in its rightful place. Ursula would serve the duty for which she had been created. Others would see to that.

Joan stepped into view and walked toward him with Mark by her side. Like the noble saint whose form she blocked from view, she had chosen martyrdom in the name of a great cause. She had gone to Westminster to save her brother's life again, knowing that if she killed Mortimer, she would certainly die, too.

She had chosen her course before she came to him last night. It had been in her heart the whole time. Thinking about her secret death watch made his throat tighten. His pride wanted to find some anger at her deception, but none surfaced. All that mattered was that she had chosen to spend her last hours in his arms.

Mark carried an old sword that he slipped into the wagon without explanation.

"I packed the bow and dagger. I rolled most of your parchments, too," Joan said. "They are wrapped in that blanket there."

He had not thought of the parchments, or of anything except her safety. "We must be gone. Get in the back with your brother. Try to get some rest."

She strode around to the front of the wagon. "Nay, I will sit up here."

He climbed up beside her and took the reins. Her hand settled on his thigh, and from its grip he could tell that she understood their danger. But the gesture spoke of trust. And of unity, for a little longer at least.

Joan's heart leapt every time a horseman overtook them, and did not calm again until the hooves clamored past. She told herself that no one knew to look for her, that no one would follow, but she experienced the fear of the hunted just the same.

She kept her hand on Rhys. She needed to feel his solidity. His presence both soothed her and added to her worry. He would protect her and Mark, but if the worst happened, and they were taken, he would now share their fate.

She needed to touch him for other reasons. The

warmth under her hand reminded her that she was alive. The surprise of that stirred her blood in powerful ways. There was a euphoria in receiving a reprieve after expecting the end. She reveled in it, even while she listened for the sounds of pursuit.

The feel of him also kept darker emotions at bay. Not just the fear. Not only guilt at having failed in her goal, and at thrusting them all into danger worse than before. Deep inside her heart she also slowly came to terms with what she had done. The image of Guy falling, and of his astonished eyes closing, threatened to haunt her.

She gripped a little tighter, and leaned against him. "I want to make love."

"Do you think it can wait until we stop for the night? It is possible up here, while I hold the reins, but passing travelers might think it very bawdy, and then there is your brother . . ."

His quiet humor almost made things seem normal again. "Aye, it can wait. But this day has made me need you in ways I can not explain." She rested her head on his shoulder. "Can you find it in your heart to give some comfort to the daughter of Brecon? Can you embrace a woman who has killed a man?"

Rhys took the reins in one hand and moved his arm to surround her. "I am honored to do so. I only waited for the sign that you did not plan to deal with this, too, on your own. And for you to decide how it would be between us, since you intended last night to be both a beginning and an end."

"I am beyond decisions now. I can not think about tomorrow, let alone such notions as beginnings and ends. As to how it will be between us, I only know what I need now, and that is to lose myself in you, and to forget everything else."

"Then I will make sure that you do. We will both forget while we can, and then remember when we must."

The sun moved too slowly. The road kept rising to meet them. She nestled alongside him, clinging with body and soul to the solace he gave her. Finally, in the last light of day, he steered the wagon into some trees set back from the road.

Sword in hand, Mark went to scout their surroundings while Rhys pulled out blankets and Joan found some cheese and bread. They started no fire, but only made a rough camp among the pine needles bedding the ground.

Mark returned to report that there was a pond nearby, where the trees met a field. He finally set down his weapon and carried a bucket away to get some water. When he returned he sat to their simple meal, with the sword again by his side.

"Where are we going?" he asked Rhys.

"West. To Barrowburgh, the estate of Addis de Valence."

"Safer to go to Lancaster, if we are going to present ourselves as our father's children."

"Addis will give you sanctuary. He is no friend of Mortimer, and he can be trusted. Lancaster might use you as pawns, and abandon you if it suits his strategy of the moment. If Addis takes you in, he will fight a war before he lets harm come to you."

"And if he does not take us in?"

"He will. I know the man. You will have to trust my judgment on this."

"So we live at Barrowburgh until Mortimer grows old and dies? Even a castle can be a prison."

Rhys brushed off his hands, and pulled Joan into the circle of his arms. "It will not be so long. One way or the other, this will be over soon."

He seemed very sure of that. She relished his embrace, and her body began anticipating more, but his words cast a pall over the peace he offered. She could not think about tomorrow, but he did, and it sounded as if he did not expect there to be very many tomorrows to share.

She turned into his body, and let his warmth obliterate the shadow that his reassurances had created.

Mark looked at them, and rose in exasperation. "Hell, I'm not staying here if you two are going to . . ." He grabbed up a blanket and his sword. "I'll sleep out near the road. If anyone comes, I'll raise the cry. Try to notice."

His movement through the trees had barely receded before Rhys laid her down. They came together, hot and impatient, in a passion that made the day's danger disappear. Nothing existed for Joan but his taste and touch, and her exultant arousal reminded her what it meant to be completely alive.

Rhys tried to slow things. He began to remove her gown, but she could not wait for that. "Nay. Come in me. That is all I want this time. I have been thinking of little else during this journey."

He came over her and filled her arms and her body and her heart. She groaned with relief, and let the fullness obscure everything else. His kiss made her forget the horrors of this day, and the dangers of the next. His touch let her hide from thoughts about the few tomorrows allotted to them. His presence became her whole world, and blocked her contemplation of the brother holding vigil by the road, and the future that he symbolized.

She climaxed before he did, and was glad for it. She loved being alert to the power of his own end, and savored the way the building desire made him move in her. He spoke her name lowly but clearly as the pleasure peaked. The tenderness in that one utterance penetrated her soul. She would never forget its sound.

She held his weight to her afterward, looking up to the treetops pointing against the moonlit sky. The rich scent of pine wafted around them on the cool breeze, and his calming breaths played in her ear. She cradled his hips between her thighs, making the unity last, making memories from the beauty of the night and the sheer joy of holding him.

He eased his weight off her. He rolled onto his back and pulled her to him.

"Are you angry about last night? That I did not tell you?" It was easy to ask him. There was nothing about him that she feared.

"Nay. I should have guessed it, though. I should have known that you would be bold enough to dare it."

"Still . . ."

"I would have preferred if you had let me take care of you, I will not lie about that. You knew that I would do whatever it took to protect you. I told you as much. But I can not resent that you came to me, even knowing what you planned to do. You honored me last night."

She snuggled closer. She could tell him anything. That was the best part of their intimacy. "I failed. With Mortimer."

"I thank God that you did, because it means that you are alive. Forgive me, but that is how I feel."

"I thank God that I did, too. I think that I would have in any case. I do not think I would have been brave enough to do it."

"You are nothing if not brave, Joan. But if a man had to die, better it was Guy Leighton. It is another's destiny to make Mortimer fall."

The mention of Guy brought back the image of his death. "I do not like what I did today," she whispered. "Even in justice and defense, I do not like it. I do not like myself for having done it."

He kissed her, then sat up and held out his hand. "Let us go to the pond. I think that you should wash this whole day off of you, and out of your mind."

"Like a purification?"

"Aye. But it will also give me the chance to see you naked in this moonlight."

Stripped of their clothes, they ran hand in hand to the far edge of the woods where the pond sparkled in the night. They slid down the damp bank, and sat to let the flow cleanse them. Facing each other, they played with the water and each other, making games out of splashes and kisses.

Her mood lightened as her fear and guilt washed away. It was not the water that purified her, and helped her reclaim some innocence. It was Rhys. It always had been.

He raised a handful of water and let it drip over her shoulders and breasts. He leaned forward and licked the rivulets. She stroked the head bending to flick her with pleasure. "You are tied to my danger now. I had wanted to avoid that."

"I am tied to you. The danger is a small part of it, and one that we will defeat."

"I think that I will always regret not giving you more, sooner."

"I do not want your regrets. Not tonight, or tomorrow. They are just more chains. You carry enough, and others await. I want you to forget about them for now, so that we can be free together for as long as possible."

His tongue circled low to catch a drop on her nipple. She pressed him closer. "I have a new chain that I will never forget or regret. I will always be bound to you. I will never be free of that."

He pulled back, so he could see her face. "Then this will bring you unhappiness."

"You can never bring me unhappiness. This chain gives me joy. I wear it with pride. Its weight will remind me that I have known the best love, no matter what life I live."

"You are sure? I would not want this to make your duty harder for you."

"I am most sure." She raised her hand, palm out, facing him. "I will swear it. Nay, I will take a vow to prove it."

Rhys went very still. "You can not do that. You know it, and so do I."

"We are free this night. Naked as the day we were born and as removed from the world's worries as Adam and Eve. The bond exists, no matter what the future holds. Don't you want to give it words? Do you hope to forget me still, like you did last night?"

"I will never forget. I will live off of this love my whole life." So there it was, their admission of love. He said it so calmly. She wondered if he had always known what this might be.

He laid his palm against hers and bent his fingers between hers. "Then let us make our own vows, Joan. Honest and true ones, so that we both can remember the words as we grow old."

His warmth flowed into her through their connecting touch. She could feel his life force like a pulse. "You are the husband of my heart, and the love of my life. Wherever I am, whatever I do, you are joined with me and I with you. The part of me that matters will live with you forever. I accept the chain that binds us with joy, because in this unity I have known the purest freedom."

Rhys laid his other hand against her face. "And you are the wife of my heart, and the love of my life. In the ways that matter we are joined forever, and will live together until death. I pledge my life to protect you, and will always answer your call. I accept this chain with joy, because in our unity I have finally known pure freedom."

He sealed their vows with a gentle kiss, so tender and loving that her heart filled her chest. He gathered her in his arms and lifted her from the water. "You are getting chilled. Come and lie on this rock so that I can see all of you in this Eden."

The low flat rock still held the sun's warmth, as if nature had arranged to provide a comfortable bed for them. They sprawled on it under the stars and moon, enjoying their unity in the timeless world that only a silent night can create.

He ran his fingertips over her body, as though he drew memories of her form onto his mind. His feathery caresses both comforted and titillated, and mixed deliciously with the breeze drying her skin and the heat rising from the stone.

That meandering touch had her halfway to delirium before he kissed her. The passion was not desperate this time, but slow and soulful and imbued with the emotions of their vows.

He used his hands and mouth to lead her into an exquisite sensuality. He slid off the rock and eased her to the edge of their stone marriage bed. He spread her legs and bent to kiss and taste the essence of her womanhood. Her consciousness soared to the stars.

He gently flipped her so that she hugged the warmth of the rock and her legs lined down its side. He lifted her hips and entered her, and held her firmly in his rough, strong hands while his thrusts joined them together in a long and beautiful consummation.

"He will not believe us. He will think that we are impostors."

Mark blurted the words as soon as he saw Barrowburgh. They had stopped at the far edge of the fields that surrounded the town and castle.

The massive walls rising in the distance presented a formidable sight. Rhys could understand how they might intimidate the youth who had lived in poverty for three years. Joan looked a little worried, too.

Rhys snapped the reins and headed for the town gate. "He will believe you. Humble garments do not make the man if wise eyes are seeking the truth. Addis will know that you are not impostors."

Actually, he was counting on Moira knowing it, and convincing Addis.

The town gates stood open, but those of the castle did not. Addis was taking no chance that Mortimer might send in spies.

It took some time for the gate guard to receive permission to let them pass. When they finally rolled the wagon into the inner yard, the Lord and Lady of Barrowburgh were waiting.

Moira ran over to greet them. She acted as if his sudden arrival, just days after her own, was not at all unusual.

Addis was more direct. He paced around the wagon, eyeing its contents. He ended his inspection by giving Joan a long, considering examination. Then he turned his scarred face on Mark, who managed not to cower—just barely.

"Your departure from London was sudden, mason. I trust that you were not fleeing for your life."

Rhys smiled at hearing his own words spoken back to him.

"Actually, we were."

That stopped the pleasantries that Moira and Joan had been exchanging. The lord of the manor raised an eyebrow.

It was time to explain. Rhys nudged Mark and Joan forward. "I present to you the children of Marcus de Brecon. They have come to ask you to extend your protection to them."

"How long have you known?"

Addis had waited until after Rhys told him of the visit to

Mortimer, and the discovery of Joan with Guy Leighton, to ask his questions. They sat alone in the lord's solar, with the ancient sword of Barrowburgh almost filling the wall above Addis's head. Addis might live in a public inn while in London, but here on his estate his power and wealth were visible everywhere.

"I guessed when you told me their story."

"Then you fell in love before you knew. Forgive me, but Moira says that is how it is between you and Joan, and she is rarely wrong."

"Aye, she is rarely wrong."

Addis reached over to pour more wine into the goblet that Rhys held. "I am sorry for your disappointment."

That simple statement said it all. The lord of Barrowburgh guessed that Rhys had been hoping for a future that would be impossible now. This baron may have married a serf-born woman, but the daughter of a baron had no choices in these things. To disobey her kinsmen to marry below her position would mean being severed from her family and her life and her past.

That had already happened to Joan once. Rhys would not let it happen again. Nor would she.

"The boy has his father's eyes. I met de Brecon long ago, when I was a squire. Joan must look like her mother, whom I never saw. Moira suspected something, although not this. She mentioned that she thought Joan harbored some secret that she feared revealing. I confess that I have been distracted by other things and did not pay much attention."

"Will you extend your protection?"

"I will. Hopefully, it will not be for long. I know what it is like to be robbed of one's home. The boy will know no peace until that is avenged."

"And if Joan is accused of Guy Leighton's death?"

"If it is learned that she was there, we will call it what it was. A woman defending her virtue. I doubt that Mortimer will come to Barrowburgh to demand that I hand her over. Not after you have made him as worried as you have. I will send a messenger to Edward tomorrow, to let him know what you told Mortimer, and that you are here with me. I think that you should stay until we see how the wind is blowing."

Faint metallic sounds began somewhere outside. Addis rose and walked to a window. Rhys joined him.

In a practice yard below, a fair-haired youth parried with a bald knight. Addis had handed Mark over to his steward after learning his story, and after hearing his request to be trained in arms.

"He shows strength and the promise of skill. He will have to work hard to make up for the lost years, though. Still, I think that he has the makings of an excellent warrior. When he gets his home back, he will be able to hold on to it."

"He has the heart for it. And the will."

Addis glanced over. The calm understanding of a friend showed in his eyes. "It was their good fortune to have met you, but perhaps not yours to have met them."

Rhys watched Mark wield his weapon, and realized that it was not only Joan that he would mind losing. Mark's departure from his life would create a void. He would miss the boy.

"Fortune smiled on me that day in the marketplace when I met them." He turned away to go and find Joan. "Tell your steward to work him until he drops. Make him the finest warrior in England."

"So that he can protect her?"

"Aye. And himself."

CHAPTER 24

"YOU ARE CONTENTED HERE?"

Joan turned at the sound of her brother's voice. He approached her along the wall walk. He still wore the padded tunic that fits under armor. His hair dripped with water from his sluicing after hours of swordplay.

"Contented enough. Not so much as you, since you get to spend the days practicing at arms. I am over-idle in comparison, and it makes me restless."

She dropped her gaze to the rooftop of the castle chapel. Rhys was in there, carving borders of ivy into the crossing's piers. It was a gift to Moira. He had found a way to avoid idleness at least.

"You have spent three years working like a serf. You are not accustomed to being treated like a lady, that is all. We have our places back, sister, and I swear to God that it feels glorious."

It did feel glorious, as though an upside-down world had been set right again. But it also felt strange and dreamy and a little distant, as if she walked through invisible mist. She lived in this keep, in the luxury she had once known as her right, but a part of her saw everything with another woman's eyes. Joan Tiler's eyes.

"Not our true places. Only one of our legs is back in that world, and only by the generosity of Sir Addis. It may be a long time before we stand there completely, on our own feet, and not propped up. As to being treated like a lady, it makes me uncomfortable sometimes. I had not noticed the deference when I was younger. It was part of the seamless fabric of my world. Now I see it for what it is."

"It is what is due you, as the lord's guest."

"The servants do not accord Rhys the same courtesies, even if they treat him like a guest, too. In subtle ways they make distinctions, and that vexes me."

"I doubt that it vexes *him*. He knows his place, as you must remember yours. He is a craftsman, and it is rare enough that he sits at a lord's high table. He does not expect the castle folk to think that makes him more than he is."

She swallowed the urge to scold him for the way he spoke of Rhys. He only gave voice to the truth. If she found that truth irritating, and saddening, it was not her brother's fault.

She gazed over the fields. "I had forgotten this, too. How different it is away from big towns and cities. What it feels like to stand on a high wall and see miles of the world spread out around you, until the earth meets the sky in the distance. When I came up here the day after we arrived, it was the view that made me believe it had really happened, more than the welcome and the promise of safety. For a moment I was back at home, and a girl again."

"You will truly be back at home someday. As soon as I can make it happen."

"Do not rush your training for me. Guy is dead, but another will take his place. Take the time to prepare yourself well. As I said, I am contented enough here."

"Too contented, perhaps."

His tone made her turn away from the awesome image of the circling world. He had on his man's face now. He wore the eyes and frown of someone much older than his years.

"Too contented? How so, Mark?"

He drew himself straight, the image of a brother forced to exercise his authority. The week here had only fed his sense of prerogatives. Everyone treated him like the head of the family.

"Too contented because your mason is with you. He should leave."

"Moira has asked him to stay."

"You have to end it."

"It will end soon enough." Too soon.

"I had hoped that once you were away from London, and that house, that you would see the futility of it. He does, if you do not. You might only have one leg back in your old life, but he can not walk alongside you any further." His mouth thinned, as if he prepared for an unpleasant task. "I want you to stop visiting his bed."

"Not yet. Not now."

"Aye, now, sister. I will make it plain. I do not request this. I demand it."

"And I defy the demand. I am fully aware of my duty to you and our family. I know what awaits. But I have been given something that I will not put aside until I must."

"Hell, Joan, the whole castle knows that you lie with a craftsman every night."

"I do not lie with a craftsman, although he is so skilled that I would be honored to do so. I lie with a man. The man who saved my life."

"I am grateful to him. Do not think that I am not.

When it is in my power to do so, I will show it. I will give him land or coin or any wealth that he wants. But I will not give him *you*."

"Nor will he ask you to. Like me, he knows that we enjoy a short reprieve. He understands you and me and the others like us very well. He does not even resent the place that we give him, because his mind and heart are not imprisoned by the world's notions of such things. When he must, he will leave. But I tell you now, brother, that whenever you speak to me of him, you had better do so with respect. Neither of us will know the likes of him again, and there will be times when you are the lord of Brecon when you will curse that you do not have men so true as Rhys beside you."

"I did not say that he is not a good man, and true. I said that my sister can not be his lover."

"Punish me if you choose, but unless you demand that Addis lock me away, I will live with Rhys while I can. However, before you make such a demand, remember whom the lord of this keep married."

"That was different, and even so his own retainers think him half mad because of it."

"Aye, it was different. I think that you are too young to appreciate how beautifully different it was."

"I am not so young. Old enough to know the risks that you take. I fear that you will get with child. I must tell you that if you do, it will change nothing. You are mine to give—"

"I am *mine own* to give, and while I can, I give myself to him. If I birth a bastard, he will take the child, and raise him stronger and freer than I ever could. I will not deny you your right to give my hand, in any alliance that reclaiming our family honor requires. But my heart rejects such worldly chains, and wears another by my own choosing."

"You are half mad yourself. You doom yourself to un-happiness with such notions. And you condemn me to be the agent of your misery."

"Ah, Mark, you are so ignorant. When I break this, I will not really give up the important things. It did not be-gin when we made love. It will not end when we stop." She turned back to the horizon. "Go and prepare. Learn what you must to make our old lives whole again. But un-til those lives or his tear us apart, I will take what I can get, and give what I have chosen to give."

Joan had told Mark that she was contented, but in truth she was not. She and Rhys lived out their love under a hanging sword, knowing that one day it would drop and sever them forever.

It made their time bittersweet, and the nightly embrace painfully poignant. Even the pleasure was shadowed by the anticipation of loss. She could not find abandon any-more. She could not lose herself in the present now that the future surrounded her. Too often as she lay in his arms a soulful melancholy overwhelmed her.

Her whole world seemed to share the heavy anticipa-tion. There was a mood in the household that she could not name. A palpable expectation filled the air. It was as if everyone waited for something. It reminded her of those days after the abdication, when her father and Piers and the knights always seemed to be listening for the sounds of an army.

At first she had assumed that it was concern for her that caused it. But when days passed and no riders followed from Westminster in pursuit of the tiler seen with Guy Leighton that day, the mood still persisted. She told her-self that she imagined it, and that her own conflicted wait-ing, her own impatience to finish what had started and her own prayers that time would stand still for her and Rhys, was the source of it. But it came from the others too. The waiting cloaked Addis, and even Moira.

Then one day it suddenly disappeared. A new mood spread in the household. A silent hum of excitement filled the air.

Mark came in the late evening to tell her that the waiting was over, and that Addis and the King and a few others planned to arrest Mortimer at Nottingham Castle, where Queen Isabella had moved her retinue.

"Isabella and Mortimer have summoned Edward to Nottingham as though he were some servant. They want him to explain rumors they have heard that he plots against them. I say that is damn bold of them. He is the King, not Mortimer. So he will go, but sooner than they expect, and he will settle with them both."

He paced with excitement, spilling the tale. "I'm to go, too. Not into the castle, but to Nottingham. I will serve as one of Sir Addis's squires, and be nearby so he can present me to the King when it is over."

"It sounds very risky. Just a few men, you say. They will be very vulnerable."

"It is brilliant. It will be glorious."

"It will be a bloodbath. They will be horribly outnumbered inside those walls. Mortimer will order his guard to cut them to pieces. With Edward dead, he will have the barons declare the Queen the official monarch, and continue as he has done."

"You do not understand warfare."

"You do not describe a war. You speak of a band of thieves stealing into a home."

Joan paced around her chamber, imagining this bold scheme easily going awry, agitated by an unpleasant excitement.

"What if they fail? What happens to you then?"

"I will be with Addis's retinue. I will be safe."

"If Addis is killed, no one in his retinue will be safe."

"Stop being such a woman. It is Addis and Rhys who face the danger, not me."

That stopped her pacing. Abruptly.

"Rhys? What has he to do with this?"

Mark looked too much like someone who knew that he had spoken unwisely.

"He is going with you?" Oddly enough, that idea made her calmer, not that a mason could protect Mark better than a band of knights.

"Nay. He departs for Nottingham at dawn. We will wait some days more."

"Why does he go at all?"

The toes of his boots suddenly fascinated him. "Don't know. Something about a project for the King."

It made no sense. Any project for the King could wait until after this action.

Mark pivoted and aimed for the door.

She intercepted him. "How much do you know of this plan?"

"What I told you."

She glared.

"A bit more."

"Tell me the bit more. *Now*. Why does Rhys go to Nottingham?"

He tried to look mature and superior. She was in no mood to play to his pride. She grabbed his hair the way she used to when he misbehaved as a boy.

"Ow! Damn! Jesus, I'm not a—"

"Then tell me what I ask."

He disengaged his locks and stepped back, indignant and embarrassed. "I've already told you more than I should. If you want to learn all of it, speak to Addis. As for why Rhys is coming, I expect it is because this was his idea to start."

He dodged her, and ran out of the chamber before she could make him explain.

She grabbed a lit candle and followed on his heels. She aimed for a chamber in the nearby south tower.

The door was not barred, but the chamber was dark. Her flame shed vague light on a mound of leather sacks heaped against the wall near the threshold.

Silence greeted her, but she knew that Rhys was there. She felt his presence, as solid and strong as the rock that he carved.

The bed where she slept in his arms was empty. She raised the light. It barely penetrated to the far wall, but it found him there. He stood with arms braced on either side of the narrow window, face turned to the moonlight and the cool breezes flowing in.

He wore only his hide work leggings. His pose made the strong muscles of his shoulders and back taut and defined.

He sensed her arrival. It showed in a subtle flexing of his body and a sudden change in the air. He turned and rested against the wall, arms crossed over his chest.

Joan gestured to the sacks. "It looks like you are leaving."

"Aye. At dawn. I was going to tell you tonight."

"Where are you going?"

"Away. It is time. We both knew the day would come when we had to part. Where I go when that happens does not matter."

"It does if you journey to Nottingham. Mark told me what Edward plans to do."

"The boy still has much to learn if he speaks so freely."

He was not making it easy. He acted distant, as though he was hiding something. Aye, he had intended to tell her, but not all of it. He had been planning to lie.

"Why do you go to Nottingham now? The King's project can wait until this is over."

"It can wait, but it does not need to. That is how it is with craftsmen. Knights and kings fight their battles, but we must continue earning our bread."

"I do not think that you go only to earn your bread."

"Perhaps you forget who I am. What I am."

She dripped some wax onto the top of the chamber's lone chest, and pressed the candle in it to stand. "You are a man who helped depose a king. I think that tomorrow you will be a man setting out to depose a usurper. Please tell me what your role will be. I want to know what danger you will face."

He turned back to the window. "Very little danger. The role is a small one."

A knot of fear had formed in her chest, and his confirmation only made it thicker. She went to him and embraced him from behind, laying her head on his back. "Tell me. Please."

He hesitated, then moved to bring her forward under his arm. He still gazed into the night. "There are passageways underground that will permit Edward to approach unseen. Trusted men will be at the inner gate and will let him pass. But once at the keep, he will be vulnerable. I will make a diversion, that is all. Something to distract the guards while Edward reaches the Queen's chambers. It should not be difficult."

"If the King's plan fails, it will be known that you were involved."

"Possibly."

"Certainly. Mark said that this move was your idea. How long have you been scheming with Addis?"

"Not so long."

"Since before we met?"

He did not answer, but she looked at his profile and knew the truth.

"Why didn't you tell me?"

"I expected it to come to nought, and did not want you disappointed. And I was sworn to secrecy. The fewer who know of such things the better."

He spoke so calmly, as though he did not comprehend his risks. She could think of nothing else but the deadly danger he faced.

He would leave at dawn. The hanging sword would finally fall, and he would be severed from her forever. If this rash plan worked, their worlds would separate. If it failed . . .

Bile rose to her throat. Images invaded her head, and the old ones that had plagued her for three years transformed into new ones. Ghastly and hideous ones.

Blood in a yard, and bodies twisted in death. A sword falling, and eyes defiant to the end. Rhys's eyes.

Except it might not come so mercifully. A king might lead this action, but a queen would mete the punishment if it failed. Addis might survive, but there would be a terrible death for a common craftsman who dared to plot against a royal person.

An unholy fear took possession of her, turning her limp. A new dread, more terrible and more raw than any she had known these last years, left her cold and shaking.

She had to stop him.

"I do not want you to do this."

"That is another reason why I did not tell you."

"I entreat you not to. It is not your—"

"Not my place?"

She would worry about his pride later. "Aye, not your place, nor your battle."

"I remember a fiery-eyed woman telling me that anyone can stand against injustice, even masons. And it is my battle because of you, if for nothing else. I may not be the champion you sought, but I can do my part."

Her heart glowed that he loved her enough to risk his life to make it right for her. But fear for him also sliced like knives, shredding her composure. She pressed her face against his shoulder. "Wait a day more. One day only. A little more time . . ." A little more time to hold him, and make memories to sustain her. A little more time to convince him not to go.

"One day, then another, and another . . . It will be no easier to leave you a day or a month hence. The sooner I get to Nottingham, the better chance this will unfold as planned."

His calm resolve made her frantic. "You do me no honor with this."

"And you do me no honor in trying to dissuade me."

"I do not want it from you." She tried to make her voice cold and firm, but it came out a whimper.

He looked at her and smoothed his hand over her cheek. "It is not just about you, Joan. That is a part of it, but it is not all of it."

"That does not reassure me. If it were just about me, I might be able to stop you," she muttered miserably, wiping her eyes.

"Do not waste the night that way. It will not happen."

She heard the decision in his tone. Recognized it. Nay, it would not happen. He stood where she had recently stood, and his path would not be diverted.

Rhys waited as she had, for the dawn. He faced an ordeal, and knew its potential cost. He had been savoring the breeze and the night when she entered, and dwelling in that poignant present that only exists when one anticipates no future.

The light showed enough of his intensity for her to know where his soul was tonight. She remembered her own dark vigil. Empathy stirred her love, and her heart swelled with the desire to protect and comfort.

She looked at him. All of him. Slowly and carefully, so that she would always remember. He appeared so splendid to her. Handsome and hard, hewn with dignity and strength. His chiseled expression showed no weakness, but his humanity still had its needs.

His words made it explicit. "I thank you for trying, Joan. I will cherish the evidence that you put my life above your quest. But I do not want to speak of this anymore. Nor of the parting that awaits. Nor of anything but love."

He stepped behind her, and began untying the lacing on her back.

He worked the lacing slowly, enjoying how his slow progress made her tremble, like a murmur whispering through her body and the night. He might not have noticed but for his raw alertness to everything. And so he also felt the sadness in her, and her aching awareness that this would be the last time.

"I wish that we were still in London. Or at the pond behind the pines," she said wistfully.

He smoothed his hand up the gap he had made, and relished the warmth beneath the thin shift's fabric. She arched ever so subtly to his touch. "Aye. But this is where we are now, and we can not change that."

He eased the gown off her shoulders. It slid down her body into a heap on the floor. He went to work on her braid. She did not turn. She knew that he wanted to savor every moment.

"I will always regret that I brought you into this, Rhys. You were content before you met me. And safe."

"Not so content. And maybe too safe. I was lacking purpose, and envied you yours, whatever it was. Protecting you gave me one. Regret nothing, pretty dove. A man who has nothing worth fighting for is not really alive."

He set her hair over her shoulder, and bent close to kiss her nape. Then her shoulder, while his fingers slid the shift off them. It skimmed down. "Do not move. You are so beautiful, and I want to look at you in this moonlight."

The moon gave her a pale glow in the darkness. Lovely. Ethereal. He would worship this image of her forever. She stood as still as a statue, but it was not stone that his hands glossed while they followed her curves. Her warmth spoke of her life and spirit and need, and her skin quivered beneath his touch, as if her pulse responded.

She was so beautifully formed. He kissed her back, to honor all that she was. Joan, daughter of Marcus de Brecon. Joan the tiler. Tonight she was still both those women. For the next few hours, at least, she was still in his world.

He kissed lower, along the entrancing, delicate bumps of her spine. He sank to his knees as his kisses descended. He took the softness of her hips in his hands and pressed his mouth to the round swells.

She wobbled. Her stillness disappeared and her body flexed with her response. The softest moans mixed with her breathing. She grasped the window ledge, bending slightly, steadying herself. He licked and nipped the tops of her thighs. With a gasping "aye" she parted them, and he let his tongue flick and explore.

Her scent made the sweet mist of desire cloud his head. The demand for more pounded through him.

He caressed her legs up to her hips. "Turn, love. I want to taste you fully."

She faced him, leaning against the wall, looking down with glistening eyes. The light from the window and the candle played over her breasts and arms and legs, creating fluid, mysterious shadows. He raised his hands and caressed as softly as the night air flowed. He glided his touch over her chin and down her neck. A flush warmed the path, and a lively pulse beat through the connection. He glossed lower, to the full softness of her breasts, and reveled in her sharp intake of breath. He eased her toward him, bending her until he could kiss her lips.

Her hungry response said where she was. She clutched his shoulders and kissed back more aggressively than she ever had before. Her little assault sent desire on a rampage through him. He moved his mouth to her neck and then to her hovering, beckoning breasts.

He teased at her with his tongue, and her sounds of pleasure filled his ears, his head, his blood. She arched and pressed forward, begging for more, her fingers clawing his shoulders, her head thrown back in abandon.

He leashed the raging impulse to rise and immediately claim what waited. Removing her hold, he set her back against the wall. Kneeling closely, he kissed lower. Over her stomach, around her navel. Lower still.

He reached down for her ankle, but did not have to guide her. She pressed against the wall, and looked down with smoldering eyes. "Aye, fully," she whispered as she bent her knee and rested her foot on his shoulder.

No thought. No restraint. Cradling her hips in his hands, he kissed up her thigh to his goal and licked. Her ascending cries and pulsing flesh absorbed his consciousness. She rocked slowly, rhythmically as he explored deeper and the hunger turned primal. He kept her on the edge, frantic with a need that aroused him more than her taste, before he finally sent her screaming into a glorious release.

He rose and crushed her to him. Her scent and gasping breaths immersed him in a cloud of sensation. Her feminine softness yielded limply into his clasping hold.

He took her hand to guide her to the bed. "Come lie

with me now. Let the husband of your heart love you while he can."

To his surprise, she resisted and stood her ground. "We will love each other, not just you me." She caressed down to the closure of his leggings. "After such a start, my blood is up. Do not expect me to be shy."

His garment loosened and she brushed it down his hips. She looked him in the eyes with a new confidence. Desire scorched through him like a brushfire.

She stepped back and regarded his body frankly. There was a promise in that inspection that stunned him, and also pushed his craving higher. The memory of being inside her swept him, and he almost pinned her against the wall to make it real.

Her gaze dropped to his phallus. She reached out and gently ran the fingertips of both hands up and down. She had touched him before, but not boldly like this. It made the pleasure maddening.

She smiled impishly. Seductively. Her finger circled. "I am wondering if I might yet be able to convince you to stay."

"If you plead your cause like that, you are welcome to try."

She laughed. His heart leapt at the sound. He had expected a soulful night, imbued with her sadness. And his. He was grateful for the sign that there would be joy, too.

And then she surprised him further. She bent to offer something that she had not done before. Her crown dipped. Time slowed. His body silently begged for it with a pounding anticipation. The sensation of her lips kissing him, and of her tongue slyly flicking, almost undid his control.

It was just a taste, no more. A torturous promise. She kissed up his body, and offered her lips to his. "Not now, I think. Not yet. I want to play first."

He grabbed her in a hold too rough and kissed her with a mouth too hungry. "It might be a dangerous game for you, pretty dove. Especially tonight."

"You can never be dangerous to me. I want us to feel everything together and be alive in each other. I do not think it will be dangerous at all, only delicious and deep."

"If we are to feel everything together, I have some work to do, since I am crazed with the want of you but you are already content."

"Not so much work. I find the contentment passes."

He would make sure it did. Quickly. He wanted her vulnerable to the pleasure. He wanted her shaking from passion as he now shook, and full of the silent howl that demanded more and more.

He lifted her and carried her to the bed and laid her down. The sight of her there, naked and willing, made his desire tight and chaotic.

Her arms rose up to receive him in an elegant gesture of invitation. He joined her, and their closeness soothed his hunger a little. The unity of skin and warmth enchanted his soul.

He wanted the night to last forever, and he tried to slow time. He caressed her smooth skin until he felt her rising to his hand, impatient for more. His touch circled her breasts eternally until her sighs grew fretful. Even then he gave her pleasure with grazing strokes and tantalizing touches, and waited for her to again reach the intensity of need that obscures the world.

He ran his tongue around the velvet tip of her breast. Her arms fell to either side of her head as she arched and offered herself. He flicked and sucked and aroused her other breast with his hand, and reveled in triumph when utter abandon claimed her.

Different this time. She proved that at once. She slid away and pushed him down. Eyes bright with passion and confidence, she straddled his hips and sat back on his thighs.

She looked glorious and wild and statuesque in her beauty. The light played on her golden hair streaming around her body. Her breasts peeked from beneath the curtain.

She pushed her hair back so he could look. And he did. At all of her, all the parts and lines. The warmest part snuggled him closely, and he could feel the pulse and moisture that his looking created.

The tips of her breasts bid him with tight, seductive promise. He guided her down so he could taste them again. Not for her pleasure this time, but for his.

He lost himself in it. The sounds of her passion became a musical cloud in which he drifted higher and higher. Her body rocked slowly, just enough to brush his phallus again and again. He reached down and stroked her cleft, and her cries grew frenzied. He sensed her need coil and begin to beg.

She eased away, and sat back again. "I said that we would love each other tonight, and not just you me. You tempt me to forget my pledge." She smoothed caresses down his chest. "I think that I know how to do it. I believe that I can guess what you want."

She dipped forward, and kissed him, and then moved her lips to his neck. Different this time, since she did not follow his lead. A subtle change quivered through the pleasure. Her boldness made it more erotic—for both of them.

Her kisses moved to his chest, and her tongue to his nipple. All the while her hands touched in tantalizing, feathery caresses over his body.

The desire turned keen and decisive. He reached to flip her and take control.

She retreated from his hold, and sat back again. "You are too hasty. I have promises to keep."

She looked down at his phallus rising in front of her belly. She gently scratched one fingernail from its base to its tip.

She glanced in his eyes. "Aye?"

"Please."

Her explorations built a delirium of sensations. Her playing brought him to the brink time and again. When she swung off his thighs, and turned to use her mouth, he thought that he would die from it.

He almost succumbed. He barely retreated from the finish being drawn out of him. The bigger desires of this night pulled him back, and he reached for her.

He laid her on her back and spread her legs and knelt between them. He put his hand to her and slowly touched until her cries filled the little chamber. She bent her knees and raised her hips. "Come in me. Please. Now. I want to feel you inside me."

He pressed her knees to her chest so that she was open and waiting. He rose up and stroked in as deeply as possible.

The chaos cleared for a moment, and profound contentment glowed like the sun. Nothing and no one intruded on the light. He had worried that their parting would shadow it this time, and was relieved that it wasn't so.

The calm did not last long. A penetrating, incessant desire took control. He rose up on his arms and withdrew, and looked down to watch her body accept him again. He made the thrusts a slow, long, series of joinings, and each one seemed deeper and tighter than the last. He wanted to stroke into her velvet warmth forever, and hear the contentment moan out of her for ten lifetimes.

It turned insane at the end, hard and grasping and noisy. Her clawing hold and crying breaths urged no gentleness, and the power in him overwhelmed all restraint.

The release came like a cataclysm, rending his consciousness.

He experienced nothing physical for a long moment. Not even her body beneath him. Her breath and scent were there, and her heart and love, but nothing that had substance.

Slowly the world intruded. Its forms reemerged. He found himself sprawled on her, wrapped by her arms and legs, her lips pressed to his temple.

A slight moisture slid between their faces. He rose up and looked into her glistening eyes.

Her smile quivered from her emotion. He kissed her, to seal and savor what they had shared. He moved to her side, and tucked her against him.

The passing hours were not desperate. They held each other in blissful silence, and then again in passion. She urged him to take everything he could imagine, and gave all that she could. He had never known such peace as he experienced in that borrowed bed. It was the night's unfettered union with her that caused that. A man can not fear death while he is dwelling in paradise.

As sleep slowly claimed them, she rested in his arms, her body sprawled over him, her cheek to his chest. "I did not convince you to stay, though, did I?" she murmured drowsily. "I did not really expect to."

He only kissed her head gently in response, and awaited the dawn in the sanctuary of her arms.

Rhys packed the wagon lightly. It would appear odd if he did not bring it, but he wanted no extra weight slowing his way.

The castle yard was quiet and empty except for a few yawning servants. One could sense the household stretching as it woke to the dawn, but the latent silence of the recent night still hung in the air. He hitched the horse, and draped the reins over a post. Then he turned back to the keep, to go and take his leave of Joan.

Probably his final leave. Whether good winds or ill waited at the end of this journey, there would be no more nights like the last. He was determined not to think about that when he kissed her on parting. He did not want their joy in each other to be marred by sorrow.

A draped figure appeared at the top of the keep steps. A woman, head and body obscured by a cloak, descended toward him. He thought at first it might be Moira, but the column of fabric was too small.

She raised her head and the cloak fell back. Smiling broadly, Joan came down to meet him.

He wished that she had waited inside. He had left her in the bed, and had promised to return. He had wanted his last sight of her to be as he had known her during the night.

She paused to kiss him, then walked over to the wagon. Something thick and bulky emerged from under her cloak. She dropped a sack in among his, then turned, looking too much like a woman braced for an argument that she planned to win.

He went to her and glared down at the new baggage. "What is that?"

"A sack with some clothes."

"I left no garments behind."

"They are mine. I am coming with you."

"The hell you are. You are staying here, where you will be safe."

"I will be safe with you. I always have been."

"I ride into a lion's den, woman. You are the last person who would be safe there."

"I am unknown to them. If anyone suspected me of Guy's death, we would have been caught on the road. The messenger heard no news of a search for me, or of anyone with my description. Even if Mortimer sees me, he will not know whom he meets."

"I do not risk you, and that is my last word on it. Now kiss me sweetly, so I can be on my way."

She crossed her arms. "I am coming. You are to do the same work as at Westminster. You needed a tiler there, and you will need one at Nottingham, too. We are partners in the tile works, and it is fitting that I should be with you."

"You are not coming, Joan. If you will not obey me, I will tell Addis to lock you away."

"I do not think that he will. I have already spoken to him, and he agrees the risk is a small one."

He aimed for the steps. "Then I will explain it more clearly."

"If you insist on questioning his judgment, you will find him in the solar. He is still abed with Moira, and I do not think that he welcomed my intrusion, if you know what I mean. I doubt that he will appreciate yours any more."

The insinuation made him pause. "Then we will wait until he finishes what he is about."

She embraced him, and looked up with beseeching eyes. It annoyed him to no end that she had him weakening at once. "Rhys, do not insist on thwarting me. My brother will be there, and I can not just sit here worrying about him and you."

"Moira will be sitting here. You can worry together, if you must worry at all."

"Moira has children. If she did not, she would surely come. She reminded Addis that she had joined him when he came to retake his home. It was that which swayed him to my plan, I think."

That was all he needed, Moira conspiring against him.

"If I do not leave with you, I will follow with Addis and

Mark. I have waited too long for this, and I will see my family's honor restored when this is done. Denying me will not stop me."

She pressed a little closer, so that her rebellion was imbued with a silent argument that was much more compelling than the verbal one.

"I will come, one way or another. I am resolved."

He knew what that meant, and saw the truth of it in her expression. He glanced up to the solar. The lord and lady making love in there would not be of any help in this.

"I will not enter the castle. I will stay at an inn, and wait for you to bring me news. We will be together at least, on the journey and then at night in Nottingham. I wasted so much time with you, please do not forbid me that which is left."

Speaking of their nights together defeated him. The chance to prolong them, even for a week, proved too seductive. His heart said that the risk would not be so great, even though his better judgment still insisted that any risk was too much.

"You are to stay in the town, away from the castle."

"Of course."

"When Addis arrives, you will wait with your brother, and not interfere."

"Certainly."

"If I sense any danger at all, you will leave at once. You must swear to obey me in this."

"I will be dutiful, master."

He helped her onto the wagon, and climbed up to take the reins. She smiled with contentment.

Master, hell. She had worked him like the clay of a statue.

And he was glad for it.

CHAPTER 25

RHYS WAS IN Nottingham Castle for four days before Mortimer even realized he was there. The King's commission had been enough to gain him entrance, and he busied himself with the project, staying invisible among the other craftsmen and servants. If not for the arrival of a chamberlain to ready Edward's apartments for his summoned visit, he might have never been noticed.

The call from Mortimer came the next day, as he prepared to return to the inn where Joan waited.

The great man was not alone. A knot of his knights filled a dark corner of his chamber where they played with dice. Rhys glanced at them only long enough to count five.

Addis could handle five. The sword of Barrowburgh was known to cut a wide swath.

"Another commission? You are fortunate in the King's favor," Mortimer mused upon hearing the reason for his presence.

"He approved of my work at Westminster, and seeks to

favor his wife with this, not me. I thought it unwise to re-fuse."

"Does he know of the service that you have done for me?"

"He surely knows of the work that I have done on the fabric of buildings, and knows that some was for the Queen. But I do not think that he suspects anything else. A master builder does not refuse his king's project, that is all that I meant."

"Perhaps you knew that he is coming here, three days hence."

"I did not know that. I was given the commission only, not any confidences. Kings do not discuss their movements with masons."

The reminder of his lowly status seemed to help. The vague suspicion fell from Mortimer's expression, and he lost interest. He did not even give a dismissal. His attention merely wandered away.

Rhys waited until his presence became no more significant than that of a piece of furniture, then strolled to the door.

As he did so, laughter burst from amidst the gambling knights.

He glanced toward the sound just as the knot loosened. A beam of light from a nearby window sliced through the gloom, illuminating a crouching figure scooping up some winnings.

The knight's head tilted back, revealing a full view of his face. His eyes lost their mirth and grew alert, as if they sensed something amiss. His gaze swung through the chamber, stopping at the craftsman standing near the door. His lids narrowed in scrutiny, and then something thoughtful and dark shadowed his expression.

Rhys continued his calm retreat, but his blood raced and his heart beat with alarm.

Guy Leighton was alive.

Somehow Rhys managed not to bolt through the castle like a madman. He headed directly for the yard and gate, all the while cursing himself in a hundred different ways.

He should have made sure that bleeding body had taken a death blow. He should have found the knife and thrust it into Leighton's heart.

He should have chained Joan up at Barrowburgh.

No wonder there had been no search. Guy would not tell Mortimer who his attacker had been. He would not admit that his lust had permitted the children of Marcus de Brecon to live—children who could testify about the massacre carried out on Mortimer's command.

Nay, he would keep silent, and make the search a quiet one.

How much had his inquiries revealed? Had he learned that Joan lived in London with a mason? Did he know about the tile yard, and her work on the King's apartments? He need only ask the right questions to learn all of it. He was probably the kind of man who could ferret out information.

Even if he had not, Joan was not safe here. Rhys had to get her far from Nottingham. Addis and Edward would have to move without him.

He found her in the tiny chamber that they shared at an inn on the town's main market street. She sat at the window, watching the bustle down below.

He walked over and pulled the shutters closed. He reached for a leather sack and began stuffing her garments into it.

"We are leaving. Now."

"What has happened?"

"Guy Leighton is not dead. I just saw him with Mortimer."

She paled. "You are sure? You saw him only once, briefly. Perhaps—"

"That brief seeing seared my mind. It was Leighton, and he looked very hale and fit for a dead man."

"It can not be. All of that blood—"

"Not enough, it appears. Or maybe he is truly a demon, and can not be killed with a knife." He dropped his tools in the sack with her clothes, and slid his dagger in, too. "We leave the rest. I do not want to delay." He threw her cloak over her shoulders and took her arm to urge her along.

"You are too hasty. We need not flee, and you need not abandon the King's plan because of this. Guy can not know that I am here. Addis should arrive tomorrow, and the King as well. One day more and it will be over. I will stay in this chamber, and not even open the shutters until then."

He remembered the thoughtful veil that had fallen over Guy's eyes. It had been the look someone gets when two halves of a mental chain suddenly link together. "One day is too long. It is a chance that I will not take. Nor will I permit it of you. Come with me now. You promised your obedience in this, and I command it of you."

He hurried her out of the inn and down the alley to the stable where the horse had been bedded. When the groom began to lead the animal to the wagon, Rhys stopped him. They would leave that behind, too. He wanted nothing to slow their departure from Nottingham.

He saddled the horse himself while the groom fit the bridle. Joan waited, arms crossed over her chest and foot tapping with annoyance.

He took the reins to lead the horse out of the stable. Her hand closed over his, stopping him.

"You abandon the wagon and your garments. You abandon your solemn word, too. For a man with big ideas, your concerns are very small suddenly."

"You are not a small concern. Not to my mind and my heart."

"Nor are you to me. My heart is glad that you want to leave. I am relieved that in seeking my safety, you too will be safe. But if Edward fails because we fled, it will be a bitter draft for us both."

"I do not seek to compromise his action. For your sake, if not the bigger reasons, I pray that he succeeds. But Leighton's breathing body changes everything, to my mind. On my own, I would take any chance, but if any harm comes to you, it will be more than bitter. It will be like poison."

"And it will be poison to me if my demand to accompany you here means the cause is lost."

"It will not be lost. They do not need me."

"They desperately need you. You have told me the numbers inside those walls. A diversion can well mean the difference. If Addis spoke lightly of your role, it was only to permit you to refuse with no embarrassment, since in failure your fate will be worse than his. You know the truth of this. They will be much more vulnerable if you do not do what is expected."

Aye, he knew it. It was why he had not refused, and what he had learned since arriving in Nottingham had only confirmed that this quick action might end badly. Five guarded Mortimer in his chamber, and fifteen more waited in the hall and chambers.

Joan's hand still covered his. It closed more tightly, and she touched his face with the other. "If you command me to leave, I will do so. But if you choose to stay, there will be no blame on you if I come to harm."

She demanded a choice that he did not want to make. His mind raced with the options and their consequences. Her gentle touch coaxed him to weigh carefully, and his few moments of deliberation seemed much longer then they must have been. The fetid smell of horse and the sweet odor of hay rose around them while he gazed into her earnest eyes and faced the horror of balancing her safety against the bigger goals.

Something sad passed in her expression. She weighed and balanced, too. Her own love's desire to protect him faced down her need to see Mortimer broken.

They made their choices in the same instant, but Joan spoke first.

"I am being foolish. You are right." She released his hand and stepped aside. "Let us leave this town. Let us flee the realm if necessary."

"We will leave the town, but not the realm, or even the county. I will find someplace away from here to hide you, and return on my own. It is your safety that matters, not mine. I will see to it, and come back to finish this."

An adorable, troubled pout played over her mouth. "I should have kept silent, if your solution is to separate us."

"Your silence would not have blinded me. Once we were a mile outside the gate, I would have seen it. With your safety secured, my fear for you would have dimmed enough for me to think straight."

Rhys circled her shoulders with his arm, and led the horse toward the alley. She leaned against him as they walked, and he let himself savor the supple length of her body pressed to his side.

A few steps of unity. A brief stroll of intimacy. He closed his eyes and pressed a kiss to the silk of her hair and let his heart feel all that it had ever felt.

The light behind his eyelids subtly dimmed. A darkness intruded on the glow that they shared.

Her body went rigid under his arm. Her steps halted with a jerk.

He opened his eyes and faced the alley. The entry to the stable was blocked.

Guy Leighton stood there, with four of his men.

CHAPTER 26

JOAN TORE A SWATH of fabric from the sleeve of her gown and gently wiped some blood from Rhys's face. He flinched, and then grimaced when the reaction aggravated other injuries.

There had been no defense against those blows in the stable. With two men holding him to the wall, he had been left with only his anger and strength to shield him.

"You are sorely wounded."

"I am sore, but not so wounded. I will live."

Aye, he would live, for a day or two. Guy wanted him alive, so that he could take his time while he made the mason pay for the insult of stealing what he considered his property.

Only the dimmest light leaked through some airholes bored high in one wall of the stone cell. They were not in the keep. Guy had thrown them into a cavity buried in the foundations of the castle's inner wall.

Rhys carefully shifted his position against the damp stones where they sat. She felt his hurt as if it racked her own body.

"He does not know why we are here," he said. "Mortimer might see a pattern to it, but Guy does not, and he has hidden us here so that his lord does not learn about you."

"He may not know why we are here, but he has you all the same."

"In less than a day it will be over. Edward should arrive in Nottingham tonight. He will move soon after dawn. Guy will fall with his lord. One day only, Joan. Do not be distraught."

How could she not be distraught when the man she loved sat battered beside her? Those blows had been methodical and punishing.

And there would be more.

"In his own way, I think that he cares for you. Enough to risk Mortimer's displeasure, which is no small thing for such as Guy."

"Whatever he feels for me, it is not a normal emotion."

"Nay, not normal. Not simple lust. He senses your strength, so making you submit has a special pleasure. I had not guessed that before. He did not punish me with the beating so much as you. He knew that blows to your own body would not defeat you."

She had been forced to watch. She recoiled from the memory of it. She would have gladly changed places with Rhys. Physical pain would be easy to bear compared with the torture of seeing him brutalized.

He lifted her hand to his mouth. He gently pressed his swollen lips to it. "You do not bargain for me, Joan. You do not go to him."

It broke her heart that he knew what this was about. "I had thought you too far gone to have heard Guy's demand. He spoke for my ears alone."

"I heard nothing, but I see the man's mind. If he merely sought revenge for your knife, we would both be dead now. If he wanted to rape you first, he could have taken you there in the stable, or forced you back to his bed in the keep. A simpler man would have, but he is not simple, is he? It was not like that before, and it will not be now, even though you almost killed him. He still wants the illusion that you are willing. He likes to pretend there is more between you than there is."

Her stomach turned as old memories loomed that proved the truth of that. Guy, solicitous and generous. Guy, wooing her as if they were lovers. His insistent caresses had been more degrading than rape. In defense her body had learned to feel nothing at all.

She had forgotten about that with Rhys, and had finally broken down the wall that had preserved her from humiliation.

"You do not go to him. No matter what happens with me, you do not."

"The last man who commanded me thus perished under Guy's sword. For nought. He merely made my brother the next prize."

"Your brother is safe now. Do what you must to save yourself, but do not let him use me to break your will. Do not forbid me the honor that you allowed that last man."

The vague light disappeared as night fell. They did not speak, and she hoped that he slept. She could not embrace him because of his wounds, but her love tried to surround him and her hand stayed in his the whole time.

She prayed that Guy would forget them. She begged the saints to have Mortimer require his best man's attendance as a guard. As the time passed and Rhys's breathing became more regular and deep, she dared to hope that there would be no more torture.

It was not to be. In the hours before dawn the stones subtly quaked with soundless echoes. The ghosts of approaching movements disturbed the crude peace that they shared. She gritted her teeth, and gazed through the blackness to the door.

A key grated harshly in the lock. She barely swallowed the plea for mercy that wanted to cry out of her.

The hand holding hers squeezed. "You do not go to him."

Cramps pulled Rhys out of the comforting oblivion. Bolts of red streaked through the blackness.

Pain. It made him come alert too fast, and his body doubled instinctively to protect itself. That only made it worse, and his eyes jerked open to a dark void that might have been the bottom of an abyss.

In the misery of renewed consciousness, he noticed nothing but the pain. He forced himself to check all his parts, testing for the damage. Relieved that he was whole, he eased onto his back and slowly pushed himself up.

It was then, as the shrieks dulled and his mind found some accommodation to his condition, that he realized that he was alone.

He did not need a light to know it. He did not bother saying her name. He was as sure of it as he had been the morning after they had first made love.

A new pain cut through him, making the others insignificant. It scored his heart with repeated gashes. It would not stop. It just kept slicing.

He gripped the wall, and forced himself to stand. The new blows were not enough to keep him down. That only increased the anguish. He should be half dead at least.

Joan must have struck her bargain soon after Guy arrived.

He should have been stronger. If he had stayed conscious, she never would have done it.

He cursed loudly, at her and himself and at the man

who toyed with them. His voice thundered off the stones. He imagined her with Guy, and a primitive roar tore out of him.

He forced himself to move. He beat back the pain, and tested his strength. He discovered that the hurt was not enough to stop him. His muscles had been battered, but not torn. Carrying stone and swinging a hammer had given him a shield of sorts.

The vaguest shadows emerged from the blackness. Tiny streams of grey light filtered through the air holes. The first glow of dawn began offering subtle illumination to his prison.

How long had he been out? How long since she left? How long had Guy had her in his power?

He tried not to contemplate that, but his mind filled with Guy's taunts. Each swing of a fist had been followed by descriptions of what had happened during those weeks before she escaped. Guy had sowed images that now tortured worse than all the bodily wounds.

The images filled him with a rage that obscured his condition. It dulled the sores and blocked the suffering. He grabbed the madness and held onto it. When that door opened again, he would kill the man, no matter how many swords came at him.

He rested against a wall and waited. Every fiber of his body prepared. He would grab that devil by the neck and haul him back to hell with his own two hands and all of the weapons on earth would not defeat him before he finished it.

He centered his will. He garnered all of his strength to attack. He waited for the sound of the key in the lock.

It came sooner than he expected. A new burst of fury crashed through him as metal clanked against metal. The noise heralded more than his own fate. It meant that Guy had finished with Joan for now. Her memories had been given life again. The fears had been realized.

She might even be dead.

He slid to where he could attack quickly, choosing a corner that an entering torch would not illuminate.

The door pushed open. A dark shadow entered. He was halfway to grabbing it before it penetrated his outrage that it was small and slim and alone, and that no boot steps rang off the stones.

Joan.

She bent low, peering along the walls for him.

"Rhys? Where are you?"

"Here, behind you."

She turned, but he could not see her face in the dark. He was not sure that he wanted to.

"Can you walk? There is not much time. We must go quickly."

"I can walk." He could fly if he had to.

She slipped out the door and he followed. They stole down the low passageway lined with other cells.

"Did he give you the key?"

"I did not count on such generosity. I stole the key. I smashed a warming brick against his head and took it. He is not dead, though, and may awaken, so we must leave at once."

A warming brick. From a bed. "I told you not to bargain for me."

"If I had not, you would not have lived to the dawn. He wore a dagger when he came, and unsheathed it when you fell. The choice was mine to make, not yours."

The images invaded again, and the rage burned.

They reached the small portal that gave out to the yard. He cracked it open. Two knights were strolling by.

He touched her arm to tell her to wait.

Her hand covered his and pressed firmly. "It was not what you think. I pretended compliance so that he would drop his guard, but nothing happened. I may have been smiling when I felt for the brick, but he had not touched me yet."

She spoke earnestly. Maybe she told the truth. Maybe not. She would never let him know if she had bought his life with more than a smile.

"All the same, you should not have gone to him. Not because of me."

"Scold me once we are away from here. Right now, getting outside these walls is more important. Do you think that we might just walk through the gate? He told only a few of his retainers about us, and the guard should not stop us."

"You will walk through. Go to the town and find your brother and the knights who came with Addis. Dawn breaks, and I must do something before I join you."

"Nay. You are no use to them in your state."

"My state is not so bad. I find that I have the strength of a horse despite my injuries. No pain enters my mind, Joan. There is no room in there for it, because of the fury that owns me."

"Put your anger aside and find some sense. Guy may be looking for you. I did not hurt him badly, I fear, and even now he might be on his way here. You must come with me, and we must go now."

"I hope that he is looking. If he is not, I will find him instead."

"God have mercy, Rhys. I beg you, flee with me while we can. I want no revenge against him. That part of the past died for me. Our love killed it. I will not risk you to its horrible power. It does not matter to me anymore. I do not care."

"*I* care. It matters to *me*."

He opened the door a body's width. Light streamed between them, and he could see her distress and fear. He caressed her face, and savored her soft, smooth skin beneath his fingers. He bent to kiss her lips.

He lingered an instant, then pushed her into the light. "To the gate, darling. I command it of you, as the wife of my heart. Do not run. Let it appear that you are just a servant strolling to the town. Become Joan Tiler again. Become invisible."

There was no danger of her running. She could barely move. Her feet might have been made of lead.

The yard was waking to the morning, and Joan saw every detail with eerie precision. A brown hound trotted along the keep's wall. Knights stretched at the door atop the stairs. A slow line of servants entered through the gate, ready to begin their labor.

It appeared such a normal castle yard. Calm and sleepy and quiet. No attention being given to much of anything, least of all the humble woman dragging herself along the wall toward the gate.

She could not bear to leave Rhys. She prayed that he would change his mind and come with her. If he did not, he would die here. And it would be her fault. No matter what else he claimed, he did this for her.

Somehow her legs moved in obedience to his command. She waited to hear his step behind her. She begged him to find his sense and join her in this flight.

She neared the gate, and he still had not come. She faced the open portcullis. Her heart emptied out.

She hesitated taking the final steps. A chaotic battle waged in her.

A voice bellowed across the yard, cutting the morning's peace and silencing her heart's debate.

Joan pivoted at the sound and her attention snapped to

its source. Guy stood atop the keep steps, shouting for the gate to be closed.

His gaze swept the yard. It stopped on her, pinning her in place. Danger glared down on her. His expression said there would be no forgiveness for this last betrayal. Even the price of her body would not buy her life.

The portcullis began descending.

The servants pressed against the wall, seeking sanctuary from the trouble that shout had portended. No one moved except Guy. He paced down the steps toward her. The heads of knights and castle folk bunched in doorways and windows, drawn to the disturbance.

He reached the yard and aimed for her. Only a fool would not have feared what burned in his eyes.

Another movement. Another man. Rhys stepped from the wall. He strode to the center of the yard, blocking Guy's path.

He just stood there, strong despite his wounds. She doubted that anyone but she would detect the stiffness that indicated it was only the power of his will that kept him upright.

Guy stopped, knowing a challenge when he saw one. The silence broke as scuffing boots and shoes marked the arrival of more soldiers and servants. Knights wandered down the steps from the hall. A circle of watchers took form.

The two men took each other's measure. Joan measured, too, and knew that her love would be destroyed soon. Guy wore no sword, but his dagger dangled from his belt. Rhys would die if this went any further. His fury and determination could not protect him from a blade.

She took a step toward him. His arm angled out from his side, straight and firm. His palm faced her with the command to stay back.

She looked desperately around the crowd, hoping to find someone who would stop this.

Masks of excitement beamed back. All attention centered on the open circle of yard and the two men who promised some blood sport. No one noticed her beseeching gaze, or anything else.

Nay, not everyone watched. Along the wall, behind the crowd, some bodies moved. Very slowly, one by one, some of the servants who had just arrived eased toward the keep stairs. They appeared no more than shifting forms of brown and grey, their bodies and heads obscured by old cloaks.

Edward. He was inside.

She pulled her gaze away, so she would not draw attention to them. How many had she seen? Five? Seven? Had Rhys recognized the bowed knights shuffling in among the servants? Did he know that they were here?

Aye, he knew. He waited as long as he could before starting it. He let the crowd's expectation peak, and begin to fall, before goading it higher again.

"You have much to answer for, Leighton."

"Not nearly enough, if you can still stand."

"I am not speaking of myself."

"An anointed knight does not answer to his inferior, mason."

"You do today."

A group of knights laughed. Guy grinned at them, then cocked his head while he considered Rhys. "You must know that you will die. And for what?"

"For my lady."

"For that murdering bitch? She may have the blood, but her soul is that of a whore. I had her again, you know. Just this morning. She begged for it. She moaned for me."

"You lie, but it is of no account. You are finished with her. Here, today, you will answer for all of it."

Guy turned to the onlookers, and held out his arms. Like a player in a mystery pageant, he appealed to his delighted audience. "He is an odd champion, but the challenge is clear. He is not worthy of my efforts, and she not worthy of his sacrifice, but still he insists on forcing this. I have been generous in giving him the chance to remove himself, nay?"

The knights certainly thought so. Most of the servants agreed.

He ceremoniously removed his dagger and laid it at the feet of the knights. "I would not want it said that I had an unfair advantage."

The gesture gave Joan scant comfort. He would not need a dagger against a man whom he had already beaten to unconsciousness just an hour ago.

Guy faced Rhys again—no longer angelic in his beauty, no more humor in his face. Excited expectation burned in his eyes, and anticipation transformed his expression.

"Then defend your lady's honor, mason. Let God's judgment show you the truth of it. Die knowing that whatever she told you was a lie to hide her guilt at how quickly, and how eagerly, she surrendered her virtue."

The crowd did not know how battered Rhys already was, but Guy did. He paced forward with impunity, and swung.

Rhys took the blow. He staggered, but did not fall. Joan felt that fist land, heard its dull thump, and it knocked the breath out of her.

Cloaked figures slipped up the keep steps.

Rhys let three more blows fall, until the last of Edward's band was swallowed by the dark at the top of the stairs.

When Guy swung the next time, his fist met the implacable barrier of a hand that could break stone.

Guy stared in shock at the hand gripping his in its vise.

Eyes alight with the fires of hell looked up. The fires of justice blazed back.

The crushing hand immobilized Guy. Pain broke in his expression, and his body buckled.

"I think that you should beg her forgiveness," Rhys said.

"You are mad."

"A madman is dangerous. He feels no pain, like a sensible man. He knows no restraint. Beg her forgiveness."

"At the command of a stonecutter? The hell I will."

Rhys smiled, and those crinkles formed. Not charming this time. Dangerous. His eyes appeared like polished steel reflecting the sky. "I am glad that you will not. Now this stonecutter has an excuse to break every bone in your body."

He lifted Guy's arm until the man stretched, and swung a fist at his stomach. Had Guy been a statue, a large chunk of stone would have flown.

Another blow sent Guy sprawling in the dirt.

The crowd's silence broke. The real contest had begun. A din filled the yard as shouts urged it on. Somewhere in the keep, men moved through deserted chambers to a queen and a usurper whose commands would not be heard.

It seemed to go on forever. The fight was not all one-sided. Guy was quick, and Rhys, for all of his madness, had been badly weakened during the night.

Rhys never went down. Joan's eyes filmed. Her sickening worry could not completely obscure her pride. He stayed standing for her. He had taken those first blows for the King's cause, but now he defended her. Protected her. He fought for her honor and her freedom and her life.

No knight in England could have shown more courage.

Guy flew again, and landed near her. Rhys staggered over, and lifted him by the neck of his tunic. He swung.

Not a blow, but a hard slap to the face that made Guy's head snap back. "Moan for you, did she?" He slapped again. "I want you to moan, so that you learn to hear the difference between pleasure and despair."

Guy had gone limp, and did not defend against the punishment. A movement on the edge of the crowd drew Joan's attention. Two knights broke away, and began to approach Rhys from behind.

A voice rang through the yard, instantly silencing the crowd. A firm command ordered the knights to stay back.

Addis and a young, tawny-haired man stood at the top of the steps. No cloaks covered their armor. The young man's surcoat bore the royal coat of arms.

It was Edward who had issued the command. His presence, and his armor and sword, announced what had occurred. Then, in an even tone of authority, his words did.

Shock spread through the crowd. Suddenly no one cared about the fight between a knight and a mason anymore.

Rhys still hovered over Guy. Joan walked over to them. She looked down on the man who had destroyed her life. She could not deny that she knew some satisfaction in seeing him humbled like this. The woman she was today did not need it, but the girl she had once been still did.

Rhys seemed not to have noticed that things had changed. She touched his shoulder, calling him back from the place he had gone to find his strength.

"It is over. Edward has taken Mortimer, and the guards know it. They are not resisting."

He glared down at the half-conscious man in his grasp. He did not seem to hear her.

"It is done, Rhys. The gate is open again, and the men of Barrowburgh are entering to secure the castle."

His attention did not waver from his enemy. The fury in

his expression did not dim. She thought that he would hit Guy again.

A new presence warmed her side. Addis stepped into place beside her.

Rhys still gripped Guy.

Addis unsheathed his sword and offered it. "Finish it, if you want. There will be no judgment on it. He is a dead man anyway, and this may be a mercy if he faces his lord's fate."

Rhys turned his steely gaze on the sword. She expected him to reach for the hilt. She could tell that he wanted to.

He released his hold and Guy fell back into the dirt. "Let the executioner have him."

His false strength deserted him at once. He began to sink. Joan hurried to offer herself as support. He leaned on her, and together they followed Addis and headed toward the steps.

Confusion surrounded them. The yard teemed with agitation. Word of Mortimer's downfall buzzed in the air. She heard it all, but felt no excitement or triumph. It seemed such a small thing suddenly. She only cared that Rhys was alive, and that his arm circled her shoulders, and that his steps fell beside hers.

A rush behind her. A surge of danger. Her instincts knew it before her senses.

Rhys knew, too. His arm pushed her forward, into Addis. She staggered and turned and saw Guy lunging, arm raised and dagger glinting.

It happened fast, too fast to see clearly. Her shock took in only bits of it. Fractured details loomed, precisely and slowly.

The dagger falling, toward her. Rhys catching the blade itself in the grip of his left hand, and hurtling his body into Guy. Blood streaming down his arm, and the dagger moving again. Another grab, a quick twist, and two men sprawled on the ground in a death struggle.

Then stillness. No movement at all. They both looked dead.

A soundless cry tore through her. Her breath would not come. She felt as though her heart had stopped beating.

Slowly, Rhys rolled off the body beneath him. The dagger lay so deeply imbedded in Guy's chest that only its hilt showed. Guy stared wide-eyed up at the sky. The fires died, and his eyes turned into violet ice.

Addis lifted Rhys out of the dirt and blood. He hoisted a limp arm around his neck, and began dragging his friend toward the keep. His voice boomed above the confusion, ordering his men to send a surgeon at once.

CHAPTER 27

"ONE CAN NEVER TELL, of course," the surgeon said. "I have seen sword cuts like this that healed well enough for the hand to hold a weapon. If not, thank God it was not your right hand."

Rhys did not speak, nor watch the new shroud take form. The few minutes of washing and anointment with balms had told him what he needed to know. Free of the wads of cloth and stitches, he had tested his hand's movement.

The surgeon appeared annoyed by his patient's lack of response. He did not realize that it was not indifference that kept Rhys silent.

He gathered up his bowls and ointments. As he left the chamber, Addis entered.

He gestured to the white bandage. "How is it? There is no corruption?"

"It looks and smells clean."

"Thank God for that. That butcher wanted to take it off, but I said I would do to his head whatever he did to your hand, and he rethought it. Do not listen to the leeches and such. They are ignorant of these things. Let it heal and then see how it works. I was told once that I would never walk right again, but I did."

"Even if the damage is permanent, it is not so horrible. Edward will name me his principal builder today. I will have little time for the chisel anymore, and I will not starve for losing my craft."

Addis pretended that was good news, but the expression in his eyes said that he understood the truth of it. Losing one's craft meant losing part of oneself.

Grieving over that would come later. A different sorrow waited today.

"Will you ride with us?"

"Nay. I will come and see her brother recognized, but when you take them home, I will not come."

"Have you spoken with her about this?"

"I have seen little of her since Edward's queen arrived. Philippa has finally found a friend whom she can trust, and is jealous of Joan's time. A lady-in-waiting to the Queen of England does not desert her duties without explaining why, and I am not a suitable explanation. She slips away when she can, but I do not waste those moments by speaking of what awaits."

Addis nodded vaguely. A silent sympathy cloaked him. He might not speak of it, but he understood what would soon be lost.

"Do you return to London, then?"

"I have been thinking that I will first visit the home of my youth. I have not been back in years, and as I lay here I found myself longing to see it again. My parents are dead, but I have kin there."

"Then you head west. That makes it easier to ask a favor of you. I will bring my men with me when I escort Mark and Joan to their father's lands. Can you go to

Barrowburgh on your way to the marches? Moira waits for word about me, and I do not want her growing anxious."

"I will gladly bring her word of your safety, and of what has transpired." It would give his journey some purpose. In truth he headed west mostly because he did not want to return to London yet. After today, he would need more time before he went back to that house.

Addis sat and they spoke of the last days' events. Mortimer had been sent to Westminster to await his execution, and Queen Isabella had been banished to Castle Rising. Guy Leighton had been buried, the only fatality of the action. Edward had sent a decree throughout the land, announcing that he had taken the reins of power, and barons had begun streaming into Nottingham to show support for their king. The first to arrive had been some loyal to the usurper, and Edward had been magnanimous in his forgiveness. A few select heads would roll, but there would be no new bloodbath.

The chapel bells tolled. Their conversation dried. Addis rose. "Let us see it finished, then. It is good and right that you will be there, for the loss in the doing was mostly yours."

People of all degrees jammed the hall. A festive atmosphere filled the space, and tables of food waited. First, however, Edward would hold an audience, and favor those who had helped him, and listen to petitions as a good king should.

He entered with his young queen. She had brought his crown and robes with her, and they walked to the chairs set forth to serve as their thrones. To the shouting joy of the barons, the King finally took his rightful place.

Rhys barely heard the rest. Even when he was called forth, and given the King's favor, he did not fully listen.

His attention had become absorbed by a woman amidst the ladies who had trailed Philippa into the chamber.

Joan.

She looked incredibly beautiful. The Queen had decked out her new friend in the finest garments. A gown as blue as sapphires flowed like water down her narrow body, and its bejewelled decorations dipped along her breasts and hips. He realized that he had never seen her in a garment that fit before. Her blond hair had been worked into an intricate roll around her crown, and another roll, of precious blue silk and golden threads, rested atop it beneath a transparent golden veil. More silk wove through the long braid hanging down her back.

She had been transformed, turned into someone precious and noble and more valuable than pearls. A woman of beauty and dignity to be desired from afar by many. A prize to be won only at the table of alliance and politics.

She appeared a little sad. Her expression brightened only when he approached to receive his new position. He did not remain near her long, however. For all of Edward's gratitude, a mason was a minor matter, and more important things waited.

The petitions began, and Addis stepped forward. He called Mark to join him. Hand on the youth's shoulder, he explained the story that Edward already knew, but which the other barons must hear. He asked Edward to return the lands of Brecon to the son of a man who had done nothing wrong, but had only obeyed his oath as he understood it.

The King gestured Mark forward. Fewer than three years in age separated them. For a moment it was a youth looking at a youth, and not a King examining a petitioner. Edward offered his hand in friendship before he positioned it in a demand for fealty.

Mark rose after the oath, and held out his arm toward

the ladies-in-waiting. "This is my sister, my lord. I beg your blessing on us both."

Joan came forward, to finally reclaim her life. Elegant. Breathlessly beautiful. Something painful and proud swelled in Rhys's chest. He glanced around at the barons and knights. Every male eye settled on her.

It had begun. But then, Philippa had probably planned that, and made the display more magnificent with that intention. A queen's generosity demanded such efforts for a friend. Influencing alliances by arranging marriages was the most important power that she wielded.

Edward broke into a boyish grin. "I welcome you, lady. And I find myself half dazed by you. After my queen, you are the most lovely lady in the chamber today."

"Thank you, my lord."

"Is your husband here with you?"

She hesitated. Mark answered for her. "Her betrothed died."

"Recently? I sense a melancholy in you."

Again, Mark had to answer. "Three years ago, but she still mourns all that was lost."

Comprehension entered Edward's eyes. "Well, that is over now. Your brother will sit in your father's chair soon, Lady Joan. And you will sit beside a lord of our choosing. Beauty such as yours should not be wasted in grief."

Again she hesitated. Rhys could see only her lithe, shapely back. Finally her voice spoke clearly and firmly, with more resolve than gratitude. "Thank you, my lord."

Edward said something else, but Rhys did not listen. He turned away, and angled through the people toward the door.

It was finished. Joan Tiler was completely gone, and the daughter of Marcus de Brecon had been resurrected, in all her glory.

He walked down to the yard. He leaned against the

keep wall, and took deep breaths of the crisp air. The ache in his chest did not come only from his healing wounds.

It was finished, but it was not over yet.

Philippa would not leave Joan alone. The Queen was a sweet girl, but too grateful to find a friend who had been separate from the suspicions and deceptions of the last few years. The quick bond had become invasive.

Joan suffered the continuous introductions to lords and knights. Time and again she tried to ease away, only to have Philippa beckon another man forth.

She kept searching the milling crowd for Rhys. She needed to see him. Mark had said that Rhys would not accompany them west when they left today, and she had to convince him to change his mind.

It could not end now, like this. She had sat by his bed those first days while he began to heal, but since the Queen had arrived, there had been only snatched minutes drenched with the horrible awareness that she had lost control over her future.

Another man. Another introduction, and another courteous bow. Another appreciative inspection, and another flowery flattery.

She could not bear it. Soon, too soon, she would deal with the life that these suitors represented. Right now she wanted to cling to another man's attention, and a different life's memories.

An ache wedged in her, deep and low beneath her heart. She was losing her hold on what had been. She had felt it slipping away since Mortimer fell, despite her clutching grasp. It had lost its solidity. It flowed away like the finest sand finding paths through her fingers.

The meal was ending. The dancing had stopped.

Outside, horses and wagons waited. They were due to leave as soon as the festivities were over.

She needed to find Rhys. Speak to him. Bask in his presence, just the two of them alone together, for a few moments at least. She needed to beg him to come with her, for a few days at least. She needed to hold him one last time, for one more night at least. She needed . . .

Another man. Not a suitor. Addis de Valence stood in front of her. Flowery words flowed from his mouth, but not for her. He addressed the Queen.

He glanced to Joan, and then to the door, and she understood. He was not a man given to courtly games, but he could play them if he chose. He chose to now, to distract Philippa. He soon had the Queen giggling and blushing.

Joan quietly slid away.

She ran through the hall, and out to the stairs. Below in the yard the men of Barrowburgh waited. The procession that would take her home prepared to depart.

She scanned the yard, and found Rhys. He stood against the wall, his arms crossed and his bound hand propped against his chest. He had spoken lightly of that wound, but she knew that it pained him.

She ran down the steps, praying that Philippa would keep Addis a very long time. Hours. Days.

Forever.

He saw her coming, and opened his arms to her. She sank into his warmth and strength, and savored every bit of his touch as it gently caressed her back.

He set her away, and looked her over. More than a man's appreciation showed in his eyes. "Edward lied. You were the most beautiful woman in the hall, and no queen surpassed you."

She fingered the blue silk. For some reason, she felt

very embarrassed by its luxury. "It is her gown, fitted to me by her seamstresses. I do not like it so much."

He gently touched the crown of silk and gold, and the veil. "You belong in a tapestry, pretty dove. One where gallant knights woo their ladies, and angels sing in the sky, and banners and bedecked horses announce the coming of the best blood."

He spoke of who she was, and where she was going. He smiled, but a cloud of sorrow descended on them both.

His intense eyes gazed into hers. Knowing. Accepting. He was stronger than she would ever be.

"The King and his wife favor you and your brother. All will be well now."

"How can it be well if you are not with me? Please come with us. A day only. It can do no harm."

"A day only. Then another day. And another. Parting will get no easier for the delay."

He spoke gently, but with finality. Her heart became heavy, as though it absorbed a grief that would never relent.

She would not have him severed from her. She could not. The pain of it would kill her. Already she felt a suffocating anguish that left her struggling to breathe.

Tears brimmed, and she could not hold them in. "I will not go. I have fulfilled my oath to my father's memory. We have it all back, and Mark has his place. I will stay with you. We will return to London and live together and know happiness again."

He brushed his lips against her, silencing her gush of words. "Your brother is still young, and he needs your guidance. He will badly need the alliance that Edward plans for him. Your duties can not be thrown off so easily, and we both know it."

"They can, if I will it. I need only decide, and choose freedom with you."

"It is not so simple, love. Not only duty calls you. For three years, regaining your life is all that sustained you. It is a part of your soul and your heart, even if you do not acknowledge it now. You can not turn your back on the goal now that it is in hand."

She clung to his chest, and wept into his tunic. The notion that this would be the last time that she held him ripped her composure to pieces. "I *can* turn my back on it. I do not care about it. I do not want it. I hate this gown and veil. I hate those lords inside the hall."

He nestled his face against her head. "Do you hate your brother? Can you turn your back on him? On your family's honor, and your place in it? That is what you speak of. He is here now, not far behind you. Turn and see him."

Slowly, she looked over her shoulder. Mark stood by the horses, impatient to be off. He did not watch them, but she could tell that he had seen their embrace in the shadow of the wall.

We will reclaim our home as we left it, hand in hand.

Rhys brushed some tears away, but they kept flowing. "You can not abandon him, nor the rest of it. You will not be whole if you deny it now. You must go home. You must reclaim it all, and stand in triumph where you were defeated. Once you do, you will know that you belong there, as I know it already."

Sounds behind her. Movements. She heard Addis's voice, calling the men to mount.

She pressed against Rhys, and ran her palms over his shoulders and arms, feeling his solidity with desperate intensity. Images of him, carving in the garden, standing below the stocks, looking down on her in love, filled her head. The tears could not come fast enough. They backed up into her throat and then her heart, scalding her with their unspent power.

He kissed her. A last kiss. One to taste for a lifetime. "Go now."

She could not. He had to push her away from him.

She could not move. She resented the waiting duty. If she took one step, all of the others would follow, and their path led away from this man who had saved her in so many ways.

His expression tightened and his eyes filmed. "Go, pretty dove, before I start weeping with you. I will always remember the private vows that we made. We will be together forever in the ways that matter."

He turned her shoulders, so that she faced Mark.

She stood immobilized, tearing in two.

Her brother watched and waited. His hard expression softened. He extended his hand to her.

She looked back, for a final decision.

It was denied her. Rhys had left.

Chapter 28

"I THANK YOU for making this journey to tell me all of it. I heard of Edward's decree, but of course I worried about Addis."

Moira's fingers gently soothed a balm over Rhys's healing palm while she spoke. She had insisted on tending to this herself when she saw the bandages upon his arrival. He had spent the last hour drinking her wine with one hand while she bathed the other. He had diverted his attention from the raw scar by regaling her with lively stories about the great events that she had missed.

She prepared the binding to wrap his palm. "I think that your story is incomplete, though, from the way that you rode in the gate. Those days in the saddle took more strength than you had. You have suffered much, my friend, and must stay a few days and rest."

He could tell that she suspected the real reason for his condition. It had not been the journey that had tired him, nor the healing wounds, but a lack of sleep. Thoughts of Joan plagued him at night.

He had almost veered north while he rode. Time and again he had to stop himself from heading to the road where she journeyed. Only the pain of their parting kept him from doing so.

He never wanted to go through that again.

"Will you stay as I ask?"

"Aye, a few days."

They sat in the solar, bathed in light pouring through the large windows. A nurse rocked the fussing baby in a corner, and little Patrick played with a toy on the floor.

The domesticity soothed him. So did Moira's friendship.

She set aside the little pot of ointment, and held his hand in hers. "How long since you received this cut?"

"A fortnight."

"It looks like it was cleanly sewn."

"The man did his best."

"Not good enough, I fear. You have lost the strength in this hand, haven't you?"

"It does not close as it should. I think that it never will."

"It is too early to know that."

"So Addis says. But I do know it."

She must have seen how certain he was, and did not offer any more false hope. "I am sorry."

"I can still hold a quill. I can still create with my mind if not my hands. Being the King's principal builder will bring me wealth, and status equal to a courtier. I have not lost so much."

"That is not true, Rhys. You have lost a great deal, and the fact that you will never carve again is only a part of it."

The sorrow in her voice touched him. It probed his hidden grief.

Something in him began cracking, as if the thin edge of a metal wedge had started a fissure in a soft stone.

He looked down at the child playing nearby. Little Patrick smiled up at the attention. He pushed to his feet, and toddled the few steps to come closer. He beamed with a big smile, and smacked Rhys's knee. "Up."

Rhys raised his knee. The child laughed, and pushed it, showing what he meant.

"He wants you to cross your legs so that he can ride your boot," Moira explained. "It is a game that Addis plays with him."

Rhys crossed his legs. Patrick straddled his booted foot and leaned into his leg, arms extended. Rhys rocked him up and down.

The child's squeals of delight rang through the chamber.

Rhys laughed. Then, suddenly, the mirth died and the sound caught in his throat. Patrick still rode, giggling with pleasure, but the child's voice and face dimmed. The fissure grew and grew, like a hammer pounded the wedge down, and profound sorrow poured through the increasing gap, engulfing his mind and dulling his senses.

Hands removed the child from his foot. Steps receded. Patrick's indignant howls and the baby's fussing disappeared behind a closing door.

Silence surrounded him. He stared blindly at the spot where the child's innocent face had just been.

Motherly arms slid around him. A woman's hand pressed his head to a soft shoulder. His battered heart relished the comfort, but it only weakened him more.

He took a deep breath, and began to pull away. "Hell, Moira, your husband will never understand. He will kill me if he hears of it."

She firmly eased his head back down. "Ah, Rhys, you still do not understand him. He took three messengers to Nottingham, and did not need you to make this journey for his sake. He sent you to me, so that you could share your sorrow with a friend."

The depth of Addis's generosity moved him more than he could contain. It defeated his defenses. The fissure reached his heart.

And then, because it was Moira, he broke.

Snow dusted the city of London, and the overcast sky promised an early nightfall. Rhys turned his horse onto the lane where he lived, and let the horse find his way home.

He had delayed his return as long as he could. He had stayed with Moira more than a few days, and then gone to the town of his youth. His uncle had received him with warmth and given him a bed for as long as he wanted. There had been some good times there, surrounded by the cousins born of his uncle's second wife.

The young ones had thought his role in Mortimer's downfall a splendid adventure, but his uncle had followed him to the graveyard one evening to have a private talk. While they gazed down at the graves of his parents, and of a dark-haired woman and a nameless babe, his uncle had spoken his mind.

"If you did it for yourself, to advance your station, so be it. But if you did it for her, and what happened all those years ago, you've still got notions in you that need fixing. Let lords and bishops worry about the big world. Men like us live in a small one, and there is contentment in our gardens that nobles never know. Go and serve the King now, and build his castles and churches, and grow rich from his favor, but make your life in your craft and in a family if you want to know any peace. There is no point in risking your neck over who holds the power, boy. One's the same as the next to us, and justice comes and goes at their whim. You find a good woman and take care of what's important now."

Maybe he would. Perhaps it was time to put aside boyish notions and accept what life was about. His new position at court meant that he could even marry above his degree if he wanted. Not too high above, but there were gentry knights who would accept him for their daughters. He would look for a practical woman with property, who sought only security, and who did not mind that her husband's love lived forever with someone else.

He paused a few buildings away from his house, at the place where an alley would take him back to the stable. Aye, he should start a family and find the peace his uncle spoke of. In a year or so, he might be able to do it. Not in this house, though. There would be no contentment in its garden, ever again.

Some boys strolled by. One broke away and came to greet him. It was Mark's friend, David.

"Back finally, are you? You missed all the feasts. The ward was drunk for a week after the decree got read, and everyone went to the execution. The men kept looking for you, since we heard you'd been in the thick of it, same as last time. They'd have bought you all the ale you could drink. Where have you been?"

"I went to visit my boyhood home."

"Ah, well, then you celebrated with them there. Anyway, it was a grand time. Do you want me to take your horse back? Mark showed me how to groom him."

The idea of avoiding the garden entrance appealed to Rhys. He dismounted and handed over the reins.

David made to lead the horse down the alley, but paused. "I heard that Mark's a baron now."

"So he is."

"He always said he had secrets that would surprise me. I can't wait until he comes back and tells me of it."

"He will not be back. He has returned to his home."

"He can visit when he comes to court." He pulled on the reins. "You go in and get warm. I'll see to the horse proper for you, and leave your bags outside the garden portal."

The youth led the horse away. Rhys walked down the lane to his door.

He still did not want to go in. All of the time away had not lessened that one bit. Well, it could not be avoided forever. Until he bought another house, he had to sleep somewhere.

He turned the latch, stepped inside, and waited for the void to assault him.

It was not emptiness that flowed over him. Not absence. She filled the air. He stepped into a place haunted by the phantom of her presence, and into a cloud of memories.

Her brief return to the house the day that they fled had left its remnants. He half expected to smell bread baking.

He closed his eyes, and savored the feel of it. Touching the breath of her fading ghost was worth the wrenching heartache.

He absorbed it fully, because it would not last. It would seep away with every minute that he lived in this place without her. Very soon this would once again become the house too wide for one person.

He forced himself to look, and to let that begin happening. He walked into the hall, to accept the future.

A sound. Quiet and vague.

Another, more distinct. It came from the kitchen.

His heart began pounding. Slowly. Hard. He told himself it was only David, bringing the bags in rather than leaving them in the garden. Or the wind hitting a loose shutter.

The vague sounds continued. He stared at the hearth,

explaining them away, resenting the pitiful hope that just built and built.

A new sound. A voice. A woman humming. Its meandering melody drifted toward him like the growing tendril on a vine.

Forcing himself to move, he walked toward the kitchen.

CHAPTER 29

WARMTH AND LIGHT. It did not come just from the fire in the big hearth. The woman in the chamber produced her own brilliance, and his whole being flushed in response.

Joan stood beside the window. The table had been moved close to it, and one shutter stood open to the cold, overcast day. A workboard rested on it, holding the clay shape of a figure.

She molded with deft fingers, intent on her task. Lost in her craft, she had not heard him enter the house.

She wore a dove-colored gown of fine cloth, with embroidered blue lines braiding along the neck. She had unlaced the sleeves and pushed them up, revealing a lady's creamy arms and hands, but blotches of clay had still smeared the costly fabric. A rich blue surcoat, and a wimple and veil, lay piled at the end of the bench. The ensemble looked expensive enough to be court dress.

She must have come to Westminster, to visit the Queen. He imagined her making some excuse, and slipping away for this visit, not knowing that he was on a journey. He saw her waiting, and growing bored, and finally going out to the garden and the barrel in which some clay still soaked, and deciding to pass the time doing that which she loved.

Then again, maybe she had known he was away, and had come for the clay alone.

If so, he did not care. He indulged in the joy of seeing her. He would pay dearly for this visit, but he did not care about that either. Watching her mold the clay, feeling her intensity, was worth the pain of a hundred partings.

He stood at the threshold a long time, sharing her craft vicariously, experiencing the soul through her quiet rapture, watching the little figure grow more defined. He had thought never to know that power again, but she unknowingly gave him the gift of tasting it once more.

Finally the day's light grew too dim. She drew back and considered her progress with her hands on her hips. She glanced at the hearth, but knew that its heat would dry the clay too fast, and that she could not continue in its light.

Her expression changed while she looked at the flames. She realized that she was not alone. Her gaze darted about, and found him in the shadows by the doorway.

She smiled, but her eyes glistened with moisture. And with something else. Her hands went back to her hips, smearing more clay on the dove-toned fabric.

"You take your time returning home, Rhys Mason."

He went to her, and took her face in his hands, and tasted the lips that he had kissed so often in his dreams these last weeks. She might have duties to her family's honor now, but their love permitted him this intimacy at least.

She let him, and lingered, and seemed sad when he forced himself to pull away.

"You have been in town long?" he asked.

She began wrapping the statue in damp cloths. "Seven days."

"I am glad that I returned before you left."

She completed her task in silence. Something poured out of her, and it was not just happiness in their reunion.

Finally, when the board had been cleared, and the statue placed on a shelf, and the table wiped clean, she began fixing her sleeves.

His heart dropped. Night would fall soon. No doubt the Queen expected her attendance.

Her life awaited her return.

She did not put on the surcoat. She looked out the window to the garden. She appeared to be an elegantly worked statue illuminated by the evening's silver light.

"You should not have made me leave with them. At Nottingham. You should have let me stay with you."

She had not brought her love to him, but her anger. "God knows that I have hated doing it, Joan, but you had to go back. Telling you to do so was the right thing."

"I did not want you to do the right thing. I wanted you to do the selfish thing, so that I could, too. My heart broke when you left me there. I knew nothing but pain for weeks. I hated you for being strong and good, and for making me go through with it."

"If it was a mistake for you to return, I am sorry. If seeing your home brought you pain . . ."

"It was not that which pained me, but that you would let go of me."

"I have never let go of you. If my judgment in this proved wrong, I have suffered for it as much as you."

She sighed, and turned and sank down on the bench. "Your judgment was not wrong. It was as you said. I needed to ride through those gates, and see Guy's men displaced, and watch my brother sit in the lord's chair. I needed to visit my father's grave and tell him it was done, as I had sworn it would be." She paused, and gazed down at the clay-speckled hands on her lap. "I needed to reclaim my chamber, and . . . and my bed, and the person I had once been. I needed to close the circle, and complete it. It is good that I went home, I can not deny that."

He sat beside her, and took her hand in his. The clay had made it very smooth. "Then I am happy for you."

They sat together in silence, sharing a delicious connection. She placed her other hand over his, so that she enclosed him.

"I visited the tile yard. I had more clay brought in, so that the King's pavers might be finished. It will take some time with the cold weather, but they should be right. It would not be good for the crown's principal builder to leave a project incomplete."

He had not thought about the tile yard, or the King's project, in all these weeks.

"It would not do for that investment to be lost," she added.

He had not thought about that either. "I suppose not."

More silence. There was profound peace in just sitting with her, holding her hand. They had shared the deepest passion, but he had never needed that to love her.

"They have chosen a husband for me."

The peace shattered. Its falling pieces cut like blades.

"He came to Brecon. I met him. He holds lands near York, and is one of Edward's favorites. It will be a great alliance of families."

"So soon? Your brother—"

"Addis has been given wardship of my brother, until Mark learns what he must know. Barrowburgh will protect him, and give the advice and guidance, not me. It is just as well. He does not hear a woman's voice anymore."

"This lord is a good man, you think?"

"Aye, a good man."

The depths of his reaction stunned him. A visceral anger split through his mind. He had known she would be given to another, but hearing of it sent flames jumping through his blood.

She had come to tell him this, not to work clay or visit an old lover. When their hands separated this time, it would truly be the final parting.

He gazed at her delicate profile. She could do it. She could do anything if she put her will to it. She had proven herself stronger than the despair wrought by misery and degradation. This fate, decreed by birth and duty, would be a small thing in comparison, and she would flourish in that man's home if she chose to accept him.

A decision formed in him, as solid as rock. It was not one hewn out of good and right, but out of selfish desire and heartfelt need.

He hoped he was right, and that the chains of their love were stronger than those of duty and blood.

He touched her cheek, and turned her face. He prayed that what he planned to do would never bring her unhappiness.

Sitting with him, holding him, filled Joan with that sense of being protected and vulnerable at the same time. She reveled in the security, but his touch evoked longings that could not be ignored. Not today, after all this time apart. She wanted to be absorbed completely by him, not just loved quietly.

Didn't he know why she had really returned to this house?

She kept hoping that he would kiss her again. She wondered if she would have to be bold about it. Surely he could feel what kept building between them. The press of their hands became imbued with it. The connection changed from comforting to sensual.

His fingertips touched her cheek. He turned her face, and looked into her eyes. Warmth and love gazed at her, but a bit of that steely glint showed too.

"If you are to marry this lord, you should not have come here."

"There is no harm in visiting a friend."

"I can never know you just as a friend. You are not Moira, and I will never love you as in kinship."

"I do not ask you to."

"It is good that you do not, because speaking of that man has raised the devil in me. But I think that you knew it would."

Aye, she had known it would. She had counted on jealousy making him less good.

He kissed her. Not like the first one. Not in greeting, or restrained affection.

For weeks she had filled her senses with memories of him. She had waited impatiently for the times alone when she could give herself over to the fantasies. Savor them. Immerse her mind in the spirit of his touch and scent and caress. Her love had become another world to which she escaped every night, and often during the day. It had become more real than the hall and chambers in which she dwelled.

It had been a sad world, though. One full of wistful longing and aching grief. Living in the spirit of love, but never tasting its reality, had kept the pain of their parting alive and sharp.

She tasted love's reality now. She clutched a solid man, not a phantom. She accepted deep kisses, and possessive caresses, and felt anew what the memories had lost. The physicality of the intimacy undid her. The beauty of it, the realness, made her composure break.

She buried her face in his chest so he would not see, but he knew anyway. He held her tighter, and pressed a kiss to her hair.

"I am making you unhappy."

Holding in the tears choked her. She could only shake her head. Didn't he know that it was joy that overwhelmed her, not sorrow? Couldn't he tell?

He guided her face up, and brushed away tears with his lips. "I want you to sleep with me tonight. In my arms, and in my bed. I want to wake in the morning and find you naked beside me. You will not deny us this night. I think that it is why you came here. Am I wrong?"

"You are not wrong." She had come for that, but also for much more. One night, and then another. And another . . .

She reached up and ran her fingers over the planes of his face. She had forgotten how just looking at him could make her blood sparkle.

They did not rush it. They held each other, and she relished a contentment that she thought never to know again. Ecstasy could wait for the night and the feather bed. A quieter rapture bound them together on this bench.

"It will be dark soon. We should send word to the palace that you will stay here, or the Queen might have her guard looking for you."

"She will not, because I never went to the palace and she does not even know that I left home. I have been in this house all week, waiting for you."

He lifted a bit of her skirt. "It is a court dress. I just assumed that you had come to Westminster."

"It is all I have, this and others like it from the old days.

Mark would not let me keep my other gowns. He said that they reminded him of the bad years."

"Does Mark know that you came to visit me? I am surprised that he would permit it."

"I did not ask his permission. He saw my resolve, and did not try to stop me. He even bid me to ask a favor of England's best mason. Come, I will show you what it is."

She rose and took his hand and led him out into the early twilight. She had almost forgotten the favor. In truth, it was really a gift. She looked forward to his surprise.

She brought him to the workbench over near the hawthorn tree. Canvas draped the large object propped up on it.

"Close your eyes."

He eyed the bench curiously, then his lids dropped. She pulled the covering off to reveal not his Saint Ursula, but a shimmering white block of stone.

"Look."

He did. She saw his shock, but none of the delight that she expected.

"It is marble," she said.

"I know."

"Mark's first act once we got home was to move my father's grave. He wants a statue put in the chapel near the floor vault where he now lies. Saint George, in armor, to honor the way father died. Marble, he said, the finest there is, to be carved by the finest mason, which means you. It was not easy finding this block. A bishop had brought it in from Italy for his own tomb."

"It is a fine stone, Joan."

His lack of enthusiasm confused her. "Have you never worked marble before?"

"I have. Twice. But I can not carve this statue."

"Why? It will be magnificent, and you can do as you like. Mark trusts your judgment, and asks for no drawings. He knows that you will have building projects, and that it will take a long while, if that is what concerns you."

He strolled over to the stone. He touched its surface, running his fingertips down its length. Regret shadowed his expression.

He held up his left palm. The scar from Guy's dagger showed thick and red, slashing from the base of his thumb to that of his smallest finger.

"I cannot carve it for you. I cannot hold the chisel."

His flat statement stunned her. She took his hand and studied the scar. She felt along its ugly ridge.

"It does not look maimed. The bones are whole."

"It is not the bones. Something else."

"You said the surgeon had told you it should be right. You said Addis had suffered much worse, and time had healed him."

"Both the surgeon and Addis offered hope, but I knew. Even before the healing began, I knew."

"You knew wrong. It is too soon to despair. You have only to work it again, and use your tools, and with time—"

"God knows that I tried. I borrowed the tools of a mason in my uncle's town and I tried for days. It takes strength to hold a chisel under the force of a hammer, and my hand no longer has it. See. I can not close my fist tightly."

He could make no more than a claw. He tried to force it. His whole arm tensed from the strain. His efforts broke her heart.

She bent and rested her cheek on his palm. "It was for me that you lost this."

"As losses go, it was a small one."

Not small. Huge. The magnitude of it filled her.

"I will be building still. Palaces and churches, as I have dreamed. More has been given than has been taken away."

She looked up at him and their gazes met. For all his brave words, they both knew the truth. He might build, but he would never carve. With his drawings and geometry he might see the mind, but he would never again know the soul.

She released his hand. She went to the wooden box near the table, and opened it. She lifted the hammer and chisel that it held.

"It will not be so. I will not accept it. You will try and try until your hand is right. You will carve my father's statue."

"Your resolve will not change this, pretty dove."

"It will. You will see." She handed the tools to him. "Take them. You will see."

Rhys reluctantly took the tools in his hands. His calm expression broke when he felt their weight and forms. "Joan . . ."

"Please, try. I can not bear that you have lost this part of yourself. It is unfair. Unjust. Surely it was not meant to be."

He became angry at her insistence. She was afraid that he would throw the tools down and walk away.

"Please. For me."

His right hand tightened on the handle of the hammer. His left closed on the base of the chisel. Anger burned hotter in his eyes.

"Aye, I will try once more, for you, so that you can see how it is. And after you do, you are never to speak to me of this again."

He gazed at the stone, and a special intensity slowly replaced the anger. He measured the block, judging its depths and strength, making his decision. His expression reminded her of that wonderful Sunday when she had watched him carve while she molded.

"Do you see the figure in it?" she asked.

"Aye, your Saint George is in it."

"So he needs only to be freed."

He stared down at the tools. Then he lifted the chisel, and placed it obliquely near a corner of the block.

He swung the hammer.

It landed on the other tool.

The chisel slid and flew, landing in the dirt.

Its dull thud hit just as a silent one shook her heart. It was true. His hand did not have the strength to hold it.

A brittle silence filled the garden. He appeared resigned, and resentful. He did not like being made to face this again, in front of her.

A deep sorrow, hidden beneath his strength, leaked through his barriers and flowed toward her.

His efforts to contain it twisted her heart. "It is not fair that you should be the only one to lose, when you had nothing to gain."

"The world is not always just. You know that better than I. And I gained much. All that I wanted for you. I regret nothing, and will not have you pity me over this."

Still brave. Always strong. But she knew that he grieved.

She yearned to find some way to comfort him. She wanted to give him back this essential part of his life. Surely there was some way to right this injustice.

She walked around him and picked up the chisel. Its cold metal length rested heavily in her hands.

"Take it again. Place it on the stone, where it should be. I will hold it for you."

"It does not work that way, darling. When I carve, my two hands become one. It is all a single action, and a single thought."

"Take it. Do it. You have nothing more to lose but another moment of pride."

He sighed deeply, and gestured. "Then stand here, and I will put your hands where they should be."

She stepped in front of him, within the curve of his left arm, and lifted the chisel in both her hands. His palm closed over her grip, and settled the tool on the stone.

"Nay, we cannot do this. If I miss, your hands will be broken."

"You will not miss."

He hesitated. She held firmly, refusing to budge.

His hand covered hers more fully, to shield her. She centered all her strength on keeping that tool in place.

He swung. The impact jarred her whole body, but she did not let go. A break appeared, and the chisel slid into the stone. Four more swings, and a small chunk of stone slid away.

She stared at what they had done, then back at him. He appeared as shocked as she felt.

A laugh burst out of her, along with her joy and amazement. "I did not really think that it would work."

That made him laugh, too. He shook his head with amused exasperation. "Jesus, woman, your stubbornness is both a curse and a blessing. Who would have thought that making tiles would give you such strength."

"Again. Let us do it again."

He placed the chisel.

Over and over, they chipped off white chunks. She became an extension of him. One body, not two, really worked the stone. Two hands, not four, actually held the tools.

The connection grew intense. A unity of purpose bound them together. First their bodies acted as one, and then their souls.

The trance of creation slid into her like it always did when she worked her craft. She greeted its arrival with a smile. Only it was different this time. She was not alone in it. They had shared it before, but not like this. They did not meet each other within that euphoria, but entered it entwined together.

She did not need his guidance for the next cut. Her hands moved, knowing where to go now. She saw the saint imprisoned in the stone, but she did so through Rhys's eyes. She sensed how to move, as if his mind silently spoke to her.

The experience enthralled her. They had merged in the ultimate intimacy.

She glanced back at him. Their gazes met. Aye, Rhys felt it too. Its heady power glinted in his eyes. Total understanding flowed between them.

She began to move the chisel once more. The hand covering hers stopped her. He pried the tool away and cast it aside.

The hammer fell to the ground. His arms circled her. He embraced her to him and bent to kiss her neck.

The intimacy did not disappear. It changed and deepened and she melted into him so thoroughly that she lost herself.

His embrace aroused more than desire. Pressing her back against him, feeling his body, evoked the pain of their separation. Experiencing once again all that this could be, knowing it today at this deepest level, made her ache from the thought of what they had too easily forsaken.

He held her close, wrapped in his arms, lips pressed to her neck, his emotion surrounding her.

"You should not have let me go. You should not," she whispered.

"Nay, I should not. I should have gone with you, and let you finish it, and then taken you away with me."

He still bound her closely, but his caressing hand slid up her back to work at her gown's lacing. Anticipation bubbled through her. They would not wait for night and the feather bed. They could not now.

The gown loosened. He turned her, and pressed her against the marble. He slid the fabric off her shoulders and peeled away her shift.

Watching him look at her tantalized more than his hands holding her breasts and his fingers stroking her skin.

"I am going to make love to you now. I spoke of one night, but after I possess you again I will never let you go." He dipped to kiss her two nipples. She felt that brushing warmth all through her body. It kindled a blaze. A desperate need for total closeness instantly pounded in her.

He lifted her skirt, and caressed up her naked leg. Cold air licked at her, but she did not care. Soon she would have his warmth enclosing her. Filling her.

His hand moved higher, until he cupped her. "I decided in the kitchen that I cannot let you leave again, Joan. I am not that strong and good. I plan to love you so well that you will stay here. Not just for a visit, but forever."

His touch took her breath away. She could barely speak. "It is why I am here, Rhys. Why I came back. To know freedom with you forever."

He gazed into her eyes while he intensified the pleasure. "You will tell your brother that this is your home now."

"I already have, my love. I already have. Mark does not approve, but he will understand someday."

He leaned her against the stone. He lifted her knee and entered. All of her, body and soul, moaned with relief. She clutched him and rested her head on his shoulder. The joining made them one form, rising out of the marble like a living statue of the act of love.

The pleasure pitched too high for words and restraint. Her body cried for more, but the sweetest fulfillment already saturated her soul.

"I want you to marry me, and add wedding vows to the ones that we made that night. We will stand together in our love before the world."

His proposal floated to her on the sharp breaths of his passion. Her eyes misted at the sound of the words she had prayed to hear spoken. She held tighter and they moved harder. "Oh, aye."

"You will be my wife, truly and legally, and bear my children."

"Aye, love," she gasped. "Aye."

"We will live together forever, and find our happiness in this garden. You will be all that matters to me." His voice came low and ragged. "All that matters."

He kissed her so that at the end they were totally joined. The power shot through her so violently that the stone wobbled at her back.

She held him to her, feeling his breaths slowly calm on her neck and beneath her arms. Tears streamed down her face, and she did not try to hold them back.

He kissed her wet cheek. He did not ask why she wept. He did not need to. He was with her in the joy. She could feel that this loving had moved him as much as her.

He touched his forehead to hers. No part of her lacked a connection to him, and it would be so forever, even without physical touch.

"I am so grateful that you came back," he said. "So grateful I was wrong about the future you should have."

"I had to come back. If I had not, I would have once more lived one life while dreaming about a past one."

She touched his face, to mold a memory of how he appeared in the sweet aftermath of this perfect union. It was not necessary to cling desperately to the emotions swelling her heart. She could look forward to a lifetime of such moments.

"I had to come back because I belong with you, Rhys. My heart could be happy nowhere else, nor could I ever feel safe away from your strength. I had to come back to our home, darling. You are the husband of my heart, and you are my champion."

*Be sure to look for Madeline Hunter's other
enchanting romances. . . .*

BY ARRANGEMENT

and

BY POSSESSION

now on sale

Read on for previews of these spectacular novels.

BY

ARRANGEMENT

now on sale

"Master David, I have come to ask you to withdraw your offer of marriage."

He glanced to the fire, then his gaze returned to her. One lean, muscular leg crossed the other, and he settled comfortably back in his chair. An unreadable expression appeared in his eyes, and the faint smile formed again.

"Why would I want to do that, my lady?"

He didn't seem the least bit surprised or angry. Perhaps this meeting would go as planned after all.

"Master David, I am sure that you are the good and honorable man that the King assumes. But this offer was accepted without my consent."

He looked at her impassively. "And?"

"And?" she repeated, a little stunned.

"My lady, that is an excellent reason for you to withdraw, but not me. Express your will to the King or the bishop and it is over. But your consent or lack of it is not my affair."

"It is not so simple. Perhaps amongst you people it is, but I am a ward of the King. He has spoken for me. To defy him on this . . ."

"The church will not marry an unwilling woman, even if a King has made a match. I, on the other hand, have given my consent and cannot withdraw it. There is no reason to, as I have said."

His calm lack of reaction irked her. "Well, then, let me explain my position more clearly and perhaps you will have your reason. I do not give my consent because I am in love with another man."

Absolutely nothing changed in his face or eyes. She might have told him that she was flawed by a wart on her leg.

"No doubt an excellent reason to refuse your consent in your view, Christiana. But again, it is not my affair."

She couldn't believe his bland acceptance of this. Had he no pride? No heart? "You cannot want to marry a woman who loves another," she blurted out.

"I expect it happens all the time. England is full of marriages made under these circumstances. In the long run, it is not such a serious matter."

Oh, dear saints, she thought. A man who believed in practical marriages. Just her luck. But then, he was a merchant.

"It may not be a serious matter amongst you people," she tried explaining, "but marriages based on love have become desired—"

"That is the second time that you have said that, my lady. Do not say it again." His voice was still quiet, his face still impassive, but a note of command echoed nonetheless.

"Said what?"

" 'You people.' You have used the phrase twice now."

"I meant nothing by it."

"You meant everything by it. But we will discuss that another day."

He had flustered and distracted her with this second scolding. She sought the strand of her argument. He found it for her.

"My lady, I am sure a young girl thinks that she needs to marry the man whom she thinks that she loves. But your emotions are a short-term problem. You will get over this. Marriage is a long-term investment. All will work out in the end."

He spoke to her as if she were a child, and as dispassionately as if they discussed a shipment of wool. It had been a mistake to think that she could appeal to his sympathy. He was a tradesman, after all, and to him life was probably just one big ledger sheet of expenses and profits.

Well, maybe he would understand things better if he saw the potential cost to his pride.

"This is not just a short-term infatuation on my part, Master David. I am not some little girl," she said. "I pledged myself to this man."

"You both privately pledged your troth?"

It could be done that way. She could lie. She desperately wanted to, and felt sorely tempted, but such a lie could have dire consequences, and very public ones, and she wasn't that brave. "Not formally," she said, hoping to leave a bit of ambiguity there.

He at least seemed moderately interested now. "Has this man offered for you?"

"His family sent him home from court before he could settle it."

"He is some boy whom his family controls?"

She had to remember with whom she spoke. "A family's will may seem a minor issue for a man such as you, but he is part of a powerful family up north. One does not defy kinship so easily. Still, when he hears of this betrothal, I am sure that he will come back."

"So, Christiana, you are saying that this man said that he wanted to marry you but left without settling for you."

That seemed a rather bald way to put it.

"Aye."

He smiled again. "Ah."

She really resented that "Ah." Her annoyance made her bold. She leaned toward him, feeling her jaw harden with repressed anger. "Master David, let me be blunt. I have given myself to this man."

Finally a reaction besides that impassive indifference. His head went back a fraction and he studied her from beneath lowered lids.

"Then be blunt, my lady. Exactly what do you mean by that?"

She threw up her hands in exasperation. "We made love together. Is that blunt enough for you? We went to bed together. In fact, we were found in bed together. Your offer was only accepted so that the Queen could hush up any scandal and keep my brother from forcing a marriage that my lover's family does not want."

She thought that she saw a flash of anger beneath those lids.

"You were discovered thus and this man left you to face it alone? Your devotion to this paragon of chivalry is impressive."

His assessment of Stephen was like a slap in her face. "How dare such as you criticize—"

"You are doing it again."

"Doing what?" she snapped.

" 'Such as you.' Twice now. Another phrase that you might avoid. For prudence's sake." He paused. "Who is this man?"

"I have sworn not to tell," she said stiffly. "My brother . . . Besides, as you have said, it is none of your affair."

He rose, uncoiling himself with an elegant movement, and went to stand by the hearth. The lines beneath the pourpoint suggested a lean, hard body. He was quite tall. Not quite as tall as Morvan, but taller than most. She found his presence unsettling. Merchants were supposed to be skinny or portly men in fur hats.

He gazed at the flames. "Are you with child?" he asked.

The notion astounded her. She hadn't thought of that. But perhaps the Queen had. She looked at him vacantly. He turned and saw the expression.

"Do you know the signs?" he said softly.

She shook her head.

"Have you had your flux since you were last with him?"

She blushed and nodded. In fact, it had come today.

He turned back to the fire.

She wondered what he thought about as he studied those tongues of heat. She stayed silent, letting him weigh however he valued these things, praying that she had succeeded, hoping that he indeed had a merchant's soul and would be repelled by accepting used goods.

Finally she couldn't wait any longer.

"So, you will go to the King and withdraw this offer?" she asked hopefully.

He glanced over his shoulder at her. "I think not."

Her heart sank.

"Young girls make mistakes," he added.

"This was no mistake," she said forcefully. "If you do not withdraw, you will end up looking a fool. He will come for me, if not before the betrothal, then after. When he comes, I will go with him."

He did not look at her, but his quiet, beautiful voice drifted over the space between them. "What makes you think that I will let you?"

"You will not be able to stop me. He is a knight, and skilled at arms . . ."

"There are more effective weapons in this world than steel, Christiana." He turned. "As I said earlier, you are always free to go to the bishop and declare your lack of consent to this marriage. But I will not withdraw now."

"An honorable man would not expect me to face the King's wrath," she said bitterly.

"An honorable man would not ruin a girl at her request. If I withdraw, it will displease the King, whom I have no wish to anger. At the least I will need a good reason. Should I use the one that you have given me? Should

I repudiate you because you are not a virgin? It is the only way."

She dropped her eyes. The panicked desolation of the last day returned to engulf her.

She sensed a movement and then David de Abyndon stood in front of her. A strong, gentle hand lifted her chin until she looked up into his handsome face. It seemed to her that those blue eyes read her soul and her mind and saw right into her. Even Lady Idonia's hawklike inspections had not been so thorough and successful. Nor so oddly mesmerizing.

That intensity that flowed from him surrounded her. She became very aware of his rough fingers on her chin. His thumb stretched and brushed her jaw, and something tingled in her neck.

"If he comes for you before the wedding, I will step aside," he said. "I will not contest an annulment of the betrothal. But I must tell you, girl, that I know men and I do not think that he will come, although you are well worth what it would cost him."

"You do not know *him*."

"Nay, I do not. And I am not so old that I can't be surprised." He smiled down at her. A real smile, she realized. The first one of the evening. A wonderful smile, actually. His hand fell away. Her skin felt warm where he had touched her.

She stood up. "I must go. My escort will grow impatient."

He walked with her to the door. "I will come and see you in a few days."

She felt sick at heart. He was making her go through with the farce of this betrothal, and it would complicate things horribly. She had no desire to play this role any more than necessary.

"Please do not. There is no point."

He turned and looked at her as he opened the door and led her to the steps. "As you wish, Christiana."

She saw Thomas's shadowy form in the courtyard, and flew to him as soon as they exited the hall. She glanced back to the doorway where David stood watching.

Thomas began guiding her to the portal. "Did you accomplish what you needed?"

"Aye," she lied. Thomas did not know about the betrothal. It had not been announced yet, and she had hoped that it never would be. Master David's stubbornness meant that now things were going to become very difficult. She would have to find some other way to stop this betrothal, or at least this marriage.

David watched her cross the courtyard, her nobility obvious in her posture and graceful walk. A very odd stillness began claiming him, and her movements slowed as if time grew sluggish. An eerie internal silence spread until it blocked out all sound. In an isolated world connected to the one in the yard but separate from it by invisible degrees, he began observing her in an abstract way.

He had felt this before several times in his life, and was stunned to find himself having the experience now. All the same, he did nothing to stop the sensation and did not question the importance of what was happening.

He recognized the silence that permeated him as the inaudible sound of Fortune turning her capricious wheel and changing his life in ways that he could only dimly foresee. Unlike most men, he did not fear the unpredictable coincidences that revealed Fortune's willfulness, for he had thus far been one of her favorite children.

Christiana Fitzwaryn of Harclow. The caves of Harclow. There was an elegant balance in this particular coincidence.

The gate closed behind her and time abruptly righted itself. He contemplated the implications of this girl's visit.

He had understood King Edward's desire to hide the payment for the exclusive trading license that he was buying. If word got out about it, other merchants would be jealous. He had himself suggested several other ways to conceal the arrangement, but they involved staggered payments, and the King, desperate for coin to finance his French war, wanted the entire sum now. Edward's solution of giving him a noble wife and disguising the payment as a bride price had created a host of problems, though, not the least of which was the possibility that the girl would not suit him.

His vision turned inward and he saw Christiana's black hair and pale skin and lovely face. Her dark eyes sparkled like black diamonds. She was not especially small, but her elegance gave the impression of delicacy, even frailty. The first sight of her in the fire glow had made his breath catch the way it always did when he came upon an object or view of distinctive beauty.

Her visit had announced unanticipated complications, but it had resolved one question most clearly. Christiana Fitzwaryn would suit him very well indeed.

BY

POSSESSION

now on sale

The hearth glow suddenly illuminated the stranger.

Moira gasped. *Surely not. It was impossible!* A handsome face composed of sharp planes emerged from the retreating shadows. Deep-set dark eyes met her gaping stare, the low fire highlighting golden sparks that brightened while he considered her. He turned slightly and she gasped again when she saw the pale scar slicing down the left side of his face from forehead to jaw, contrasting starkly with his sun browned skin.

Impossible!

"You know who I am?"

She knew who he appeared to be, who the scar and eyes and dark hair said he should be. But that was all that reminded her of him. Certainly not the suspicion and danger quavering out of him and giving that face a harsh, vigilant expression.

Especially not the crude garments that made him appear like some marauding barbarian. In the hearth light she could see that they were made of buckskin, not woven cloth. The hip length sleeveless tunic displayed the sinewy strength of his arms. More leather clad his legs to the ground in two narrow tubes. The tunic was decorated with orange beads that picked up the fire.

"You spoke boldly enough before, woman. Do you doubt your own eyes?"

"I doubt them, since the man you appear to be is dead eight years now."

"Well, I am not dead, nor a ghost."

"If you are who you appear to be, you should know me as well."

The eyebrow bisected by the scar rose. "Come here."

She stepped closer and he scrutinized her face. She managed not to flinch as his gaze pierced hers, invading and probing with a naked contemplation. Still, he didn't look quite so fearsome up near, and her own examination revealed something of the handsome, blessed boy she remembered. Leaner and harder, but the same high cheekbones and strong jaw defined the face.

"You are the daughter of Bernard Orrick's leman," he said. "But you are well grown these eight years, and not the plump child you were when I left." His intense gaze drifted down and then returned to her face until their eyes met in a frank connection of familiarity. She saw recognition and maybe something else in his expression. Her nape prickled.

Another count against him and she doubted anew. The man he claimed to be had never looked at her like that, and never would.

"Raymond no doubt told you where you were coming and who I am."

"So you do not trust Raymond either? No wonder you have kept the boy safe. In these times you are smart to suspect everyone. But Raymond would not know the name I called you when you were underfoot and in the way, would he?"

Nay, Raymond would not know that name which spoke volumes about her youth, her appearance, her status in the Orrick household. Her insignificance.

He reached out and touched the tip of her nose like he had done on occasion when she was a child. "You are little Moira, Claire's Shadow."

A stunned acceptance swept her, splashed with relief and joy and heartbreak.

"Now, where is the boy?"

The heartbreak submerged the other emotions. She turned away, castigating herself. She had been keeping Brian safe for a reason, hadn't she? He was not really hers and did not belong here. This man above all others would ensure that he someday sat in his rightful place and lived the life he was born to live.

She should be happy, not devastated, but her spirit began a silent, grieving moan as she realized that she would lose Brian forever. "I will show you. Tell the others to stay here. They may frighten him."

Raymond and his men remained in the house while she led the way around to the shed in back. She called Brian's name when they approached the stacks of reeds drying for her baskets. The bundles shifted and a blond head stuck up. Young blue eys examined the stranger cautiously.

"It is all right. Come out now."

He scrambled up and came over to her. Moira stepped away. Man and boy examined each other. She was glad that Brian had the good sense not to comment on the scar or garments, even though both obviously fascinated him. He looked so small and brave there, struggling not to shrink from the hard countenance above him. Her heart swelled at the image of them taking their mutual measurements.

She slipped back beside him and knelt, placing her hands on his shoulders, closing her eyes and savoring the feel of his small frame under her palms. *Probably never again.* She wished she had known that it would be today. She would have taken him to the stream to play yesterday, and cooked him a special meal. Tears puddled in her eyes and she looked away, biting her lip for composure. Then she pressed his shoulders and smiled at his questioning face.

"This is Addis de Valence, Brian. This is your father."

"My father is dead. He died on the Baltic crusade."

"Nay."

He frowned up. Realization began dawning. Fear and panic masked his face and he lunged into her arms, burying his face in her breast. She embraced and rocked him and silently pled with her eyes for Addis to be patient.

The scarred face turned toward the house and she twisted and saw that Raymond and the others had followed. Perhaps they thought Addis de Valence needed help subduing one seven-year-old boy. She tried to disentangle Brian, but he burrowed in deeper. Perhaps they were right.

Addis reached down and pried the boy loose. Brian squirmed in resistance but Addis lifted him and gave a sharp look that quelled the rebellion. He began walking away with little Brian's distraught eyes locked back on her. She reached out a reassuring hand to the boy who had been her son for four years.

Addis walked as if indifferent to the boy's tears. When he passed Raymond, he glanced back. "Bring the woman."

ABOUT THE AUTHOR

MADELINE HUNTER has worked as a grocery clerk, office employee, art dealer, and freelance writer. She holds a Ph.D. in art history, which she currently teaches at an eastern university. She lives in Pennsylvania with her husband, her two teenage sons, a chubby, adorable mutt, and a black cat with a major attitude. She can be contacted through her web site, www.MadelineHunter.com, where readers can also find more information regarding the historical events and characters used in this novel.

Bestselling Historical Women's Fiction

□AMANDA QUICK□

___28354-5 SEDUCTION . . . . . $6.99/$9.99 Canada

___28932-2 SCANDAL . . . . $6.99/$9.99

___28594-7 SURRENDER . . . . $6.99/$9.99

___29325-7 RENDEZVOUS . . . . $6.99/$9.99

___29315-X RECKLESS . . . . $6.99/$9.99

___29316-8 RAVISHED . . . . $6.99/$9.99

___29317-6 DANGEROUS . . . . $6.99/$9.99

___56506-0 DECEPTION . . . . $6.99/$9.99

___56153-7 DESIRE . . . . $6.99/$9.99

___56940-6 MISTRESS . . . . $6.99/$9.99

___57159-1 MYSTIQUE . . . . $6.99/$9.99

___57190-7 MISCHIEF . . . . $6.99/$8.99

___57407-8 AFFAIR . . . . $6.99/$8.99

___57409-4 WITH THIS RING . . . . $6.99/$9.99

□IRIS JOHANSEN□

___29871-2 LAST BRIDGE HOME . . . . $5.99/$8.99

___29604-3 THE GOLDEN BARBARIAN . . . $6.99/$8.99

___29244-7 REAP THE WIND . . . . $6.99/$9.99

___29032-0 STORM WINDS . . . . $6.99/$8.99

Ask for these books at your local bookstore or use this page to order.

Please send me the books I have checked above. I am enclosing $_____ (add $2.50 to cover postage and handling). Send check or money order, no cash or C.O.D.'s, please.

Name _____

Address _____

City/State/Zip _____

Send order to: Bantam Books, Dept. FN, 400 Hahn Road, Westminster, MD 21157
Allow four to six weeks for delivery.
Prices and availability subject to change without notice.   FN 16 1/01

Bestselling Historical Women's Fiction

□ IRIS JOHANSEN □

___28855-5 THE WIND DANCER .... $6.99/$9.99

___29968-9 THE TIGER PRINCE .... $6.99/$8.99

___29944-1 THE MAGNIFICENT ROGUE ... $6.99/$8.99

___29945-X BELOVED SCOUNDREL .... $6.99/$8.99

___29946-8 MIDNIGHT WARRIOR .... $6.99/$8.99

___29947-6 DARK RIDER .... $6.99/$8.99

___56990-2 LION'S BRIDE .... $6.99/$8.99

___56991-0 THE UGLY DUCKLING .... $6.99/$8.99

___57181-8 LONG AFTER MIDNIGHT .... $6.99/$8.99

___57998-3 AND THEN YOU DIE .... $6.99/$8.99

___57802-2 THE FACE OF DECEPTION .... $6.99/$9.99

□ TERESA MEDEIROS □

___29407-5 HEATHER AND VELVET ...... $5.99/$7.50

___29409-1 ONCE AN ANGEL .... $5.99/$7.99

___29408-3 A WHISPER OF ROSES .... $5.99/$7.99

___56332-7 THIEF OF HEARTS .... $5.99/$7.99

___56333-5 FAIREST OF THEM ALL ...... $5.99/$7.50

___56334-3 BREATH OF MAGIC .... $5.99/$7.99

___57623-2 SHADOWS AND LACE .... $5.99/$7.99

___57500-7 TOUCH OF ENCHANTMENT. . $5.99/$7.99

___57501-5 NOBODY'S DARLING .... $5.99/$7.99

___57502-3 CHARMING THE PRINCE ...... $5.99/$8.99

Ask for these books at your local bookstore or use this page to order.

Please send me the books I have checked above. I am enclosing $_____ (add $2.50 to cover postage and handling). Send check or money order, no cash or C.O.D.'s, please.

Name _____

Address _____

City/State/Zip _____

Send order to: Bantam Books, Dept. FN 16, 400 Hahn Road, Westminster, MD 21157

Allow four to six weeks for delivery. Prices and availability subject to change without notice. FN 16 1/01